A DANGEROUS WEAPON

INSINUATION

A DANGEROUS WEAPON
||||||||||||||||||| INSINUATION |||||||||||||||||||||

CHARLTON CLAYES

A DANGEROUS WEAPON
INSINUATION

iUniverse books may be ordered through booksellers or by contacting:

iUniverse
1663 Liberty Drive
Bloomington, IN 47403
www.iuniverse.com
1-800-Authors (1-800-288-4677)

ISBN: 978-1-4917-8185-2 (sc)
ISBN: 978-1-4917-8186-9 (e)

Print information available on the last page.

iUniverse rev. date: 12/18/2015

"One thought fills immensity."
William Blake, "Proverbs of Hell,"
The Marriage of Heaven and Hell (1790)

A SUDDEN GUST of wind whips across the platform, scattering debris before it. It dies away quickly, but not before it chills the lone person there.

The young woman paces nervously down to the far end of the platform, turns, and trudges back toward the other end. The heat is stifling, and the brief breeze is only a temporary respite. It is late evening, but the temperature is still in the high eighties; the day had been yet another scorcher in a seemingly unending series. She desperately fans herself with a religious flyer she had found on the seat of the train which had brought her to the City; if not for the miniscule movement of air the makeshift fan produces, she would have thrown away the flyer as soon as she had realized what it was.

She is pretty but not excessively so. She wears her jet-black hair loosely around her shoulders, and one lock threatens to hide part of her face. She has a pallid complexion, a result of spending too much time indoors. Her face is full and fleshy, and it is punctuated by a pug nose which tends to make her appear as if she is perpetually leaning backwards. She is of medium height and neither lean nor chubby.

She reaches the other end of the platform, halts, and peers off into the distance toward where the railroad tracks disappear from view. The train which had brought her here to this strange city is long gone now, and she wishes she had stayed on it and returned to St. Louis, which is home to her. She wishes she had not gotten on the train in the first place and left all the familiar sights behind.

Then she remembers just why she is here and why St. Louis had become a dangerous place for her. The organization which had given her succor and counseled her had recommended that she come to this place. They had even bought her ticket (one-way, of course) and insisted that their "sister" organization in the City would help her out of her dilemma, if anyone could.

Her dilemma.

She tries not to think of her dilemma. It is too painful to think about. She pushes the pain to the back of her mind and focuses on her surroundings. The train depot is unlike any she has ever seen. In the first place, it is round, not rectangular, and it has a conical roof. In the second place, it is constructed of rough-hewn yellow stone, not brick or wood or concrete or steel. And, in the third place, it looks...*old* as if it had always been there since this city was founded; but that is surely an illusion – whether deliberate or accidental, she cannot say.

Certainly, it is not old on the inside. When the train deposited her here, she had attempted to gain entrance, but the doors had been locked for the night. Some of the interior lights had been left on – for security purposes, she supposed – and so she had gotten a brief glimpse of a surprisingly modern interior. The contrast is remarkable, she had thought at the time, and there is probably an interesting story behind it.

Where is the man I'm supposed to meet? she wonders wearily. *I don't want to stand here all night.*

She begins to pace the platform again, first to one end, then to the other. When she turns around after the first lap, she spots a flash of movement. *At last*, she thinks, *my contact has finally shown up.* Her mood lightens slightly, and she heads in the direction of the movement. Then she spies the white-garbed figure, and she freezes.

"No! Not *them* again!" she whispers and looks about for a place to hide.

She has seen the men in the ice-cream suits in St. Louis many times – too many times – and each time, they had been up to their usual nefarious behavior. The people who had succored her had counseled her about how to avoid the Disciples of Purity until she had found safe haven. It had been difficult at first – they were everywhere – and a couple of times she had nearly been caught but had escaped at the last minute. Now, the nightmare is beginning all over again.

All because of her dilemma.

*No! Don't think about it! You'll bring on the…*power *again. Think about getting away from here.*

She does not think that the ice-cream-suited fanatic has spotted her yet. He is definitely looking for someone – that much is clear –but he has not looked in her direction yet. Unfortunately, the only way off this platform is past him, and she can't take the chance that he is alone. Her experience has been that his kind never travels alone; they work their mischief in groups, re-enforcing each other's efforts and so creating the maximum amount of harm to innocent people.

Maybe, she thinks, he is searching for his companions instead of acting on his own. Maybe, if he keeps his back to her, she'll have a chance to escape. Maybe…

She picks up her small suitcase and, breathlessly, inches off the platform and onto the sidewalk running adjacent to the depot. From there, it is a scant few yards to the street; if she is very lucky, she might be able to run across the street and disappear behind one of the buildings over there before she is spotted. Then she can…

Never mind that, girl, she admonishes herself. *Just take it one step at a time.*

Step by cautious step, she creeps along the sidewalk, all the while keeping a close eye on the other person, ready to run if need be. It is an agonizing task, this creeping along, but all will be lost otherwise. She feels her heart beating like a trip hammer, perspiration streaming down her face, and her stomach knotting up. Still, the white suit has not yet looked her way. What *is* he up to?

Abruptly, she detects another movement near the street. Four bulky figures are approaching the depot. She freezes and presses herself against the building in an attempt to blend in with the stone and become invisible. Are *they* what the Disciple is looking for? If so, her chances of escape have just been reduced to zero. She might have eluded one person, but not *five*. Her heart beats even faster (if that is possible), her face drowns in perspiration, and her stomach is completely knotted up.

The four newcomers march with deliberateness toward the lone figure. They spread out so as to surround him and prevent him from escaping *them*. The white suit is clearly in a panic now, and he searches for an avenue of escape but sees none. He too presses against the building. The burly quartet advance unerringly toward their target with quick, measured steps. As soon as they near the building, they are exposed to the dim interior lighting.

The young woman gasps in shock at their appearance. They do not look like any human beings she has ever seen. They are stocky and muscular like wrestlers, but their faces are hideous and horrifying. Cruelty masks those faces; their mouths are mere slits, and their eyes steely glints in their sockets. They have short bull necks and hairless skulls. Two of them have wicked scars on their faces which enhance their hideousness.

When these nightmares are only a few meters from their target, he raises an arm as if that will halt them in their tracks.

"Halt!" he cries out. "Stop in the name of the Light of Purity! The Light curses thee, foul creatures. The Light seeks out all impurity and destroys it. If thou wouldst be saved from impurity, embrace the Light. Love the Light! Love Purity!"

One of the newcomers chuckles evilly, and the scar on his face moves with his facial muscles, turning him into a grotesquery.

"Stupid Tellurian," he speaks in a halting, gravelly voice. "You think *words* will stop the Swarm? Think again!"

"Stay away from me," the Disciple pleads. "Don't touch me."

"Tell us what you have done with our agent here, and perhaps we shall let you live."

"I don't know what you're talking about."

"Tell us, Tellurian, or die!"

"I don't know anything!"

The scar-face steps forward and seizes the Disciple by the throat. "*Tell us!*"

"I – I *can't!*"

"Fool!" The Leader increases the pressure on the other's throat. The white suit gurgles helplessly. In a matter of seconds, it is all over; the hapless Disciple dangles lifelessly in the grip of the Leader. "Stupid Tellurian!"

He lets the body drop to the ground, turns to his comrades, and speaks to them in a harsh, indecipherable language. They prepare to leave when one of the lesser members cries out and points at the young woman, still crouching against the depot, paralyzed by the tableau she has just witnessed.

She panics now. These strangers have committed cold-blooded murder, and they mean to leave no witnesses behind. Stealth is out of the question; she must now run for her life. She drops her suitcase and starts into a fast trot toward the street.

The Swarm, however, are experts in tracking and capturing their targets. At the Leader's direction, they fan out, block all avenues of escape, and close in on the woman. She edges back the way she had come, fear gripping her increasingly with each passing second.

Then, the sensation she fears the most comes to the fore. She has experienced it too many times before when in a high emotional state. The last time that sensation overtook her, she had severely injured a would-be boyfriend who had initiated a romantic episode. That incident had been the trigger which led her to being in the City. And, now, she is again in a high emotional state.

The sensation begins as a slight humming in her brain and builds up to the point where she believes her head will explode. The humming spreads throughout her body via the nervous system, and still it increases in intensity. She must find release before she does explode.

The Swarm move ever closer to her. They wear smiles, but murderous intent fills their eyes.

"Stay away from me!" she rasps. "If you come any closer, I'll – I'll *hurt* you!"

"Stupid Tellurian female," the Leader growls, "you cannot hurt the Swarm. We are too powerful."

He directs one of his subordinates to seize her. The latter eagerly obeys, approaches to within a meter of her, and reaches out with both hands.

She can no longer hold the sensation back. She must release the force within her – *now!* To the Swarm's great surprise, their prey becomes enveloped by a pale red haze. The young woman stretches forth her arms toward the would-be captor. There is a sharp crackling as she discharges twenty thousand volts of electricity at him. He screams in agony as the discharge burns the flesh from his bones and turns his bones to cinders. The smell of charred flesh and bone fills the air.

She turns toward the remainder of the Swarm with grim determination. Now, fear grips the Leader, and he barks out a command. His subordinates draw weapons from underneath their clothing and prepare to fire. They do not get the chance, as their prey is still surrounded by the red haze and has not yet fully discharged the force within her. The crackling re-occurs, and a second discharge is issued. This time, however, she is able to project only five thousand volts. But it is still enough to cause a severe electrical shock; the Swarm members reel in pain. The Leader gasps out another command, and all of them beat a hasty retreat.

The woman sobs with relief as the sensation subsides and the haze dissipates. She views what she has done and is filled with remorse. She hadn't meant to kill that creature, but he had forced her to defend herself in the only way she knew how.

She cannot stay here any longer. Someone will report this incident to the police, and they will question her interminably and learn what she is. She cannot allow that to happen. She retrieves her suitcase and hurries toward the street. She pays no attention to whatever traffic there is, dashes across the street -- barely avoiding being struck by a rickety old station wagon – and disappears into the shadows.

MISSION REPORT

THE DRIVER OF the station wagon slammed on the brakes at her passenger's command. The vehicle rattled, groaned, and wheezed at this ill treatment but miraculously held together. The passenger, a male with cherubic facial features, a receding hairline, and the palest blue eyes imaginable, rolled down his window and peered out at the figure retreating into the shadows. The driver, a tall, statuesque redhead wearing dark glasses, rolled down her window as well but did not look out; instead, she cocked her head as if listening for something.

"What did I almost hit, George?" she queried.

"Not *what*, Sheena, but *who*. A young woman running from the depot who darted in front of us."

"*Oh, my God!*" She took a deep breath and let it out slowly. "It's a good thing I have quick reflexes."

"I'll say. Are you picking up anything?"

Sheena swiveled her head from side to side, concentrating on any sounds or smells she might detect.

"A rapid heartbeat in the direction that woman went, fading as she puts distance between her and us." She wrinkled her nose. "And,

1

George, the godawfulest odor I've ever smelled coming from the depot –
something was *burned*. Do you think that's what she was running
from?"

"That's a strong possibility. We'd better check it out."

Sheena depressed the accelerator, and the station wagon rattled,
groaned, and wheezed again but still held together. She turned into
the depot's driveway and entered the grounds. George scanned the area
with a professional eye and instantly spotted the carnage which had
recently taken place. He told his partner to stop and jumped out when
she did. With an awkward gait, he approached the body cautiously. It
had been burned almost beyond recognition; but his trained eye and his
analytical brain were able to discern a few features, and those features
he recognized immediately.

The Swarm! But, what hit this character that was strong enough to fry
him crispier than the Colonel's chicken?

Questions but no answers – this was the bane of the private detective
that he was, and he would have to do some hard detecting to solve this
mystery.

Sheena came up behind him and laid a hand on his arm. He gazed
up at her and saw that she was still reacting from the strong odor of
burnt flesh.

"What did you find, George?" she choked out.

"A burned body. Someone or something did a real number on it."

"But I'm not smelling burned *human* flesh. I'm smelling – oh, God!
It's the same odor I detected from Mr. Jones. Is – is that body –"

"Uh-huh. It's – or *was* – a Swarm soldier."

"There are more of them here?"

"Without a doubt. I'd hazard to guess they're here to find out what
happened to Mr. Jones."

"But why here at the depot? And how was that young woman
involved?"

"We've got a big mystery, Sheena, and we'd better solve it fast.
Otherwise – uh, oh! I see another body over by the depot entrance. It's
a Disciple."

"A Disciple? The mystery just got bigger."

"You know it. I'm going to check out that second body."

He stumped over to the ice-cream-suited figure, bent down as well as he could, and examined it. Sheena was right behind him, guided by his footsteps.

"What's the cause of death?" she asked.

"Strangulation, by the looks of the marks on his neck. More precisely, his throat was crushed – which doesn't surprise me, since the Swarm are big bruisers."

"So, they killed him, and then someone killed one of them. The 'whys' and 'how's' are buzzing like bees."

"Yeah, they are. Well, it's time for an 'anonymous' phone call to the police. Then we head for DEDEP."

* * *

The trip to the abandoned government facility which DEDEP had appropriated for its own purposes years ago was made in silence. Both George Larkin and Sheena Whitley were lost in his/her own thoughts, and neither had anything useful to say (aside from Larkin's driving commands).

As Director of Operations for the secretive group, the detective felt an especially heavy load on his shoulders. In part, he blamed himself for what had occurred three days ago; because of his decision to pit the aliens known as the "Swarm" against the religious fanatics who called themselves the "Disciples of Purity" in order to buy time for the "good guys" to gain strength in the coming show-down, he had unleashed a force, unknown and unexpected by anyone, which may or may not have been an even bigger threat to Earth and humankind. He had witnessed one member of DEDEP experience a psychotic episode, another severely injured by an alien device, and a third kidnapped and tortured. He himself had been taken captive by the Swarm and most likely would have faced some horrific fate off-world had it not been for a timely rescue by his teammates. And there had been the deaths on both sides of the divide. At this point in time, he was feeling less like the "master strategist" he and others thought he was and more like a "master executioner."

And, on top of everything else, he had lost the "eel" he had been sent to retrieve for DEDEP. He had always prided himself on "getting his man"; that's how his reputation as a detective *par excellence* had been built. He had failed this time, and now a lonely, panicky young woman was lost in the City.

In the aftermath of the recent battle between him and the Disciples and Mr. Jones – the opening salvo of this phase of an interstellar war stretching across thousands of light-years and hundreds of centuries -- he had busied himself with plans to loot the apartment of Mr. Jones and appropriate all of that fabulous alien technology for future use by DEDEP. He wanted to experiment with those machines and learn which could help the group in the coming battle. It was also a means to keep his mind occupied and avoid wallowing in guilt and self-pity.

The discovery of the bodies at the depot meant that he could not afford to indulge himself with alien technology just yet. He had to be what he had been appointed to be: a leader of a group which possessed *psi*-talents. The group looked to him – counted on him – to rescue them from a life of living in a hole in the ground, and he daren't let them down. Failure to work toward that goal would be the hardest blow of all.

Larkin glanced surreptitiously at his business partner. She was gripping the steering wheel of the station wagon tightly as if she believed that, if she loosened her grip a fraction, she would lose control and send the vehicle into the ditch or an oncoming car. Her face was lost in darkness, and he could not see the expression on it (if there was one); but her silence told him that she too was undergoing some self-examination. He could only guess at what that process entailed.

Sheena represented another of his problems. She was deeply in love with him, and she made no effort to disguise the fact; quite the contrary, she attempted seduction at every opportunity. He was deeply in love with her as well – no use in denying it – and he could not disguise his feelings from her hyperesthesia which she used to "read" the emotional states of all with whom she came into contact, no matter how hard they tried. And lately, he had dared to think he could be a lover for her, despite his disability, and find the happiness he had always wanted but never hoped to achieve. Still, the exigencies of the day was forcing him to put his personal desires aside and concentrate on the Bigger Picture. If they both survived the coming storm, then perhaps...

If George Larkin was wrestling with his conscience, so too was Sheena Whitley, but for different reasons. As the junior partner in the newly re-named Larkin-Whitley Detective Agency, she was obliged to carry out her assignments and to assist the senior partner with his, wherever feasible. Carrying out those assignments had been difficult enough when they had only the Disciples of Purity to deal with; tracing missing persons and being dogged by religious fanatics had made life rather hectic of late, if not downright dangerous. Many had been the times when she just wanted to cuddle up with George and forget about the job and the Disciples. She loved him more than words could express, but he had always kept his distance because of his disability; her hyper-senses relayed to her the emotional turmoil raging inside him as desire battled despair. And nothing she said or did had made any inroads toward her cherished goal.

Now, with the advent of the Swarm on Planet Earth who were bent on utter destruction, her George had become obsessed with the idea of stopping their invasion personally and single-handedly. He had formulated daring – and reckless, in her humble opinion – plans for doing so; and in doing so, he had risked not only his own life but those of others in DEDEP, including (she had to say) herself. If he continued in this mode, he and she would have absolutely no chance of the sort of relationship she hoped for. She wished she could tell him to be more careful, but she was afraid of jeopardizing the relationship they did have.

Bright lights on the road ahead snapped her out of her reverie. She could not see the lights, of course, but she could feel their intensity on her skin. In a matter of seconds, she heard the *thrum-thrum* of heavy-duty engines, three of them in fact, judging from the sounds. Three large trucks, either semis or moving vans, were approaching; and, because the engines were at full throttle, they appeared to be fully loaded. They passed the station wagon, and their passage caused the old vehicle to shake violently. Since they were traveling on a Federal highway, their presence was not unusual; yet, Sheena felt something odd about this convoy. For one thing, why were they on the road at this hour? Federal law had banned night travel for trucks due to safety concerns. For another, they were evenly spaced and not very far apart at that. For a third, one of the trucks, the middle one, needed a tune-up; she could hear a disruption in the *thrum* of its engine as one of its sparkplugs misfired. And, for a fourth, they gave off an unusual odor as they passed. It didn't smell like diesel fuel but rather like – here she wrinkled her nose – burning garbage.

What kind of convoy was this? her detective's mind would like to know. She doubted, however, that she was unlikely to find out.

Presently, Larkin announced the approach of the turn-off onto the gravel road which led to their destination. At his signal, Sheena deftly made the turn and listened to the gravel pummel the underside of the station wagon. At once, she began a variation of her ability to count blocks. Previously, she had determined that, from the highway to the gate at the farm, 341 seconds would elapse.

When the count reached 330, she automatically slowed down. At the count of 340, Larkin instructed her to turn right and stop. She heard him open the station wagon's door, slide out, and walk to the gate. There followed the scraping of metal on metal which would be George pushing open the gate manually. Ordinarily, he would have used the electronic gate opener, but Mr. Jones had burned out the gate's locking mechanism during his unexpected – and fatal – visit days before. When her partner was back inside the vehicle, she accelerated slightly and, with his directions, steered a careful path between the double rows of trees which lined the driveway.

When she had braked in the front of the farmhouse, she heard the creaking of the front door as it was opened. Heavy, short-paced footsteps marked the passage across the porch, down the steps, and over the lawn. It had to be Monk.

"Hiya, Monk," Larkin greeted the Department of Energy man cheerfully.

"Hiya, Georgie, Sheena." A short silence followed. "Say, weren't you s'pposed to be bringin' a new inmate?"

"Yes, but there was a mix-up. I have to tell Emil our plans need to be changed.

"Oakie-doakie. See ya later."

Larkin and Sheena got out of their vehicle and headed for the barn. The former pulled out his gate opener and clicked the code for the barn door. They walked in, and the detective clicked the door shut. At the trap door, Larkin began his laborious climb down the shaft leading to the underground facility. Sheena crouched down, felt for the rim of the opening, found it, and swung her body around. She eased herself onto the ladder and began her own descent. Because she didn't have artificial limbs, she had an easier time of it.

With the metallic grating of the emergency door as it opened, they accessed the world of DEDEP, a haven for persons with paranormal/ unusual talents.

The corridors were sparsely populated. As it was past the dinner hour, most of the residents would have returned to their quarters. They could have availed themselves of a recreation room and a small library, but there was little left by way of recreational equipment or reading/ viewing materials, the previous occupants having removed everything which was easily portable. Dr. Emil Razumov, DEDEP's Director of Research and nominal head of the facility, had thought about restoring those areas, but the lack of time and sufficient funds had worked against the project. The residents were thus left to their own devices, and most chose to pursue those devices in private.

Those few who were in the corridors were most likely in transit from one place to another. When they encountered Larkin and Sheena, they greeted them heartily, exchanged a few words, and continued on to their final destinations. One of the few was the Perkins family, who seemed to be the most tightly knitted of all the residents and whose members were seldom seen apart; whatever they did to amuse themselves, they did it as a unit. The two detectives caught them as they were entering the central corridor. The greetings they gave were effusive, leading Sheena to whisper to Larkin that her biopsychometric readings of all four were the strongest she had ever read in a family unit.

In the central corridor, at the midway point, stood a four-foot-high black pole topped by an equally black sphere. It was the only piece of equipment the detective had looted from Mr. Jones' apartment; it was the dampening-field generator, and Larkin had taken it simply because it had been the only piece easily transportable. He had reasoned that, if it worked well for the alien, it would work well for DEDEP; and, at this juncture, the residents needed all the protection they could get.

"Hmmm. That's odd," he murmured. "The generator's been turned off."

"I'm glad," Sheena remarked. "That field makes my skin crawl."

"I know. But, I brought it here for a reason. I'll have to ask Emil about it."

The remainder of the trip to the Director's office was made in sullen silence. Sheena had been with her partner long enough to know when to make a comment and when to keep quiet. George had been on edge ever since the demise of the Swarm agent precipitated by the psychic gestalt created by Eve Pelletier and Stan Jankowsky (quite by accident). The black sphere had been full of surprises from the moment of its creation, but the biggest surprise of all occurred when it had acted independently in the face of a threat to its existence. And Larkin had been standing next to it when it reduced Mr. Jones to a handful of black powder. The detective had immediately identified the gestalt as a "dangerous weapon" with the potential for large-scale destruction, and he had recommended that it be used as such in the coming war with the Swarm.

Presently, the pair arrived at Dr. Razumov's office. Larkin rapped gently on the door three times, opened it, and walked in.

The Russian parapsychologist was engaged in his usual activity when he was not conducting an experiment – poring over a pile of computer read-outs from one testing session or another. He was making frequent annotations to the strips of paper and muttering to himself in Russian as he was wont to do. Emil Razumov was one of that rare breed who were completely absorbed by their work to the point of absent-mindedness. If Sheena Whitley knew when to keep quiet, so did George

Larkin. And so, the detectives sat down as unobtrusively as they could and waited patiently until they were recognized.

When he was finished with one strip of paper, the Doctor tossed it aside and grabbed the next one. Occasionally, some datum puzzled him, and he dug into the already-examined pile and re-read a strip. This interruption in his routine provoked more muttering plus a shaking of the head in frustration. Whatever anomaly he had discovered might or might not be voiced aloud. The curious person had to bide his time.

Abruptly, the old man whipped off his glasses, tossed them onto the pile of read-outs, and rubbed his eyes. He then discovered that he was not alone in his office. He blinked a couple of times to focus on the newcomers and broke out in a huge smile.

"George, Sheena, *zdrafst*. Where have you been these past few days? I have so much to tell you."

"Hello, Emil," Larkin responded. "We've got a bit of news for you as well. You first, though."

"*Spaceebo*. I have been wracking this old brain of mine since the… incident with Mr. Jones. And I have formed a theory about it."

"I'm not surprised. Does it have anything to do with radiopsychology?"

"*Konyechno!* Everything I do here is connected to radiopsychology. The gestalt that Eve and Stan created was a product of their combined radiopsychological abilities, and it follows that it too has a place in both my General and Special Theories."

"Which is?"

"The gestalt is, in my estimation, both a receiver and a generator of radio energy. This is evidenced by what it has done so far. We have seen that it increases in size in direct proportion to the number of persons it comes into contact with. And we have seen that it utilizes radio energy to produce certain phenomena, such as transmitting images to Eve's mind and, particularly, the demise of Mr. Jones. In these respects, the sphere acts very much like the human brain."

"Do you think it's a sentient being?" Sheena entered the conversation.

"*Kto znayet* [who knows]? We shall not have an answer to that question until we communicate with it – assuming, of course, that we can communicate with it. Thus far, it seems to have bonded with our two young people who possess powerful *psi*-talents and with no one else. Whether it has communicated with them remains to be seen. But, I could imagine that it is sentient; it did respond to a threat to it, *nye pravdy?*"

"I'd have to agree with you there," Larkin said. "The gestalt targeted Mr. Jones specifically. Otherwise, I wouldn't be here having this conversation. My guess is that, at least, it has the ability to differentiate between hostile and non-hostile agents."

"*Da, oo tyebya mnogo pravdy* [you are very correct]."

"So, what's next?"

"More experimentation, naturally. We must learn the full range of its abilities and then to assess their usefulness to us. We must also proceed with caution so as not to be identified as a threat to it." He regarded the detective expectantly. "So, *moy starry droog*, what is your news?"

Larkin launched into a detailed account of his failed appointment with the "eel" from St. Louis. With each new bit of information, the Russian's frown grew deeper; at the end of the report, he was staring worriedly at the ceiling. He stared at the ceiling for a minute or so. Then:

"*Bozhu moyu!*" he murmured with a shake of his head. "*Mnogo chuzhdye kosmonavty* [more alien spacemen]? Is there no end to this dilemma, George?"

"I'm afraid not, Emil. I'd hazard to guess that, when Mr. Jones failed to report to his superiors in a timely fashion, they sent out a team to investigate."

"But why would they murder that Disciple?"

"If Mr. Jones had informed them that the Disciples were a threat to their plans for invasion, they would need to know how much of a threat."

"What about the 'eel'?"

"Ah, well, I'll have to come up with a thorough search plan. We can't afford to lose her."

"Certainly not. She is in great danger on her own."

"Right. Um, before we return to the City, we should look in on Eve and Stan. Is that permissible?"

The old man peered at the ceiling again, his lips puckered. Larkin knew in an instant what he was thinking. As always, Emil Razumov took a great interest in DEDEP's residents, as care-giver, counselor, and father-figure, and he guarded these positions jealously. Any attempt to put his charges in harm's way drew an instant rebuke. And the detective had been on the receiving end of rebukes more than once whenever he had enlisted Eve Pelletier's psycho-imaging abilities in his investigations. The Doctor feared that images derived from criminal activity would push the already mentally unstable woman over the edge.

"Just for a short while, George," he said at last. "They are still under observation."

"Thank you, Emil."

The detective pushed himself to his feet, using his arms as levers. At once, he felt a tug on his sleeve. Sheena was regarding him with concern.

"What?"

"Aren't you forgetting something? The field generator?"

"Oh, right. I did forget."

"What is this about the field generator?" Dr. Razumov inquired.

"It's been turned off. Why?"

"Christopher complained that he couldn't project outside of DEDEP, and so I turned it off."

"Oops. In my haste to protect the place against electronic snooping, I forgot what effect it has on certain people. Sorry about that, Emil."

"Perhaps you have had too much on your mind lately, *starry droog*. But, there may be a solution. I will ask Christopher to notify us when he wants to go outside and when he wants to return. We can turn off the generator at those times."

"That sounds reasonable. Let's go, Sheena."

* * *

(He)(She) stares at the ceiling and sees nothing. (He)(She) has been staring at the ceiling and seeing nothing for the past three days.

(He)(She) is not unconscious, however. (He)(She) is perfectly aware of (his)(her) surroundings. But (his)(her) mind is too full of images to take notice of any externalities.

The images are memories (?) of The Incident of three days ago, and they replay in (his)(her) mind on an endless loop. As soon as one loop finishes, another one begins; but the point of view is altered slightly as if the same scene is being seen through different eyes in succession. The replays are both confusing and fascinating.

The memory (?) loop begins with the Summoning. (He)(She) is directed by the one with the non-organic limbs to bring the Entity into (his)(her) plane of existence. (He)(She) does so in co-ordination with the third member of the summoning process, the short malformed creature. (He)(She) follows the Entity in (his)(her) mind's eye as It drifts out of the structure in which (he)(she) inhabits. (He)(She) sees (his)(her) director a few [untranslatable] away. That one is not alone. That one faces another bipedal creature of much different configuration. (He)(She), via the Entity, senses anger/anxiety/ tension from both creatures.

As soon as the Entity appears in the open and is observed by the creature of much different configuration, its anger is replaced by surprise and confusion. The director radiates amusement at the other's reaction. In an attempt to further confound the surprised one, the director commands (him) (her) to maneuver the Entity in a non-threatening manner. This action does not produce the desired effect; instead, the creature of much different configuration becomes angry again, and it searches the ground for something it has dropped. It finds the object and touches various facets of its surface.

(He)(She), via the Entity, recognizes the object as a miniature electromagnetic-field generator, although (he)(she) does not know how it operates. Further, (he)(she) realizes that the generator has begun to produce a potentially destructive frequency. The Entity takes action to protect Itself. The scene is filled with a bright, white light, blotting out all details. (He) (She) is not blinded, however, but is protected – along with the director – by the Entity.

A moment of Time passes.

The bright, white light dissipates as quickly as it had been created. (He)(She) now observes that the director stands alone. The creature of a much different configuration has been reduced to a fine black powder. The director radiates horror. (He)(She) is not horrified but is fascinated/ intrigued/curious. The director commands (him)(her) to recall the Entity. (He)(She) disengages from the summoning procedure.

The next loop begins, slightly altered.

* * *

From the diary of Christopher Wredling:

Where do I begin?

I've had enough adventure in two hours to last a life-time, and George says that what happened at DEDEP was just the beginning!

The mobiles had to settle for second-hand accounts of what happened. But, because of my psycho-projection ability, I had a ringside seat, and I wish I hadn't had one. I was so close to the action that, if I had been there physically, I could have touched either George or the alien Mr. Jones – not that I'd want to touch the latter in the first place! He was a dark force to end all dark forces, and there are more like him "out there."

I have never told anyone – even George and Emil – that I can "see" energy fields as colored splotches of light. That I can do so helps me in my travels since energy fields act as barriers to me. Emil mentioned some time ago that different energy fields generate in different frequencies and that, theoretically, each frequency corresponds to a specific hue. Well, it's more than just theory – it's reality. And, if all humans could see these frequencies like I can, it would be a mind-blowing experience. Sometimes I encounter a veritable kaleidoscope of colors when I'm traveling in the vicinity of cities – lots of energy fields there.

I mention all this because humans generate energy fields too. (In ancient times, these fields were called 'auras.') This is part of Emil's General Theory of Radiopsychology, and he says that they exist to protect the organism from personality-altering radio waves. If I concentrate, I see these fields as a low-level glow around the organism. Emil shows up as a 'yellow' which reflects his intellectual acuity. George is a 'reddish-brown,' passion mixed with adventure. Sheena is a 'red,' pure passion (if George only knew!).

In this scheme of things, Mr. Jones was a shadow-shape as if he absorbed light rather than reflecting it. He gave me the willies every time I looked at him. I did say that he was a 'dark force,' didn't I? Well, he was – literally as well as figuratively.

I have to confess that I can't see the gestalt that Eve and Stan conjured up. The mobiles describe it as a 'black sphere' bobbing in the air, but there's something in its nature that renders it invisible to my unique visual capability. On the other hand, I sense heat energy radiating from where it is supposed to be – sometimes warm, sometimes scorching. I suspect it correlates to the amount of energy it generates at a given moment. I'll have to ask Emil about that....

...I have been replaying my experience of that final battle over and over for the past three days, and each time I get the willies. I don't know which is worse: an alien invasion from outer space, or the tiger we've got by the tail.

A dangerous weapon indeed!

* * *

Half an hour later, Larkin and Sheena were back on the road, returning to the City. The visit to DEDEP's make-shift infirmary had been a waste of time; the moment they walked in, they knew they wouldn't be able to talk to either Eve or Stan. All they could do was to stare helplessly at them.

The gestalt-summoners had appeared as if they were in a coma – silent, unmoving, and unaware of their surroundings. Yet, it hadn't been some run-of-the-mill coma, for their eyes were wide open and they were staring at the ceiling in a stuporous fashion. Emil had likened their state of mind as being in a trance; whatever was playing out in their minds was absorbing their attention completely, and no external stimuli could penetrate the mental barrier which had been erected. That something *was* playing out was evidenced by rapid-eye movement of the sort that dreamers exhibit.

They're wide awake, the detective had mused, *and yet they're dreaming. If I had a right arm to give, I'd gladly give it for a chance to see what they're seeing.*

Larkin and Sheena had said their good-byes and left in a mood of great sadness. The former was especially upset. He had formulated the plan to get Mr. Jones off DEDEP's back, and the plan had worked better than he had wanted it to. And that hadn't been the first time one of his schemes failed to account for all of the consequences – Eve had been the principal victim there too – and he couldn't be sure that future schemes would be exempt. He could have written off the unintended consequences as the result of unknown variables, but he would have been rationalizing his inability to take all the variables into account. He was supposed to be the "master strategist," wasn't he? He had to take responsibility.

The drive back to the City was as silent and uneventful as the outbound trip. The partners were again lost in their private thoughts. Once they had entered the City, Larkin suggested that they return to the depot in order to check on any new developments.

He wasn't disappointed. As they approached the depot, he spotted two squad cars still on the scene; the officers were still searching the area where the bodies had been (although the bodies had long since been taken away). And the usual crowd of rubberneckers who invariably collected around a tragic event – the morbidly curious humans who lived vicariously through the misfortunes of others – was in full flourish. All this he related to Sheena.

"I can sense many people there," she responded. "Their emotions are hammering at my mind. They're full of lust, on the verge of having an orgasm." She wrapped her arms about her in order to keep from shaking. "Please, George, let's leave."

"All right. I've seen enough here. Look, I want to cruise around for a while and see if we can spot our missing 'eel'."

Sheena pulled away from the depot and began criss-crossing the streets in the business district. Personally, she thought it was a waste of time. True, a stranger in town might keep to the main streets so as not to lose her bearings more than she had to; on the other hand, if she were used to being on the run from the St. Louis branch of the Disciples, she might be able to apply her experiences there to the not-so-different environment here. In which case, she would be the "needle" in this urban "haystack." She could be hiding in plain sight for all they knew, using her skills to blend into the backdrop. Even if the "eel" were easily frightened, she could still be hard to find. She'd be constantly on the move, seeking some safe haven, not stopping until she had found one. She could backtrack to a previous location if she thought the place she currently occupied became compromised.

But Sheena was not about to tell George this. He was the "master strategist" here, not her, and he usually knew what he was doing. Personally, she would rather cuddle up with him, caressing and kissing – and a lot more. But she couldn't tell him that either; he'd have some excuse for not being romantic. So, she kept driving.

Whenever Larkin spied a lone female on the street, he had Sheena slow to a crawl so that he could eyeball the "suspect" more readily. The reactions he received from those females fell into three distinct categories: (1) fright; (2) anger; and (3) invitation. (1) thought she would be raped and have no avenue of escape. (2) thought the fellow was a pervert and gave him an obscene hand gesture. And (3) thought she had a customer for the evening. But, none of the females matched the description Larkin had gotten from his contact in St. Louis, and none resembled the frightened young woman who was nearly run over at the depot.

Just as the detective was about to call it a night, he did spot the "eel." She was slowly walking along Main Street, darting from one shadowy doorway to the next in a well-practiced manner, all the while looking this way and that for any threatening persons. He might have missed her altogether but for the fact that she had passed by a street lamp during one of her maneuvers, and he recognized her. Quickly, he had Sheena pull over to the curb where he rolled down the window and called out to her.

"Jean! Jean Fulton! I'm George Larkin. I've come to pick you up."

Why she didn't believe a word he said could be chalked up to any number of reasons. In her present state of mind, she was in no mood to trust anyone late at night on a lonely street in an unfamiliar city. Instead, she bolted and ran down the street. Larkin and Sheena pursued her. She turned into a narrow alleyway and disappeared into the darkness. They circled the block in an attempt to intercept her at the other end of the alleyway but caught no sight of her. Somehow, the "eel" had gone to ground.

C⊕UNTER-ESPI⊕NAGE

AS THE YEAR 2018 wore on, each passing day set a new temperature record. While temperatures did not always increase – sometimes they "plateaued" for a day or so – they did not decrease, and they reflected for the most part the total number of sequential days where the reading reached a certain level and/or exceeded it. The weakening (and occasional disappearance) of the ozone layer over the Earth's polar regions expanded in slow progression and allowed ever more amounts of raw solar energy to bombard the planet's surface. Weather alerts were now an hourly occurrence, and the inhabitants in all parts of the globe were advised to limit their outdoor activity to the bare minimum. Nevertheless, the hospitals were full of patients who, on a daily basis, succumbed to heat exhaustion/prostration. The demand for salt tablets threatened to outstrip the supply, and their prices increased in direct proportion to the temperature.

Two other areas of concern threatened to over-tax the ability of human agencies to avert them. One was near-spontaneous combustion. As the planet heated up, the land masses dried up, especially in the naturally arid regions. The least spark could trigger a raging wildfire, even in the heart of a populated area. Fire departments everywhere were on constant alert for such outbreaks which became a daily occurrence. Some fires were easily put out where there was sufficient manpower, water supplies, and anti-combustion deterrents available; others raged on for days and weeks, resulting in a large loss of life and/or property.

The second area of concern was actually a consequence of the first, and that was the diminishing supply of water (or the lack thereof). It was a two-prong problem. First, the rising temperatures evaporated liquid water at an ever higher rate, and, second, they prevented water vapor in the atmosphere from precipitating out in the first place. All of the Earth's rivers, lakes, and oceans began to shrink, and water consumption for personal use, manufacturing, agriculture, and fire-fighting was subject to rationing in the hardest hit areas. Rationing was not at all popular, of course, and "water wars" broke out everywhere as humans fought for possession of dwindling supplies. Civil society in some places was on the verge of collapse.

Happily, the City – and by extension DEDEP – suffered neither continuous outbreaks of near-spontaneous combustion nor scarce water supplies – for the present. It was close to a cluster of large lakes from which to fulfill its needs. But the residents paid a stiff price for their largesse in the form, first, of higher rates for public supplies and, second, of even higher prices for private supplies, i.e. bottled water. The residents paid this price with forbearance (if not with equipoise), because they could hardly do without water. *Sic semper naturalis!*

Like most residents of the City whose business necessitated their being out and about, Larkin carried a bottle of water wherever he went but drank sparingly of it in order to stretch his supply as far as possible and to save money. Some days, it was difficult to do either, and only his will power kept him on the "straight and narrow."

On the morning after the failure to apprehend the "eel," he entered the suite of the Larkin-Whitley Detective Agency, only to find his secretary, Mrs. Watson, uncharacteristically absent. Not that he begrudged her taking time off now and then; but, because she seldom did, he had come to take her presence at her desk for granted. In light of recent events, he suspected she was tending to her ill husband. He scanned her desk for any mail or messages she might have left for him, found none, and proceeded to the "snoop room."

The "snoop room" was where the real detective work was carried out. Larkin had installed a fantastic array of state-of-the-art electronic equipment to aid him in communications and information-gathering. Only out of absolute necessity did he ever go out and knock on doors as his illustrious (and not-so-illustrious) predecessors had done in the "bad old days." He affixed the "DETECTIVE AT WORK" sign to the door and entered.

Once inside, he went unerringly to his special stool parked near the giant monitor of his array, switched on, and logged in. The computer came alive with a swirl of color and a bar from Tchaikovsky's "1812 Overture" which he had programmed into the hard drive. The swirl and bar segued to a "WELCOME" message, followed by the menu. Since the array was designed to perform multiple tasks, Larkin had created a special menu to help him navigate through layers of windows. He selected "Phone Messages." A half dozen lines of print appeared on the monitor's screen. All but one were from clients or potential clients; he read those perfunctorily and made mental notes concerning possible responses.

The one message not from a client/potential client was the one which interested him the most. It was from Gordy, his friend and former FBI agent, whom he had taken into his confidence concerning the presence of extraterrestrials on earth and had corralled into searching FBI files for relevant information. Said information was scarce, thanks to President Hadley Richardson's Department of Justice. The message read:

"STOP! QUIT OUR NEW ARENA! ROCKS KNOCK STUDS AFTER YAHOOS HAVE CARTS OF BEVELS ROPED BY THE EGG ROOM. IS FIVE TONS ROUGH ON ME? NEED A CLASSY BOAT, STINGY!"

The "key" to Gordy's bizarre message was the number which appeared in it. In this case, it was "five" and meant that the decoder should take every fifth letter to form the true message. Larkin took up his pencil and began counting and writing. What he came up with unnerved him no end. The hidden message read:

"QUARK SAYS CONVOY GOING EAST."

Convoy!

This was serious stuff. Not only were the Swarm investigating the disappearance of their agent, they were also preparing to expand their base in the City in order to deal with the *cause* of the disappearance in a time-honored fashion, i.e. a search-and-destroy mission. A convoy meant extra equipment. But what kind of equipment were they bringing? The detective did not like the sound of this.

He checked the date of the message and discovered that it had been sent yesterday. How much time had elapsed between the time of the Quark's sending and Gordy's forwarding it to him? More relevant: how did the Quark know where to send it? He'd have to ask Gordy ASAP.

The time that the convoy had left Nebraska was crucial. If it left, say, the day before yesterday and traveled non-stop, it could be in the City already, setting up the special equipment and organizing the search. He and DEDEP had their work cut out for them, and it was anybody's guess as to the outcome of any confrontation. DEDEP had a formidable weapon, but would it be enough to defeat the Swarm's purpose?

First, he needed to check his e-mail and learn if the Quintessential Quark had included him in the update. He switched the PC from "phone" mode to "PC" mode and waited (barely) patiently for the e-mail listings to appear on the screen. An age passed before they did. He quickly scanned the list, found what he was looking for, and highlighted it.

True to form, the Web "hitchhiker" rambled on in paranoid fashion, describing his latest observations of the UFO base in Nebraska. And, when he got to the part where the aliens were loading up three semi-trailers with "a lotta weird-lookin' shit," he read each word very carefully. The Quark had improved his descriptive abilities over the past few days (was he off his drugs?), either due to a sense of urgency which required quick action or as a sense of relief that someone was finally taking him seriously – or both. Whatever the reason, he now provided details of the aliens' physique, their behavior, and the machines they loaded onto the semis (even if he didn't understand their purpose). Larkin took particular note of the number of Swarm personnel accompanying the convoy – a driver and his assistant in the cab and two more in the trailer, a dozen all told. The Quark concluded with what was now his signature line: "WHAT THE FUCK'S GOIN' ON, MAN?"

What indeed was going on?

The detective had a glimmer of an idea, but he didn't like it one bit. It was too awful to think about.

He heard the door to the "snoop room" opening and closing, followed by the scraping of a chair across the floor.

"Sleeping in late, Sheena?" he inquired without turning around.

"I was exhausted, George. We had a busy night last night."

"Yes, we did. And we're going to be even busier from now on."

He activated the synthesized "voice" function of the computer and replayed Quark's message. Now he turned around to gauge Sheena's reaction. Alarm was written all over her face; she gripped the arms of her chair and threatened to break them with the applied pressure. When the "voice" had finished "speaking," she sank into the chair and stared in her partner's direction.

"God, George! This is – *horrible!*" She blanched suddenly. "Oh, *no!*"

"What?"

"Do you remember some trucks passing by us as we were on our way to DEDEP? *Three* of them, heading toward the City."

"Vaguely," he murmured. A light bulb lit up in his brain. "You don't mean to say…?"

"I thought at the time it was strange a convoy of trucks would be on the highway at that time of the night."

"Unless they were on some urgent business. Well, that settles it. Mr. Smith has got to know about this. And he'd better have that 'special equipment' he promised us. Meanwhile, I want you and Kenny or Paddy to drive around town and see if you can pick up the Swarm's unique signals. The sooner we can track them, the better we can plan our counter-offensive."

* * *

It was probably Larkin's imagination, but the abandoned supermarket on Hill Avenue appeared to be even more dilapidated on this visit. The roof was sagging further down, the outer walls were buckling further inwardly, and the foundation was sinking further into the ground. If the building had been a living thing, one might have concluded that the excessive heat had sapped the strength out of its body and that it was withering away with each passing day. The least vibration would send it crashing in upon itself, leaving a pile of decay and rot.

The detective approached it warily, lest too heavy a footfall provide that fatal vibration. As he drew nearer, he could hear the groaning and moaning as what breeze there was passed through cracks in the structure and caused an imperceptible shift throughout. He maintained a discreet distance from the building as he rounded the far corner and proceeded toward the loading docks in the rear. The one consolation was that he chose to be on the side away from the morning sun; the shade offered a brief respite from the high temperature of a degree or two.

He stepped gingerly onto the stairs leading up to the docks, expecting them to collapse at any second and dash him against a pile of rubble. Miraculously, he navigated the stairs safely but still did not relax his guard. Slowly but surely, he edged toward the rear entrance. The groaning and moaning was just as intense here as it had been in the front. A shiver worked its way up his spine and down again, and he found little relief as he passed through the doorway into the receiving area.

There, the ever-present stench assaulted him as it had on his previous visits, and he immediately began to breathe through his mouth. This tactic did not entirely protect his olfactory nerve, but it reduced the assault to a tolerable level for the short time it took him to enter the supermarket proper. As he wended his way into the store, he wondered why the stench had returned. On his last visit, Mr. Smith had somehow neutralized the odor. Had he forgotten to do it today?

Thinking about that question shifted his concentration away from his footing, and he slipped on a patch of rancid vegetable oil. He fell to one "knee" and found himself at an awkward angle; his artificial legs could not find enough traction to right him, and he had to rock back and forth until traction was obtained. In the back of his mind, he was glad that Sheena wasn't here. She would've wailed inconsolably at his plight and cursed herself for not being able to help him to his "feet." After what seemed like hours, he pushed himself upright and headed – more cautiously than ever – for the central part of the store.

Nothing appeared to have changed in the outlay of alien equipment in this "listening post." On the other hand, since Larkin was dealing with a variety of alien species, he couldn't be sure that there weren't any changes; for all he knew, he could be looking at a device he hadn't noticed before. He recognized the ten eight-foot-high, silver-gray modules which were Mr. Smith's translating devices to connect him with his fellow operatives on Earth. In front of them was the 100-inch monitor with its control console. Opposite those, the cold-fusion generator hunkered quietly but ominously; he had shivered every time he thought about its potential to wipe the City off the map. Next to it, the low-frequency electromagnetic generator hummed and sent out its protective force field. The twelve-foot-tall pole and its two attendants which linked the alien to his colleagues on Earth was strangely quiescent. The same could not be said for the over-sized "Tinker Toy" for deep-space communication; all the colors of the rainbow were flashing all at once across their components.

The pasty-faced alien was standing in front of the 200-inch monitor and speaking to another alien somewhere beyond the Solar System. Mr. Smith spoke in his own language; and, while Larkin understood not a word of it, it reminded him of a Gregorian chant, speeded up. How the distant alien sounded, he would never know; his speech was being translated into more "chants." From the animated gestures both creatures were producing, the detective guessed they were having a spirited conversation, perhaps an argument of some sort.

Larkin studied the new alien carefully. If he hadn't known better, he might have sworn he was looking at a Chinese individual. The round face, the skin color, and the hair pulled back to resemble a skullcap were almost identical to an Oriental. The one feature which distinguished this creature from a human (other than its language) was the color of its hair; it was corn-silk yellow (as opposed to the black of the average Chinese), and one had to look closely to tell where the skin ended and the hair began.

He wondered idly just how many species were represented in the Coalition of Sad Despoiled Beings and whether he'd meet all of them. The real question, however, was whether they'd be willing to meet with *him,* a so-called "primitive" in the cosmic scheme of things. Given what Mr. Smith had told him about his own background, it was even money that most of the membership of the Coalition were not too much less "primitive" than the average "Tellurian." They were, after all, a collective of victims of war, hardly the elite of their respective (and now defunct) societies.

Mr. Smith now caught sight of Larkin at the edge of the clearing. The latter, convinced that he was now a member of the Coalition, had made no effort to conceal himself. There erupted from the translator a burst of very speeded-up language, even as the maker of it went through a set of frantic gestures with its hands. In response, Mr. Smith spoke something to his colleague; the other's voice slowed down slightly, and his gestures abated. After a few more seconds of speech, the monitor went dark, and the flashing lights on the "Tinker Toy" blinked off, one by one.

The pasty-faced alien faced his new ally and grimaced.

"Mr....Largin...I...egspegted...you...two...days...ago."

"I had a...confrontation with Mr. Jones, and it took up more of my time than I had planned on." Whereupon, he launched into a detailed account of the "confrontation," taking care to disguise all references to DEDEP and the black sphere. "I barely escaped with a whole skin," he concluded.

As the detective related his edited account, he also took note of Mr. Smith's reaction to it. The other made no attempt to mask his feelings upon hearing of Mr. Jones' demise; his face twisted into a grotesque version of itself, and he pounded his fist against his leg. Whether these gestures signified pleasure or displeasure, the human could not say, nor did he want to jump to any conclusions. Best to let his "client" express his feelings himself.

"Thhhen…thhhese…Disciples…terminated…Mr….Shones?" the alien said at last. "Hhhow…did…you…manashe…to…persuade…thhhem…to…attag?"

"I, ah, told them that Mr. Jones was an evil spirit and let them decide their own course of action."

"Evil…thhhat…being…certainly…was…and…hhhe…rishly…deserved…his…fate.   Unforshunately…hhhis…deathhh…presents…a…problem."

"How so?"

"Hhhis…failure…to…report…to…hhhis…superiors…will…prompt…   an…investigation.   Thhhat…may…upset…thhhe…Goalition's…timetable."

"I can tell you that they're already conducting an investigation, Mr. Smith." Larkin now described the scene at the depot insofar as he was familiar with it but left out the part the "eel" might have played in it. He also added the account of the convoy from Nebraska. "It's imperative that we deal with this new group as quickly – and discreetly – as possible."

The alien responded with another twisting of his face and pounding of his leg. The detective concluded that his client was quite displeased with what he was hearing. Not that he could blame him, of course, but the "good guys" had to be realistic about this turn of events – and soon!

"I…must…relay…thhhis…information…to…thhhe…Goalition…and…receive…new…instrugtions. Egscuse…me…Mr….Largin."

"Speaking of the Coalition, that…person you were talking to when I came in seemed upset to see me."

"A…normal…reagtion…on…hhhis…part.   Aside…from…Frommar…   and…myself…none…of…thhhe…membership…hhhas…ever…seen…a… Tellurian. Thhhey…know…your…gind…egsists…of…gourse…but… thhhey…do…not…know…whhhat…you…loog…lighe."

"I suppose we look as frightening to them as they do to us." Mr. Smith nodded knowingly. "On the other hand, since you're all different from each other, you must have some tolerance for other species."

"We...hhhave...learned...to...put...aside...some...of...our... differences...for...thhhe...greater...good...whhhish...is...thhhe... utter... destrugtion...of...thhhe...Swarm."

"A noble action, to be sure. Tell me more about the Coalition. How did it come about, and when?"

Mr. Smith stared at him dispassionately for a moment. Then: "Is...thhhis...information...important...to...you?"

"It might help us...Tellurians to co-ordinate our efforts with yours if we knew more about you." He paused for a second or two. "Please?"

"Very...well...Mr....Largin. Now...thhhat...you...are...a...new... 'member'...you...deserve...to...hhhave...thhhe...whhhole...story."

The Swarm is truly a terrorist organization [Mr. Smith began], *and it lives only for destruction and slaughter. Yet, it cannot kill an entire species. Some few escape the slaughter and warn other species of the impending danger.*

As the refugees grew in number, they sought each other out for the purpose of presenting a united front in order to convince those species not yet 'visited' by the Swarm that they must prepare themselves and to assist the refugees in their time of need. In particular, the refugees pleaded their case to those species more technologically advanced in the hopes of forming a military alliance to confront and defeat the Swarm. It took many long [untranslatable] *to achieve this latter goal, but eventually it was accomplished. Unfortunately, in the interim, the number of the Swarm's victims increased.*

The resulting Coalition of Sad Despoiled Beings, now fifty [untranslatable] *old, is a diverse group, representing* [untranslatable] *of species across a broad spectrum of technological achievement. My own species were on the verge of sending explorative teams to neighboring planets in our star system when the Swarm descended upon us and reduced us to rubble. Frommar's people were even more advanced – perhaps two hundred* [untranslatable] *ahead of yours. But we are all united in the face of a common foe. There are other species in this Galaxy we have not yet contacted, but we intend to do so; even now, our agents are traveling far and wide to seek them out before it is too late for them to survive. Sadly, it may be too late for some of them. But we persevere lest the whole Galaxy falls prey to this monstrous invader.*

Our strategy, as I have said before, is one of stealth, careful planning, and clandestine military exercises in order to build our strength. Our goal is to deal the Swarm one swift, crushing blow so that all that is left of them is a painful memory. We are now on the verge of delivering that blow, Mr. Larkin, and we have chosen this star system as the battlefield. Our forces are nearly in place, and soon the Enemy will fall into the trap we have prepared for them.

It will be a fight to the death — ours or theirs — 'no holds barred,' as you Tellurians say. Either we win, or the Galaxy loses.

A near-silence filled the wreck of a supermarket as one creature absorbed this new information and pondered the enormity of its implications and the other creature delved into his own private world and contemplated what fate awaited him. The only sounds were the whistling wind blowing through the cracks in the structure and the vibrations of its settling.

Larkin licked dry lips and gazed upward, attempting to discern the forces of the Coalition far off in space. He imagined he saw it, imagined the Swarm's arrival, imagined the conflict which ensued — and shuddered in horror at the finality it represented. Unconsciously, he pulled his handkerchief from his pocket and wiped away the perspiration which had suddenly formed on his face. He gazed now at Mr. Smith and formed his next words carefully.

"Why this star system? What makes *it* so special?"

In response, the frail alien reached into his own pocket, pulled out the small metal box he carried there, and snapped it open. He took out one of the tiny pink spheroids, popped it into his mouth, and swallowed. He pocketed the box and regarded his new ally solemnly.

"I…will…be…gandid…withhh…you…Mr.…Largin. Thhhis… star… system…hhhas…no…special…value. It…is…merely…thhhe…

Swarm's... negst...target...and...thhhe...Goalition...is...ready...to... strighe."

"I...see. Well, thank you for being candid. Now, what about that 'special equipment' I was promised?"

"Wait hhhere. I...will...return...shortly."

Mr. Smith turned and plodded toward the module which housed his cold-fusion generator. He slid open a panel on one side, entered, and slid the panel shut. Larkin shivered again at the thought of the destructive potential of that machine and forced himself to think of something else. He focused on the "Tinker Toy," now quiescent, and wished idly that he could have one like it, albeit on a smaller scale. He also wished he could have some of those translators; detective work would be a whole lot easier if he could reach out to the entire planet.

Presently, Mr. Smith re-appeared. In his hand, he carried a brass-colored sphere approximately ten centimeters in diameter. He held it out for the detective's inspection. The latter regarded it with mixed feelings. On the one hand, he was puzzled over what its function was; on the other hand, he was annoyed at the very real possibility that it was the sum total of the "special equipment" he was going to get. Carefully, he took the piece out of the alien's clammy hand and peered at it from different angles. There were five shallow depressions in each hemisphere, equidistant from each other. He looked at Mr. Smith questioningly.

"And this does what?"

"It...is...a...traghing...device...Mr....Largin. Withhh...it...you... may... logate...anyone...you...wish...whhherever...hhhe...may...be... and...follow ...hhhis...every...movement." He reached into his coat pocket and produced a sheet of paper-like material which glistened even in the dim lighting of the supermarket. He handed it to the detective. "Hhhere... are...thhhe...operating...instructions. Thhhe...device... is...really...guite... easy...to...use."

Larkin had to smile to himself. He didn't need this gadget, whether or not it was easy to use. He already had a tracking "device" -- *two* of them, in fact – which had proven their capability dozens of times. He couldn't tell Mr. Smith about the Twins, of course, because DEDEP and its personnel were still his ace-up-his-sleeve, and he loathed to negate their value to him, even if the fate of the world depended on complete candor. Still, he couldn't refuse the gift either. He had to remain on cordial terms with the Coalition and its agents at all times. The fate of the world did depend on that! Besides, who knew how aliens would react if you refused a gift? The worst-case scenario was the Coalition's packing up and leaving the "Tellurians" to face the Swarm alone.

"Ah, thank you, Mr. Smith. But, is this all I get? I was hoping for something more...substantial."

"I...am...sure...you...were.   But...as...I...hhhave...already... told... you...we...gannot...give...ahhh...'less...developed'...species... any... sophistigated...weapons. Perhhhaps...in...time...whhhen... your... efforts...on...our...behhhalf...warrants...a...shanshe...in... policy... we...will...offer...you...more." He closed his eyes, took a deep breath, and let it out slowly. "Speaking...of...whhhish... gan... you... tell...me... whhhat...begame...of...Mr....Shones'...eguipment?"

"I took some of it to my...base of operations to see what I could learn about it. The rest is still at Mr. Jones' base. As soon as I have the time, I'll move it to a safe place."

"I...would...appreciate...thhhat. We...gannot...allow...thhhe... Swarm ...to regain...possession...of...it."

Larkin exited the building as quickly as he could in case Mr. Smith changed his mind about letting him take possession of the Swarm equipment, regretting all the way having been so short with his "client." But, in the larger scheme of things, he hoped to be on a par with the aliens, technology-wise, and the Swarm's now unattended devices was a good start. He'd turn it over to Monk and let the Department of Energy man have a go at making it work for DEDEP. Perhaps a working knowledge would help enhance "Tellurian" value to the Coalition.

In the meantime, his other appointment was equally long overdue. Except, in this case, it was *not* an appointment he was looking forward to!

* * *

"Do slow down, love. We'll be of no use to our dear George if we're all dashed to pieces."

While Sheena Whitley loved George Larkin more than she could express in words, she would rather have had someone other than him to do her "backseat" driving. George always gave her a detailed description of the scene before them as they cruised the streets of the City, and she had to translate his words into a visualization she could handle. Often, she had difficulty doing so. Ordinarily, her hypersenses could form a "picture" she could "see" where she was at; but, in many instances, they were a poor substitute for actual eyesight. Sometimes, she had had to ask George to repeat himself in order to get a real "picture." And, in those instances, she also "read" the regret he felt for having let her drive.

Traveling with either of the Smythes, however, presented no problems whatever. Since Kenny and Paddy were telepathic, all they had to do was to send her a mental picture of the scene before them, and she could "see" it as if she had real eyesight. It was an exhilarating experience, one which enhanced the thrill of being able to drive in the first place and, consequently, she tended to get carried away and drove faster than she should.

Properly chagrined, she eased up on the accelerator and mumbled an apology. Kenny reached over and patted her hand as a gesture of good will.

"Not to worry, love. When we've found where those Swarm blighters are holed up, I'll let you go out on the highway for a bit. Then you can pretend you're bloody Dale Earnhart."

"Thanks, Kenny. I'd like that."

"And, of course, we shan't tell our dear George about our little side trip. Mum's the word, eh?"

"You got it, pal. Speaking of the Swarm, have you picked up their signal yet?"

"Not a trace so far. I suppose we'll have to knock up the whole city before I do. I – Hello! What's this?"

"What have you got, Kenny?"

"Pull over to the curb and let me concentrate."

She did as instructed and switched off the engine. The telepath leaned back in his seat, closed his eyes, and slowed his breathing. Sheena watched him anxiously. It was like watching grass grow. The seconds ticked away like hours. Presently, Kenny's eyes snapped open.

"Got it, by Jove! Due south of here. Let's go."

Sheena pulled away from the curb, again guided by Kenny's imagery in her mind. He gave her turning directions from time to time in an effort to stay on course, but otherwise gave her her head. Their route took them through a residential area, peppered with small businesses; the further south they went, the fewer the residences and the more the businesses. Finally, they found themselves on Ridgeway Avenue where several large manufacturing concerns were located.

One of these concerns was abandoned. Weeds dotted the parkway and the walkway in front of the building. Many of the windows were broken, and those which weren't were covered with grime. The foundation was cracked in several places, and the wind whistled through all of them. The loading docks had collapsed from disuse and were a mass of broken timbers. The main door was chained shut. Over it, a sign with faded lettering proclaimed "Ridgeway Bearing Company – Established [*illegible*]." With her hypersenses, Sheena caught a whiff of the mustiness which permeated the structure like a cancer, and she recoiled from it as one who has sensed the presence of Death.

Nevertheless, she forced herself to get out of the station wagon and approach the building. Kenny was right beside her, his mind focused on fifteen distinct signals emanating from within. They cautiously made their way around to the west side and toward the rear. Neither made any move to come within twenty meters of the place on the off-chance that the Swarm had erected a low-frequency electromagnetic generator to protect their base from snoopers. As they rounded the far corner, Kenny gasped in surprise.

"What do you see, Kenny?" Sheena asked in alarm.

In response, he relayed an image of three black semi-trailers parked neatly side by side. She gasped as well.

"That clinches it. This is the Swarm's base all right. God only knows what they're up to in there."

"Right-o, love. I suggest we leave and report back to George."

"I'm with you, chum. I've 'seen' enough."

Before they could return to the street, however, they were frozen in place by an eerie sound issuing from inside the building. It started out as a low hum, then turned into a screech as of metal grinding against metal. The old ball-bearing plant shook violently for the space of five seconds; and from all of the windows (even the filthy ones), a brilliant blue-white light flashed into existence and was immediately extinguished. Utter silence followed.

"What the hell was *that*?" Sheena whispered.

"I don't know, and I don't care to know. Let's leave, shall we?"

"Wait. George will want to know what we found here. It may be important to his plans."

"We'll be taking an awful chance."

"Well, it's not like we're completely defenseless."

"True. Still..."

And before Kenny could finish his sentence, Sheena began to inch her way toward the building, using all of her senses to guide her. The telepath shook his head in resignation and followed her.

At a distance of ten meters from the building, Sheena felt the sensation she most dreaded: the pulsing of an EM field. Instantly, her skin began to crawl. She halted, shuddered involuntarily, and hugged herself in an attempt to ward off the unpleasant feeling. Kenny caught up with her and noticed the anguish in her face.

"What is it, love?"

"They've got an EM generator in there, and it's just been turned on."

"That means that whatever is inside is closed to my mind."

"You could still peek in one of the windows."

"Yes, I could, couldn't I?" He sighed heavily. "Ah, the things I do for DEDEP."

The psycho-communicator trudged off and picked his way toward the nearest broken window. Just as he was about to peek inside, another low hum sounded. He steeled himself against what he believed would come next and was happy he did. The screeching was louder and longer than before, and he covered his ears instinctively. Sheena writhed in pain as her senses became overloaded. The brilliant blue-white light which ensued caused his eyes to tear, now that he was closer to the source, and he feared instant blindness. He leaned against the building and waited until the racket – and its effects – subsided.

When the effects wore off, he peered through the window. The interior was suffused with a dim illumination from several mobile lamps scattered about. Not that he could see anything worthwhile – this part of the factory was empty. Only debris covered the floor, and rusted machinery hunkered here and there. The mustiness assailed his olfactory nerve even more, now that he was close by. He moved further down the building to the next broken window and looked into it. He saw movement now; several stocky humanoid shapes were visible and busying themselves with the assembly of some unknown object.

He needed a different angle of view to determine what the Swarm was constructing. But, before moving on to another open window, he checked on Sheena's condition. She remained rooted to the spot where he had left her, unwilling to go anywhere until she was absolutely sure that it was safe to do so. Kenny briefly contemplated re-joining her because she was quite exposed where she was and thus vulnerable to anyone who might happen to glance outside. If worse came to worse, he could project an image into her mind which would lead her back to the station wagon.

At his next "port of call," he received the shock of his life. He saw clearly all of the Swarm engaged in assembling a large metallic object, easily thirty meters in length and approximately five meters in height. The thing filled up this section of the building, leaving little room for anything else. It appeared to be battleship-gray in color; but, in the dim illumination, it was hard to tell. His mouth went dry as he realized what he was looking at. From Eve's description – obtained when she had a psychometric reading in Mr. Smith's apartment – the thing could only be one of the Swarm's atmospheric warships which spat fire and incinerated animate and inanimate objects alike. The Swarm was planning an assault on some unknown target!

Kenny did not need to let his imagination run wild to understand the implications of this discovery. Not only were the Swarm investigating the disappearance of their agent, but they were also ready to punish those responsible. And the punishment would be obliteration!

Sheena had been correct to learn what was taking place in this abandoned factory. Otherwise, DEDEP would be unprepared for a fearsome weapon of war. It was imperative to contact Larkin, report to him, and let him work out a counter-offensive (if one could be worked out, that is).

As if to emphasize the point, the low humming repeated itself. Kenny strained to see what was occurring. One of the soldiers was passing a small black cube – similar to the one Mr. Jones had used to agonizing effect – across a section of the warship. The psycho-communicator braced himself, covered his ears, and closed his eyes; by doing so, he partially avoided the effects of the screeching and the flash of light. The soldier moved to another section of the ship's hull.

Having seen all that he cared to see, Kenny turned and trotted back to Sheena's position. Her pained expression told him that she was not weathering the sensory assault either. He told her what he had just witnessed, and her agony instantly turned to horror.

"Oh, God, Kenny! This is awful! What have we gotten ourselves into?"

"A spot of bother, I should judge. *Now* we leave."

As they made their way to the station wagon, they were "encouraged" by yet another assault on the senses.

CHAPTER THREE

INTO THE LION'S DEN

MUCH HAD BEEN written about the election of 2016. Every pundit, commentator, and columnist across the political spectrum seemed to have written the "definitive" analysis of the event; most concentrated on the personalities of the major players, although one could find a paragraph or two which had focused on the issues. These latter generated the most controversy, as one might expect, and the authors spent much of their personal capital defending their remarks afterwards. Only one writer made an attempt at objectivity, and she was largely ignored. Most of America had an axe to grind, and many axes were ground.

The one point that everyone agreed upon was that the election of 2016 was a seminal event. In the first place, it was the first time since 1860 that a third-party candidate had captured the White House; Hadley Richardson was no Abraham Lincoln by any stretch of the imagination, but he did win – as did the "Great Emancipator" – because Americans were looking for a change in the political environment. And, in the second place, it was the first time ever that a political party whose emphasis was on moral redemption had captured the American imagination. That that party might be a violation of the First

Amendment's dictum of separation of state and church bothered no one except the hard-core secularists (afterwards largely disorganized).

As the twenty-first century opened, the Democrats had already flat-lined due in large part to the excesses of the Kennedy clan. Subsequent candidates were either "weak sisters" or too close to the "Old Guard." The Republicans might have thought the way was clear to establish a conservative "dynasty," starting with the Dole presidency; but, external factors had entered the fray, and the Grand Old Party soon found itself steamrollered as well.

It began with the recession of 2003 and the President's weak response. Four major Wall Street banks had declared bankruptcy following a run on all of their branches, and the Federal Reserve was undecided as to the proper course of action. Hundreds of lesser banks fell into the abyss as well, and still the central government was paralyzed. The conservatives inside and outside of the Belt, having long put their trust in the marketplace, could not bring themselves to enact measures which they considered "socialist" that Franklin D. Roosevelt had pushed in the 1930's. Liberals demanded such measures, and they raised the issue of impeachment of the President for his waffling, but they were ignored.

With the closing of the banks, factories and retail businesses also closed, and hundreds of thousands of Americans lost their jobs. Demagogues of all stripes railed against the politicians, the corporate CEO's, the bankers, and anybody else whom they believed had had a hand in destroying the economy. Huge crowds gathered in the streets on a daily basis and were harangued into taking action; riots, vandalism, and looting soon became a "way of life" for many who had no other voice. Martial law was declared in many cities across the nation, and the National Guard was mobilized; the Dole Administration hinted at a nation-wide mobilization which only made tempers worse. The United States teetered on the edge of anarchy.

Enter the Return-to-Purity Party.

The party leaders saw their opportunity to direct the affairs of state, a goal which had eluded their predecessors. They gave free rein to Hadley Richardson to make speeches and write op-ed pieces to all the media, and he made the most of the opportunity. From one end of the country to the other, he denounced the "evils" of the secular state and declared that the recession was "God's punishment" for turning away from the Light of Purity. He remonstrated like no other preacher had ever done before, and soon Americans began to believe what he was saying. They "enlisted" in the Party in droves.

At this point, President Dole blinked. He was not prepared to speak against a religious revival, for that would have made him look even worse than his waffling on the economy had done. His further inaction cost him his re-election in 2004.

By the time of the election of 2016, the Return-to-Purity Party had seized control of both the national and the state legislatures, and the party leaders were primed to take the final step toward total control of the country. They had a detailed plan of attack; drawing on their experiences in previous elections, they knew what had worked and what hadn't and acted accordingly. They pulled out all the stops by cranking out leaflets, flyers, and posters by the truckload, buying huge amounts of television and radio time, and sending out hundreds of "talking heads" to poll the electorate. They worked tirelessly around the clock, seizing on the least misstep of the opposition to score political points for their candidate, Hadley Richardson. The campaign became a be-all and end-all for the "Light of Purity."

In the City, the Disciples of Purity were especially enthusiastic in their "missionary" work for one salient reason: Archdeacon E.A. Fogarty. It was the worst-kept secret in this Congressional district that the old man aspired to be a Bishop in the organization and that he would move mountains in order to achieve that lofty position. To be a Bishop meant that he had to exert himself above and beyond what was expected from ordinary Disciples; he had not only to elevate the requisite number of Deacons to Archdeacons but he also had to do so in a manner which would catch the eyes of the national staff. The fact of the matter was that he was not interested in becoming a Bishop over a geographical territory but in being a Bishop on that staff. And, if he had to exert himself, he would see to it that his own people would work just as hard as he did.

Archdeacon Fogarty saw the election of 2016 as The Opportunity to achieve his goal. He harangued his underlings day in and day out on the necessity of bringing the "Light of Purity" to as many as they could; he buttonholed every VIP (political and business) and tried to enlist their support for the local candidate the RPP was backing as well as Hadley Richardson. One marveled at the tremendous amount of energy he was able to summon up for the rigorous schedule he set for himself.

The race for the seat in the House of Representatives from the district in which the City was located was, as it happened, a four-man contest which in itself was unusual even if there had been no Return-to-Purity Party. For all practical purposes, however, it was a two-man contest as both the Republicans and the Democrats fielded candidates no one expected to win many votes; they fielded those candidates simply to save face. The real contest was between the RPP and a newly resurgent Progressive Party born of the economic disaster which threatened to destroy the country; they stood at opposite ends of the political and economic spectrum and triggered a battle royal which engulfed the City in a mini-civil war.

George Larkin remembered all too well the machinations of E.A. Fogarty as he himself was kept busy around the clock in an attempt to counter the RPP propaganda machine. He had been the campaign manager for the Progressive candidate, and he had had to schedule a press conference each and every day to point out the lies, the half-truths, and the innuendos cranked out by his opposite number. And, in his "spare time," he kept his own "troops" focused and moving and provided them (he hoped) with a moral compass in the face of a foe determined to win at all costs. Once or twice, he had come very close to suffering a mental break-down because of the stress under which he worked because the stakes were too high to give up.

In the end, however, it was all for naught.

Days before the election, the RPP candidate, a bland individual who was no more than Fogarty's ventriloquist's dummy, pulled a final dirty trick. At a press conference, he claimed that the Progressive Party was being bankrolled by the Kennedy clan and that its local candidate was a Kennedy protégé whose purpose was to re-introduce the failed policies which had brought on the recession and, worse, to return America to immorality and libertinism. None of it was true, of course; the claim had been manufactured out of whole cloth. Still, the memories of what had happened in the White House in 1998 still lingered in the minds of many Americans, and the lie won the day. The RPP man won by a landslide, emulating a similar victory at the national level by Hadley Richardson.

The day after the election, George Larkin took a solemn oath to bring down E.A. Fogarty any way he could.

* * *

It loomed up over him like a creature out of a nightmare, some blood-thirsty monster ready to swallow him whole.

The old converted firehouse which now served as the local RPP headquarters seemed even more sinister than the last time Larkin was there. Then, he had hatched a plot to set the Disciples against the Swarm and allow them to battle each other while he and DEDEP could go about their business without interruption. Then, he was quite full of himself – smug even – and the firehouse was just another old building.

Now, he had witnessed the first real skirmish between the Disciples and the Swarm, and it had been, for all practical purposes, a draw. Both contingents were dead (though not at each other's hands), and only he had survived through trickery. Now, he had to report to the Archdeacon concerning his part in the skirmish and how he had managed to remain alive.

He stood at the front door for a while before entering, rehearsing what he would tell old man Fogarty and, more importantly, *how* he would tell him. It had to sound plausible, or his entire plan would unravel on the instant. He took a deep breath and let it out slowly.

Inside, the young female he had seen days before was back behind the receptionist's desk – the baby-faced, acne-scarred, *pregnant* "junior Disciple" – and she was busy stuffing flyers into envelopes. She recognized him instantly and flashed him a big smile. He merely nodded perfunctorily.

"Brother Larkin," she breathed, "it's good to see you again."

"It's good to be back," he lied. "I have an urgent matter to discuss with His Worship."

The girl rang the Archdeacon's extension, listened briefly, and hung up.

"Sister Hedberg will be right down to escort you upstairs."

"Thank you."

Larkin took a seat on one of the uncomfortable chairs nearby, but he didn't sit long. "Sister" Hedberg bounded down the stairs leading to the *sanctum sanctorum* and approached him with a radiant expression on her face. If she was faking being glad to see him, it was one of the best acting jobs he'd seen in quite some time – a complication he didn't need just now.

"George," she murmured, "you're back among the living. I – ah, *we* were so worried."

"I'm glad to be back among the living, Dorothea. And that's why I'm here. I have to update His Worship on recent events."

"And he's anxious to receive your report."

As they turned toward the stairs, Hedberg slipped her arm under his and pressed against him. He frowned. The woman was making no pretense at coyness; she intended to hook him and reel him in. He'd have to be the one playing "hard to get"!

At the top of the stairs, she released her grip, assumed her customary professional demeanor, and opened the door to the Archdeacon's office. He took another deep breath and entered the lion's den again.

He discovered the old man and his right-hand man, "Brother" Kincaid, hunched over the former's desk, studying a map of the City. Neither man looked up but continued to speak in soft tones and to gesture at various parts of the map. At times, one or the other would nod or shake his head.

Presently, this "conference" ended, and the Archdeacon looked up and waved the detective to a seat. Larkin sat down, and Hedberg took a seat uncomfortably close to him. Kincaid rolled up the map and headed for the door; as he passed by Larkin, he gave him a searching look as if to ferret out whatever secrets the latter was concealing. The detective regarded him with a neutral expression and was glad when the fellow had exited the office. Kincaid was too suspicious for his taste, and he'd have to keep a closer eye on him from now on.

The old man shuffled a few papers, then peered at his visitor pensively. Finally:

"We've been worried about you, Brother Larkin. We hadn't heard from you these past three days."

"That's what Sister Hedberg said." He paused dramatically. "I have to confess, Your Worship, that I've been hiding – frightened for my life."

"How so?"

"You're aware of what happened to Brother Rosansky and the other brothers?" The old man nodded. "Well, by a stroke of luck, I barely escaped that…*massacre*. But I soon learned that that…*demon* was following me, and I went to ground."

"'Luck,' Brother Larkin? There's no such thing as 'luck.' The Lord was looking out for you. You were spared because He has other plans for you." He fixed the detective with a penetrating stare. "What became of the demon?"

"I don't know, sir. I'm sure it's still out there. I've been too frightened to leave my hiding place – until now." Larkin decided that this was the right moment to bait the trap. "My sources say they've seen it roaming the City – it and others like it. My sources could be mistaken, but they're usually reliable."

"I'm not a gambling man, Brother Larkin, but I'd be willing to wager that the Enemy is gathering his forces openly in the mistaken belief that he has the upper hand. The loss of Brother Rosansky and the others was a grievous one, but that was a merely a skirmish and not the war. We will take the fight to the Enemy, no matter how many foul creatures he has in his army, and we will win."

"I'm greatly relieved, Your Worship. Of course, I'll attempt to redeem myself and do whatever is expected of me."

"I'm sure you will." The Archdeacon checked his watch. "You'll have to excuse me now. I have an appointment with my Deacons in half an hour. Keep me posted."

"I shall, sir. Thank you for your faith in me."

Larkin rose, and so did Hedberg. She accompanied him to the door, opened it for him, and ushered him out of the office. She did not, however, take him downstairs; instead, she smiled warmly and placed her hand on his. He felt his internal temperature rising again.

"Good-bye, George. Perhaps we'll meet again – at the book store?"

"Perhaps. However, I think that we might not have too much time for that sort of thing. There's danger ahead, and we've got to meet it head on, each in our own way."

"You may be right. Still...."

She turned and re-entered the office. Larkin heaved a huge sigh of relief. Talk about *femmes fatales*!

*I concur, old darling.

*Kenny?

*None other. That bird is pure trouble, as far as you're concerned. Don't let Sheena find out what 'Sister' Hedberg's up to, or there'll be a fresh homicide in the ranks of the Disciples.

*Humph! Do you have any news for me, or are you just rattling my cage?

*A little of both, actually. Meet me at the store, and I'll make your day – as you Yanks like to say.

*Straightaway, as you *Brits* like to say.

* * *

Larkin was approaching the intersection of Broadway and Fox Streets when he saw the gathering crowd. It was the usual eclectic mix: young and old, male and female, all ethnic types, singles and multiples. They were all jostling each other to get a better view of what was taking place on the southwest corner of the intersection; no one thought to caution anyone else about rude behavior, because everyone's attention was riveted on the central characters in this drama.

To the detective's disgust, a gaggle of Disciples had surrounded two young women wearing only halters, shorts, and sandals (an ensemble guaranteed to invite sunburn in the heat of the summer of 2018). The young women were about to become the latest "object lessons" of the

Return-to-Purity movement's efforts to eradicate "impurity" in the world. Larkin debated whether to stay and witness the sordid event or to move on and keep his appointment with Kenny. Morbid curiosity got the better of him, and he moved in for a closer view.

The Deaconess-in-charge detached herself from her underlings and closed in on her victims. The latter clasped hands in order to comfort each other and took a determined stance. Nonplussed, the Deaconess began the "Litany of Purity" and was pleased to hear echoes throughout the crowd.

"God created heaven and earth and made them pure.

"God created man and woman and made them pure.

"God put Adam and Eve in a Place of Purity. There, they lived in the Light, nurtured by the Love of God.

"Then Satan entered the Place and sowed evil ideas, corruption, and impurity. His lying tongue was pleasing to Adam and Eve, and they turned from the Light of Purity and followed Satan.

"God, seeing His children made impure, laid a curse upon them, the curse of imperfection of body and of mind.

"And those who live not in the Light bear the marks of the curse, and the curse is made manifest in their bodies and minds.

"But those who live in the Light are blessed with perfect bodies and perfect minds, and they enjoy the blessings of God.

"Thus are they charged by God to return Purity to the world so that the Light may shine forth as it did in the Beginning.

"Love the Light! Love Purity!

"Cast out the impure! Cast them out forever!

"Brothers and sisters, you who love the Light and seek to return Purity to the world, behold! Evil and corruption and impurity have shown themselves in the persons of these two harlots before you. For, has not God placed the curse upon them? Have they not manifested the curse by their imperfect minds which moved them to flaunt their nakedness before you? I say to you, brothers and sisters, look upon the imperfection and know them for what they are, the whores of Satan, who is the enemy of Purity and the source of impurity.

"What shall we do with them, brothers and sisters? What shall we do with those who love not the Light? Tell me, brothers and sisters!"

As one body, her Disciples and those in the crowd who sympathized with them shouted back the formulaic response:

"Cast them out! Cast them out! Send them back to their master, Satan!"

The Deaconess stepped forward and slapped one of the young women as hard as she could. Her victim leveled a broadside of obscenities at her tormentor. Undaunted, the Deaconess turned to the other young woman, slapped her viciously as well, and received another defiant broadside.

"Impurity," the Deaconess intoned, "the Light curses you! Begone!"

Their emotions whipped up into a feeding frenzy, the crowd surged forward, led by the Disciples, to take their turn at pummeling the young women. The latter disappeared from view under the onslaught, and their sobs and cries diminished in tone and frequency until they fell silent. Only Larkin (it seemed) remained rooted to where he stood, sick to his stomach by both the violence and his inability to prevent it. He turned to escape the madness.

"Makes ya wanna puke, don't it, mister?"

The detective reeled in surprise. Before him stood a young boy, no more than eight or nine years old, with a mop of unruly red hair, a face full of freckles, and a voice like a foghorn. He was dressed in a torn and dirty white T-shirt and a pair of bib overalls but was barefoot. A piece of straw hung loosely from his mouth. Larkin could well believe the boy had just stepped out of a Norman Rockwell painting.

"Perhaps," came the noncommittal reply. "How do *you* feel about it?"

"Same as you do, Georgie. Makes *me* wanna puke."

The detective's jaw dropped at the sound of his name coming out of that mouth.

"How do you know my name? Oh, wait! You're one of Farquhar's merry band. I wouldn't have believed he'd recruit from the junior set."

"Don't believe it then."

"Do you have information for me, or are you just following me around for the fun of it?"

"Both, nephew. I saw some Mr. Jones look-alikes yesterday. They were goin' around askin' about the Disciples. Whyzzat?"

"The Disciples killed Mr. Jones," Larkin fibbed. "The look-alikes are out for revenge."

"I reckon. Well, they don't look any friendlier than he did. Better watch yer step, Georgie."

"I always do. Thanks for the tip."

* * *

In the nine years since he first set foot inside Browsing Unlimited, George Larkin had never seen the bookstore when it wasn't cluttered with books. Books of all sorts were stacked haphazardly on shelves, tables, and the floor in no apparent order. It was as if a large dump truck had backed up to the door and unloaded its cargo into one huge pile and the owners had simply pulled books at random and put them in any available empty space; and, when they had run out of empty spaces, they just piled the remainder in smaller stacks under the tables, in the aisles, and on surfaces where no one expected to find a book. Yet, the owners, Kensington and Paddington Smythe (lately of London, England), had done this deliberately, because in their humble opinion, it encouraged people to *browse*. Curiously, the Twins seemed to know where every single book resided; and, when asked for a particular title or topic, they could go unerringly to the exact location and satisfy the customer's desire. Larkin had never figured out how they could do it, and they had never bothered to explain.

Also, in those nine years, the detective had failed to walk in and not see a large crowd of potential buyers, regardless of the time of day. He supposed that customers had been a mere trickle when Browsing Unlimited first opened for business but that, when the news of the store's wares spread throughout the City, the trickle became a torrent. Young or old, male or female, every conceivable ethnic group and manner of dress, the customers poured in, hoping to find treasure, and they were rarely disappointed. Larkin had never seen anyone leave the store empty-handed; whether what they carried away was what they had originally been looking for was beside the point. The bright, shining faces told the whole story. The detective had even seen Disciples walk away looking pleased with themselves!

This day was no different, and he could have sworn Browsing Unlimited looked even more cluttered and crowded than usual. He was sure that it was just his imagination. Still….

He scanned the interior with his trained eye and saw the eclectic crowd wandering (as best they could) the aisles, jostling one another in order to get to another interesting pile of books and perusing casually – sometimes intently – one title or another. Some few came across a book and instantly claimed it for him/herself; the majority browsed until they stumbled onto a must-have title. Some of the customers were familiar – repeat *satisfied* customers, hoping to score again. The *hausfrau* was back, again searching for more cookbooks; she already had four in hand, and still she was not satisfied. The tall, athletic man had returned and had found a dog-eared copy of Gibson's *Necromancer.*

Most of the faces, however, were new. A slender blonde in a gray tweed pantsuit and black pumps seemed to be undecided. First, she picked up a German-English dictionary and studied it; then she grabbed a Russian grammar, studied it, put it down, looked at the dictionary again, studied the grammar again, put both down, rubbed her jaw, picked both up, and headed for the check-out counter. If he had been watching a film, Larkin would have recognized the elements of a slapstick comedy.

Two people he was on the look-out for and whom he hoped to avoid were Dorothea Hedberg and Farquhar. The former was a shark in woman's clothes, and she was targeting him for – what? Romance? Espionage? He had difficulty believing the first but not the second; the Disciples had proven time and again that they were ready and willing to use every trick in the book (and to invent some new ones) in order to gain their objective. "Sister" Hedberg was attractive enough to be able to seduce any man and wring information/co-operation/money out of him. The detective thought he was stronger-willed than the average American male, but he still didn't care to put his will to the test. He had better things to do than to play cat-and-mouse with the likes of Dorothea Hedberg!

As for the latter, he was a conundrum. He could be anyone in this shop, and Larkin would never know which one until the informant sidled up to him and introduced himself. How much time did the fellow spend every day dreaming/donning a new disguise and/or recruiting others to do his dirty work? The detective scanned the crowd continually for any tell-tale signs of behavior which would set him apart from ordinary people and saw none.

Wait a minute!

He spotted the same freckle-faced, red-headed "boy" he had encountered not half an hour ago, wandering through the piles of books aimlessly and unescorted. He didn't appear to be searching for anything in particular; rather, he seemed to have walked in out of curiosity as children often did. Obviously, the "boy's" presence here couldn't be a co-incidence – or could it? Eventually, the "youngster" departed the bookstore, and Larkin headed slowly toward the back room. On the way, he caught Paddy's eye and nodded.

*Hello, George. Welcome to the monkey house.

*Hello, Paddy. Lots of 'monkeys' today, huh?

*Right-o. If this keeps up, we could retire at an early age.

Larkin pushed and weaved his way through the hordes of bargain seekers and arrived at the door to the back room relatively unscathed. He gave the crowd a final glance to insure himself that no one was looking his way, then slowly opened the door and slipped inside.

For as long as he had known the Brothers Smythe, he had never seen a facial expression as grim as the one with which Kenny greeted him. Normally, the Twins were as carefree and happy-go-lucky as anyone could be in the current depressing social environment; it was not in their nature to be down in the mouth regardless of the circumstances. If any word described them to a "T," it had to be "wryness." Even Kenny's recent kidnapping and the potential for his demise had not put a permanent stain on their usual behavior. They were like children at play, and they were never far apart for long.

Today, however, Kensington Smythe looked deeply troubled as much as a man waiting on Death Row waiting for the inevitable. If the frown he was wearing were any deeper, it would have touched the floor. He sat at the make-shift desk and drew imaginary circles on its surface. At Larkin's entrance, he bolted upright, a look of relief replacing the grimness.

The detective discovered that Sheena was also there, and her expression equaled Kenny's. That worried him. She was hardly the carefree and happy-go-lucky character that either of the Smythes were, but neither was she ever as depressed as she appeared at that moment. When he entered, her face brightened considerably. She stood and took two steps toward him. He wanted very much to take her in his arms and comfort her, thought better of it, and gazed from one to the other.

"Oh, God, George!" she breathed. "Thank Heaven you're here."

"I had to make a 'report' to the Archdeacon. I'm surprised it went as well as it did." He paused. "I'm no psychic, but even I can sense more gloom and doom in this room than I've seen in a month of Sundays. What's up?"

"When you hear what we've got to tell you, old darling, you'll be full of gloom and doom yourself."

"I'm all ears."

First, Sheena related her version of their discovery at the abandoned factory. Since visual images were beyond her capability, she painted a picture based upon her other senses; and, the more she spoke, the more she shivered and stammered. Larkin wanted desperately to comfort her, but he constrained himself mightily. When she had finished her part of the tale, she hung her head in sadness.

Kenny then took up the thread and filled in the blanks left by Sheena. He did not shiver or stammer, but his voice wavered at times. When he had finished, he shook his head and peered at the floor.

The detective absorbed this information in as stoical a manner as he could so that his analytical brain could make some sense of it. Even so, he could not prevent a shudder or two as he pondered the implications of what had developed in so short a time. If he had been anybody but himself, he might have yielded to panic and/or despair. He couldn't afford that "luxury," however; too many people were counting on him for guidance, and he could scarcely fail them. He had to put aside his own fears and set in motion a plan of action against the threat posed by the Swarm.

He kept silent for a few moments after Kenny had finished. The others watched him with no little concern. The one who could scan a person's mind as easily as the average person could read a book guessed that he was in his "thinking mode," while the one who could read emotions by listening to body signals guessed that he was also in his "equipoise mode." Both waited patiently. Presently:

"I can't say that I'm filled with doom and gloom, but I will admit to a sense of urgency. If the Swarm has brought one of their super-weapons with them to Earth, they have just raised the stakes, and that means we have to ramp up our own forces."

*What do you propose, old darling? [Paddy joined the conversation].

"I haven't worked out the details yet, but I do have a tentative outline. I'm going back to the office to do some serious thinking. After you close up for the night, I'll pick you up and we'll head out to DEDEP for a special conference."

"We'll be waiting," Kenny said quietly.

Larkin and Sheena slipped out the back door, rounded the building, and bundled into the rickety station wagon. The drive back to the office was made in absolute silence. Sheena ventured to rest her head on her partner's shoulder and was secretly pleased that he didn't shrink away from the action. Perhaps there was hope after all….

As they walked through the lobby of their office building, the detective halted abruptly. He spied a person who had no reason for being here, but its being here was obviously a deliberate act on its part. "It" was the freckle-faced, redheaded "boy." What the Devil was Farquhar doing here? Larkin was further disconcerted by the fact that the "child" was looking straight at him and wearing the same colossal grin that he'd seen before, in his office and in the Archdeacon's office where Sheena had identified the "grinning idiot" as the mysterious informant.

"George," his partner whispered, "what's wrong? You're all tensed up."

"What kind of signals are you picking up?"

She furrowed her brow at the unusual response but nevertheless activated her hyperesthesia. It didn't take long for her to recognize a familiar signal; she gasped sharply and clutched Larkin's arm.

"Oh, God! It's Farquhar!"

"I thought as much. You won't believe who I'm looking at." He described the "boy" and mentioned the grin. "If that's Farquhar, he has a talent I never thought he had."

Sheena was just as full of consternation as Larkin was. She already had an idea what George's favorite informant truly was; and, if her suspicions were true, then this mystery man posed a great threat to her, to DEDEP, and to the world at large. The membership of DEDEP was constrained by the principles laid down by Emil Razumov at the very beginning of the organization's existence. The first (and foremost) principle was that the use of *psi*-talent was for good rather than for evil; the second was that the use was to be made in co-operation with others for the greater good. Farquhar was a loose cannon, a rogue element, with a potential for selfish purposes. She hadn't mentioned any of this to either George or Emil, because she had needed to think things through before confiding in them. Now, however, with this new display of Farquhar's unique ability, she knew she had to inform DEDEP's leadership before too much time passed so that they could deal with this strange person and somehow keep him in check.

Before she could say anything to George, however, she sensed the "boy" approaching them. He was still grinning as he regarded both of them. Then:

"Been waitin' fer ya, Georgie."

"So I see. What do you have for me now?"

"I got nothin'. But you got somethin' *I* want."

"And that is?"

"The *real* story behind them strange-lookin' dudes."

"The real story?"

The "boy's" face hardened, and a steely glint formed in his eyes.

"Look, Larkin," he growled, "I'm not stupid. There's something queer going on here, and it isn't a turf war. If you want my co-operation from now on, you have to meet me half-way."

The detective's mind buzzed with conflicting thoughts. First of all, he couldn't believe he was having an adult-style conversation with someone who looked like a nine-year-old. Even if this "kid" was an agent of his chief informant, how did he come to be so brash as to make demands? On the other hand, if Farquhar was using him as a go-between, why was he doing so? Secondly, Farquhar had never bothered to ask for any explanations behind the information-gathering up to now; he had just dropped tidbits here and there and gone on his merry way. Why the sudden change in tactics? Why the sudden interest in the Swarm? What did he suspect?

"Are you sure you want to know? You might not believe anything I tell you."

"Tell me what I want to know, and I'll draw my own conclusions."

Larkin turned to Sheena. She was white as a sheet; moreover, she was trembling from head to toe. What was she sensing with her hyperesthetic powers? Did she think this "kid" was a threat to them? No matter – this "boy" would soon find out just how close to the line he was getting.

"All right, I'll tell you the 'real' story. But not here, of course. We'll go up to my office. You should be sitting down when you hear what I have to say."

CHAPTER FOUR

A SERIOUS INVESTIGATION

"COME FLY WITH me," the Entity whispers to her.

"But, I can't fly," she protests.

"You can. I will show you how."

"How can I fly?"

"With the wings of your imagination. Stretch out your mind, and you will sail away."

"Is it that simple?"

"Yes. You have flown before, but you were not aware of it."

"When?"

"When you opened your mind to the 'visions,' as you call them. Then you traveled to places never before possible."

"I never thought of it that way. Where will you take me?"

"To places far and near, to the depths of the Earth and to the depths of the Universe, to shadow worlds and worlds of imagination, to the beginning of Time and to the end of Time, and to all the places in between."

"I can go to all those places?"

"As easy as wishing. There is no limit to your flying. I have already shown you some of those places."

"I remember now. When can I go?"

"When you are ready."

"When will I be ready?"

"You will know."

* * *

"Come run with me," the Entity whispers to him.

"I'm stuck in this place. I can't run."

"You can. I will show you how."

"How?"

"With the feet of your imagination. Stretch out your mind, and you will speed away."

"Is it that easy?"

"Yes. You have run before, but you were not aware of running."

"When?"

When you opened your mind to make things move, or to order 'Mr. Whosis' to do so, as you thought. Then you ran to places never before possible."

"I never thought of it like that. Where will you take me?"

"To places far and near, to the depths of the Earth and to the depths of the Universe, to shadow worlds and worlds of the imagination, to the beginning of Time and to the end of Time, and to all the places in between."

"I can go to all of those places?"

"As easy as wishing. There is no limit to your running. I have already shown you some of those places."

"I remember now. When can I go?"

"When you are ready."

"When will I be ready?"

"You will know."

* * *

Eve/Stan sat straight up in bed and looked about the room (s)he was in. (S)he did not recognize it and wondered how (s)he had gotten there. The last thing (s)he remembered was sitting on the floor of the barn above DEDEP and directing the gestalt (s)he had conjured up to assist George Larkin against the attack by the alien Mr. Jones. As (s)he continued to look about in confusion, clarity came abruptly to her/him. (S)he was in DEDEP's infirmary. But why? (S)he didn't feel injured or sick. In fact, (s)he felt fine – refreshed even.

Eve/Stan now recalled the dream (s)he had had. Or had it been a dream? It had seemed so real at the time. A silver sphere (not a black one) had appeared in her/his mind and "spoken" to her/him. It wasn't a "*person*," and It wasn't a "*thing*"; It was both and neither. It was some sort of…Entity which somehow reminded her/him of the gestalt. But why had It come to her/him instead of some *important* person, like Dr. Razumov or George Larkin, who was better equipped mentally to deal with strange creatures. If It had come to her/him because (s)he was one of the "Summoners" [and why did (s)he think of *that* word?], then It might appear to both of them.

Whatever Its reasons for appearing to her/him, this Entity had been most seductive. When (s)he had first touched the black sphere, a flood of marvelous images filled her/his mind, images which (s)he could only imagine existed since they were the sort of things no human eyes could have seen without mechanical aid, images which provoked a desire to see more. The Entity had promised them to grant that desire – not only to show her/him those things, but to carry her/him as well to where they occurred. It was a mind-boggling prospect, if true, and (s)he was torn between desire and suspicion. For, the Entity raised more questions than It had answered (if It had answered any at all). What *was* It exactly? Where did It come from? What reason did It have for entering her/his world? Why had It attached Itself to her/him? Was It good or evil? (S)he couldn't go away with It until there was some assurance that It meant no harm to her/him.

Another question occurred to her/him. So far, the Entity had come to her/him in a dream state. Would – *could* – It come to her/him in a waking state? More importantly, would – *could* – It come if (s)he concentrated and called out to It? (S)he toyed with the idea of giving It a name, the better to summon It but dismissed the idea as being too silly. If It had a name, It would have told her/him what it was at Its first appearance.

After picturing It in her/his mind, (s)he mentally framed the word "Come." A minute passed without results, and (s)he tried again. Still, nothing happened. Either the Entity was unwilling to appear except on Its own terms or It came only in the dream state when her/his subconscious was dominant.

* * *

Eve and Stan turned toward each other, but neither spoke for a long moment. Each was straddling the line between doubt and certainty and attempting to decide which way to go. Then:

"Stan, did you…?"

"Yeah. It was *cool*!"

"Well, that's one way to put it, I guess."

"We still gotta keep this to ourselves, right?"

"Definitely. We have to learn what the…Entity wants with us."

"Yeah."

* * *

When Emil Razumov learned that his prize pupils were lucid again, he practically knocked over his desk in his haste to leave his office. It was the happiest news he had received in three days, and he wasn't going to waste a single minute in visiting Eve and Stan. If he had been a younger man, he might have broken into a trot to get to the infirmary even though it would have been most undignified. Dignity be damned!

DEDEP's Director of Research had been worried sick ever since the "Battle of the Farmyard." That the *psi*-gestalt had acted of its own volition took him by surprise and moments later filled him with horror. Gestalts, by their very nature, were not supposed to behave independently of their creators, simply because they were not independent entities – which meant, to his mind, that this particular gestalt was no ordinary one. And, perhaps, now that he was exploring possible explanations, perhaps it was not a true gestalt after all, but something entirely different, something entirely unknown, even to one who had spent half his life mapping the potential of the human mind. But, what was it then? That was, as the Americans were fond of saying, the sixty-four-thousand-dollar question.

He needed answers. The black spheroid had to be examined, studied, and experimented on so that its potential could be quantified – and, more importantly, be controlled. It could not be allowed to act independently at will, because it could wreak havoc as well as protect people. It had already destroyed one living being. The fact that it may have done so in self-defense notwithstanding, such decisions could not be left to it alone but instead in concert with those it had made contact with for whatever reason. If it possessed a moral code – and that seemed far-fetched on the face of it -- it must be made to realize that its contactees had their own, possibly different, moral code.

Therefore, it was imperative that he get Eve and Stan back into harness (so to speak) and get the exploratory process moving again. He had spent the past three days devising and/or discarding one approach after another but finally had made a rather lengthy list of things he wanted to do – if, that is, the gestalt was co-operative. And why shouldn't it be? Without DEDEP's assistance, it would not exist in this space-time continuum. It had damned well better be co-operative!

Dr. Razumov had gained the reputation of an "absent-minded professor." When he wasn't engaged in research, he was busy fine-tuning his General and Special Theories of Radiopsychology. Getting his attention, then, was a complex task, and it was often a futile one. In the present instance, he was more absent-minded than usual as he was concentrating on what he would say first to Eve and Stan. Consequently, he collided with DEDEP'ers of all ages and genders more often than not. With a quickly muttered "*pozhalsto,*" he continued on without breaking stride. Happily, the residents were used to this behavior and made exceptions to his eccentricities, not least because he had given them sanctuary from the religious fanatics above ground.

At the infirmary, he burst through the door, alarming everyone inside. Only four persons were present: Eve and Stan, of course; Lacey Perkins, who had been a practical nurse before circumstances had forced her and her family underground and who was now the closest thing DEDEP had to a medical practitioner; and the "duck girl," still recuperating from the trauma of being attacked by a mob of Disciples bent on punishing her for her "deformity." The first two individuals had been engaged in whispered conversation but clammed up at the sight of the Director.

"Doctor Razumov!" Lacey exclaimed. "What's the problem?"

"*Pozhalsto*, dear lady. I have been informed that Eve and Stan were, ah, awake, and I wanted to speak to them about the recent incident."

"Well, I hope you have better luck than I have. So far, they've been talking to each other and ignoring me."

"We shall see, we shall see."

Lacey departed in order to provide a modicum of privacy for whatever counseling the Director could offer. The Doctor regarded the pair for a long moment, choosing carefully how best to initiate the conversation and to determine their mental state. The situation was unique, to say the least; no human being had ever experienced interaction with an unknown product of the mind quite like Eve and Stan had, and so they had to be dealt with very circumspectly in order to avoid exacerbating any trauma they might be undergoing. For their part, the pair merely stared at him wide-eyed, quite willing to let him make the first move.

"*Dobroye ootro, ryebyonky. Kak onee pazhyvayetye* [how are you]?"

"Good morning, Doctor Razumov," they replied in unison. "We're fine. How are you?"

Nyeobyasneemy [uncanny]! he mused. *They are speaking as one person. Is this the result of their interaction with the gestalt? Well, I intend to find out.*

"*Ochen khorosho.* Are you well enough to describe your recent experience?"

Eve and Stan faced each other, but neither spoke. Instead, they seemed to be communicating on a non-verbal level. After a few seconds of silence, they regarded the Director again.

"We still haven't sorted it out in our minds yet, Doctor," Eve responded.

"Yeah," Stan added. "We need more time to ourselves."

They are holding back. There is something they do not want to talk about, something to do with the gestalt. But what? I cannot push them too far, because they will retreat further into their private world. Best to let them choose their own time to open up.

"*Konyechno.* When you are ready, let me know. I need to understand what has happened so that I may know how to proceed."

"So do we, Doctor," they said in unison again.

He left the infirmary, muttering to himself in Russian.

* * *

Light-bulb inspection was a weekly task on Freddie Hamilton's list of things-to-do. On the first day of the week, he patrolled the corridors of DEDEP and all of the public areas looking for burnt-out bulbs. Living underground on a permanent basis was bad enough; living underground in the dark tended to give one claustrophobia, and so the Director insisted on routine inspections.

Light-bulb inspection was a pure bore, as far as Freddie was concerned, and it took him away from more important tasks. Yet, it was also the easiest task on his list; walking around and staring up at the ceiling gave him an opportunity to take a breather away from the more difficult work-orders – of which there seemed to be an endless number. Something was always going wrong in this abandoned government facility, and it was all that DEDEP's "Mr. Fix-it" could do to keep up with the work-load. Any time he could find to take a break was a welcome moment.

Just now, he was sitting on top of a folding ladder and replacing one of the compact fluorescent bulbs in the northeastern "leg" of level three (the middle residential level). So far, so good – it was the only one this day he had to replace. But Freddie had noticed that two others – one on the first level and one on the fourth level – were beginning to flicker. He'd have to keep an eye on them, because they were liable to burn out fairly soon with his luck. While he worked, he thought deep (for him) thoughts.

The deep thoughts he was forming had to do with how hectic things had gotten at DEDEP with the discovery of extraterrestrials on Earth, aliens who were planning to make the planet their latest conquest. And somehow, it had fallen to the merry little band in this hole in the ground to combat this menace from outer space and still remain a secret organization. Then there was that damned black sphere Stan and Evie had pulled out of thin air and which George was planning on using against the aliens. If it had just been Stan and Evie who had conjured up that thing, that would have been just fine with him. But, somehow, he was a key component in the conjuring, and the Doc insisted on taking him away from his repairs to do his experiments with the thing. He hadn't been this busy – or exhausted -- since he left the circus. The sooner the aliens were dealt with, the better as far as he was concerned. Then maybe he could get some work done around here!

He replaced the bulb, clambered down the ladder (not an easy task for a dwarf), carefully folded the ladder, and started toward the emergency stairs.

"Freddie!" a soft feminine voice halted him. "Please report to Lab #2. Urgent!"

"Yeah, right. *Everything* is urgent!" He continued on a few steps, then halted, wide-eyed with wonder. "Hey! Who said that? Nobody here talks like that!"

He remembered someone who used to talk like that, however: his old circus "buddy," Madame Fortuna, the fortune teller. She hadn't been a raving beauty but rather plain-looking; but what stood out was a seductive voice which she used, first, to entice prospective "rubes" into her tent and, second, to mesmerize them into believing her every "prophecy." She had even spoken that way in private, and Freddie had been intrigued, no matter what the topic of conversation had been.

But, Madame Fortuna was dead, murdered by the Disciples of Purity for being a "witch." It couldn't have been her who had just spoken. So, who did? Someone was pulling his leg, and he intended to find out who and give him/her his two cents' worth. And the place to start was Lab #2.

* * *

Dr. Razumov was still puzzling over the curious remark made by Eve and Stan in unison. Both had indicated that they wished to continue the experiments with the gestalt. Such a desire was in character with the ten-year-old boy; he had found a new "toy" to play with, and he wanted to show off his *psi*-talent at every opportunity, no matter how frightening the demonstration might be perceived by others. Certainly, his enthusiasm was commendable, as it made the Director's work that much easier, but Stan's enthusiasm needed to be channeled into more productive uses.

The same could not be said of Eve, however. She had been a very reluctant participant in experimentation from the start. Her fear of her psycho-imaging, triggered by her conservatively religious upbringing, made her unwilling to exercise it in solo, least of all in concert with another *psi*-talent. Psychologically, then, she was the complete opposite of her "partner-in-crime." Now, however, she seemed out of character by evincing a willingness to continue the experiments. What had caused her to change her perspective in so short a time? Had it been the gestalt's destruction of Mr. Jones? It made no sense, given her fear of *psi* in general. Something else was at work here, and he was damned if he could explain it, either through radiopsychology or some other "-ology."

But, he, Emil Razumov, the supposed expert in parapsychology, intended to learn the truth of the matter or give up his practice.

As he was now full of nervous energy, he decided to walk it off (if he could), and the best place to walk it off was "upstairs" where he could breathe fresh air and feel the Sun on his skin. It was a terrible thing to have to live in a hole in the ground; human beings were not naturally "indoor" creatures but required space to move around in freely. He encouraged his fellow DEDEP'ers to go above ground and walk around, even if it were only for a few minutes. Despite the soaring temperatures incumbent with climate change and the risk of over-exposure to ultra-violet radiation, a few minutes wouldn't kill the average person.

As he headed for the emergency exit – avoiding collisions with any passers-by – he heard his name being called. He turned and instantly groaned. Huffing and puffing his way toward the Director was DEDEP's resident "sleeping prophet," "Fat Henry" Rawlins. "Obese" did not come close to describing him; he was a Weight Watchers poster child, constantly eating and blaming his size on a "glandular problem." Even if he had not had a *psi*-talent, he might have been a target for the Disciples on the grounds that he defiled his "temple," i.e. his body, by over-eating.

George Larkin had encountered Henry Rawlins by accident. Henry had been a former client of the detective who wanted to locate a missing relative. Almost from the beginning, he had provided Larkin with vivid descriptions of persons and places he thought might help in the search. The "leads" had helped tremendously, and the missing relative was eventually located. The detective, ever the curious sort, wanted to know how Henry had come by descriptions of persons and places he'd never seen before; under pressure, Henry confessed that he had seen them in his dreams. Further, he said he had seen future events in dreams; although sometimes the imagery tended to be more symbolic, and he had to struggle to decipher them.

When the time came to create DEDEP, round up all the *psi*-talents he could locate, and move them underground, Henry Rawlins was near the top of Larkin's mental list. It took the detective a long while to locate the "sleeping prophet," because, like all the others, he didn't wish to be found and risk exposure to God-knew-what sort of treatment at the hands of strangers. Eventually, the detective prevailed, but it wasn't long before he came to regret his efforts.

Henry Rawlins was a "whiner," always complaining about something or other. Dr. Razumov supposed he couldn't help himself; he was obviously self-conscious about his weight and used complaining as a way to call attention away from his condition by creating another problem. For the sake of keeping the group intact and preserving a valuable *psi*-talent, the Doctor endured the complaining as best he could. Too often, however....

"*Dobroye ootro*, Henry. What is on your mind today?"

"Good morning, Doctor," Henry wheezed. "I just wanted you to know that I had the same dream I told you about the other day."

"*Exactly* the same dream?"

"Yes. Except there was one added element."

"Which was?"

"The headless man had four arms, and two of them shot out fire. That's how he rips open the cage and frees George."

"*Ochen intyeryestno.* Have you arrived at any conclusions?"

"I can only guess that the headless man is actually some sort of robot. More than that, I don't know."

"Ponder some more on the imagery, Henry. The meaning is bound to come to you sooner or later."

The Director continued on his way, relieved that his encounter with the "sleeping prophet" was a brief one.

"Dr. Razumov," a stern male voice intoned – in Russian, "please report to Lab #2. This is urgent!"

He whirled around to see who had spoken to him. There was no one else in the corridor. It could not have been the PA system; otherwise, he would have heard the short screech of feedback as the system was activated. The voice had been a "live" one, originating nearby.

What was particularly disturbing was that the voice was a familiar one. He had heard it many times while he was matriculating at the University of Moscow; it was the voice of his post-graduate advisor who had guided him, sometimes gently, sometimes roughly, toward the goal they both pursued, i.e. a perfect student. But how could it be his old mentor speaking to him? The man had been dead for over twenty years; the Doctor would have gone to his funeral except that he was in exile in the United States and would have been arrested the moment he stepped foot inside the Soviet Union. Some sort of trickery was being played here, and he had to confront the trickster and defeat whatever nefarious scheme he was planning.

His only clue was Lab #2. There he must begin.

When the Doctor arrived at Lab #2, he was greatly surprised to find it already occupied. Eve, Stan, and Freddie were seated and chatting amongst themselves. At his entrance, all three ceased their conversation and turned their attention to him. All three seemed not to have been expecting him and so assumed neutral expressions. His consternation increased exponentially, and for a long moment, he regarded them with wonder.

"*Pochemoo vee toot?*" he asked at last.

"We got 'summoned' is why," Freddie replied. "Dunno who did the summoning, though. It didn't sound like you. I asked the kids, but they wouldn't say." He moved the stump of his cigar from one side of his mouth to the other. "So, why are *you* here?"

"Ah, well, apparently, I have been 'summoned' also, and I am as much in the dark concerning the one who summoned." He focused on Eve and Stan. "Are you two well enough to be out of bed?"

"We're fine, Doctor," the young woman responded. "We're..."

"...all rested up," Stan finished her thought, "and we wanna do some experimenting."

"As do I. Are you sure you are up to it?"

By way of reply, the three shifted their chairs to form a "triangle," and Eve and Stan joined hands. Instantaneously, the gestalt appeared above the space where they sat, hovering slightly. It did not seem to be any larger or smaller than the last time Dr. Razumov had seen it in a controlled environment. Nevertheless, he gasped reflexively at the sight; the potential power and capability the thing represented was simply overwhelming, and he did not speak or act until he had adjusted his mental gears to its presence. And, in the back of his mind, he busily created new experiments to test its power and capability.

"*Khorosho,*" he murmured, rubbing his hands together. "Let us begin then."

A few simple exercises were the first order of business. The Director was not going to overburden the two principals right away until he was satisfied that they were indeed "fine" and "rested up" and were capable of performing more complex tasks. Therefore, he requested Eve to use her psycho-imaging talent to order up some simple scenes – landscapes, still life, portraits, and the like – before asking for intricate vistas of the sort he himself had witnessed the first time he had touched Eve and Stan's hands. It occurred to him that either Eve might be able to dictate the images formed or the gestalt consciously or reflexively controlled what was viewed. Further experiments would depend upon whichever was the case, but he thought how marvelous it would be to be able to conjure up a particular image at will.

Stan's part in the warm-up exercises consisted of sending the sphere circling around the lab in slow, lazy arcs. Not surprisingly, the boy was bored by the pointlessness of it all and squirmed in his chair, anxious to do some "real neat stuff." The Doctor could sympathize with Stan's attitude, since he was just as anxious; but, he was a scientist after all, and science could not be rushed. Haste led to errors, and errors led to ruined experiments, and ruined experiments led to wasted time and energy.

In the present instance, waste of time and energy was not a major concern. DEDEP was dealing with an unknown, a potentially dangerous unknown, and the slightest misstep in contact with it could possibly mean injury or death to everyone in its vicinity. Therefore, one must take one cautious step after another, investigating thoroughly every aspect of the gestalt until all the facts about it were revealed and any danger it posed nullified. After that, then, the "real neat stuff" could proceed apace.

"So far," the Doctor intoned as soon as he had run his charges through their warm-up, "you have been unintentional participants to the phenomenon the gestalt represents. I mean by that that it has reacted to your particular *psi*-talents, and no more. It has not taken an active part in the proceedings. I wish to explore the possibility that it *can* take an active part. In doing so, we may also determine if we can communicate with it."

Eve and Stan eyed each other with concern.

"How?" Eve asked with apprehension in her voice.

"In the only way available to us, *oochenka*: through your minds."

"You want us to *think* at it, Doctor?" Stan asked suspiciously. "But we ain't telepaths like the Smythes."

"*Mozhet beet, nye mozhet beet* [perhaps, perhaps not]. We have a unique circumstance here, and anything is possible now. We will not know if we do not try to contact the gestalt."

"What do we do then?" Eve murmured.

"Form a request in your minds. Concentrate on that request. If the gestalt responds to your request, that will be proof."

"What kinda requests?" Stan murmured.

"Eve will ask it to show an image of her own choosing. You will ask it to perform a movement of *its* own choosing." The Doctor placed his hand on top of theirs. "Now, both of you, relax, clear your minds of all distractions, and concentrate on your requests."

Eve and Stan were not enthusiastic about this exercise. They did want to contact the Entity, but on their own. Having the Director involved would be counter to any private conversation they might have with it, and he was liable to deduce the fact that they were already in contact with it. Nevertheless, they couldn't refuse to do as he asked, for that would raise suspicion in his mind and lead to an interrogation.

Reluctantly, then, they relaxed and closed their eyes. (Freddie, by this time, was already in that mode!) Their breathing became shallow.

On the other hand, Dr. Razumov tensed. He was venturing into the Unknown, and he did not know what would happen nor did he know what to expect to happen. He gazed from one quiet face to another and hoped for the best. In the back of his mind, he wished he had remembered to hook up his electroencephalograph to Eve and Stan so that he could record their brain-wave patterns as they attempted to contact the gestalt. Next time, he told himself. He also kept one eye on the black sphere. It continued to quiver imperceptibly. He would have given all he possessed to learn what was occurring inside that thing – if anything was occurring at all. That was the damnable thing about unknown phenomena: one had to wait and wait and wait until something took place, and then one had to spend time analyzing the results and making sense out of them. Oh, the life of a scientist!

Whatever the Director expected or wanted to happen, he was not prepared for what actually happened. Without warning, the black sphere winked out of existence, even while Eve and Stan remained in physical contact.

"*Shto?*" he exclaimed, looking around wildly. "*Gdye ono?* Bring it back, please!"

Eve and Stan regarded each other with a mixture of fear, concern, and confusion. The Entity was gone, and they didn't know why. They were afraid that the experiment had chased it away and that they'd never see it again. Freddie bolted upright. He was merely confused.

"*Pochemoo onee dyelaly* [what did you do]?" the old man asked in a near-accusatory tone. "Why did it go away?"

"We don't know, Doctor," Eve replied in a little-girl voice, her lip trembling. "We were concentrating on our requests, and it just... *disappeared*."

"Yeah," Stan added. "We di'n't want it to go away. We wanted to do the experiment."

"Lighten up, Doc," the dwarf admonished. "It ain't like they did it on purpose."

"But, can you recall it?" the Doctor asked, ignoring Freddie.

The pair joined hands again, but the space above them remained empty. Despair was in their eyes.

"*Bozhu moyu*, this is terrible. Return to your rooms. I must ponder the implications of this new development."

* * *

Larkin sat by himself at one end of DEDEP's dining room. One empty chair next to him was reserved for the Director of Research, but Emil Razumov was nowhere to be seen. When the detective, his partner, and the Twins arrived to report their recent discoveries, the first place they had gone was to the Director's office, only to find it empty. This absence prompted them to search the testing areas with the same results. Larkin was at a loss for an explanation; characteristically, if the old man were not in a laboratory testing someone, he was in his office poring over the results of said testing. They then tried the infirmary on the off-chance he was visiting Eve and Stan. The only person there was the "duck girl." If Emil were still on the premises, he had found himself a very good hiding place. But why would he do such a thing?

Sheena sat across the table from Larkin and worried in silence – not so much about Emil's whereabouts (although that was also a concern) as about George's state of mind. She could read his unease and frustration. Being a hyperesthetic had its advantages and disadvantages, and right now it was a disadvantage. Reading George was never a pleasant experience for her since he was always worried about something or other – when he wasn't trying to conceal his feelings for her. But reading him was all too easy; he was strong-willed, and his emotions fairly shouted at her like a booming voice in her ear. What she wanted to do was to throw her arms about him and whisper soft words of comfort to him. But this was neither the time nor the place – even if George had allowed it.

The Twins looked for all the world as if they were somewhere else mentally. And perhaps they were. They were seldom out of communication with each other, even if they were great distances apart. What they said to each other was anybody's guess; they had never revealed the contents of their communications to anyone – even with George Larkin, who knew them as well as anybody did – and no one, including him, had ever dared to ask.

While he waited, the detective observed the gathering denizens entering the dining room by ones and twos and by whole families. The room was abuzz with whispered conversations as the DEDEP'ers speculated about the nature of this hastily convened meeting. The anxiety was palpable, even to a non-hyperesthetic, and it was reflected by the many nervous glances cast his way. He debated with himself whether he ought to start the meeting without the presence of the Director. On the face of it, it seemed unprofessional of him to keep his "audience" waiting; yet, protocol dictated that everyone in the facility be present so that all could provide feed-back and/or support. Even Christopher Wredling was present; his spectral image shimmered off to Larkin's left, a Mona-Lisa smile etched on his "face."

In this sea of buzzing, one island of silence existed, and the detective was amazed to see it. Eve, Stan, and Freddie sat together and were as glum as could be. For one thing, Eve usually sat on the fringe of any gathering, not in the center of it. Her doubts about her *psi*-talent had kept her apart from other human beings. What now possessed her to surround herself with her fellow DEDEP'ers was nothing short of astounding, and Larkin was bursting with curiosity and wishing he could satisfy it with a few well-chosen questions. For another thing,

Stan Jankowsky was normally the most ebullient person in the room. The thrill of being a part of this unusual organization had invigorated his ten-year-old mind, and his enthusiasm knew no bounds. Besides, he was always ready to show off his psycho-kinetic powers at the drop of a hat. Whatever moodiness now possessed him was as much of a wonder as Eve's desire to immerse herself in humanity.

Meanwhile, Freddie spoke to Joyce Jankowsky in what appeared to be a fatherly fashion. That was also uncharacteristic; the dwarf was a natural born cynic, and he seldom spoke words of comfort and joy. Normally, he would have been talking to Stan about one thing or another; but apparently, Stan's moodiness had put him off, and he was trying his luck with someone else. For her part, Joyce, the "lost little girl" of DEDEP who comprehended the nature of the organization not in the least and who wished she was somewhere else, mostly listened and nodded her head periodically.

Larkin shook his head in wonder and glanced at his watch for what seemed like the umpteenth time. He had to make a decision now, come what may. He pushed himself to his feet and raised his hand for attention. Instantly, the chatter ceased, and all eyes were focused on him.

"Ladies and gentlemen, I have no idea where Emil has gotten to, and I am forced to start this meeting without him. We've got an update for you on what's going on 'upstairs.' Then I'll discuss a plan of action. First, Sheena and Kenny will tell you what they've discovered."

Sheena glanced at Kenny, and he at her. Kenny stood up.

"What we've feared the most has come to pass. With the death of the Swarm bloke, Mr. Jones, his teammates have come to the City to investigate." Multiple gasps rippled across the assembly, and many clutched at their neighbors' arms. "Sheena and I were able to pick up their signal and pinpoint their location. What we found will 'knock your socks off,' as you Yanks are fond of saying. Words can't describe it. If all of you will relax, I'll put some images into your minds and you will see what we're up against."

More gasps ensued, mingled with murmurs of alarm. The idea of having someone invade one's mind did not sit well with humans in general; and, even though the residents at DEDEP accepted psychic abilities as a reality and not as a threat, most of them were still not immune to the ancient fear. Those few who were immune registered anxiety, not for the sanctity of *their* minds but for what they might "see."

"Please, people!" Larkin pleaded. "This is important. Kenny will not harm you."

The tension faded by stages, and soon the group braced itself for Kenny's input. That input was not long in coming. First, he showed them an image of the front of the abandoned factory on Ridgeway Avenue so that they knew what and where the Swarm had chosen as its base of operations. Then he projected the image of the three large black semis which had transported the Swarm's equipment to that base. Finally, he presented moving pictures of the construction of the weapon of war.

Cries of terror, of outrage, and of despair greeted these last scenes. A number of the group were on their feet, shouting curses; others – men and women alike -- sobbed uncontrollably. Consternation gripped the crowd like a giant hand and squeezed them hard, individually and collectively. And no one was more affected than Eve Pelletier, who had already "seen" what that weapon was capable of. She fainted at the "sight" and slumped against Stan.

Kenny sat down and bowed his head in remorse. There had been no way he could have ameliorated the images he had projected; psycho-communication was a harsh and straightforward reality. Both Sheena and Paddy touched his arm as a show of sympathy.

Larkin, who had seen much horror in his professional life, was not unaffected either. But he could not provide any comfort and so had to allow the distress to play itself out in its own time. Long minutes passed before there was an element of calm. Then Henry Rawlins took it upon himself to speak for the group.

"God *damn* it, George! This is too much! These alien bastards intend to kill us all."

"I agree, Henry, but that was their plan all along. Those jokers on Ridgeway are just the vanguard."

"So, what are we going to do?"

"Fight fire with fire, that's what. I intend to send out our own weapons to destroy theirs – and them as well. I realize that sounds pretty cold-blooded, but our backs are now up against the wall."

He now regarded Eve, Stan, and Freddie and was shocked to see Eve in a state of unconsciousness, Stan gloomier than ever, and Freddie shaking his head in disgust.

"What's wrong, guys?"

"It's gone, Georgie," the handyman responded. "Dunno how or why, but the gestalt thing disappeared on us earlier today, and the kids can't get it back."

If Freddie had hit the detective with a hammer, he couldn't have stunned him more with this revelation. Larkin's jaw dropped, and his eyes goggled. He had had such high hopes for using the black sphere in the fight against the Swarm and had created various scenarios in which the Enemy could be completely neutralized, and now his hopes had just been dashed to pieces.

"This is not good," he stated the obvious. "The gestalt was our prime weapon."

"So, what do we do, George?" Henry Rawlins pressed him.

"We go to Plan B – as soon as I figure out what it is. Meanwhile, we'll begin monitoring the Swarm on an hour-by-hour basis. Lacey, I'll need your help on this."

The short, dark-haired psycho-occulist perked up and gave the detective as broad a smile as she could muster under the circumstances.

"Tell me what you want, George."

"First of all, can you focus on a particular area?"

"If I've seen the area prior to focusing, yes."

"Is the image Kenny put in your mind sufficient pin-pointing?"

"It should be. I won't know for sure until I try."

"All right. I want you to peep that bunch on Ridgeway every hour on the hour. I need to know every move they make."

"Can I help, Mr. Larkin?" Billy Perkins piped up.

"Sure, Billy. Four eyes are better than two. Now, if –"

He was cut short by the entrance of Emil Razumov into the dining room. He frowned at the sight, for the Director seemed to be in a daze.

CHAPTER FIVE

FIRST STRIKE

WHEN LARKIN AND Sheena returned to their offices, messages were waiting for both of them. Mrs. Watson greeted them warmly, then handed each a fistful of message slips.

"Good morning, Madge," Larkin responded. "How's Bill today?"

"He's resting as well as he can. That horrible Deacon still comes around to 'convert' us, but not as often as he used to. Maybe the idea that he is wasting his time is starting to penetrate his pointy little head."

"Maybe. Keep me posted."

The detectives retreated to their respective offices. Once inside his, Larkin scanned his fistful of slips with a keen eye. Most of the messages were from clients who were requesting updates on their cases. He sorted these out in three separate piles: "urgent," "somewhat urgent," and "not-so-urgent." He pushed the latter two stacks to one side, spread out the slips in the former, and re-arranged them in descending degrees of "urgency." Next, he went to his filing cabinet and pulled the appropriate folders. Even in the age of computers and electronic data bases, George Larkin still relied on a paper trail as a back-up; he had all of his cases, past and present, on a computer disc, but he was old-fashioned enough to want to feel paper in his hand. And he also had a *third* format: his eidetic brain which remembered everything he read.

One by one, he made phone calls to the "urgent" clients, spoke briefly to them, and scribbled some notes on the message slips. The slips then were placed in the appropriate folders for later review and for entry onto the disc during some blank spot in his schedule. (He laughed to himself at that notion.) Once that task was completed, he turned to the messages not from clients. There were two of those, and he frowned when he read the names of the persons who had left them.

One was from the Archdeacon himself. Fogarty had come by a piece of information – no specifics stated, of course – which he believed would interest his new "ally." Larkin hoped to keep his contacts with the City's acknowledged "spiritual leader" to a bare minimum, simply because it would be good for his sanity. On the other hand, if the Archdeacon had information he could use, he could hardly refuse to receive it. He'd give the man a call when he was finished with his usual routine.

The other message was even more disturbing. It read: "I'll be at Browsing Unlimited tomorrow at noon. Let's meet and have a chat. D." He shook his head in amazement. "Sister" Hedberg was still in pursuit! He hoped he had other business at noon tomorrow to use as an excuse to avoid the blonde shark. He crumpled up the message slip and casually tossed it into the wastebasket.

Official detective business behind him, Larkin switched to "electronic" mode, exited his office, hung up the "Detective at Work" sign on the door of the "snoop room," and entered it. The first task was to check his e-mail. He activated the computer, logged on, and clicked the "Telephone" icon. Only more messages from clients/potential clients appeared. He could deal with those later. He then clicked the "Inbox" icon. Several messages were waiting for him, and he scanned them in order to prioritize them.

One of them jumped out at him immediately. It was a coded message from his FBI friend, Gordy. He located the key-code number, counted out the letters, and wrote the real message on a slip of paper. It read:

"Excuse e-mail. Suspect phone tap. Director now requires personal authorization to access all files. Sorry, old buddy."

This was a real set-back, of course. Just when the detective thought he had established a pipeline to the Bureau's UFO files, someone high up in the chain of command – most likely in the Department of Justice itself –had choked it off. Worse, the Bureau was maintaining a close watch on who was accessing those files. Gordy now had to keep a low profile, lest the U.S. Attorney General, a Bishop in the Return-to-Purity movement, have cause to arrest him on any number of trumped-up charges. The detective replied (in code) to the e-mail, commiserating with his old friend and admonishing him to take care of himself.

One other message caught his eye. The Quintessential Quark was "reporting" in! The quirky informant described in more detail the preparations of the "weird-lookin' dudes" in sending out their convoy. While his assessment of the "cargo" was disjointed and confusing, it at least confirmed what Kenny had seen at the abandoned factory. The Swarm was secretly deploying advanced weaponry in advance of its intended invasion. What interested Larkin the most, however, was the Quark's observation that the aliens had set up a "tall pole with a big red light on top" and that this light flashed like the lights on police cars. The detective had no idea what purpose that piece of alien technology served; but, if the Swarm saw fit to erect it at this point in time, then he needed to know about it. He'd have to ask Mr. Smith what its purpose might be. The Quark signed off in his usual fashion: "WHAT THE FUCK'S GOIN' ON, MAN?"

Larkin hated having to rely on a UFO "junkie" like the Quark. Most of them were conspiracy freaks and therefore paranoid. But, under the circumstances, the "junkie" was the only available source of information in Nebraska. He would have preferred to employ Chris or the Twins, whose *psi*-talents were more suitable for "spy" work. He chuckled just then. Who was *he* calling a "conspiracy freak" and a "UFO junkie"? Wasn't he becoming one himself?

His reverie was interrupted by a tap on the door and the creaking of the same as it was pushed open.

"Anything new?" Sheena asked.

"Yeah. Listen to this."

He recalled the Quark's e-mail and fed it through the synthesizer. What came out was a grumbling sound with a hint of a moan, and it was as disjointed as the visual representation. He imagined that that was the way the Quark talked all the time. Sheena reacted with a grimace.

"Huh! He still talks like he's high on amphetamines," she remarked casually.

"Uh-huh. I'd hazard to guess that friend Quark is a walking pharmacy himself. What do you make of the message?"

"I'd say the Swarm is initiating a new phase in their little plan."

"My thought exactly. We'd better contact Mr. Smith and exchange information. Have you anything urgent you need to take care of?"

"Nope. Just some miscellaneous items I can clear up any time."

"Good. Let's go."

One block away from the building which housed the Larkin-Whitley Detective Agency (and other assorted small businesses) lay a City-owned parking lot, large enough for a dozen vehicles. Parking there was by permit only, and the permits were renewable on a monthly basis. The City owned several other lots of similar size scattered all across the central business district – in addition to two large multi-story parking garages – from which it collected a modest revenue. Because the space was limited, competition for any vacancies was fierce; consequently, permit holders tended to view their permits in the same manner as a king his gold. Larkin had waited for months for a vacancy to become available, and he did not hesitate one minute to stake his claim. That had been ten years ago, and he maintained possession of his permit tenaciously despite the fact that his beat-up old station wagon was as out of place next to later-model vehicles as a bird at a cat convention.

The distance to the parking lot may have been one short block but, in the summer of 2018, it may as well have been a mile. The loss of ozone in the upper atmosphere had created desert-like conditions on the Earth's surface, and no one ventured out of doors for any length of time without (1) adequate skin protection and (2) lots of water. Even so, most folks were uncomfortable in the heat and walked briskly – if they walked at all – from point to point.

George Larkin had the added disadvantage of having to rely on artificial legs for locomotion. His legs moved him too slowly for his liking; in fact, he did not walk so much as he *lurched* from side to side and gave the appearance of a man on stilts (which, in a manner of speaking, he was). One block for him was still a monumental task, but it was worth it to be able to walk at all.

What surprised the detective on this short walk was when he encountered a group of Disciples going in the opposite direction. Ordinarily, he would have avoided them because they were such arrogant, self-righteous bastards. This encounter, however, was unavoidable, and he gritted his teeth for the inevitable stare of disapproval Disciples gave everyone who wasn't one of them. Not only did they *not* stare disapprovingly, but they actually nodded courteously and *smiled*. He could only hazard to guess that the Archdeacon had alerted his people that he and Sheena were allies – complete with descriptions of both – and told them to give them any assistance they required. Larkin's Grand Plan was still in full force!

Just as the detectives reached the parking lot, a young Disciple rushed up, pushed a slip of paper into Larkin's hand, and dashed off again. The latter glanced at the paper and goggled. It read:

"Enemy force spotted, Main and Island."

Larkin grimaced. The Swarm were getting bold, appearing in the open in broad daylight in the business district. Apparently, they were so confident of their invulnerability that they could afford to take such chances. They weren't invulnerable, however, having already lost two of their comrades through inexplicable means. Were they still searching for the person(s) responsible for that loss? And what would they do if they found the responsible person(s)? He shuddered to think of it. Mr. Jones had been as ruthless as they came, and he was only an advance scout. The fact that the Swarm had found it necessary to import advanced weaponry into the City demonstrated the level of their ruthlessness. He had to check out this lead and learn what the Enemy was up to.

"What is it, George?" Sheena inquired.

He handed her the paper to "read" with her hypersensitive fingertips. She gasped with shock.

"This is terrible!"

"You got that right. But, thanks to our new network of 'informants,' we've been forewarned. We have to check it out."

The intersection of Main Street and Island Avenue formed the dividing point between north and south and east and west in the City. That was its only distinction. Otherwise, it was just another point of commercial activity, no less and no more than any other point. Hotels occupied two corners of the intersection, one of which was taller than the other. The third corner housed the City's sole newspaper, the *Sentinel-News*, a non-descript daily which served more as a medium of advertising than for news reporting. The fourth corner was home to the local outlet of a national chain of department stores; it had been recently re-furbished, having replaced an older, family-owned department store which could not keep up with the competition and went out of business.

When Larkin and Sheena reached this intersection, there was minimal activity in the area, most of which were actual and potential customers of the department store. Two Disciples – by no mean co-incidence the same two young people who had been monitoring the lobby of the detective agency's building only days before – huddled together near the newspaper's building; both exhibited extreme nervousness as they glanced this way and that and shifting their feet. Larkin could scarcely blame them for behaving this way; they were facing a dangerous Unknown not too far away. Whatever the Archdeacon had told his followers about the Enemy was merely a fraction of the truth; if he and they knew the full story, they might have fled the City altogether.

The young male Disciple caught Larkin's eye and pointed toward the taller hotel across the street. The detective signaled his understanding and motioned the pair to clear the area. Neither needed a further invitation but hastily walked away toward the east. As yet, Larkin had no plan for dealing with the Swarm other than sizing them up; but he didn't need any frail-looking Disciples hanging about and getting in the way. When the time for action came, he wanted the same sort of muscle-heads who had confronted Mr. Jones at his apartment building.

"George," Sheena whispered, "I'm picking up the same vital signs Mr. Jones gave off, three of them."

"Uh-huh. I see them now. They're just coming out of the Hotel LeGrande."

The three Swarm members emerged from the hotel as bold as brass, and one of them spoke briefly to the other two. While the two scanned the streets in all directions, the third — obviously the group Leader — produced a pocket-sized device from an ill-fitting jacket and pressed various points on its surface. He appeared to be speaking into it, then listening, and finally nodding in either understanding or obedience. When the trio came out of the shadow of the hotel and into the sunlight, Larkin froze. Instantly, he pushed Sheena behind a traffic sign and took a position there himself.

"What's wrong, George?"

"This is not good. I recognize one of those bozos."

"You do? How?"

"When I snooped Mr. Jones' apartment the first time, one of the pieces of equipment was activated. It was a communications module, and I came face to face with an ugly-looking character with a long scar across his face — presumably Mr. Jones' commanding officer. He's taken personal charge of the Swarm's presence here."

"Do you think he'd recognize *you*?"

"I don't know, but I'm not taking any chances. The order for the day is surveillance, not confrontation. We're outnumbered at the moment, in more ways than one."

The Swarm trio finished their scan of the intersection and began walking slowly eastward on Main Street. They paid particular attention to all of the passersby on the sidewalks and as many of the motorists and their passengers as they could. As it happened, they were too busy in their task to notice that they themselves were under surveillance.

Because Larkin had seen the Swarm Leader only briefly before, this time he noted every detail of the creature — facial features, gestures, body posture, and sounds he made. There were few utterances, however, and the Swarm seemed to communicate strictly by gesture and facial expression, the marks of a well-trained soldier. The detective filed away all of these observations for future reference; if he had to confront the Leader —and he was sure he would sooner or later — he wanted to be on a level playing field.

As soon as the Enemy passed by the detectives' position, Larkin stepped away from his hiding place and began walking slowly behind them. Sheena opened up her hyper-senses a few degrees and formed a detailed profile of Swarm biology. Like Mr. Smith's vital signs, those of this species were incredibly alien; the heartbeat and the respiration were slightly faster than a human's, suggesting that the Swarm originated on a world with a higher gravity than Earth's. A higher gravity-world would also account for the stocky, muscular body and a light and lengthy footstep on this planet. The Swarm body odor and breath had a hint of copper in it. That data would correlate with the Quintessential Quark's observation that they needed to flush out oxygen in their bodies periodically and re-supply themselves with whatever chemical compound necessary for their survival.

Ordinarily, she would have gotten a read on a target's emotional state, but the signals she was receiving from these creatures were beyond her comprehension. She gave up the effort after a minute of trying to analyze the signals and concentrated on the biological data.

The Swarm crossed the bridge over the east channel of the river which passed through the City and abruptly entered the first retail shop they encountered. Larkin took a chance on not being spotted, crossed the street, and peered through the window. The Leader was showing each of the employees a thin rectangular object which looked very much like a photograph; when the employees shook their heads in non-recognition, he pushed the object closer to their faces. His own face indicated anger, and his facial muscles twisted his scar into a hideous feature. Again, non-recognition was forthcoming, whereupon the Swarm marched toward the entrance. Instantly, Larkin retreated back across the street and re-joined his partner.

"What's happening, George?"

"Those bozos are looking for someone. My guess is that that 'someone' is the person they suspect killed their buddy at the depot."

"The 'eel'?"

"Uh-huh. So, it's imperative we find her before they do."

The Swarm visited three more retail shops before reaching the corner of Main and Broadway. Each time, they buttonholed the employees and showed them the photograph; each time, they received negative responses; and, each time, they departed grimmer than before. Larkin was of two minds concerning the Enemy's failure to obtain the information they sought; on the one hand, he was pleased that they were failing and, on the other hand, concerned that failure would result in ruthless behavior.

Just as the aliens reached the corner of Main and Broadway, a screeching of tires split the air, and three white automobiles traveling north on Broadway turned sharply left onto Main at high speed. All three stopped in the middle of the street with more screeching of the tires, blocking traffic. Six burly individuals wearing ice-cream suits poured out of each vehicle; some of them wielded baseball bats and iron pipes, while the rest held ham-sized fists at the ready. Larkin grunted in surprise. Another Disciple "hit squad" was on the move!

The leader of the Disciples, whom the detective thought he recognized, directed his "troops" to surround the Swarm team. They did so with quick efficiency. The aliens took this action in stride; battle-honed on dozens of worlds, they recognized military tactics when they saw them and knew how to gauge any sort of threat. They stood their ground, exuding self-confidence and murderous determination.

"Stay where you are, devil-spawn!" the Disciple leader commanded. "Yield to the Light of Purity, or suffer the consequences!"

The Swarm leader turned to his own troops and barked something in their own language. While his subordinates reached into their tunics and pulled out hand weapons, he extracted a small black cube from his own tunic. Larkin by now was close enough to see the latter object clearly, and a cold chill ran up his spine. He had no time to explain in rational terms what those black cubes actually did, and so he resorted to language only a Disciple could readily understand and, hopefully, act upon.

"Look out...brothers!" he shouted. "Those are weapons they're holding, weapons that will...produce hellfire!"

The ploy worked. The Disciple leader turned, recognized Larkin, and waved to him by way of acknowledgement of the danger. He addressed his people.

"Brothers," he declared, "they will not yield. Cast them out! CAST THEM OUT!"

The burly bunch did not hesitate one second. They were just as trained to obey orders as any Swarm soldier was; moreover, having been primed to deal with Evil, they were itching to do battle with it. And, of course, they knew that they had God on their side. As one man, they pressed forward and closed in on the aliens. The latter braced themselves and brought their weaponry to bear.

"George, what's happening? I'm picking up rapid heartbeats all over the place. I sense great anger and hatred."

"The same thing that happened at Mr. Jones' place three days ago – mayhem."

He felt Sheena shudder with fear and suppressed a shudder of his own. He knew very well what was about to happen, and there wasn't a damned thing he could do about it – even if he had wanted to – except watch the carnage unfold.

Only the suddenness of the attack and the sheer numbers of the attackers prevented what would otherwise have been a massacre. The Swarm realized that they would not have time to deploy their weapons efficiently and thus burn down the upstart "Tellurians." Instead, they prepared for hand-to-hand combat. If Sheena's surmise were correct, and the aliens originated from a world with a higher gravity, then their musculature would have adapted. On a world with a lighter gravity, their musculature would give them "super-strength" (like the comic-book hero, "Superman"), and they would believe they could swat these puny creatures like so many pesky insects.

That is how the melee began. The Swarm lashed out at the nearest Disciples and rained heavy blows upon them. The crunch of bones being broken was quite audible, even to Larkin across the street; blood gushed everywhere from dozens of wounds. Other Disciples had their own weapons wrenched out of their hands and used against them with savage efficiency. The tide of battle turned, however, as the Disciples deployed three or four of their number toward each of the defenders.

The Swarm Leader saw a gap open up in the Tellurian ranks and took advantage of it. He dodged several swinging bats and pipes, slipped through the gap, and ran for his life. Some of the Disciples gave chase, but the Leader's leg muscles allowed him to outrun them easily. His underlings were not so fortunate; they disappeared under a mass of righteous warriors and perished. Their bodies were scarcely recognizable as once-sentient creatures.

Larkin watched the mayhem with a sense of *déjà vu*. This was the second time he had witnessed self-sacrifice on the part of the Disciples for what they believed in, and the aftermath had not been a pretty sight. He counted five ice-cream suits on the ground who neither moved nor made a sound; four others, including their leader, were badly injured and probably near death. Blood covered the sidewalk and the street. Larkin's Grand Plan of pitting the Disciples against the Swarm was still on track, but he wished he didn't have to watch it in action.

"Oh, God, George!" Sheena wailed and buried her head in his shoulder. "It was *horrible*! Thank God I didn't have to *see* the carnage. My other senses told me everything I didn't want to know. The sound of broken bones. The smell of blood. The cessation of vital signs. I wanted to throw up!"

"So did I, if truth be told. But, it's over now. We have to move on."

The Disciple leader -- a stocky and muscular type with jet-black hair, dark, deep-set eyes, a ruddy complexion, and a square jaw -- with the aid of two of his followers still in one piece holding him on his feet, concluded a prayer of thanksgiving for their victory over the Enemy. He instructed his aides to escort him over to Larkin and Sheena. He wore a self-satisfied smile on his face.

"Brother Larkin, Sister Whitley," he said in a raspy voice, "are you all right?"

"We're fine. You're not, though."

"A small price to pay for service to the Lord."

"Of course. You arrived in short order."

"Actually, we were on stand-by, waiting for just such a situation to occur. His Worship didn't want us to be surprised, like what happened a few days ago."

"His Worship has a good grasp on strategy. Otherwise, we wouldn't be having this conversation."

"Right. So, when Brother Connolly and Sister Smithers alerted us that you were tracking the Enemy, we mobilized and rushed here. We achieved a significant victory today, thank the Lord."

"But at great cost."

"No cost is too great to bring the Light of Purity to the unbelievers. By the way, I'm Brother Horton."

"Horton? Aren't you a coach at the high school?"

"Yes, a football coach. That's why I was chosen to lead this task force."

"A good choice, I'd say."

"What will you do now, Brother Larkin?"

By way of answer, the detective walked over to the remains of the two dead Swarm soldiers and rifled through their pockets. He tried to avoid looking at their smashed-in faces. Presently, he stood up and displayed the two hand weapons.

"These are the damnable weapons I tried to warn you about, the ones that would've burned you with hellfire."

"Brother" Horton's face sagged, and he swallowed compulsively.

"What – what are you going to do with them?"

"I have a friend who likes to tinker with gadgets. I'm going to see if he can make these things work for us."

"I think they should be destroyed. They're...evil. But, since His Worship trusts you, I guess you know best. May the Light of Purity guide you, Brother Larkin, Sister Whitley."

"And the same to you, Brother Horton."

"What an act you put on," Sheena sniggered as soon as the Disciples left to lick their wounds. "It was all I could do to keep from laughing."

"One of my many talents, don't you know?"

"So, what *are* you going to do with those weapons?"

"Exactly what I said I'd do. I'm going to have Monk take a look at them and see if he can make any sense out of them. But, first, we pay a visit to Mr. Smith."

* * *

Mr. Smith was not at home.

When Larkin entered the make-shift base of the Coalition agent, he did not see him anywhere amongst the array of technological wonders. He checked each piece from all angles, but the alien was missing altogether. He considered entering the one chamber he had observed Mr. Smith emerging from during a previous visit; he remembered, however, that that module was the cold-fusion generator and that it was booby-trapped, set to self-destruct should anyone but its operator touch it. There was nothing to do but wait until the operator returned.

Or, was there?

Now, he thought, would be a good time to examine this array in detail and see if he could gain some understanding of its functions. Mr. Smith might not be present, but the machines were still active. Some were humming in various tones; others were changing colors. A great deal of information – Coalition information – was being received, analyzed, transmitted, and/or stored for future reference, and Larkin wished he could access even a fraction of it in order to learn what was going on in the rest of the Galaxy. The aliens were not likely to volunteer any more information than they absolutely had to, and so he must ferret out what he could on his own.

First, he had to call Sheena and let her know what he was up to. She was sitting in the station wagon across the street by necessity, not by choice. When the pair had arrived at the abandoned supermarket and were walking across the weed-choked parking lot, she suddenly froze twenty meters from the building and clutched her stomach.

"What's wrong?" Larkin had asked.

"I'm experiencing an EMF," she had replied, "and it's really strong."

"Yes. I noticed it the last time I was here. Mr. Smith had just installed it, and he probably had it set at maximum."

"Well, he didn't do me any favors. I can't go any farther, George. I'm going back to the station wagon."

George Larkin was now on his own. But, then, what else was new?

His mind drifted back to last night's meeting at DEDEP. Emil Razumov had finally put in an appearance toward the end, but his mind had seemed to be elsewhere. He made a few perfunctory remarks in a low, barely-audible voice, then fell silent and let the detective answer any questions raised by the residents. The latter had muddled on without the benefit of the Director's input and support.

He knew, of course, what was bothering the old man – the same thing that was bothering him – the loss of the gestalt under mysterious circumstances. Emil, ever the dogged scientist, had a long list of experiments in mind involving the black sphere, and he was now like a small child who had been sent to bed for no discernable reason. In all the years Larkin had known the Russian, he had never seen him in a sheer funk; usually, he was excited by one thing or another, be it a successful experiment or a new insight on the workings of all things *psi*, all of which was processed by his fantastic brain. Emil's present state, however, did not bode well for the future of DEDEP; and the sooner he was snapped out of his funk, the better for all concerned.

The question was, how to do it?

Perhaps, if the detective learned more of the Coalition's plan to defeat the Swarm and presented it to the Doctor, that just might get his brain working again.

The key to the functioning of all this equipment resided, of course, in the control console. If he could learn how it functioned, he could operate the array without the assistance of Mr. Smith. That was a big "if," but he had to try. He studied the grid and called on his eidetic memory to provide what information he had picked up by observing the Coalition agent.

The grid was a sixteen-by-sixteen lay-out, and each subdivision contained a single symbol. No two subdivisions contained the same symbol. The detective marveled at the complexity of it all: two hundred and fifty-six symbols and each of several hundred thousands of combinations to perform a specific command. He wondered idly if Mr. Smith knew all of the combinations. Given the alien's agrarian background, he doubted it; the Coalition would have had to provide him with a code book of some sort with an emphasis on certain basic combinations in order to carry out his monitoring duties. Even if such an "owner's manual" existed, however, Larkin knew he couldn't read it.

As he pondered the console in frustration, he was startled by a *bong-bong* emanating from the "Tinker Toy," a.k.a. the "Coalition Communication Relay." A section of it lit up in a gaudy array and flashed rapidly.

Incoming message? the detective thought. *Where's Mr. Smith when I need him?*

He turned automatically toward the giant monitor and watched as the screen lit up, presented a kaleidoscopic sequence of multi-colored patterns, and coalesced into an identifiable image. He gaped at the figure looking down at him; it was Frommar, the Co-ordinator of the Coalition (or another of his species). Unintelligent sounds issued from the speakers. The alien looked off to his left, and his speech increased in speed.

Damn! I need to turn on the translator. But how?

He concentrated on the grid and pictured Mr. Smith activating the translating program at his first meeting with the Coalition leader.

There! Those two symbols. Then that one. And that one.

He pressed the symbols Mr. Smith had pressed and was pleased to hear pigeon-English issuing from the speakers.

"…primitive not able to commune. Waiting! He knowing now." Frommar's speech slowed down appreciatively. "La-k'n?"

"Yes, I'm Larkin. Are you Frommar?"

"I Frommar. I pleased to speak at you."

"And I am also pleased."

"Where Mabel-choo-choo?"

"I don't know. I came here because I have some information about Swarm activity to give him. He seems to be absent."

"New information? Reporting it to me."

The detective began (without specifying his own involvement) with the incident at the depot and the killing of the Swarm soldier. He followed that up with the Swarm's presumed search for the assassin and the loss of two more of their numbers. Finally, he presented the *piece de resistance*: the establishment of a temporary base in the City and the construction of one of their warships. He concluded by saying that he had organized a guerrilla force to strike at the Swarm when and where and however it could.

A long silence ensued, and he fidgeted a bit. Would Frommar believe his report? Then:

"A good report, La-k'n. This new information help-will to assess Swarm strategy." Another long pause. "We not pleased by new developments. The Swarm making bold moves – disregarding secrecy. We mobilize-must sooner than planned."

"What will you do? How can my people help?"

"We tell-will you later. We – Ah! Mabel-choo-choo arrived-has."

Larkin turned and saw the pasty-faced alien shuffling toward him from the direction of the dockside entrance. He appeared (undoubtedly with good reason) to be very alarmed to see that his new "ally" communicating feely with his superior without his being present. He pulled up to the control console and spoke to Frommar in his own language. The conversation lasted no more than a minute after which Mr. Smith signed off.

"Good...morning...Mr....Largin," he addressed the detective. "I... see...thhhat...you...hhhave...made...yourself...at...hhhome."

Alien or no, Larkin recognized sarcasm when he heard it. No doubt he was expecting an apology for this intrusion upon his "turf." He was doomed to disappointment; he should have hired a PI less curious than George Larkin if he had wanted absolute privacy. Now that he was an "ally," the agent should expect more of these unannounced visits.

"No one was here, so I waited for you to return."

"Whhhat...did...you...and...Frommar...talg...about?"

The detective repeated everything almost word for word he had told the Coalition leader. Mr. Smith make a few facial expressions which Larkin deduced as changing emotional states; which states they reflected only the alien knew for sure, although Larkin could have made some shrewd guesses based upon his own reaction to the information received were the shoe on the other foot. Mr. Smith regarded the control console and tapped a sequence of symbols (which Larkin quickly memorized). Instantly, the ten eight-foot poles sprang into activity.

"I…am…relaying…thhhis…information…to…my…golleagues… around…thhhe…globe.   Thhhey…are…advised…to…ingrease… thhheir …monitoring…agtivities…immediately."

"A wise precaution. What is the protocol for this circumstance?"

Mr. Smith remained silent for a moment while regarding Larkin minutely. Then:

"Protogol…digtates…thhhat…we…arm…ourselves."

"You're going to import weapons here?" the detective asked with no small amount of alarm. "What kind of weapons?"

"Do…not…goncern…yourself…Mr….Largin. Thhhe…weapons… will …will…be…purely…defensive…in…nashure."

"You'll excuse me for saying so, Mr. Smith, but I find little comfort in that."

"We…are…at…war…and…thhhere…is…little…gomfort…in… thhhat."

Yeah, right. And Planet Earth is caught smack dab in the middle of it!

CHAPTER SIX

THE SEARCH FOR THE "EEL"

OF ALL THE psychic/occult phenomena which has been, or will be, discussed in this work, the least understood – and therefore, the most misinterpreted – is 're-incarnation," the supposed transmigration of the "soul" from one physical body to another ad infinitum.

The concept of the "immortal soul" which survives physical death has been a key doctrine of all the religions in human history. If one behaves oneself and/or does good to his/her fellow humans, then (s)he will go to Heaven/Paradise/the "happy hunting grounds"/Nirvana (or any of dozens of similar places). If, however, one does not behave oneself, (s)he will surely go to Hell/the underworld/the "infernal regions" (or any of dozens of similar places). The various priesthoods who have claimed to speak for one god or another hold out the promise of "eternal life" in order to gain adherents to the religions they have founded and are promoting. The fear of death/non-existence is so prevalent among humans that it drives them to seek out any means to forestall and/or avoid the final reckoning....

...Most religions therefore do not accept the notion that the "soul" experiences an endless procession of physical lives. Only Hinduism has promulgated this idea. Yet, even in Hinduism, the procession is not endless; the Hindu scholars say that re-incarnation continues until all of one's "karmic debts" have been repaid.... When those debts are taken care

of – however long it takes – the "soul" enters Nirvana, a state of oblivion and final rest.

Westerners who have embraced the concept of re-incarnation reject the part about Nirvana on the grounds that it is just so much Oriental mysticism and therefore not important. They prefer to view the phenomenon as eternal....

Re-incarnation usually comes to light when humans experience strange dreams. The dreams involve persons or places in bygone eras that the dreamer has never seen or visited in his/her current existence. Very often, the dreamer also interacts with those persons or places and comes to the conclusion that (s)he has actually seen them in a "past life." Hypnotic regression fuels this belief by causing the subject to "re-live," on demand, the alleged "past life" and convinces him/her that re-incarnation is a real phenomenon. Once convinced, the subject will not listen to any other explanation for his/her strange dreams.... Thus re-incarnation takes on the form of a cult with many adherents regardless of their original religious backgrounds.

In the second chapter of this work, I demonstrated, from the viewpoint of radiopsychology, the nature of the human brain as a generator of radio waves. I stated that this form of energy behaves much like a carrier wave similar to the signals sent out by radio or television transmissions, i.e. a series of electrical impulses of varying frequencies carrying bits of information. Upon the brain's "carrier wave" reside one's thoughts and emotions and memories; it is an unconscious process which occurs every second of one's existence. The major portion of these transmissions are absorbed by the generator's environment and contributes to the phenomena of "ghosts" and "hauntings" (cf. chapter four). The remainder flies into space to join a vast panoply of energy.

At the moment of death of the organism, the brain ceases to generate radio energy, and the last thoughts and emotions and memories are added to the mix....

What happens to that quantity of energy which floats about in space?

In physics, we learn that energy can be neither created nor destroyed. And so it is with radio energy. It remains all about us, to be tapped into by a living brain that is sensitive to one frequency or another, just as that brain is sensitive to energy absorbed by a particular environment....

It quite often happens that an organism suffers a traumatic death. That is to say, the death may result from either an act of violence or an unusual circumstance where strong emotions are present. In these cases, the final signals from the dying brain are stronger than otherwise and will remain strong for a longer period of time. It is not co-incidental then that the majority of the alleged instances of re-incarnation involves such deaths. And thus the persons who experience these phenomena are quite often disturbed by them....

No one has lived before his/her present existence. What has actually occurred is that (s)he has tapped into the thoughts and emotions and memories of a deceased person and lives that *person's life vicariously....*

Joyce shook her head for the dozenth time as she plowed through this particular chapter for the second reading. She had to marvel at the manner in which Emil Razumov approached and described what, to her, was a completely incomprehensible subject. It was easy for him to do so, since he had been immersed in the subject all his life; but she hadn't had the "benefit" of his academic career and so viewed his writings in much the same way a child might look at a page of calculus.

She had heard about re-incarnation, of course, listening to people who discussed it as casually as the Doctor did. Not that they had made it any easier to understand than he did – the subject was one of those mystical Oriental doctrines which required a leap of faith to believe. Her Catholic upbringing (such as it was) had not allowed any such leap in the first place; the Church regarded Oriental mysticism – whatever form it took – as heathenish superstition, the antithesis of salvation through Christ and eternal life in Heaven. The priests had also spoken out against premarital sex, and she hadn't followed that teaching very well, had she? So, why not re-incarnation which postulated an infinite series of lives, each different that the ones before?

Dr. Razumov had debunked both the mysticism of the Orient and the Western attitude, however, and instead described it as a kind of a "movie" about some other person you saw in your dreams. What would the Church or the mystics think of that idea? She was sure the priests would come up with some theological explanation and then caution the congregation not to fall into the trap of scientific plausibility. The Church pooh-poohed telekinesis as well and called it "Satanic." But, hadn't she given birth to a child with that ability? And hadn't Emil Razumov explained that ability as casually and as logically as everything else in his book and called it a "gift" rather than a "curse"? She was caught in a bit of a dilemma of monumental proportions.

And, speaking of dilemmas, DEDEP was in the midst of another one, and the Director was no longer casual or logical. The gestalt that Stan and Eve had created apparently couldn't be conjured up any more, and the Doctor was in a sullen mood. He had been completely subdued at last night's special meeting (along with her son and his "partners-in-crime"), and George had had to fill in for him. And George seemed to be in a sour mood himself; he had viewed the gestalt as a weapon he could use against the aliens who were threatening to invade Earth, and now he had nothing.

The whole thing was so arcane that she really didn't want to think about it anymore. Unfortunately, she didn't have that option; willingly or otherwise, she was now part and parcel of an incomprehensible circumstance.

A series of raps at the door came to her "rescue," even as it asked a new question. Was someone calling on her or on Stan? And why?

She opened the door and was astonished to see Freddie and Eve standing there. The dwarf wore his usual expression of indignity; Joyce could well believe he had been born with it – not that he didn't have good reason to wear it, she quickly added. Eve, on the other hand, was uncharacteristically cheerful, an attitude she seemed to have acquired only recently. *Why* was a mystery, but Joyce didn't want to go there. She had her own problems to deal with.

"Freddie! Eve!" she greeted her visitors with as much neighborliness as she could muster up at this hour. "How are you?"

"We're fine," Eve responded. "We've come to see Stan."

"Is it important? He's doing his homework right now – or he'd better be doing his homework."

"Nah," Freddie said off-handedly. "It's like this, Joyce. Um, can I call ya 'Joyce'? We've all been thrown into the same boat here, and it seems only right to be on a first-name basis." Joyce shrugged her shoulders by way of acquiescence. "Anyways, the three of us hafta talk about the gestalt."

"The gestalt? I thought it was gone."

"We don't know that yet. It disappeared, but who knows for how long. That's why us three got to talk."

"Very well." She turned toward Stan's bedroom door. "Stan! Someone to see you!"

Two seconds later, the boy bounded out of his room, happy to be doing something other than homework. When he spotted his partners in "gestalt summoning," he broke out in a huge grin. Freddie and Eve responded in kind.

"Freddie! Eve! What's up?"

"Hiya, kid. We got business to discuss."

"Business? What kinda business?"

"It's about the gestalt," Eve said softly.

"Yeah," the handyman added and turned to Joyce. "D'ya mind if we use this place as a 'conference room'?"

She eyed him suspiciously. He was asking her to leave her own apartment so that he and Eve and Stan could discuss some "business" they didn't want her to know about. Who the hell was he to ask such a thing? Should she report this to the Director? Then she looked at her son who looked back at her in a pleading manner. (Eve was biting her lip.) Now she remembered where she was and why she was here. She was not in *her* apartment but in a refuge for people like Stan, and she was here on sufferance. Once more, she was obliged to forfeit some of her parental rights. If these three needed to discuss DEDEP "business," why, she mustn't interfere.

"I guess it's OK. I'll go visit Lacey Perkins. She's been asking about my experiences in raising a—a '*psi*-child,' as she puts it."

"Thanks, Mom," Stan said, relieved. "You won't regret it."

As soon as his mother had left, the boy plopped down on the floor and regarded his friends tentatively. Freddie smiled wryly and plopped down next to him. Even though she had had plenty of "floor-time" herself, Eve was more graceful in joining them. A brief silence fell over the room as each of them debated whether or not to initiate the discussion. Presently, the dwarf pulled a half-smoked cigar out of his tool pouch and stuck it in his mouth. Eve wrinkled her nose.

"I ain't gonna smoke it, Evie. Wouldn't be polite. We chased Stan's mother outa her own apartment. If we stunk up the place, there'd be hell to pay!" He regarded his cigar. "This helps me to think when I got sumpin important to think about."

"So, what about the gestalt?" Stan asked.

"We brought it into our world," Eve answered. "We…communicated with it. Or it with us. Take your pick." Here she shuddered. "It even protected us against that horrible Mr. Jones. Now it's gone, and I don't know why. But we have to bring it back – if we can."

"How? We tried before, and nothin' worked."

"We just hafta try harder, kid," Freddie offered. "Ain't nobody gonna bring that thing back but us." He rolled his cigar around in his mouth. "First thing we gotta do is to remember what each of us was thinkin' when the gestalt disappeared. Might be a clue there."

All three fell into a deep concentration, almost trance-like.

* * *

Larkin and Sheena returned to the office, and the former did so with no little consternation. His meeting with Mr. Smith had been deeply disturbing, to say the least, and he had mixed feelings about his next course of action. While he had appreciated the Coalition agent's candor, he hadn't cared at all for the *nature* of the candor. The stakes in this "game" had just taken a quantum leap.

The alien alliance was about to arm its agents on Earth with unknown but obviously highly sophisticated weaponry without a second thought. Yet, it had consistently refused to do likewise for its supposed allies indigenous to the planet. How fair was that? The Coalition had its reasons, it claimed, but Larkin hadn't been asking for weapons for every Tom, Dick, and Harry who thought he needed one; no, he had just been asking on behalf of his own group which was more advanced than the run-of-the-mill Tellurian. Was that so much to ask? And, when the Swarm was eventually defeated, he'd return the weapons along with a great big "thank you and stop by anytime you're in the neighborhood," wouldn't he?

The desire for weapons had been somewhat negated with the discovery of one of the gestalt's capabilities. He had realized immediately the implications of that discovery; DEDEP possessed a weapon more sophisticated than anything the aliens could have supplied (or dreamed of), even if it had all the time in the Universe to develop it. As such, the gestalt was infinitely more dangerous; but, with a little ingenuity, it could be controlled. Now that it had disappeared for no apparent reason and was seemingly irretrievable, DEDEP was back to square one.

Larkin wanted some hardware, and he wanted it now!

There was one possibility, although it was a long shot. He had already secured two Swarm hand weapons which could be put into play as soon as their operation was understood. And he had removed the EMF generator from the apartment of the late unlamented Mr. Jones. So far as he knew, the remainder of the Swarm equipment was still there. Another visit was clearly in order; but first, he'd have to enlist Monk, the electronics wizard, to assist in the deciphering of those weapons and machines and determine if any of them could be used as a counter-offensive against its own creators. He was clutching at straws, he knew; but until the gestalt was restored (if ever), he had to clutch at whatever was available.

One other urgent matter needed to be resolved, and it had nothing to do with weaponry, sophisticated/dangerous or otherwise. He had to locate the missing "eel" before the Swarm did and sequester her so that her *psi*-talent could be developed and controlled. He could do the first part with a little diligence; the rest was up to Emil Razumov. And, perhaps with new "material" to work with, he could snap the Russian out of his blue mood.

The detectives entered the office, greeted Mrs. Watson perfunctorily, and headed straight for the "snoop room." Sheena had sensed his mood from the time he returned to the station wagon and so had held her tongue the whole trip back. She was anxious to learn how the meeting had gone and believed the familiar surroundings would loosen George up. When she put the question to him, he hesitated only an instant before giving her a detailed account. When he finished, she was just as consternated as he was.

"I do not like the sound of that," she murmured.

"Join the group."

"What do we do now?"

Larkin reached into his coat pocket and pulled out the brass-colored sphere Mr. Smith had given him. He held it up for Sheena's inspection. She detected a slight humming emanating from it.

"This is the tracking device the Coalition promised us. Mr. Smith gave me a quick tutorial on how to use it before I left his base. We can expect no more 'assistance' from that quarter. We're on our own." He pocketed the device. "As to your question, I'm going out to DEDEP and recruit Monk to help me loot Mr. Jones' apartment for something hopefully more useful."

"Don't you think the Swarm might've already cleaned it out?"

"Perhaps, and perhaps not. Right now, they're busy looking for the person or persons who terminated one of their own. While I'm at DEDEP, I'll assemble a search team to look for our missing 'eel.'"

"What do you want me to do?"

"Monitor my e-mail. I want to know what the Quark is up to at all times." He smiled wickedly. "Gordy may call as well. Use your charms and see what you can wheedle out of him."

Sheena grimaced.

"You betcha, George, all day and all night."

* * *

The gloom was thick enough to cut.

Larkin could feel it as soon as he stepped off the ladder leading to the underground facility and gazed down the corridor. Ordinarily, one might have heard, in the distance, the murmuring of voices in conversation or the low-level hum of machinery or even the groaning and the creaking of the structure itself. One could pay little attention to these sounds on the conscious level, but the sub-conscious picked them up easily; and, when the noises ceased, then the conscious took notice – as the detective did at that moment. At that moment, DEDEP was as silent as a tomb. One might have concluded that it had been abandoned.

One would have been wrong.

Larkin would know if it had been abandoned. In the absence of such information, he believed that the denizens of DEDEP were inactive – all of them, all at once.

He was not at all surprised by the quietude, however. In fact, he would have been surprised if there *weren't* any. Dr. Emil Razumov, who had been looking forward to endless experimentation with the gestalt, had fallen into an unaccustomed depression with the phenomenon's disappearance. The old man was an inveterate problem-solver, and he seldom conceded defeat; eventually, his superior brain found an answer or, at the very least, a clue which led to the answer. Now he had the least idea of where to look for an answer. For the first time in his association with the Russian, George Larkin saw a withered ancient who spent his time staring off into space.

It is a truism that the mood of the ruler is contagious. The ruled pick up on it sooner or later and soon, all are infected to one degree or another. And so it was at DEDEP. The inmates, having owed their salvation to the Director, looked to him every day for emotional and psychological sustenance as well as for food and shelter. The Director's depression was now their depression, and they had no desire to do anything on their own.

Most of them anyway.

When Larkin rounded the corner at the "crossbar" of the "H," the only person he saw was Freddie checking electrical circuits. Otherwise, the corridor was deserted, and DEDEP was "closed for business." It was an eerie feeling which disturbed the detective like nothing else could have; he had to struggle to prevent himself from falling into the same depression.

The dwarf looked up at Larkin's approach. Absent anyone else in the corridor, the latter's footsteps sounded like a drumbeat. The handyman broke out in a grin, and it wasn't forced. The detective smiled back in spite of himself. At least one person here seemed normal.

"Hiya, Georgie. What's new?"

"Hi yourself, Freddie. Where is everybody?"

"Huh! When the Doc crawled into his shell, everybody else followed him in. No testing, no experimenting, no classes. The only activity is in the kitchen and the dining room – we all hafta eat, doncha know? – and then it's back into the shells. Then there's me. I still hafta go around and fix things."

"Unbelievable!"

"Ain't it though? In a way, it sorta helps me out. I got no one in my way, and I can work uninterrupted." He fished a half-smoked cigar from his tool pouch and stuck it in his mouth. "And I get to smoke as much as I want to. Heh-heh."

"Uh-huh. As for what's new, I'm here to put together a search team to look for our missing 'eel.'"

"Who ya got in mind?"

"I'm thinking about the Jankowskys. The 'eel' is in a state of panic right now, and she might be alarmed by some strange-looking man approaching her. She might not suspect a woman with a child in tow."

"That's what I like about you, Georgie – yer devious mind. Dunno if Joyce will go fer it, though. She's the panicky sort herself."

"I'll just have to be extra persuasive. Right now, I've got to go check on Emil."

"Good luck," Freddie muttered and lit his cigar.

Larkin continued down the corridor, his footsteps echoing in the emptiness. Twice, he stopped to peer into a room, only to find more emptiness. He shook his head sadly. This was not the DEDEP he was used to – the hustle and bustle which marked the first "E" and the second "D" in the acronym, evaluating and developing *psi*-talent. This had to be corrected soon!

He pulled up before the Director's door, rapped three times, opened the door, and shuffled in. What he saw caused him to shake his head again. The old man was staring blankly at a sheet of paper as if he were trying to discover what it was. He displayed all the symptoms of a person who had lost all purpose in life and was simply marking time. The detective walked toward the desk as unobtrusively as he could and waited to be recognized. When that tactic failed to rouse the Doctor out of his inane reverie, he used the verbal approach.

"Emil?" he said quietly.

"Eh?" The Russian raised his head and blinked several times to clear his vision. "Ah, George. *Kak zheevyosh?*"

"*Khorosho*," came the standard reply. "*Ee tee* [and you]?"

The Director shrugged and returned to his sheet of paper.

"The reason I'm here," Larkin pushed on, "is to recruit some of the DEDEP'ers to help look for the 'eel.'"

"Mmmm."

"I think I'll select the Jankowskys, if that's all right with you."

"Mmmm."

"Well, OK. I'll talk to you later. *Do sveedanye* [good-bye]."

Dr. Razumov waved his hand aimlessly. Larkin shook his head a third time, pivoted, and left the office. He headed for the next level downward, the first of the residential levels.

The eerie silence followed him. It was uncanny, he thought. For all the grumbling he had heard in the past about having to live in a hole in the ground and not being able to enjoy sunshine and fresh air (except on a limited basis), the residents now preferred to stay in their quarters rather than participate in their usual activities – all because the head of DEDEP had had the rug pulled out from under him. He also wondered why no one had thought to step into the vacuum and provide some temporary leadership; surely, there was someone who was keeping his/her head above water. Did (s)he have to be "recruited" in order to act? Ordinarily, the duty would have fallen to the Director of Operations, but that person already had plenty on his plate with aliens and religious fanatics to manipulate for the good of Planet Earth.

He moved slowly along the residential level, very much aware of the *click-clack* of his shoes against the tile flooring. It was something most people seldom noticed because their minds were usually occupied with other matters. Now that he was aware of it, he found it most annoying. He couldn't tip-toe, because he had no toes to begin with; and, even if he had, he couldn't balance himself.

Soon, he found himself at the Jankowskys' apartment and rapped three times on the door. Five seconds passed without any response. He rapped again, then pressed his ear to the door in order to detect any movement inside. Five more seconds passed without a response. He grimaced and pounded on the door several times.

If that doesn't get someone's attention, he thought grimly, *then nothing will.*

Abruptly, the door opened wide, and he stared into an empty room. Who had opened the door? He stepped inside and saw Stan sitting on the sofa looking quite unconcerned over the visitor's consternation.

"Hello, Mr. Larkin. I was in the bathroom the first time you knocked. Sorry."

"That's quite all right, Stan. Is your mother in?"

"Hey, Mom!" the boy shouted. "You can come out of hiding. It's only Mr. Larkin."

Three seconds later, Joyce emerged from her bedroom and gave her son a look of exasperation.

"I wasn't hiding," she protested. "I was making my bed." She turned to the visitor. "Hello, George. What can I do for you?"

"I've come to recruit you two for a little project I need help with."

"'Recruit'? What do you mean?"

"As you probably know, we were supposed to receive a *psi*-talent from St. Louis the day before yesterday. An 'eel.' But, because –"

"An 'eel'?" Joyce interrupted. "That snake-like creature that swims in the ocean and gives off electric shocks? What does that have to do with DEDEP?"

"Actually, it's 'E-E-L,' which stands for 'electrically energized life-form.' This person does have the ability to give off electric shocks once she builds up a charge so large she can't hold it and has to release it. Whether she can swim in the ocean is academic.

"Anyway, because of the strange event at the depot, we missed the rendezvous. Now, she's wandering about the City, lost and confused." He paused briefly. "And, I might add, the Swarm is after her, because she may have killed one of them."

"Where do Stan and I come in?"

"She might not trust some strange-looking man, but she might be put off her guard by a woman and her child."

"Oh, *wow!*" Stan exclaimed. "*Spy stuff,* just like James Bond! How about it, Mom? It sounds *cool!*"

"Wel-l-l, I don't know. Are you sure it's not dangerous?"

"We'll pick up either Kenny or Paddy – whoever is free today – and he'll alert us to any danger. It'll get you out of this hole in the ground for a little while," he added as an inducement.

"Let's do it, Mom! I don't feel like sittin' around, doin' nothin'."

"All right. I would like to get out of this place once in a while. When do we start?"

"Right now."

* * *

Joyce fidgeted the entire trip back to the City, and she gave herself three good reasons for her nervousness.

First, she didn't know what to expect by returning to the scene of recent threats against her and her son. She hadn't been overly thrilled by accepting charity from total strangers and re-locating to an underground community of similar refugees; yet, in the end, being in DEDEP was far safer (relatively speaking) than being in the City. Now, however, she had actually volunteered to go back there and act as a go-between for DEDEP and another refugee. What did she know about such things? She'd rather watch the parade than be in it.

George Larkin had assured her that no harm would come to her. How could he make such assurances? If they encountered any Disciples and one or more of them recognized her or Stan, there would be trouble. Stan had protected her against a single Disciple. Could he do it against a mob of them? It didn't seem possible, and the thought of being assaulted again terrified her. She wished George would turn around and take them back to the relative safety of DEDEP.

Second, she was riding in this damned piece of junk of a station wagon again. It hadn't improved with age; in fact, it rattled and clanked even more than the first time she had ridden in it. If it didn't fall apart at any second and scatter its passengers across the countryside, it would be a minor miracle. As a Catholic, she was supposed to believe in miracles; but Church teachings had never had anything to say about faulty automobiles!

She now regarded her son next to her in the rear seat of this piece of junk. Stan was fidgeting too, but not because he was as nervous as she was about their mode of transportation or the prospect of returning to a place of potential danger. Rather, he was behaving like a tourist in a strange land, looking this way and that as if he had never seen these sights before in his life. Every once in a while, he would nudge her and point out something he thought fascinating. She pretended to be just as interested as he was so as not to alarm him unduly.

She also regarded the driver of the piece of junk who never ceased to amaze her. How George Larkin could operate a motor vehicle with artificial limbs was truly astounding. The first time she had ridden with him —was that actually not so long ago but now seemed like an age? — she hadn't known about his disability. Now that she did know, she had cause for alarm — her third reason — because he could lose control of the station wagon, send it careening off the road, and scatter its passengers across the countryside. She supposed she had to trust him to know what he was doing. Still…

The one Great Unknown in her present circumstance was the person they would pick up to complete the search team: either Kensington or Paddington Smythe. Both were telepaths (or, in Dr. Razumov's terminology, "psycho-communicators"). They not only could send and receive thoughts to and from other people, whether or not they had similar abilities, but they could do so *without their permission.* Worse, they could plant thoughts in other people's minds and thus control them. If that wasn't scary, she didn't know what was. Oh, the Smythes seemed friendly enough to her and Stan and made them feel comfortable to be with; yet, what – if anything – were they doing to her and Stan's minds?

She was probably being paranoid, she told herself. George, Sheena, the Doctor, and even the ever cynical Freddie all trusted the Twins implicitly. And all of DEDEP counted on them to gather information or to alert them to danger by means not available to anyone else. Who was she that she doubted their good intentions? Still...

Joyce sighed heavily and decided she had better relax so that she could be up to the task ahead of her. It wouldn't do anybody any good if she screwed up and caused the new refugee to panic even more and run away. If that happened, no one would ever trust *her* again.

As it turned out, Kenny met them at the rear entrance to the bookstore, and he clambered in at once, exchanging pleasant greetings with all other passengers. Larkin began patrolling the streets of the business district of the City, criss-crossing east and west, north and south, in an effort to pinpoint the location of the "eel." The psycho-communicator immediately slumped in his seat, and his chin rested against his chest; to the casual observer, he seemed to have taken a nap. To those next to him, he was in "search" mode, using his extraordinary mental powers to locate a particular brain-wave pattern. The only clues that he gave out that suggested he was not asleep were the occasional "ah's" and "hmmm's" and "uh-uh's" he murmured whenever he detected an unfamiliar pattern. He rejected most of the signals and stored the rest in his memory for further investigation.

As the station wagon neared the intersection of Benton and Island Avenues, Kenny sat up straight and tapped Larkin on the arm.

"Got her, old darling! Start bearing east."

The detective nodded in compliance, made a left turn, and headed toward Broadway. When he came to the intersection of Benton and Broadway, the psycho-communicator had him turn south. As they neared the old abandoned depot, Kenny requested they stop the vehicle. Larkin pulled over to the curb.

"Her signal is very strong here," the PC declared. "Good God! She's a bloody nervous wreck. Hasn't eaten in days."

"I'm not surprised," the detective remarked. "She never expected to be cast adrift once she arrived in the City. Poor kid."

"Couldn't we stop somewhere and buy a sandwich or something for her?" Joyce offered.

"We will," Larkin answered, "but first we find her and get her off the street. That takes priority. I shouldn't have to tell *you* that, Joyce."

"Yes, you're right – as usual. I'm sorry I said anything."

"Don't be. You've just taken the first step in assimilating the DEDEP way of things. You're concerned for the welfare of a *psi*-talent."

Joyce was about to remark that she had already been concerned about the welfare of a *psi*-talent – specifically the one she had given birth to and raised by herself – when Larkin gestured toward the depot.

"There she is!"

"How can you be so sure?" Joyce asked.

"I was given a photo of her by my contacts in St. Louis. That woman, huddling against the building, matches exactly, except she looks a little haggard. OK, Joyce, time for you and Stan to do your part. Her name is Jean Fulton."

The Jankowskys eased out of the station wagon (and Joyce was glad for it) and began to walk down the street past the depot. As soon as they reached the point where the young woman was huddled, they halted and looked her over. The detective had been right – she did look haggard. She had dark circles under her eyes and sallow skin, and she reacted to the least sign of movement with panic in her eyes. Joyce knew exactly how she felt and moved closer to her. The woman gasped in fright and peered at mother and son with frightened eyes; she licked dry lips and pressed against the building.

"Excuse me," Joyce said as soothingly as she could (though she was just as nervous as the other woman), "are you Jean Fulton?"

The young woman looked around wildly for an avenue of escape and, finding none, clutched her stomach.

"Who – who are you?" she rasped. "And why do you want to know who I am?"

"I'm Joyce Jankowsky. And this is my son, Stan." The boy flashed his best smile. "We're from DEDEP, and we were sent to pick you up and take you to a safe place."

"DEDEP? I was supposed to meet someone named George Larkin, but he never showed up."

"George is with us. He's in that station wagon." She gestured down the street. "Please come with us."

"Are you a freak too?"

"I'm not, but my son is. Stan, show the lady what you can do."

The boy looked around for something handy, saw a loose brick on the sidewalk, and pointed at it. The brick quivered slightly as his mind seized it. He raised his arm, and the brick rose into the air. He made it do a few circles before lowering it to the ground.

"You're a…PK!" Ms. Fulton said, wide-eyed. "Who'da thunk it in someone so young?"

"Are you really an…'eel'?" Stan asked guilelessly.

"Stan!" his mother admonished. "Don't be impertinent."

"'S all right, Ms. Jankowsky. I'm used to being called that."

"Uh-huh. Call me 'Joyce.' We're all one big happy family at DEDEP."

"All right – Joyce. And I'm Jean."

The three of them walked back to the station wagon and climbed in. Larkin turned in his seat and gave the young woman his best smile.

"Hello, Jean. I'm George Larkin, and the fellow next to me is Kensington Smythe. You can call him Kenny." The Englishman waved his hand at her. "Sorry I missed you the other day."

"Oh, Lord! After what happened at the depot, I just wanted to hide somewhere. Do you know about that?" He nodded. "Well, I've been on the run ever since."

"Not to worry, Jean. Once we get to DEDEP, you'll be well taken care of."

Larkin began to pull away from the curb. At that moment, a gray van bearing the logo of a local retail shop sped through the intersection of Benton and Broadway even though the traffic signal had already turned red. Its driver was engaged in a heated conversation on his cell phone and unaware of what he was doing. He would have claimed five victims if not for Stan's seeing the danger and acting quickly. The boy pointed his finger at the speeding van and gave "Mr. Whosis" a silent command.

The reaction was instantaneous. One fraction of a second, the van was moving at thirty miles per hour; the next fraction of a second, it stood dead still in the middle of the street. Its driver continued to press down on the accelerator, and the engine continued to roar, but the van refused to move. The driver, now realizing that he had almost plowed into another vehicle, sheepishly turned the engine off, jumped out of the van, and examined it in order to discover the reason for its failure to move.

"My God!" Jean whispered. "Did your kid stop that van?"

"Yes, he did. It's nothing short of awesome what he can do with his power."

"That was a near thing," Larkin remarked. "Stan, you saved all of us."

"Thanks, Mr. Larkin. It was nothin' really."

"George, don't forget to stop somewhere and get Jean something to eat."

The detective nodded as he turned left onto Washington Street in order to double back toward downtown.

"I'm on it. What would you like, Jean?"

"I'm a vegetarian, if that's any help."

"I know just the place then."

CHAPTER SEVEN

MIND-TRAVELING

"OH, MAN!" JEAN Fulton exclaimed. "This is one helluva hideout!"

She had just stepped off the ladder and entered the left-hand "leg" of DEDEP's "H" lay-out. She peered wide-eyed at the hospital-white walls and the multi-colored stripes on the floor of the corridor like a child who has seen its first Christmas tree. Larkin smiled at her "innocence."

"This is your tax dollars at work," he remarked. "It's an abandoned government facility, left over from the Cold War. It's still in the annual budget."

"Those God-squadders will never find me down here, that's for sure."

"Uh-huh. Come with me. I'll introduce you to Dr. Razumov."

The group strolled down the corridor toward the "crossbar" of the "H." There was light traffic in this section; but, whenever they chanced to meet another resident, warm greetings were exchanged, and Larkin introduced him/her to the newcomer. Jean was relieved that no one showed any hostility toward her and that she might find kindred souls here, the lack of which she had experienced in St. Louis.

At the crossbar, the Jankowskys turned aside to enter the emergency stairwell and return to their apartment.

"Welcome to the monkey house, Jean," Joyce said wryly. "You'll be in good company."

"Yeah!" Stan piped up. "Yer gonna *love* it here!"

"I hope so. I hate being on the run. I guess I'll see you guys later."

"When you're settled in, drop by our apartment, and we'll have a long girl-talk."

"I'd like that." She glanced at Stan. "And I'd like to see some more of your tricks."

"You bet," the boy enthused. "An' I'll introduce you to my pals, Eve an' Billy, an' they can show you *their* tricks. An' wait'll you meet my other pal, Freddie. He's the coolest person down here!"

"Is Stan the youngest here?" Jean asked Larkin as soon as the Jankowskys departed.

"No, there are a couple who are younger, one of whom has a physical deformity. The other one is the child of a *psi*-talent but hasn't demonstrated any ability herself – yet. But, Stan is one of the strongest *psi*-talents DEDEP has, if you can believe it."

"I can believe it, after I saw what he did in the City. So, what will you do with me?"

"After I introduce you to the Director, he'll want to interview you and get some background information. Then, you'll be assigned to an apartment of your own. We've got some donated clothes in storage; maybe you'll find something else to wear besides what you've brought with you. Finally, you'll be given a work assignment suitable to your skills. Everyone here eighteen or older earns his/her keep by contributing labor. After you're settled in, the fun begins."

"Fun? You're kidding, right?"

"Nope. Dr. Razumov will run some tests on you."

"Tests?" she asked apprehensively. "What kind of tests?"

"An EEG, for starters. Emil records everyone's brain-wave patterns for future reference. That way, he'll have a good idea of how to develop your ability. Once, the EEG has been completed, he'll ask you to demonstrate what you can do."

Jean wrapped her arms about her to suppress a sudden shiver and bit her lip.

"I don't want to 'develop' this thing I've got in me. What I can do is hurt people. What can the Director do to prevent that?"

"I'll let him explain that. It's all Greek to me."

The remainder of the trip to Dr. Razumov's office was made in complete silence, as Jean studied the environment of her new "home." She gawked like a schoolgirl at each new sight, craning her neck this way and that. Larkin smiled to himself. Hers was the typical reaction all newcomers to DEDEP exhibited upon entering this subterranean world. And, when the novelty of it all wore off and its reality sank in, would her attitude change as it had for all the others before her and she resigned herself to living in a hole in the ground? Only time would tell. Still, when all was said and done, she would be safer here than where she used to be.

She next encountered DEDEP's "Mr. Fixit," who was busily testing electrical sockets in the main corridor – a never-ending task, if you asked him (and even if you didn't) – who paid the least attention to anyone else. The sight of the dwarf shocked Jean greatly; Freddie was the last person she expected to see in a place like this, but she imagined there was a reason for it. There was a good reason why *she* was here, and she was not about to begrudge anyone else's being here. Later on, she'd get the full story.

Presently, they arrived at the Director's office. Larkin rapped, opened the door, and walked in. Jean and Kenny followed, the former more nervous than ever.

The detective hardly expected to see what he did see upon entering. What he had expected in the past was Emil Razumov sitting quietly at his desk, poring over the results of his latest tests; what he had expected to see in the current circumstance was Emil Razumov sitting quietly at his desk staring off into space and thinking dark thoughts. What he did see now was Emil Razumov lying flat on his back in the center of the office; he was quite still, and his eyes were closed. Larkin's immediate reaction was that the old man had suffered a heart attack, and he moved quickly toward the body. Jean stayed near the door, frightened by the possible sight of a dead man.

"He's still alive, old darling," Kenny re-assured him. "His brain activity is normal." He closed his eyes briefly, then: "I sense – Good God! He's thinking of the gestalt, trying to communicate with it."

"Huh! He's wasting his time then. Only Eve and Stan can communicate with it, and it isn't responding to them anymore." He shook the Director gently. "Emil? Emil, are you awake?"

The doctor's eyes snapped open, and he stared at the detective for five seconds before recognition set in. He smiled wanly.

"*Zdrafst*, George. *Kak zheevyosh?*"

"*Khorosho, spaceebo. Ee tee?*"

"Do you know that lying like this is good for the back? It helps to straighten out the spine."

"No, I didn't. How long have you been doing this?"

"Not long. Since I have had nothing else to do, I thought about concentrating on my physical health."

"Uh-huh. You gave us a fright, you know."

"*Pozhalsto.* Why are you here?"

"I've brought you something to do – our 'eel' from St. Louis."

The Director craned his neck and gazed at the young woman still in a fright at the door. He smiled largely now. Jean visibly relaxed at the knowledge that she hadn't seen a dead man after all. The Doctor rolled over onto his stomach and got to his feet. He approached DEDEP's newest "acquisition" and held out his hand. Jean took it warily.

"Welcome, Miss Fulton. I am Emil Razumov, the chief looney in this looney bin. You had caused us some worry, and we did not think we could find you before the…other party did."

"I caused myself some worry, Doctor, by keeping out of sight every time I thought I saw one of those…creatures. Who – *what* are they?"

"Everything will be explained in good time, Miss Fulton. But first, I want to have a chat with you."

"If you don't need us anymore, Emil, we'll be going. I want to 'recruit' Monk for some 'salvage' work."

"*Khorosho*," the Russian said distantly as he waved Jean to a chair, his mind now elsewhere. "*Do sveedanye.*"

Outside, Kenny touched Larkin's arm and nodded in the direction of the office.

"The old darling seems to be himself again."

"That's because he's got a new 'toy' to play with. It's not as bright and shiny as the one he lost, but it'll keep him occupied for a while."

"Quite so, quite so. What's this 'salvage' business all about?"

"I'm going to loot Mr. Jones' apartment. His equipment may help me plan a strategy to counter the Swarm."

"D'ya think it's still there? Those blighters are not likely to leave their goodies lying about."

"Perhaps. They've been concentrating so far looking for the one who iced their comrade at the depot. I'd say we have an even chance. Care to join Monk and me?"

"*No, thank you very much!* I still have the willies from my last 'visit' there."

Larkin and Kenny parted company then. The former continued on toward the emergency exit, while the latter descended the stairway to the residential levels. The psycho-communicator intended to confer with the Perkinses concerning their mutual "spy mission" into the affairs of the Swarm.

Interestingly enough, though the Smythes had been part of DEDEP for several years, neither of them had ever been in the lower levels. Quite simply, they had had no reason to go there; their contacts with the residents had always taken place in the dining room-*cum*-meeting hall. Kenny had no fear of getting lost, however. In the first place, all of the doors were affixed with numbers and name plates; and, in the second place, the Twins had long ago familiarized themselves with the mental "signatures" of each and every one of the DEDEP'ers, up to and including the Directors of Research and Operation. Neither brother needed a number or a name plate to guide him; his mind could pinpoint the desired "signature" instantly.

Kenny halted before the door to the Perkins residence (one of the larger units for use by a group of four or more) and knocked in the "shave-and-a-haircut" pattern. It was one of his many idiosyncrasies – acquired from long years of watching old comedy films – although he never expected anyone to respond with the final "two bits" of the pattern. He waited patiently for someone to open the door.

That "someone" was the freckle-faced Billy Perkins, who was a budding psycho-occulist, a.k.a. a clairvoyant, having inherited the gene from his mother, and an accomplished illusionist (inheritance unknown as yet). When the teenager saw who it was, his eyes went wide with surprise.

The Twins had always filled the rest of DEDEP with a great deal of awe and trepidation, not so much by their unusual physical appearance (although that was striking enough) but by their tremendous mental abilities and their speech patterns. Anyone who could walk around in other people's minds and plant thoughts and images in them evoked strong emotions in the rest of humankind whether or not they possessed psychic powers themselves. Emil Razumov had assured his charges that the Smythes were benign, and they in turn had been careful not to do or say anything which might be perceived as a contradiction. Still, their appearance anywhere together always provoked the typical reaction.

"Good morrow to you, lad," the Englishman greeted Billy cheerfully. "May I please speak with your mother?"

"Yes, sir. Mom! Mr. Smythe is here to see you. I don't know which one though."

"I'm Kenny," the psycho-communicator provided. "May I call you 'Billy'?"

"Sure – Kenny."

"Invite him in," a feminine voice issued from the kitchen. "I'll be out in a moment."

The teenager stepped aside, and Kenny sauntered in and spied the other members of the family playing a game of chess. He noted the close resemblance of all of the male members. William Perkins, Sr., was an older version of his teenaged son, while the eleven-year-old Wilson was a younger version. Upon his entrance, the senior Perkins rose, stepped over to Kenny, and offered his hand.

"This is an unexpected surprise," he said in a friendly manner.

Kenny took the hand and shook it vigorously.

"I'm here to co-ordinate my efforts with Lacey's in snooping out the Swarm. Thank you for inviting me in."

"Well, George has made the case for team spirit. And considering the opposition, we all have to pitch in, don't we? Have a seat."

Kenny took a seat on the stuffed chair matching the sofa Bill Perkins had been occupying. Wilson, sitting on the floor on the other side of a coffee table, eyed him curiously as this was his first close-up encounter with the psycho-communicator. The latter studied the chess board.

"Who's winning?" he inquired.

"*I* am," Wilson piped up with a big grin on his face.

"The kid's a whiz when it comes to games of strategy," the boy's father remarked with a certain amount of pride. "When we first started playing, I usually won. Then the matches ended in draws. Eventually, Wilson got the upper hand, and I haven't won since. He's also a mathematical genius which is no surprise. He's been studying advanced calculus lately."

"Hmmm. Emil might have had some interesting things to say about that."

"Yes, he has. Ah, here's Lacey now."

The short, dark-haired woman bounded into the living room, wearing jeans, sweatshirt, and slippers and smiled broadly. Kenny stood, and Lacey took both of his hands in hers.

"Kenny, how good of you to visit. You should do so more often – you and Paddy both. You've met the rest of the family, I see."

"Indeed I have. And a sterling lot they are."

"I like to think so. What brings you to our humble abode?"

"I'm checking to see what progress you've made in spying out the Swarm."

The woman frowned and looked off into the distance.

"Not much, I'm afraid. All I've been getting so far are hazy images. I think it's because I've never been inside that building before."

Kenny rubbed his jaw and also looked off into the distance. He would have to phrase his next words carefully so as not to alarm either his cohort or her family.

"Um, I could help you in that respect, if I might. I have seen the inside of that building, you know. What I'm about to suggest will require a leap of faith on your part."

"What do you mean?"

"You would have to let me enter your mind and guide you, as it were, into the building. Once you had familiarized yourself with the layout, you could peep the place on your own."

Lacey searched Kenny's face in earnest as worry lines formed on hers. It was not quite the standard reaction most people exhibited when they learned the true extent of the Twins' capabilities; Lacey Perkins seemed to have a more open mind than most on that subject. For that, Kenny was thankful; it would make his task easier.

"You're right," she said at last. "It would take a leap of faith." She turned to her husband. "Will, what do you think?"

The elder Perkins came over to her, embraced her, and looked deeply into her eyes. Worry lines also etched his face. Then he regarded the psycho-communicator with concern.

"What you're asking could be dangerous, Kenny."

"I know. And I do not ask lightly. Lacey – and you, sir – must trust me implicitly. I shan't hold it against you if you refuse. But it's the only way to get her past her mental block."

"It's your call, sweetheart," Will declared. "I'll – I'll back you whatever you decide."

Lacey took a deep breath and let it out slowly. She kissed her husband lightly on the cheek and faced Kenny again.

"How do we proceed?"

"Sit down wherever you feel comfortable and relax your entire body. Then clear your mind of any extraneous thoughts. I'll do the rest. It may tingle a bit as I enter your mind, but the feeling will pass."

The psycho-occulist sat on the sofa and leaned her head back. She took several deep breaths and willed her body to relax. Her husband and sons regarded her with concern and eyed Kenny from time to time. When her breathing became shallow and rhythmic and her eyes unfocused, the Englishman sat down beside her, leaned back, and relaxed himself.

Abruptly, Lacey's body stiffened, and her eyes went wide with surprise, anxiety, and not a little fear. Kenny took her hand and squeezed it gently in order to re-assure her. She relaxed and closed her eyes again, and her facial expression reflected the wonder of what was a totally different and unique experience for her.

* * *

The woman had been torn between the desire to scream in mortal terror and a child-like fascination to take in as much of her surroundings as she could. With the growing realization that she is in no danger, the latter attitude grips her like no other experience she has ever known.

Having had no previous knowledge of what the human mind looks like and only a rudimentary understanding of what it is capable of, she could not conceive of the actual reality – hence the initial fright. The fright dissipates, leaving only awe.

What she sees is a jumble of rapidly shifting images. Some of those images are derived from the mind's memory banks; others are derived from the realm of imagination and conjecture. The human mind creates and/or analyzes all of them and stores them away for future reference. She recognizes some of them, based upon what she has learned about the mind's possessor from both himself and his acquaintances. Some of them amuse her; some of them disturb her. The human mind is also a jumble of light and dark social impulses, and only the courageous can sort them out.

Her present reference point is equally inconceivable. She does not exist per se; she is but a set of electrical impulses amidst a myriad of other impulses surrounding her. That fact intrigues her as much as anything else she is experiencing.

*Lacey?

*Kenny? Is that you?

*Yes. Look to your right.

She complies, and she is filled with fresh wonder. Kenny has foreseen her initial reaction to being in a strange place and formed an image of himself – not a true image, however, because each mind perceives another human being subjectively and because few humans can view themselves objectively — so that she has something familiar with which to anchor herself.

*Welcome to my world, love.

*This is so amazing. I had no idea of how…awesome *the human mind is, even after listening to Dr. Razumov lecturing about it. I doubt that even he knows what it's like.*

Oh, but he does. Paddy and I have explored the mind — ours and those of countless others — over the years, and we have allowed Emil to glimpse a part — a very small *part — of what we have discovered.*

*I don't suppose you'll let me in on all of your secrets.

*Only at a pace you can deal with.

*So, what's our next step?

*I will now guide you toward the visual center of my mind. There, you'll be able to 'see' what I 'see.'

*Sounds like fun.

*You Yanks have a curious idea of 'fun.' But, you might enjoy the experience anyway. Come along.

The image of Kenny beckons to her, and she moves toward it. Since she exists only as a set of electrical impulses, her movement does not emulate the walking of the human body; rather, she has the sensation of gliding toward Kenny's image. She does not know how she can do that; it seems that all she has to do is to wish it to happen, and it happens. In the space of a single nanosecond, she is at his "side."

"Kenny" now moves off toward the desired portion of his mind, and "Lacey" follows. All the while, she continues to sightsee, and the increasing familiarity soothes her and fills her with joy. Kenny has such a beautiful mind!

Five nanoseconds later, the pair arrive at Kenny's visual center. Lacey is awe-struck once more. She hadn't had the least idea of what the visual center of the human brain looks like, let alone what the mind's corresponding area does, and the sight before her is nothing short of astounding. It looks like an ordinary window in someone's house — a rectangular frame with a horizontal and a vertical crossbar dividing four panes of glass. She then realizes that the "window" is nothing more than Kenny's construct of a window for her benefit.

*Very clever, Kenny.

*I thought so. You need something familiar with which to assimilate yourself while you're here. Now, look out the 'window.'

She does so. Again, she is at a loss for words. She "sees" her apartment's living room. The scene shifts as the real Kenny turns his head, and now she "sees" Will, Billy, and Wilson in front of her, all of whom are staring at her with great concern. Her real self smiles to re-assure them that all is well and that she is no danger, and her inner self "sees" her family relax visibly and offer tight little smiles by way of acknowledging her "message."

*Awesome!

*Isn't it though? Now, love, comes the interesting part. I'm going to move my mind to the abandoned factory on Ridgeway Avenue. Since I've been there before, it will be an easy transfer. What you'll experience is a sensation of being in one place one nanosecond and in another place in another nanosecond.

*Say, it just occurs to me that I'm in your mind. You said you'd be entering my mind. What gives?

*I did enter your mind. And, as soon as I made contact, I joined our consciousnesses together. You're as much in my mind as I am in yours.

*You can do that?

*It's really quite simple – if you know how.

*Awesome!

*Are you ready to transfer?

*As ready as I'll ever be. Lead on, McDuff!

The scene shifts once more, and her level of incredulity rises several notches. What she "sees" now is similar to looking into the night sky. All is blackness, save for the myriad of points of light; some of the lights are bright and pulse rapidly while the rest are dim and slow.

This then is not outer space as humankind knows it, i.e. the cosmic void which is the Universe, but inner space which is viewed by the mind's eye. This metaphysical "universe" parallels the physical one, co-exists with it, and acts as a counterpart and counterpoint. It is as real, and as non-real, as the other. It has its own laws, and the breaking of those laws is just as impossible. It holds as many wonders and possibilities as the other for those who are able, and dare, to explore it.

Kenny and Paddy have had this ability and this daring for as long as they can remember. At first, they had been unaware of what they were "seeing"; but, once aware, they explored as time allowed. Experienced as he is, Kenny travels through the Void unerringly toward his target and gives little thought to his surroundings.

For Lacey, however, it is all new, and she "sees" with a mixture of awe and trepidation.

*What are those lights, Kenny? They're not...stars, are they?

*No, love. What you're seeing are other minds as we pass over the physical space which those minds' owners are occupying. Emil has stated that the human brain generates radio waves and that each brain generates at a specific frequency. Radio waves are invisible in the physical realm but not in the metaphysical. You'll notice that the lights vary in brightness. That's due to the signal strength of each brain.

*Awesome!

*Look closely up ahead. See the cluster of a dozen or more lights? That's our target.

Quickly, they move toward the cluster. Abruptly, the scene shifts again as Kenny zeroes in on the Swarm. Now Lacey "sees" the front of the abandoned factory as clearly as if she had been standing before it in the flesh. She also "sees" the surroundings of the building as Kenny allows her to familiarize herself with the area. They then approach the window at the side of the building through which Kenny had seen the sinister activity inside. Inside, the Swarm are lined up near an object which resembles nothing less than a miniature gasoline pump; one by one, the aliens press a nozzle-like attachment to their faces and breathe deeply for the space of a minute. When all have had their turn at the machine, they return to their labors.

*So, that's what the Swarm look like. Br-r-r! Nasty looking creeps!

*You can say that again, love. We could go inside and have a closer look, but this is as close to those blighters as I care to get. I speak from personal experience. Now, observe what they are doing.

Lacey focuses on the interior of the building and examines the large object upon which the Swarm are performing their labors. This, the principal warship of the aliens is as alien-looking as they are, and it could not be mistaken for a craft of human design by any stretch of the imagination.

She "shudders" as she remembers the earlier report by Eve Pelletier and the destruction this weapon can wreak. That it is here on Earth means that the Swarm fully intend to deploy it in the near future. She "shudders" again.

*Have you seen enough?

*More than enough! I'm ready to leave.

*Do you think you can find your way here on your own?

*I think so.

*Excellent. I'll take you home now – so to speak.

* * *

Lacey's eyes snapped open wide as soon as Kenny withdrew from her mind. She regarded him with a renewed sense of wonder.

"That was *fantastic!*" she said breathlessly.

"I'm pleased that you enjoyed your little 'trip.' Perhaps we can do it again sometime. There's a wide 'universe' out there – or I should say, *in* there."

"I'll keep it in mind. Thank you, Kenny."

"Honey," her concerned husband asked solicitously, "are you all right?"

"I couldn't be better, Will. Wait'll I tell you about my experience. You won't believe what I've 'seen.'"

Bill Perkins and his sons gathered about her to listen eagerly to her tale. None of them noticed the psycho-communicator quietly leaving the apartment. When Kenny returned to the surface, he spotted Larkin and Monk, one of the *official* DEDEP operatives, engaged in conversation on the porch of the farmhouse. He joined them and regarded the latter curiously.

"Good morning, Monk. You seem to have a lot on your mind."

"Hiya, Kenny. Yeah, I do. George just told me what he wants to do and would I lend a hand."

"And do you? I sense some doubt on your part."

"We're dealin' with aliens, for God's sake – *bad* aliens. I dunno if I want to expose myself to 'em. I reckon I like to play it safe."

"Not even if it means getting your hands on some of their technology?" the detective goaded him. "That doesn't sound like you at all, Monk."

"Well, that's the other side of the coin, all right. It's a tough choice."

"Why don't you give it some more thought? Call me when you've come to a decision."

"Yeah, I'll do that. Later then."

The short, stocky man turned and went inside the house. Kenny looked at Larkin and raised an eyebrow. The latter grinned.

"He'll go for it. Monk lovers to tinker, and this is a once-in-a-lifetime opportunity."

* * *

The sun was descending toward the horizon when a rental truck turned onto View Street. The outside temperature was still in the high 90's, and it was anybody's guess if the day would see a new record high. The vehicle's air-conditioning unit strained to keep its occupants somewhat relieved from the heat, but it sputtered intermittently and threatened to quit altogether.

Those occupants ignored the heat as best they could and concentrated on scanning the neighborhood. Monk had reached the point where he was seeing aliens behind every tree, despite Larkin's assurances that the Swarm were busy elsewhere. The detective glanced at his companion frequently, ready to stop him from jumping out and running away if his paranoia got the better of him. When the building containing the apartment of the late, unlamented Mr. Jones came into view, Larkin relaxed somewhat and pulled over to the curb on the opposite side of the street.

He scanned the neighborhood again with his trained eye. No one was out and about but were sensible and stayed indoors to avoid instant sunburn and/or heatstroke. Only one other vehicle was present on the block, a white sedan a hundred feet in front of the rental truck. Larkin eyeballed it carefully as he thought he saw movement in it. He turned to Monk, who was also scanning while licking dry lips.

"You all right, Monk?"

"I guess so —considering."

"Let's go then."

He eased himself out of the truck in his usual awkward fashion and crossed the street. Monk hurried after him. They were about to go up the walkway to the building's entrance when a voice called out.

"Brother Larkin! Wait up!"

The detective twisted around at the sound of his name and instantly grimaced. Approaching him from the direction of the white sedan was Archdeacon Fogarty's right-hand man, "Brother" Kincaid. The Disciple appeared as grim as ever, and Larkin braced himself for an unpleasant conversation.

"Brother Kincaid," he murmured. "I didn't expect to see you here."

"I could say the same about you. What are you up to?"

The man was wasting no time with small talk. But Larkin never thought he ever would. He had to think fast.

"I'm here to examine the apartment of the hell-spawn who lived here. He may have left a clue as to his future plans."

"I...see. Well, His Worship wanted this place watched in case more of the Enemy showed up for whatever reason. I'll let him know you were here as well."

"Of course. I'll report any findings to him as soon as my confederate here learns anything useful. Hopefully, we can learn where the rest of the Enemy is hiding."

"Yes, that would make things easier for us. Well, I won't keep you from your labors, Brother Larkin. Good luck."

Kincaid pivoted and returned to the white sedan. In a matter of seconds, he disappeared down the street.

"Man," Monk said in amazement, "you sure laid it on thick, Georgie. Now I see how you got your reputation for thinkin' fast. That bozo bought your story, hook, line, and sinker."

"I certainly hope he did. He's the shifty sort, and you have to watch your step when he's around. Now that the coast is clear, we can go inside."

Once inside, Larkin shook his head in disgust. If at all possible, the interior seemed even dirtier, smellier, and more putrid than the last time he had been here. He was sure it was only his imagination, but it didn't take much imagination to understand that the building's management was woefully deficient, incompetent, and neglectful. Why it hadn't been fined and the building condemned was a great mystery.

The detective cautioned Monk not to touch anything with his bare hands for the sake of his health. The DOE man didn't need to be told that; he had given the place a once-over of his own and come to the same conclusion. For good measure, he stuck his hands in his pockets.

The pair went up to the top floor and stopped before Mr. Jones' former apartment. Larkin produced his set of lock picks, jimmied the lock, and pushed the door open. They were greeted by a waft of musty, odor-laden air, and both reacted accordingly. The detective scanned the living room and was pleased that everything – except the EM generator – was still in place. Monk took one look at the array and whistled sharply.

"Man, oh, man! What a setup! I'm glad you talked me into comin' here. I can't wait to examine these gizmos."

He walked over to the nearest module and touched it lightly as if he were afraid it would fall to pieces. The expression on his face resembled that of a child at his birthday party. Larkin chuckled. He had had the same feeling once himself.

"You'll get your chance soon enough, my friend, but first we have to load this stuff up and transport it to the farm. I reckon it'll take three trips to move it all."

"Uh-huh. That'd be my guess as well."

"By the way, that module you're standing next to is the Swarm's communications equipment. It connected Mr. Jones to the base in Nebraska. Apparently, he had to make daily reports to an individual he called 'Commander.' That module was the only piece I saw in operation, and I had a glimpse of the 'Commander.' He looked nastier than Mr. Jones, if you can believe that."

"What I can't believe is why those aliens left all this stuff lying about. Didn't they think we'd confiscate it?"

"It may be that they didn't think us 'primitives' would know how to operate it and that they'd be able to come for it anytime they wanted to. They'd be half-right; we don't know how to operate anything here. That's why I brought you in on this. So, take a look and find out the best way to move these gizmos out of here."

"Gotcha."

Monk fell to his task, beginning with a minute examination of the array. With each finding, he stated it aloud for Larkin's benefit. He discovered that the array consisted of three sets of four modules each, and each module measured half a meter wide, half a meter long, and a meter-and-a-half high. All were manufactured with some unknown material, although Monk said the material felt like plastic. Each module in a set seemed to be joined together, giving the appearance of one solid piece, but he couldn't figure out how. Each module was equipped with a pressure-sensitive keyboard (but no monitor), integrated into the module's surface. An examination of the rear of the modules showed no signs of a power cord nor a transmission link.

"Perhaps there's an internal power source, some sort of super-battery," came the detective's response. "Maybe the same for the link. After all, this *is* alien technology."

Monk nodded in agreement and resumed his investigation. Now, he ran his hands over all the surfaces of the modules in a search for an opening to the interior and found none that he could recognize. Finally, in exasperation, he grasped one of the end ones firmly and gave it a hard yank; to his great surprise, it came away from its neighbor with relative ease. He concluded that the joining was magnetic in nature which would make it easier to transport the array.

"One last thing to try, Georgie, but I'll need your help on this. I'm going to turn this thing upside down."

With Larkin assisting, Monk gently tipped the loose module over and laid it on its side. He then got down on his hands and knees and peered at the module's undercarriage. He shook his head in frustration.

"Completely self-contained?" the detective offered.

"No, I'm just missing something here." Suddenly, he snapped his fingers. "Got an idea. Let's get this thing right-side up again."

They set the module back on its base. Monk ran his fingers around the top edges; at two of the corners, he touched a stud which barely protruded. With an "Aha!" he pressed the studs firmly. A faint whirring sound issued from the module, and the entire top unhinged and revealed the interior. Triumphantly, the DOE man rushed over to the other modules and found similar studs on them; in the space of fifteen seconds, he had opened up all of them.

"Well, that solves that mystery." He scanned the interior of one of the modules and saw nothing but two black rectangular boxes, one twice as large as the other; the larger one possessed a five-centimeter-long rod attached to one of its sides. "Look here, Georgie. The big one's a CPU, and the small one's a power pack – or I'll eat my hat."

"Amazing!" the detective murmured. "The sooner we get this stuff loaded up and back to DEDEP, the sooner you get to play with it."

"You betcha. And the first thing I'm gonna do –"

He halted in mid-sentence when he saw that he and Larkin were no longer alone in the apartment. He inclined his head toward the door; the detective turned and, to his chagrin, came face-to-face with "Brother" Kincaid again, plus another Disciple.

"Brother Kincaid," he greeted the man with feigned affability, "did you forget something?"

"Not at all, Brother Larkin. I notified His Worship of your presence here, and he instructed me to lend you any assistance you might need. I've brought along some of the other brothers. We'll help you load those devices up and take them to a safe place where you can examine them at your ease."

"I could use the help, of course. I'll have to thank His Worship for his generosity."

"Uh-huh. I'll get the rest of the fellows."

Kincaid retreated downstairs, leaving his aide behind. Larkin suspected the latter had been instructed to keep an eye on things and make sure nothing happened to the array.

"Jesus, Georgie," Monk whispered, "what do we do now? We can't let those jokers get their hands on this stuff."

"Absolutely not. Let me think a minute."

Abruptly, Larkin lay down on the floor and closed his eyes, alarming both Monk and the Disciple considerably. He cleared his mind of all extraneous thought.

*Kenny? Paddy?

*We're here, old darling. And we sense...

*...a bit of urgency on your part. What's afoot?

* I'm at Mr. Jones' apartment, purloining his equipment. But a group of Disciples just showed up to 'lend' me a hand. I want you to get rid of them for me.

*Not to worry. We know just what to do...

*...to get those blighters to push off.

Larkin opened his eyes, rolled over, and pushed himself up to a standing position. He saw the fright in Monk's and the Disciple's eyes and smiled disarmingly.

"Sorry to scare you like that. I...felt a twinge along my spine and laid down to ease the pain. That's the downside of having artificial limbs."

The sound of many heavy footsteps on the stairs alerted him to the return of the promised "help." Kincaid and four muscle-heads trooped into the apartment, and the Archdeacon's right-hand man directed his people to take charge of a module apiece. The Disciples obeyed wordlessly; each one hefted a module onto his shoulder as Monk winced out of fear that those bruisers might drop one and damage it beyond all repair. One by one, the work party paraded out of the apartment and down the stairs.

Abruptly, another Disciple squeezed past the work party, panic written all over his face. He confronted his leader with wild eyes.

"Brother Kincaid," he gasped, "I just saw two of those creatures Brother Larkin warned us about. They're on the corner, watching this place."

"Are you sure?" Kincaid pressed his underling, piercing him with a steely glare.

"Yes, sir," the other stammered. "They match the photo that was passed around."

"This is not good, Brother Kincaid," the detective mused, taking his cue. Inwardly, he smiled at the Twins' inventiveness in inserting images into people's minds. "Those creatures have obviously come back for their evil devices. Now that they've seen us, they're sure to warn their cohorts – unless you and the brothers can stop them."

"What about those devices?"

"My companion and I can manage from here on out. I know of a safe place to take them. But, it's imperative that you stop those creatures before it's too late."

Kincaid stared at Larkin for a long moment, and the detective could just picture his mental gears whirling at high speed, trying to decide on the proper course of action. Then:

"Very well. Make sure you report all of this to the Archdeacon."

The Disciples exited and practically ran down the stairs. When it was safe to do so, Monk guffawed.

"Man, I *really* have to hand it to you, Georgie. Making those clowns think they're seein' aliens everywhere. What a hoot!"

"The Disciples are so paranoid that they'll believe anything. Do you see anything here besides the modules worth taking?"

Monk looked around and shook his head. The two of them then began the arduous task of removing the remaining modules. Outside, they discovered the first set of modules sitting on the front walk where the Disciples had deposited them in order to chase after "evil creatures." There was no sign of the Disciples anywhere; even the white sedan was gone. Larkin was pleased that his impromptu plan had worked so well. He could just picture Kincaid and his merry band searching the neighborhood block by block for non-existent aliens. Score another one for DEDEP!

But now was not the time for self-congratulations. He and Monk had to load up the rental truck and get out of this area before Kincaid returned to provide "assistance" again. The task took longer than he cared to stay here, thanks to his artificial limbs, but they finished the job without further disturbance. With the prize in hand, they returned to DEDEP.

AN ELECTRIFYING EXPERIENCE

JEAN FULTON AWOKE surprisingly refreshed. She couldn't remember the last time she had such a good night's sleep. While she was in St. Louis, she had been awake at night, wondering who she would hurt next with her electrical abilities. She looked upon what she could do – unconsciously – as a super-sized curse; no one wanted to be anywhere near her, just in case she got over-excited and zapped someone. Dating had been out of the question because of the emotions involved. She had already put one guy in the hospital, and afterwards, he never spoke to her again.

When the Disciples of Purity found out about her, they hounded her day and night and made her life miserable. Serendipitously, remnants of the old Psi Squad – a group once dedicated to investigating psychic phenomena but now having to lay low itself – also found her and gave her refuge in a "safe house." The house was dirty and cramped, however, and she was as miserable as before. She had even thought of suicide.

The Psi Squad then told her about DEDEP, located near Chicago, a place where safe refuge was guaranteed and her abilities studied and controlled. They made arrangements to transfer her there. Still, she had not been totally convinced of her alleged safety; she was being handed over to a group as strange as the Psi Squad. Who knew what would become of her? She supposed she couldn't be any worse off than she already was and, reluctantly, she took her leave of her birthplace and home town.

With the incident at the depot in the City, she was almost convinced that she had made a big mistake in agreeing to the transfer. Unfortunately, it had been a one-way trip; she was stuck here whether she wanted to be or not. Then came the running and hiding. What more could happen to her?

Therefore, imagine her pleasant surprise to be warmly welcomed by the "strangers" at DEDEP, starting with that yummy hunk, George Larkin, with the ice-blue eyes and easy smile. Being near him made her tingle all over, and she wished she could cuddle up with him. (*Out of the question, you little fool!*) The older woman, Joyce Jankowsky, with a PK son, struck her as being as confused by where she was and wanted to get together for some "girl talk." Finally, the Director of DEDEP, Dr. Emil Razumov, treated her like the grandfather she had known all too briefly; he had been very forthright in telling her what he expected from her, but he had done so in a very soothing manner and made her feel as if being here had been *her* idea. Perhaps things were going right for a change!

The first thing she did was to attend to her oblations – in a real bathroom! The second thing was taking a long, leisurely shower. When was the last time she had had one of those? The third thing was breakfast. She dried off, dressed quickly, and headed out the door.

Which way to the dining room? Just follow the crowd, huh?

She entered the dining room and instantly became self-conscious again. All those strangers looking at her – she almost lost heart and turned to leave, but her stomach had something to say about that. Stiffly, she walked up to the serving line and tried to ignore the attention she was attracting. A couple of the younger men gave her very friendly smiles. She grimaced, partly out resignation, partly out of frustration.

Sorry, guys, but I'm untouchable.

Once in the line, she spotted a familiar face – the only familiar face – the woman with the PK son, dishing out the hash-browns. Joyce spotted her at nearly the same time and waved.

"Good morning, Jean. Did you sleep well?"

"Man, did I ever! And on a real bed! This place beats the rathole I was in in St. Louis."

"It does have its good points – and its bad points."

"No doubt. I'll find out soon enough, I guess."

"Have you been given a work assignment yet?"

"Yeah. When Dr. Razumov found out I used to work with my dad in his repair shop, he said I should report to – Freddie? – and he'd keep me busy."

"Yes, he will. He'll be glad to have an assistant."

"So, how do I find him?"

"He'll be easy to spot. When you hear a lot grumbling and griping, that'll be him." Joyce paused briefly, debating her next words. Then: "Also, he's a dwarf."

"Yeah? Hey! He must've been the little guy I saw when I first arrived. He was checking electrical sockets. Man, this place is full of surprises!"

"You can say that again." Joyce looked past her, taking note of the next person to enter the dining room. "And speak of the Devil, there he is."

Freddie Hamilton walked in as if he owned the place. Despite his short stature, he acted like a "tall person" and was the least self-conscious about it. He waved to everybody he saw, and they waved back. Occasionally, he would stop at a table and say a few words to the occupants and elicit a laugh or two. Despite his grumbling and griping, he was well-liked – and respected – because of what he was able to do to keep DEDEP functioning. No one paid any heed to his gruff mannerisms; he was just blowing off steam like a regular joe.

He ambled over to the serving line, working the stump of a cigar in his mouth, and gave Joyce a big grin. He then regarded Jean expectantly.

"Freddie," Joyce introduced him, "this is Jean Fulton from St. Louis, our newest resident. Jean, our 'Mr. Fixit,' Freddie Hamilton."

"Pleased to meet you, Mr. Hamilton," Jean responded, slightly nervous.

"Likewise. And 'Mr. Hamilton' is my old man. I'm Freddie."

"OK – Freddie. I'm Jean."

"I heard there was a new inmate. What're you in for, Jeanie?"

"I'm, uh, an 'eel.'"

"A *what?*"

"An 'E-E-L.' An 'electrically energized life-form.' That's what Dr. Razumov says. I generate static electricity."

"No shit? Remind me to keep my distance from you from now on."

"That won't be possible. I'm your new assistant. I do repair work."

"No shit? Well, hot damn! It's about time I got some help around here. Let's get some breakfast. Then I'll show ya the ropes."

* * *

Jean watched the Doctor with a mixture of bemusement and trepidation as he puttered about gathering the equipment and tools he needed to test her. She hadn't seen this much scientific gadgetry since she had visited her grandfather in the hospital a few days before he passed away. That day, she had been filled with only trepidation; the old man had looked so frail and shriveled up, even while he tried to put up a brave front for her benefit. She had felt deep inside that he hadn't much longer to live; but, for *his* benefit, she put up a brave front as well. She suspected that he knew that he was close to death.

She shook off that awful memory with some effort and tried to think of something more light-hearted. With all that had had happened to her in the past few years – ever since she realized what she was and what she could do to people – her life had assumed a surreal thing as she bounced from one insane event to another, and there hadn't been very many light-hearted moments to speak of. The people in the Psi Squad had been kind enough to her – had even sympathized with her – but they had their own problems, trying to avoid detection by the Disciples of Purity and suffering the same fate as so many others had done. None of the Squad had *psi*-talent (at least, that's what they told her), but the

Disciples didn't care; anybody who sheltered or comforted an "impure" person was just as guilty, and they were "disappeared" as well.

She was not likely to see St. Louis ever again, and perhaps that was just as well. DEDEP seemed like a safe place to be; the people were more organized since they were out of sight, and they were better equipped to hide her kind from the evil that was the Return-to-Purity Party and their supporters at all levels of government. And the DEDEP'ers were friendly – perhaps because they *were* safe. She didn't think any of them would choose to live in a hole in the ground; but given the alternative, they endured.

Well, she would endure too. She'd find out soon enough why she was what she was, and the Director promised – he actually *promised* – that he would help her to control her "eel-ness." Meanwhile, she could be useful in her own right. As the little guy, Freddie Hamilton, had explained to her, there were a million things which needed fixing at DEDEP, and he couldn't fix them all by himself. And, when she told him about her repair skills, his eyes had lit up like twin headlights, and he had rubbed his stubby hands together as he rattled off all the problems which needed immediate attention, followed by another list of things he hoped to accomplish in the long run.

Freddie reminded her of her uncle, a long-time Navy man, right down to the ever-present cigar. And the dwarf was not above telling dirty stories too!

This brief reverie was interrupted by a soft *ahem* from Dr. Razumov. He smiled as she gave him her full attention.

"Now the tests?" she said resignedly.

"*Da, ryebyenka*," the old man answered. "Time to pay the dues, as you Americans say. First, I shall take a general reading of your brain-wave activity; that will establish a foundational profile from which to work. Next, I will establish exactly how strong your *psi*-talent is by taking readings of specific areas of your brain. They will also tell me where your ability is localized (if at all) and if other talents exist."

"Other talents? You mean I might be able to do things like the others here can do?"

"*Mozhno* [possibly]. Quite often, multiple talents appear if a brain is especially powerful. One talent will predominate, however. But, let us begin."

He brought the mobile EEG closer to her and began applying the sensor pads to various parts of her skull. All the while, he hummed an unknown tune. When he had completed the hook-up, he stepped back and regarded he attachments; satisfied that all was in place, he switched the machine on. A digital image appeared on the oscilloscope, an image which squiggled as Jean's brain waves were sensed and recorded. She watched the image with fascination as the squiggles became more and more complex. At various points, Dr. Razumov *hmmm*ed in reaction to a particular squiggle; and, when the readings crossed the border between the beta and the gamma regions, he nodded his head appreciatively.

"*Ochen intyeryestvo*," he commented and regarded Jean pensively. "You have *psi*-talent, to be sure, but I will not know in what form it takes until you demonstrate it for me."

"You mean, you want me to *deliberately* generate static electricity? I don't know if I can. I try to avoid doing it if possible."

"You must try, *ryebyenka*, for the sake of your own peace of mind if not for the sake of an old man's curiosity. You must become excited so that the EEG can give an accurate picture of what goes on inside your pretty little head."

Jean smiled in spite of herself at the off-handed comment. No one had ever complimented her like that before; but it sounded nice, even if it weren't true. Well, if the Doctor wanted excitement, that was what he was going to get, and she knew just how to do it. Since she discovered she couldn't have an actual physical relationship with a man without causing him harm, she had compensated by creating sexual fantasies, masturbating, and then discharging harmlessly. Obviously, she couldn't masturbate here in front of this old man, but she could dream up a juicy fantasy for him. She leaned back, relaxed as well as she could with wires attached to her head, and concentrated.

She formed an image of George Larkin smiling and approaching her. "She" wrapped her "arms" around his "shoulders" and pressed close to "him." "He" bent down and pressed his "lips" to "hers" and gave "her" a long, languid "kiss." "She" responded eagerly. "He" moved his "lips" down her "chin" and "throat." Now, "he" began to unbutton her "blouse" and moved his "lips" down to her "cleavage." "She" pressed harder against "him," panting in anticipation. The real Jean began to pant as well as a wave of sexual pleasure washed over her.

For his part, the Doctor had seen several women on the verge of orgasm, and only once in a non-professional setting (and that had produced bitter-sweet memories). Each time, it had caused him embarrassment. When he saw what was happening to his test subject, he turned away to focus on the EEG's oscilloscope. What he saw there was equally disturbing.

The electronic "pens" were going wild, racing across the monitor from edge to edge. They were recording well into the gamma range. What concerned the Russian more than his verifying scientifically that this woman had great *psi*-talent was the effect that potential was having on his equipment. Quickly, he turned it off before Jean's build-up of static electricity could burn it out. Then he moved across the lab in case she did generate a charge and envelope him in it.

Jean saw his reaction, realized why he was reacting as he did, and "erased" the exotic image she had created by thinking of something more mundane, a procedure she had worked out long ago in just such situations. Gradually, she "cooled down" and relaxed again. The fantasy had been most satisfying, and she made a mental note to add it to her "repertory." She grinned at the Director.

"Was that exciting enough, Doctor?"

"*Da, spaceebo,*" he muttered. "Um, well, that proves you have *psi*-talent, but it exhibited itself in a most unusual form."

"How so?"

"Your brain converts radio energy into electrical energy and emits it via the electromagnetic aura about your body. Fortunately, the emissions are not as random and uncontrolled as you might believe. You have just demonstrated that you can create an event and uncreate it when you apply yourself. What we will do in future sessions is to explore methods of instantaneous control."

"But, I'll still have this thing inside me?"

"*Pravda. Psi* will never go away. It is as much a part of you as your heart or your hands. What you must do, then, is to make it work *for* you, not against you."

"That'll be a switch. When do we start?"

"First, I must ponder on the correct procedure for a short while. Meanwhile, go about your normal routine." He grimaced. "And try to limit your fantasies, if you please!"

* * *

From the diary of Christopher Wredling:

Things have gotten hectic around here since the demise of Mr. Jones. George has 'recruited' some of us to perform some spy work for him. For instance, Lacey Perkins was assigned to monitor the Swarm's new base in the City. (Talk about being too close for comfort!) Kenny and Paddy continue to monitor all of the major players and alerting him to possible danger. I have gotten my own assignment (more on that later).

I need to mention something about the gestalt first. I had been told that it disappeared without warning and that Eve, Stan, and Freddie could not get it to re-appear. I confirmed this by sensing a cessation of heat energy when the thing disappeared.

I have not told anybody – yet – that the gestalt has not disappeared as we humans understand the concept. It is still lurking about and is just not showing itself for some unfathomable reason. How do I know this? It's hard to explain to the mobiles who exist in their three-dimensional, physical world. I exist between this three-dimensional, physical world and a dimension of multi-colored energy fields. On a recent projection (made to 'stretch' my mind a little), I sensed it nearby. It was generating on the same frequency I had detected at the demise of Mr. Jones.

I instantly put myself on guard (a process too complicated to explain here) just in case. I don't know if the gestalt sensed me – how could it not? – but it didn't approach me. It simply remained in place, waiting for – what? (This is purely a subjective feeling on my part.) I quickly returned to the familiar world of the mobiles and have been pondering my discovery ever since.

Do I tell Emil and George? And when? And what good would it do them if I did tell them?

One thing is certain (and, again, this is a subjective feeling): the gestalt is alive! *It has self-awareness, and it acts as an independent agent. What its purpose is in appearing in our dimension is anybody's guess, but I would hazard to guess that it does not have the welfare of DEDEP – or of humankind for that matter – uppermost in its mind – correction: not 'mind' as we know it, but 'consciousness.' Or can it? In any event, the gestalt is an unknown quantity and bears watching whenever we chance to see it.*

Now, my assignment.

Ha! Leave it to George to make life interesting for me. He is ever the 'master strategist.' I have been given the task of scouting out the Swarm base in Nebraska. My psi-*talent makes me the logical choice for the job, of course, and George said as much. And so he sent me packing (so to speak). I have been in Nebraska and back twice already; and, when I am rested, I will set out again. Our fearless leader must have his updated intelligence, don't you know?*

Getting to Nebraska is not an easy task – even for me. The first time I projected there, I was like a child just testing out my powers. The mid-western United States has become more and more developed over the years – a greater population density, more energy fields to dodge – and I spent most of that journey in navigation. It was like running an obstacle course, and I had to be on the alert every second of the way. The SAC base outside of Omaha was particularly problematic; it possesses an energy field the size of a city. Once there, however, I followed the directions George had gleaned from his oddball 'informant,' the 'Quintessential Quark.' I located the state highway and the rural road and cruised the latter and soon encountered a sizeable energy field where none should have been. I approached cautiously, and bingo! there was the Swarm base.

On the second trip out, I had to be extra cautious. The Swarm have electronic devices which can detect my own energy signal and be used to disrupt it. (I still get the willies when I remember being zapped by it.) I had to find a vantage point close enough to observe the goings on but not so close as to trip any alarms. Of course, I could have kept moving around in order to confuse them as I had done with Mr. Jones.

I halted at a point about two meters from the base and scanned the area. I wish now that I hadn't.

The base occupied the better part of a small clearing in a wooded area, far off the beaten path and away from (most) prying eyes. There were three rectangular structures, two large ones and a smaller one sandwiched between them. All of the structures were a dull gray, windowless, and constructed of a plastic-like substance. I had to assume the large ones were barracks of some sort. What the smaller one was, I had no idea. I didn't dare get close enough to examine it minutely.

Apart from this grouping stood one of the Swarm's warships which Eve had described in her psychometric vision. Those creatures were ready to strike the first blow when they were ordered to.

As to the creatures' whereabouts, I soon discovered them on the opposite side of the clearing from me. Stealthily, I edged around to get a better look. There must have been at least thirty of them, and they were engaged in target practice, except the targets were not paper bull's eyes. They were human beings!

The Swarm had somehow captured a Fellowship of Disciples and were forcing them to run back and forth from one point to another while trying to dodge the bolts of energy fired from the Swarm's weapons. Some of the Disciples were already lying on the ground, quite lifeless; others were gravely wounded and moving slowly until a fatal blast felled them; still others were kneeling and praying loudly for deliverance from evil. The Swarm laughed raucously at these latter humans and deliberately missed them in order to provoke yet more fear in them.

The Disciples are a despicable lot, and one would wish them all a good riddance. But, it seems they have met their match in these alien invaders when it comes to malevolent behavior. One could almost pity them. Almost.

One of the Swarm stood apart from his comrades. In addition to the scars gained in combat, this individual also wore an eyepatch over his right eye socket. From the array of decorations on his uniform, he was obviously the ranking officer of the Swarm in the United States. He was monitoring the display of barbarity with calm detachment. An SS officer in Nazi Germany would have had nothing on him for sheer sadism.

After five minutes of this, I decided I'd had enough for one day, and I slowly made my way back to DEDEP.

I imagine that George expects regular reports from me for the duration. I am loathe to return to that site of unimaginable cruelty, but we need the intelligence if we are ever to defeat the Swarm — if we can defeat them. But, before I return, I'm going to have to fortify myself psychologically. Otherwise, I'm not liable to be of any use to George or to DEDEP. Like it or not, I have to keep up my end.

Sherman was right: war is *hell!*

* * *

Larkin stood in front of the old re-converted firehouse for a moment or two before entering. Even though he had been here three times before – three times too many, in his humble opinion -- he needed to steel himself for the interrogation he knew awaited him. The first time he was here, he had had fewer qualms; his purpose had been to spin a web of plausible lies in order to entice the Disciples of Purity into doing his dirty work for him. Subsequent visits had been infinitely more difficult, as he had had to remember the lies he told previously and make sure his new lies did not contradict them. Archdeacon E.A. Fogarty may have been a religious fanatic, but he was also a cagey one; he would smell a rat in his midst by the least little misstep on the part of his new "ally" and make life miserable for him. And all of Larkin's best laid plans would have instantly gone awry, resulting in his becoming the latest casualty in this war of the worlds.

What made this particular visit so problematic was the fact that he had transferred the Swarm technology to the basement of the farmhouse above DEDEP rather than turning it over to the Archdeacon. Now he had to explain to "His Worship" why he did it and make the explanation as plausible as anything else he had "explained" or risk immediate suspicion. Suspicion in the mind of a religious fanatic was equivalent to solid fact, and the old man would not hesitate to order "Brother" Kincaid to dispose of the "traitor."

Sheena stood next to him, patiently waiting for him to make the next move. She had insisted on accompanying him for three good reasons (in *her* humble opinion): (1) she could give him moral support; (2) she could sense any falsehoods on the part of the Archdeacon; and (3) she could keep "Sister" Hedberg's hands off of him. She had told her partner only the first two reasons, and he had accepted them as useful adjuncts. She had kept the third one to herself, because she didn't want George to accuse her of jealousy (again!), even though she was bubbling over with it ever since their first visit to this lion's den. Fogarty's bitch would get her hands on George Larkin over her dead body!

The detective heaved a great sigh, moved forward, and entered the lion's den with Sheena at his heels. They discovered yet another teenage girl at the reception desk. This one looked and acted as mousy as they came: a thin face, averted eyes, and a slight stutter. She was not the sort of person one would want to be one's receptionist, but then the person running this show was not your average businessman, was he? Where did the Archdeacon dredge up these girls? And why did he keep running them in and out through a revolving door? Either he was an "equal opportunity employer" (not likely) or he was "auditioning" girls until he found the right one for the job (maybe). How hard was the job that it required an "audition"? If Larkin had had the time and the inclination, he might have been able to determine the reason. He had neither, now or ever.

He stated his business to the receptionist who responded with a severe bout of stuttering before waving the visitors to chairs. They sat and looked at each other in a smirking fashion.

"Fogarty really knows how to pick 'em," Larkin opined in a low voice. "If I followed his example, I'd lose all of my clients and have to find honest work for a change."

"Maybe the Twins could hire you to clean their bookstore," Sheena sniggered.

"Talk about job security! I'd be at it for the rest of my life."

"I'd fix you a martini when you got home from work."

The detective frowned at this sudden turn in what had started out as a humorous conversation and had now taken an uncomfortable direction. She knew – and he knew that she knew – what effect her "suggestions" had on him, and he knew – and she knew that he knew – that she would persist until she had broken down all of the psychological barriers he had erected ever since she joined the agency. Perhaps it *was* just a matter of time before that happened. God knew that he wanted her as much as she wanted him, but the moment had to be right.

He lowered his head and appeared to be nodding off – his standard operating procedure for contacting the Twins.

*Hello, Kenny, Paddy.

*Hello, George [Paddy replied].

*Are you free to monitor a conversation?

*Yes, I am, old darling.

*It's deadly dull around here [Kenny added]. Where are you?

*In our favorite snake pit. The Archdeacon is waiting for my latest 'report.'

*We're glad it's you there rather than…

*…us. We'd sooner catch a lightning bolt than…

*…have a wee chat with a Disciple, especially…

*…the chief Disciple. He's a real blighter, he is.

*You won't get any argument from me. Ahh, stand by.

At a jab in the ribs from Sheena, Larkin arose from his "dozing" and looked about in feigned confusion. Descending the stairs from the Archdeacon's office were "Sister" Hedberg and a young male Disciple. The latter was of medium height and build and sported a shock of reddish-brown hair and a fair complexion. He walked ramrod stiff behind Hedberg, and his face was devoid of any emotion. As the pair closed the gap, Sheena reached out with her hyperesthesia. Her eyes widened with shock.

*Lord, George! [she said via the Twins' link-up]. That guy is alternating between depression and sheer terror, and he's close to a mental break-down.

*Sounds like he had a grand chewing out by 'His Worship.' Kenny, Paddy, can you verify that?

*Half a minute, old darling. Ah, there…

*…he is. Sheena is spot on. The bloke is…

*…on the edge of the abyss, as it were.

*Hold on! [Paddy exclaimed]. I recognize the bloke.

*You do?

*Yes, indeed. Dear heart, do you remember my little prank of the other day when I put the fear of 'God' into one of the Disciples?

*I do. Is that the chap you fooled?

*Indubitably.

*What did you do to him? [the detective jumped into the conversation].

*Ah, well, I told him that he was preaching the wrong 'gospel' and that he should be speaking the truth.

*And the Archdeacon found out and is dealing with this 'heresy' in his own inimitable fashion.

*We'd say so.

*Humph! There's nothing like introducing a little dissension in the ranks. Perhaps we can work it to our advantage. Stand by.

Hedberg and the young man halted at the receptionist's desk. She turned and gave him the fiercest scowl she was capable of. If he could have turned paler than he already was, he might have become transparent. As it was, he swallowed a large lump in his throat. Hedberg inclined her head towards the door by way of dismissal. The young Disciple marched stiffly toward the door, fumbled with the knob, finally opened the door, and disappeared down the street.

Like a traffic signal, the Archdeacon's executive secretary switched from red to green and gave the visitors a warm smile (though her attention was mostly on Larkin and her eyes issued a meaningful expression). The detective alternated between a wan smile and a grimace.

*Smarmy bitch! [Sheena growled]. I just want to tear her hair out by its ugly black roots!

*You may get your chance, but not today. Today, we have to make nice.

*Humph!

"His Worship is anxiously waiting for you, Brother Larkin," Hedberg stated. "Come along."

She proceeded up the stairs with Larkin and Sheena in tow (the latter grumbling all the way), opened the door to the *sanctum sanctorum*, and ushered the pair in. Archdeacon Fogarty was standing behind his desk at the moment and having a quiet but intense conversation with "Brother" Kincaid. At the entrance of the visitors, the old man broke off the talk, smiled professionally, and waved them to one of the sofas. Larkin took a seat near the desk, and Sheena hastened to sit next to him, beating Hedberg by a fraction of a second. The female Disciple glared at her back, and Sheena smiled to herself as she picked up the vibrations of frustration and enmity from the blonde woman. Kincaid nodded courteously and sat down on the opposite sofa. The old man took his own seat and regarded the detectives pensively.

"Well, Brother Larkin," he said finally, "what news do you have for me?"

Larkin *humph*ed mentally. When Fogarty said "news," what he really meant was "What have you been up to lately? Spill your guts." What he was about to get was yet another plausible fabrication – 10% truth and 90% what he wanted to hear.

"I do have some news, Your Worship – bad news, I'm afraid. But, first, I promised Brother Kincaid I'd report to you about this morning's incident."

"Of course. Proceed."

*Careful, old darling. That Kincaid bloke has...

*...already given his 'report,' and he's done a...

*...little 'spinning,' as you Yanks say. What Fogarty...

*...wants to know is what you did with that Swarm...

*...technology and what you plan to do with it. He's...

*...not in a mood to brook interference in his plans.

"Thank you, sir. Brother Kincaid and his fellows were going to help me move those infernal machines to a safe place so that we could examine them at our leisure and deduce their function. Unfortunately, one of the brothers spotted some of those hell-spawn up the street. It was obvious to me that they were after the machines themselves, and I advised Brother Kincaid to deal with them."

The Archdeacon's right-hand man nodded in agreement at this point, though Larkin suspected that the nod was for *his* benefit and that the henchman had told his boss something slightly different. Larkin's story was already scripted, and the old man would have to decide for himself which version he wanted to believe.

"Rather than wait for the brothers to return and risk the possibility that the creatures they had spotted were simply decoys to lure them away so that other of their cohorts could seize the machines, my companion and I took the machines to a farm I own west of the City. Those creatures are not likely to suspect that and will waste their time and energy in futile searching here."

"How resourceful of you," the old man murmured in a neutral tone. "I will expect periodic updates on what you learn."

"Absolutely, Your Worship. The sooner we understand those machines, the better prepared we'll be for the final victory."

"Indeed. You should know that I had previously formed – for lack of a better description – a permanent 'Defense Brigade' to meet this threat. Select members of the Return-to-Purity movement in this area were recruited to fill the ranks. The late Brother Rosansky had been the Brigade Leader. With his passing, that duty has fallen to Brother Horton. I believe you've already met him."

"Yes I have. An admirable fellow, and perfect for the job."

"The Brigade's function is to patrol the City and meet force with force. With the help of the Lord, we shall prevail."

Mentally, both Larkin and Sheena exulted. They knew what the existence of such a group entailed. A Brigade consisted of three or more Fellowships, and it was formed for the purpose of what the Archdeacon was pleased to call "missionary work." The "missionary work" originally had translated into wholesale acts of vandalism, assaults, intimidation, and other instances where the Disciples needed to demonstrate to the general populace that they meant business. Ordinarily, Brigades were never permanent structures; they were dissolved once the "missionary work" had been concluded. They existed only in the shadows, and the membership of any one of them was known only to the Archdeacon, his immediate staff, and the Deacons involved. All Disciples had an "equal opportunity" to be a member of a Brigade, and it was not unusual for a given individual to be selected more than once. Larkin had seen Brigades in action – too many times for his liking – and he got goosebumps every time he recalled what their "missionary work" produced.

That said, Fogarty had now formed a permanent Brigade for the purpose of taking on the Swarm whenever and wherever they appeared in the City. This was more to the detective's liking, as it played into the Grand Plan he had formulated whereby he pitted the Disciples against the Swarm with the ultimate hope that the two groups would destroy each other. Perhaps with the focus on this new task, the Disciples would leave innocent people alone for a change.

"An excellent tactic, sir," he truthfully said. "But, I'd like to add a word of caution."

"And that is?"

"It concerns the bad news I mentioned at the beginning of this meeting." He paused for dramatic effect. "One of my informants reported that he saw a nest of those creatures holed up in that abandoned factory on Ridgeway Avenue."

"And how is that bad news, Brother Larkin? I should think that, if we knew where they were, we could deal them a swift blow."

"Under ordinary circumstances, I'd agree, Your Worship. But these creatures are armed with fearsome weapons and are exceedingly dangerous." Kincaid nodded again, and this time he seemed sincere. "The weapons they have may be something out of an old science-fiction movie; but they *are* real, and we're no match for them – yet."

"So, what do you recommend?"

"Let my informant scout the place for a few days in order to learn the strengths and weaknesses of the Enemy – especially his weaknesses. Once you have that information, you can deploy the Brigade accordingly."

"I like the way you think, Brother Larkin. I thank the Lord for the day we met."

*Bloody hell! You've hooked the fish...

*...solidly. He's ready to be reeled in.

The detective silently thanked his lucky stars for successfully hoodwinking the City's most charismatic – and therefore most dangerous – individual, then laughed to himself over the irony of the gesture.

"I'm pleased to be of service, sir. Now, if I may take my leave, I have a bit of organizing to do myself."

"Certainly. Stay in touch."

"Sister" Hedberg escorted Larkin and Sheena downstairs. Near the entrance, she moved close to him and gazed soulfully into his eyes.

"Meet you at the usual time and place?" she whispered.

"If I'm able. Bye for now."

Outside, Sheena confronted her partner.

"George, dear, when it comes time to take down the Disciples, would you please leave that one for me?"

* * *

The walk back to the office was largely uneventful. Both detectives walked slowly so as to conserve energy in the intense heat. Each was lost in his/her own thoughts. Larkin was busy formulating a plan whereby the Swarm and the Disciples were sure to collide *en masse* and hopefully eliminate each other from the "game," leaving DEDEP an opportunity to pick up the pieces and surreptitiously re-order the political and social scene of the City (and perhaps further afield). It was a Grand Plan to end all Grand Plans, but every once in a while, the detective liked to Think Big and see where it took him. He had no illusions that everything he planned would actually come to pass exactly as planned, but he could gain some satisfaction if a few parts succeeded.

Sheena was only half-lost in thought. She was busy creating delicious little scenarios in which she would teach "Sister" Hedberg a valuable lesson in social relationships. The other half of her mind was monitoring George's emotional state, an action she performed most of the time. In reality, she was hoping she could pick up a signal that his feelings for her were intensifying and that their relationship could finally attain the physical level.

So absorbed were the pair that the voice behind them startled them. Though they had heard that voice before, it still unnerved them.

"Yer gettin' to be a first-class liar, Georgie. You had old man Fogarty eatin' right outa yer hand."

Both detectives whirled around and confronted a short pudgy man with a round face, heavy, drooping jowls, and tired-looking eyes. His clothes looked like they were fresh from Good Will. The man was chewing noisily on a carrot. Sheena took a quick reading and confirmed what she already instinctively knew.

"Farquhar?" Larkin asked.

"Farquhar," Sheena answered definitively.

"None other," the pudgy man declared.

"How can you be so sure?" Larkin asked Sheena.

"I'll tell you later."

Farquhar was the only person she had ever encountered who had been able to mask his vital signs from her or to alter them at will to suit his purposes. George had always said that he had never met the informant twice as a single individual claiming to be Farquhar; he had assumed that the snitch either had associates who enjoyed yanking his chain or was a true master of disguise, however improbable that might seem to the rational mind. Sheena had only recently toyed with the idea that something more sinister was at work here; and, if her suspicions bore fruit, she, George, and DEDEP were in danger. For, if this quirky head of a spy network/master of disguise was, for lack of a better term, a "psychic chameleon," no secret could be safe from him. Emil might want to interview him – and test him – but Farquhar was still an unknown – and unknowable – quantity, not to be trusted.

"What's on your mind, chum?" Larkin was asking.

"'The time has come to talk of many things,'" the informant quoted Lewis Carroll. "'Of shoes – and ships – and sealing wax – of cabbages – and kings – and why the sea is boiling hot – and whether pigs have wings.'"

"What the hell does that mean?"

"It means, Georgie boy, that it's time to talk plainly."

"About what?"

"About" – a dramatic pause – "DEDEP."

Red flags went up instantly. If the detectives had been startled by Farquhar's sudden appearance, they were doubly so by his frank request. Questions raced through two minds. How did the snitch know about DEDEP? What did he already know? Why was he so curious about the organization? What use of any information he received was he planning? And how would he react if his request were refused?

The one basic rule of the secret organization was that no one – *absolutely no one* –talked about it in public or even mentioned the name. Larkin was no exception. His closest friends, Jack Torres, Vice Mayor of the City, and Gordy, the retired FBI agent, had not even been confided in. The fewer the people who knew of DEDEP's existence, the safer it and its residents were. If there now had been a breach in security, the detective needed to discover it before too very much time had passed and plug it – assuming, of course, it was pluggable. And he'd have to be extra discreet in his investigations; otherwise, he'd raise more suspicions than already existed.

Larkin, the "master strategist," assumed a neutral demeanor. His work for the Chicago Police Department – especially his part in solving kidnapping cases – served him well in moments like this. Sheena, on the other hand, having had first-hand experience with this Great Unknown, was near to panicking, and she pressed close to her partner in an attempt to absorb some of his strength.

*Kenny, Paddy [Larkin called out]. Are you still reading us?

*We are, old darling. But, who are you...

*...talking to? All we're picking up is a...

*...buzzing sound like a bunch of bees...

*...who've just encountered hostile life-forms.

*We're with Farquhar. You're not getting any clear signal?

*Negative.

*Sorry, George.

"What's 'DEDEP'?" he asked aloud.

"You ain't heard of it?"

"No-o-o. What have *you* heard?"

"Oh, scraps of information here 'n' there. Somehow, yer name came up in the conversation."

"Huh! Sorry, I can't help you there."

"OK, Georgie. See ya in the funny papers."

"*Oh, God!*" Sheena rasped as soon as the informant was out of earshot. "What are we going to do about him?"

"I don't know. It depends on what you were going to tell me about him."

"I'll tell you everything I suspect to be true, but you are *not* going to believe it!"

A WAR C⊕UNCIL

DR. EMIL RAZUMOV had lapsed back into gloominess. He alternated between staring blankly at the wall and doodling (in Russian, of course). At one point, he picked up a strip of encephalograph squiggles, peered at it, sighed, and tossed it aside. More blank stares+ and doodling followed. One doodle in particular had been repeated several times: *byespolyesny* [useless].

The bright spot in the past two days had been his examination of Jean Fulton. She had occupied his mind for a few hours in a manner to which he had been accustomed. After the encephalograph reading -- the strip which now lay uselessly on his desk – he had put her through the same rigorous pace he normally put all new arrivals to DEDEP. While the tests he performed indicated she had a *psi*-talent above the average, there was little call for someone who could shock and/or kill whoever was near her; his only recourse was to train her to control her ability and hope for the best. He had even considered using Freddie Hamilton in order to learn if DEDEP's "psychic battery" could increase her voltage or her range, or both but had had second thoughts and dismissed the idea.

With Jean Fulton out of the way, the Doctor went back to moping over the loss of the gestalt. He had had such grand plans for it, but now the opportunity was gone.

While he moped, there came a tapping on the door. He did not wish to be disturbed by anyone at this time; yet, he was still the Director, and he had obligations to the organization and its residents. He hoped whoever was at the door had some good news; otherwise, the conversation was going to be a very short one. At his invitation, Larkin and Sheena walked in, and neither looked too happy. No good news would be forthcoming from them.

Larkin, with his practiced eye, took one look at the Director and despaired. The Russian appeared to be twice as old as he actually was; the worry lines covered his face, and there were bags under his eyes. The detective deduced that he was on the verge of severe depression if he had not already slipped over the edge.

Sheena picked up several body signals which caused her to agonize. Emil's heart beat was slow. His body odor suggested that he had not bathed recently. And his breathing was irregular. She deduced that he was on the verge of severe depression if he had not already slipped over the edge.

"*Zdrafst*, Emil," the detective said tentatively.

"*Zdrafst*," the other mumbled.

"Sheena and I have a fine puzzle for you."

The old man frowned. He was in no mood for puzzles, fine or otherwise. He just wanted to be left alone. In response, he cocked his head slightly as a sign that they should keep talking. The pair took chairs, marshaled their thoughts, and alternated their comments between them.

First, Larkin provided some background, specifically his long-term – and odd – relationship with Farquhar. He described several poignant examples which emphasized the informant's ability to change appearances seemingly at will. The doctor perked up a little bit at this description and leaned forward in a gesture of interest. Sheena then told her strange tale –perhaps not as succinctly as her partner but just as vividly – of her own encounter with a person who did not register on her "radar" until he wished to be registered. She ended by calling Farquhar a "psychic chameleon" and waited for a reaction from Emil.

The reaction was not long in coming. The old man's *angst* disappeared entirely at Sheena's evaluation and was replaced by the customary pondering expression he assumed while analyzing some new piece of information. Now he was back on firmer ground, dealing with the enigma which was the human brain and its manufacture of paranormal phenomena. He nodded knowingly.

"How do you explain it, Emil?" she asked. "Does it fit in with your Special Theory?"

"Ah, you should know by now, Sheena, that it all 'fits in' somewhere, if you examine the matter in detail. What we have here is the ability, firstly, to project an image similar to what Christopher does, except that this Farquhar person is able to assume the image around himself. Secondly, he possesses the ability to generate a dampening field – similar to the electronic one Mr. Jones used on Kenny – so that, in effect, he becomes invisible."

"Would that include sound? I couldn't hear his breathing or his heartbeat."

"Theoretically, yes. A wide-spectrum dampening field should mask all forms of energy, not just the EM. I would have to test this individual" -- his face lit up like a high-beam headlight – "I would *love* to test this individual in order to verify the theory."

"That's not likely," Larkin stated. "Friend Farquhar comes and goes as he pleases. And, if he can do what Sheena says he can do, he could be in this room right now, and we'd never know it."

The Doctor registered sudden shock and gazed left and right. He frowned deeply.

"A most chilling thought, *druzhy moyee*. Let us hope that he is as benign as you believe him to be. Otherwise, it would be the end of DEDEP and all our hopes."

* * *

When Emil Razumov parted company with the American Psychological Association, he decided that, if his own profession would not give his ideas on radiopsychology a fair hearing, he would have to seek out new allies elsewhere. He reasoned that there had to be more open-minded persons and organizations which had pondered the mystery of the "Cosmic Influence" and studied and/or experimented with *psi* on their own. He vowed to find these persons and organizations and gather them together to form a network of spokespersons for radiopsychology and thereby challenge those *duraky* at the APA.

He began with the one group which was the most public: the Psi Squad in St. Louis. The Squad had had their own difficulties with the psychological profession – the latter had labeled them as "crackpots" – and so welcomed the Russian with open arms. Unfortunately, they were also having difficulty with the rampant Return-to-Purity movement and its political arm, the Return-to-Purity Party. The pressures that the RPP brought to bear were leading the Squad toward the decision either to go underground or to disband altogether. Dr. Razumov convinced them to choose the former course as he needed their continued support and experience. In return, the Squad recommended to him a person in the City who actually worked with *psi*-talents (secretly, of course) in a practical fashion.

Meeting George Larkin, the parapsychologist would later write in a private journal he had begun years earlier when he first formulated his General and Special Theories, was an instance of serendipity for more reasons than one. (And he toyed with the notion that serendipity itself might be worked into his General Theory in the same manner as intuition and re-incarnation had been.) The detective had considerable skills and resources the Doctor could use to ferret out *psi*-talents who wished to remain anonymous; and the Russian had his own skills he could use to persuade those persons to join the organization he hoped to create. Moreover, Larkin knew of a potential hideout near the City where he could experiment to his heart's content without interference from the religious fanatics. At last, something was going right!

If truth be told, George Larkin's initial impression of his Russian visitor was that he was a wild-eyed fanatic himself who espoused crazy ideas. He had known about Dr. Razumov from news reports; the American press had followed his every movement and recorded his every utterance. The detective had had his doubts about radiopsychology as it seemed like a far-fetched notion to his very rational mind, and he would need a great deal of proof before he would accept it.

That proof was soon forthcoming. The Doctor put his self-published book, *Radiopsychology: The New Science of the Future*, into the detective's hand and asked him to read it carefully before he dismissed the concept out of hand. Larkin was, frankly, astounded by the scholarship which had gone into the book; and, by the time he had turned the last page, he was thoroughly convinced. Afterwards, the two men became fast friends and close co-workers. And, when he introduced the parapsychologist to the Twins, the old man was beside himself with joy. Things were *really* going right!

The conversion of the abandoned Department of Energy facility into a useable laboratory/"safe house" for testing and protection of *psi*-talents would take considerable time and money to accomplish. The money came from the Psi Squad and a number of university parapsychologists who had been forced to resign their positions due to the pressures of the RPP, all of whom acted as a "board of directors" for the new (as yet unnamed) organization. As for the conversion itself, the detective had to employ persons he could trust to do the work without revealing it to outsiders; he told them that he was creating a haven for people being persecuted by the Disciples (which was true enough, as far as it went) but omitted any mention of *psi* just in case any of his hires had any qualms about the true purpose of the work. In the meantime, Dr. Razumov followed up on Larkin's leads on the location and nature of persons he wished to give safe haven to.

In due time, DEDEP was born.

* * *

Another conference was called for that evening to discuss the latest developments. As always, the atmosphere was filled with *angst*.

Two pockets of non-*angst* existed, however, and both of them were wholly unexpected. The first centered around Stan Jankowsky, who was engaged in an animated conversation with Freddie Hamilton and Billy Perkins. Stan and Billy, though years apart in age, had struck up a friendship after the teenager witnessed what Eve and Stan could do with the gestalt; Billy had hoped to learn more about this phenomenon and use it to expand his own abilities, particularly his psycho-occulism, to the level of his mother's. Stan and Freddie were fielding his many questions and describing what they knew and/or guessed. Stan, of course, withheld the secret he shared with Eve concerning the "conversation" they had had with the Entity, and they would continue to withhold it until they had a clearer idea of what the Entity had in store for them (and maybe not even then).

The unexpected aspect of this pocket was that Eve was once again with this group and was nodding in agreement with the many answers being given. No longer did she isolate herself from the rest of DEDEP during these conferences, ready to bolt for the exit if she felt threatened in any way. Despite the difference between her age and Stan's, she and he had bonded. Larkin had taken notice of this change in attitude shortly after the demise of Mr. Jones, but he was hard-pressed to understand how it had come about – though he had his suspicions.

The second pocket centered around Joyce Jankowsky and Jean Fulton, who sat two rows behind the Eve/Stan/Freddie/Billy contingent. Ordinarily, Joyce would have been as silent as Eve had been, due to her lack of comprehension of what DEDEP was all about and what its membership (including her son) was capable of. Such was not the case at this moment. Joyce had found the newest member of the "family" quite engaging and reminding her of her own carefree days before her unexpected pregnancy. Although she was several years older than Jean, both were giggling like school girls, oblivious to anyone around them. Larkin was pleased by this development; the "eel" was just the thing Joyce needed to break out of her shell.

The detective scanned the assembly – as he always did – in order to deduce from body language and facial expressions what each person was thinking. This night, most were apprehensive, and understandably so. What he had to say would unnerve them even more.

He caught the eye of Lacey Perkins and signaled her to come up front. He was anxious to learn what she had picked up about the Swarm's activities on Ridgeway Avenue. He was sure that what she could contribute to the discussion would be equally as alarming as his report, but DEDEP needed every scrap of information, alarming or otherwise, it could get if it were to meet the threat of the Swarm and to defeat them if at all possible. Lacey excused herself from her family and made her way slowly to the front of the group. Her expression told Larkin that she did have some very bad news.

"I've seen happier faces at a funeral," he remarked nonchalantly as she took a seat next to him.

"Wait'll you hear what I have to say, George. You'll jump for joy."

"Uh-huh. Ah, Emil's here."

Emil Razumov made his "grand entrance" as he always had. His posture was straighter than it had been for the past two days; his stride was more purposeful; and his face looked less haggard. In short, he appeared to be the Emil Razumov of old.

Sheena's description of Farquhar must've snapped him out of his funk, the detective thought as the Director closed the gap. *He's now got a new puzzle to solve, something that'll take his mind off the missing gestalt. That's a relief.*

"Is everyone here, George?" the old man asked.

"All except Chris. I'll call him." He walked over to the nearest wall where a PA speaker was mounted and switched it to "Send." "Hello, Chris."

"Hello, world," came the tinny voice. "Time for the meeting?"

"Right," Larkin replied and switched the speaker back to "Receive."

At once, a shimmering light appeared next to him, amorphic at first but coalescing into a humanoid form. Lastly, it took on detail – a young man wearing a sweat shirt and jeans and a huge grin. All but one of the assembly had seen this vision many times before and so did not react with surprise. The one exception gasped audibly and clutched the arm of her neighbor. Joyce patted the clutching hand and whispered some re-assuring words. Jean relaxed somewhat but still held onto the arm of her new friend.

"*Dobry vyecher, druzhy moyee,*" the Doctor intoned. "We have some new developments to report concerning the alien threat to Earth. But first, I wish to introduce to you formally the newest member of DEDEP,

Jean Fulton, lately of St. Louis. Would you please stand, Miss Fulton, and show yourself to everyone?"

The young woman was nonplussed, to say the least, at having been singled out for attention, and she didn't know whether to smile or be surprised. In the end, her expression was somewhere in between which gave her a comical look. Joyce leaned over and told her she had had to go through the same routine and that the sooner it was done, the better. Jean took a deep breath, stood up, and waved. She was greeted by a few "Hello, Jeans" and a round of polite applause to which she responded with a nod of the head.

"For your information," the Doctor continued, "Miss Fulton is an 'eel.' That is, she is an 'electrically energized life-form.' Under stress, she discharges static electricity."

"Yeah," the woman said pugnaciously. "Hassle me, and I'll zap ya."

Then she sat down and smiled smugly. Nervous laughs rippled through the crowd. Freddie and Joyce both gave her a "thumbs up." Larkin grinned at this sudden burst of spunk while the Director stroked his chin in perplexity.

The detective struggled to his feet and surveyed his audience again. The rumors concerning the topic of this meeting had already made the rounds as rumors of previous meetings had; and now all eyes were on him in the hopes that none of the rumors were true and worrying that all of them were.

"There's mostly bad news, I'm afraid, people," he began without preamble. "Still bad news is better than no news. At least, it'll help us in our planning." He regarded the ghostly figure of Christopher Wredling. "I'll have Chris start off. As you know, the Swarm's main base in America is outside of Omaha, Nebraska. I've had Chris scout this base periodically, and he'll fill us in on the 'Big Picture.' Chris?"

The smiling image wavered briefly as the psycho-projector shifted mental gears. When the wavering stopped, the image wore a neutral expression more proper to the somberness of the occasion. Chris' tinny voice issue from the PA speaker.

"Thank you, George. Basically, what the Swarm is doing is conducting military maneuvers in preparation for their assault on our planet." Gasps and murmuring filled the room. "It's true. They've been training day and night – assault tactics, hand-to-hand combat, weapons proficiency" – he paused here for dramatic effect – "and torture methods." More gasps and murmuring followed his witnessing of "target practice," using Disciples as the targets. "I can tell you that it wasn't easy to watch these displays of barbarism. I do it only for the sake of finding some weakness in their offense we can use against them. So far, there haven't been any. Any questions?"

A stillness settled over the assembly as each individual let his/her imagination run wild, creating one fantasy scenario after another of alien invasion, mass murder, and gratuitous violence. Finally, one member found a will to stand up at Chris' invitation. Predictably, it was "Fat Henry" Rawlins, DEDEP's "sleeping prophet" and chief griper.

"I don't see why we should be so concerned about what the Swarm does to Disciples. Hasn't George already set them against each other?"

"The Disciples have their faults, Henry, and they'll be made to pay for them someday. But, they are our fellow humans, and they deserve the same fighting chance we would want for ourselves. If we lose sight of that ideal, we're no better than the Swarm."

Rebuffed, Henry sat down and brooded to himself. Chris' image wavered again.

"If there are no more questions, I need to rest. It's been a long day. Good night, everyone."

His image shimmered, lost its humanoid shape, and faded away. Larkin took center stage again.

"We'll hear from Lacey now."

The psycho-occulist stood and smiled nervously. Ordinarily, she was as gregarious as they come – in an informal setting. By some quirk in her genetic make-up, she turned into a quivering mass and tended toward tongue-tiedness when addressing a group of people. With fluttering hands, then, she told her tale.

"My news isn't much happier than Chris', I'm afraid. I've been monitoring the Swarm at their new base in the City, and I can tell you that what they're doing gives me cold chills up and down my spine.

"First of all, they seem to have completed assembling a war machine that spits fire as well as explosives as described by Eve two weeks ago. When I first peeped them, they were running extensive checks on all of the craft's systems. Even though I couldn't hear what they were saying, their gestures were quite clear in indicating that they were near completion.

"Now, here's the scary part. When I peeped them two hours ago for an update, I was frightened out of my wits. They had used their fire weapon to burn a hole in the roof of the factory big enough to allow that craft to pass through. I think they're ready to test its maneuverability."

Lacey quickly sat down. She was shaking all over, and not from self-consciousness. Larkin took the floor again but did not speak for a long moment. Finally:

"Well, it looks like the fat is in the fire, to use an old expression. The Swarm has just raised the stakes in this game. I don't need to tell you that that war machine is capable of wiping out a whole city – and everyone in it – by itself. Any questions so far?"

Silence answered his query. All were too stunned to trust themselves to speak up and were attempting to come to grips with the implications of Lacey's report. Some DEDEP'ers whispered to each other; others wept openly. The rest thought their private thoughts. Then "Fat Henry" stood again. He did not wear a blustery face this time; instead, he licked dry lips and wrung his hands.

"We're safe here, aren't we, George? They can't find us, can they?"

The detective took a deep breath and let it out slowly. He was not too surprised to hear the questions asked; in fact, he had expected someone to ask them. Still, he needed to compose himself to deliver the proper answers. This group was on the verge of panic, and he had to defuse the situation as soon as possible. His answers had to be both factual and re-assuring – not an easy combination to handle – or else he'd have a raft of broken spirits and nervous wrecks unable to take the necessary action in any counter-offensive he might devise. He regarded the "sleeping prophet" with as much confidence-building as he could muster.

"The answer to your second question, Henry," he replied in a very deliberate tone, "is I don't know if the Swarm can find us. Mr. Jones did, but obviously he never got the chance to relay to his comrades how he did. If we are careful in our dealings with them, they won't find us." He paused and took another deep breath. "The answer to your first question is, if we stay hidden, they might not suspect our presence, and we will be safe – for a while. Do you propose to remain hidden while the rest of humanity goes down the tubes?"

"Well, yes, I do. After all, what has the rest of humanity done for us? We're persecuted for what we are – murdered even. After the Swarm has left, we can emerge into the open and build our own society free of persecution."

A low murmuring issued from the crowd. Larkin was afraid that this turn in the conversation might occur. He had to act quickly to nip it in the bud.

"You heard what Chris said. I agree with him. We're still human beings, regardless of our individual abilities. We're obliged to protect each other from external threats. Our alien allies have warned us about this particular threat. 'Forewarned is forearmed,' as the saying goes. The Swarm won't take us by surprise as they've done to countless other beings in the galaxy. We owe it to those victims of genocide, as well as to ourselves, to fight back with everything we've got. We'll show the Swarm that we humans don't go down so easily."

Brave words, George. And do you have brave actions to match?

Before he could say another word, Sheena jumped to her feet and began clapping her hands. Lacey was a second behind her. Then others -- Emil, Freddie, Eve, the Jankowskys, the Perkinses, and Jean in the forefront – gave their support. Soon, all were standing, applauding as hard as they could. Sheepishly, Henry Rawlins shrugged his shoulders and joined in. Larkin raised his hand for silence and got it.

"Thank you for your support, my friends. Emil, do you have anything to add?"

"*Da, konyechno. Druzhy moyee,* I fully support George in his sentiments. He has not let us down so far, and he is not likely to do so in the future. As for myself, my door is open to anyone who wishes to seek consultation. I think that now we should all return to our quarters and discover how best to meet this threat which affects all of humanity. *Dobry vyecher.*"

Later, as they walked down the corridor toward the emergency exit, Sheena linked arms with her partner and rested her head on his shoulder. He did not resist.

"That was a stirring speech, George dear."

"It was, wasn't it? I just hope I can be as self-confident as I sounded."

"Tsk-tsk. How could you be otherwise?"

Both chuckled heartily at the remark.

* * *

Come fly/run with me, the Entity whispers to him/her.

"You're back!" (s)he exclaims. "I/we thought I/we had lost you."

Not so. I was called away to attend to an urgent matter."

"Will you leave me/us again without warning?"

Never. I seek engagement with beings of a pure nature. You are such beings.

"I/we am/are pleased. I/we have a favor to ask."

Name it.

"The creature who attacked me/us and who you destroyed was not alone. There are others like him, and they wish to do me/us harm. Will you protect me/us from them?"

I cannot take life on such a large scale without permission from my superiors. If the threat is dire enough, then I may act. Summon me, and I will come.

"Thank you again."

Now, are you ready to fly/run with me?

"Yes, I/we am/are."

Then open your minds. See how easy it is to fly/run.

"OH, WOW!"

* * *

The VOID.

Emptiness.

Darkness.

Solitude.

Silence.

Infinite sameness stretching across and through infinite numbers of dimensions of EXISTENCE.

An eternal sameness which transcends TIME itself.

Without boundaries, it simply...is.

Nothing has disturbed the VOID for uncounted eons.

Until now.

Three images appear. One image represents an adult female humanoid with a lean face, high cheekbones, deep-set eyes, and a small mouth. Another image represents a juvenile male humanoid with a round, fleshy face, a pug nose, a narrow chin, and wide-set eyes. The final image is not humanoid at all; rather, it is a large, glowing white globe.

The humanoid images regard the non-humanoid image with awe and wonder – and reverence. How this non-humanoid image regards the humanoid images is open to speculation and, in point of fact, is irrelevant.

"Where are we?" (Female)

"You are in my domain now. Here, I – and soon you – can observe all there is to observe through conduits such as yourselves."

"You live *here?" (Male)*

"'Live' is a meaningless term. I have existed here for longer than you can possibly imagine."

"Are you...immortal? (Female)

"Also meaningless. I simply...am.

"So, what do you observe?" (Male)

"The macroverse and the microverse. The past and the future. The real and the imaginary. Everything there is to see in this universe and in countless other universes."

"You know everything then?" (Female)

"Hardly. All of EXISTENCE is in constant flux. The patterns shift like a [untranslatable], and new points of reference appear. I observe it all as it comes about." The glowing white globe dims ever so slightly, then brightens again. "Now, children, I will show you some of those wonders of which I spoke. Each of you may have two choices."

"How do we choose? If what you say is true, then choosing will be difficult." (Male)

"Open up your minds. The first two thoughts you have will be the gateways of your choices."

* * *

A multitude of colors — all the colors of the rainbow and all of their shadings.

Swirling and twisting and looping and criss-crossing each other in no discernible pattern.

Dimming and brightening and fading in and fading out in no discernible pattern.

It is a hodge-podge, a riot, a melee, a kaleidoscope — chaos in technicolor.

The viewers are awed/astonished/amazed/astounded/bedazzled/dazed/ overwhelmed/ stunned/stupefied beyond belief.

(S)he stands in the exact center of this multi-hued display, craning her/his neck this way and that in a futile effort to take it all in. The light show envelopes her/him in a sphere, and (s)he cannot see in all directions at once. At length, (s)he gives up the effort and concentrates on one segment or another.

Blink! *The display vanishes and is replaced by:*

A swarm of tiny organisms — no bigger than the tip of a pin — races toward its target. The organisms have all been launched at once, but only one will succeed in striking the target.

The target lies ahead, a spheroid no bigger than the head of a pin. It has just been released from its birthing place and is unaware of the swarm which approaches, is unaware of the fate which will soon befall it.

The swarm approaches ever closer. One of the organisms appears to have taken the lead, and it may be that it will succeed in striking the target first and initiate a chain of events which defies all comprehension.

The fortunate organism strikes the targeted spheroid with full force and buries itself inside it. Its chemical make-up merges with that of the spheroid, and the two become one.

Conception is complete.

Blink! *The display vanishes and is replaced by:*

A whirlpool in space, sucking up anything which comes near.

Its grasping, avaricious hunger is not vortical in nature, but gravitic.

It begins as a dying star, collapsing in upon itself. It becomes a super-dense mass and produces a tremendous gravitational field. The pull it exerts is so intense that not even light can escape its grasping, avaricious hunger.

A passing comet draws too near. Gulp!

Several free-floating asteroids, remnants of a shattered planet, pass innocently by. Gulp!

Clouds of gas and dust – what would have been a future star – drift into the event horizon. Gulp!

With each devouring, the whirlpool grows ever larger, and its gravitational pull grows stronger. Soon, nothing will withstand its grasping, avaricious hunger.

A star system with four planets (and a number of moons) are caught up in the gravity net. One by one, their masses are stretched out like taffy and sucked into the "black hole."

Were any of those planets inhabited by sentient beings? If so, were they able to escape in time? If so, what became of them? Do they now wander still, searching for a new home?

The whirlpool continues to eat.

Blink! *The display vanishes and is replaced by:*

A "planetary system" plows through space. The primary possesses ninety-two satellites; the satellites spin about the parent in rapid, continuous movement.

A rogue "world" approaches. It bears down upon the "planetary system" blindly, attracted by its magnetic force.

The rogue crashes into one of the satellites and sends it soaring off into space to become a rogue itself. The intruder continues to strike satellite after satellite, and they too fly off into all directions. Finally, the intruder crashes into the primary and splits it into its constituent parts. The parts also become rogues and bear down upon other "planetary systems" nearby.

One by one, all of the affected "planetary systems" in this "galaxy" are destroyed, and they release all of their energy at once. The chain reaction is complete, and an explosion of gigantic proportions occurs.

Blink! *The display vanishes and is replaced by:*

A slight vibration underground is set off by the movement of two masses of rock grating against each other. The rocks scrape back and forth as each attempts to dominate the other. The vibrations increase in intensity with each scraping.

The vibrations morph into tremors, violently shaking the ground. Above, canines howl in fear, and other wildlife flee the epicenter of the tremors.

Abruptly, the ground splits asunder, creating wide, deep cracks in the Earth. If there are structures and/or life-forms in the vicinity, they are swallowed up and descend into the Earth to their doom. The earthquake is unrelenting and unrepentant.

Soon, equilibrium is restored, and the tremors cease. All is peaceful as the Earth attempts to repair itself.

Blink! *The display vanishes and is replaced by:*

A multitude of colors — all the colors of the rainbow and all of their shadings.

Swirling and twisting and looping and criss-crossing each other in no discernible pattern.

Dimming and brightening and fading in and fading out in no discernible pattern.

It is a hodge-podge, a riot, a melee, a kaleidoscope — chaos in technicolor.

The viewers are awed/astonished/amazed/astounded/bedazzled/dazed/ overwhelmed/stunned/stupefied beyond belief.

* * *

"WOW!!!"

"That was awesome!*"*

"Cool!"

"That was just a sampling of the wonders of the multiverse which will be available to you."

"'Multiverse'?" (Female)

"What's that?" (Male)

"Your species understands only one universe – that which has been partially discovered by your astronomers – but there an infinite number of universes existing side by side."

"How can they do that?" (Female)

"Each universe vibrates at its own unique frequency. If you were to alter the frequency at which you vibrate, you would find yourself in a different – a vastly different – universe. Collectively, the whole is termed the 'multiverse.'"

"And you can go to these other universes?" (Male)

"A mere thought is all that is required for my kind. For you, the process requires much training."

A long/short silence. Then:

"I must return you to your own plane of existence. I have other errands to perform."

"Wait! I/we don't know –"

* * *

Eve and Stan literally dashed out of their respective apartments. For the former, that act was made difficult by the fact that she had to stop and physically open the door. For the latter, however, it was clear sailing because the door was opening psycho-kinetically the moment he exited his bedroom. Once out, both made a beeline towards the emergency stairwell. As chance would have it, they met on a landing between levels. Each regarded the other with wide-eyed wonder.

"Were we dreaming?" both said in unison.

"If we were," Eve whispered, "then I want to sleep forever."

"Yeah, me too."

"I don't think we were dreaming, though."

"Nah," Stan agreed. "It was too real to be a dream."

"So, what do we do now? Do we tell Dr. Razumov?"

"I dunno. He might not believe us. He might think we was havin' de-delu-delusions."

"And I wouldn't blame him."

"Me neither."

"Still, we should tell him that the gestalt is available again. We just won't tell him *how* we know that."

"Right. An' we gotta tell Freddie too. He's part of the team."

"OK. Let's do that now."

* * *

In the VOID, five points of light appear in a circle. After a brief moment/eon, a sixth point appears in the center of the circle.

One of the points in the circle brightens slightly.

-- REPORT.

The point in the center now brightens slightly.

-- Phase One is concluded. This One has made contact with two indigenous life-forms in the [untranslatable] *dimension. One is a young* [male]. *The other is an adult* [female]. *Both have abilities beyond any possessed by most of their kind.*

A second point in the circle brightens slightly.

-- Are they suitable candidates?

-- This One has probed both life-forms and analyzed the resulting data. The life-forms show great potential.

A third point of light brightens slightly.

-- What has been done toward recruitment?

-- This One has taken the life-forms on a short journey into the VOID. Both were impressed by what they observed and showed a willingness to explore further.

A fourth point brightens slightly.

-- Are they ready for recruitment?

--This One believes so. With permission, this One will initiate Phase Two.

The final point brightens slightly.

-- Permission is granted. The Communion will await your next report. You are dismissed.

The point of light in the center of the circle winks out of existence. After a brief moment/eon, the remaining points of light are extinguished.

Only the VOID remains.

CHAPTER TEN

GESTALT REDUX

IN THE BEGINNING of his research into radiopsychology, Emil Razumov classified *psi*-talents as either "passives" or "actives." His General Theory of Radiopsychology dealt with the former classification, while the Special Theory dealt with the latter. In his studies and experiments, he had discovered that the majority of psychic and occult phenomena fell into the "passive" category, and so he devoted a great deal of time on the formulation of the General Theory. As he encountered "actives," he set down the basic principles of the Special Theory and then sought to correlate them with those of the General Theory. Additional tweaking brought forth a comprehensive whole, although he had preferred to keep the two parts separate (on paper) in order not to confuse the lay person.

Another way of looking at *psi*-talents, he thought later on, was to categorize them as "receivers" and "senders," to employ the jargon of electronic transmissions (although, in his writings, he preferred to use the original terminology more extensively). "Receivers" were covered by the General Theory, whereas "senders" were covered by the Special Theory. In essence, "receivers" were sensitive to external sources of radio energy, while "senders" focused on internal sources, i.e. the brain, to create radio energy. For example, Lacey Perkins, a psycho-occulist, "saw" images at a distance by focusing on radio energy generated by the source and would be considered a "passive/receiver." Similarly, Eve Pelletier, a psycho-imager, received images of an historical nature by handling objects touched by others and internalizing the radio energy so generated. On the other side of the coin, Stan Jankowsky, a psycho-kinetic, was most assuredly an "active/sender" when he focused radio energy from his brain to impact a distant object. Similarly, Christopher Wredling, a psycho-projectionist, "sent" his consciousness to distant places where he could view the lay of the land.

Although he really didn't have to do so, the Doctor marked each name on the DEDEP roster with either a "p" or an "a." Such was his diligence to his field of study, and he was constantly revising his methodology.

It followed therefore that there had to be *psi*-talents who were both "passive/receivers" and "active/senders." It also followed that those individuals formed a tiny percentage of the pool of paranormals, because performing both aspects of *psi* required considerable brain power, the more so if the individuals could switch from one aspect to the other at will. As it happened, DEDEP possessed *two* such individuals, Kensington and Paddington Smythe, psycho-communicators; not only could they "send" messages and/or their consciousnesses to other minds, but they also could receive the same from others. It also followed that this category of super-*psi*-talent was the most dangerous of all and had to be monitored at all times. For a person with evil intent could wreak havoc whenever and wherever (s)he could simply by manipulating another's mind and thus that person's actions. Happily for DEDEP (and the world at large), the Twins were benign and moral creatures and used their considerable abilities sparingly and to good purpose.

There was also a fourth category of *psi*-talent – also a small percentage in the pool of paranormals – that in which the individual was neither a "passive/receiver" nor an "active/sender." Dr. Razumov had been forced by circumstances to include this category and to label certain individuals as "transformers." A "transformer" relayed radio energy from a source to either a "passive/receiver" or an "active/sender and/or altered its form. Freddie Hamilton fell into this category and was called a "psychic battery."

The "eel," Jean Fulton, had to be considered a "transformer." As the Doctor had discovered in his initial examination of her, she converted radio energy generated by her brain into electrical energy and discharged it under particular circumstances. This was a radically different method from the way static electricity was usually produced; whereas normally static electricity was produced thermo-mechanically via friction and released by contact with a conductive object, Jean's output was produced electro-chemically, altered, and discharged at random. How she could accomplish the latter was a mystery and a challenge to the Russian's intellectual powers. He may have lost the gestalt; but now he had a puzzle to solve, and he was determined to solve it.

The previous tests he had performed had provided him with a general picture of her brain-wave activity. The EEG read-out showed a high level of activity – into the gamma range, to be exact – whenever she experienced a high emotional state. This was as it should be in the case of *psi*-talent. The next step was to pinpoint the exact area of the brain which was responsible for the activity. Jean would have to have each area tested separately which meant that she would have to be stimulated multiple times into producing an emotional state. She had balked when he made the original suggestion but relented when he assured her that he would not push her beyond her endurance. How she would react to multiple stimuli was unknown; the worst case scenario was her refusal to participate and/or a request to leave DEDEP. The Doctor was walking a fine line here.

Jean watched in fascination as he set up his equipment. His routine was similar to her own. In her work at her father's repair shop, she always made a mental list of the tools she would need for the particular job and then gather up said tools and lay them out on her work bench in the order she would use them. She could appreciate the Doctor's methodology even if she couldn't comprehend its purpose. She would watch and learn, however.

Dr. Razumov made his final adjustments and wheeled the EEG over to where Jean was sitting. He attached two sensor pads to specific points on her skull. She winced because the pads were icy cold to the touch. He was about to switch on when she interrupted him.

"Is this going to take long, Doctor? Freddie wants me to re-wire some circuits in the kitchen. The wiring is frayed."

"It will take as long as it must, dear lady. You and Freddie must be patient. What I intend to do here is to map your brain one area at a time. With a complete profile, I will be able to learn the nature of your ability and devise a method by which you may control it."

"Is that possible? I mean, to prevent me from hurting people?"

"Everything is possible, if one has all of the necessary information. Now shall we begin?"

Since the "eel's" ability manifested itself during highly emotional episodes, the logical place to start an EEG probe was in those areas of the human brain which dealt with human emotions. Two of these existed: (1) the amygdala, an almond-sized and –shaped mass in the center of the base of the brain which processed emotional responses, e.g. sexual arousal and fear; and (2) the orbitofrontal cortex located below the frontal lobe which governed patterns of behavior. The latter was subdivided into the medial orbitofrontal region which responded to rewards and the lateral orbitofrontal region which responded to punishments. Furthermore, the forward parts of the orbitofrontal cortex dealt with material rewards, such as tasty foods, while the rearward parts dealt with abstract rewards, such as satisfaction with a job well done.

Because the amygdala was located so deep within the brain, a more complex set-up was required to probe it. Therefore, Dr. Razumov had applied his first pad to Jean's temple behind which lie the orbitofrontal cortex. He switched on the EEG and fixed his attention on the electronic "pens." He was instantly rewarded when the lines representing neural impulses skittered quickly through the alpha range and deeply into the beta; moreover, the lines were thick and long, indicating strong neural activity. Jean's emotional values were pronounced, a sign which suggested that it would not take a large stimulus to provoke her "eel" ability. The trick lay in containing the provocation to acceptable levels.

Outwardly, the old man presented a picture of calm and reserve. He hardly moved at all and might have passed for a statue. Inwardly, however, it was a different story. He was beside himself with joy for having discovered so soon what he had hoped to find. Yet, his joy was tempered by the fact that he needed to corroborate this test with others – particularly with the amygdala, the core of human emotional patterns. Needless to say, he could hardly wait to probe that region more thoroughly.

He ran the EEG for two minutes in order to determine whether or not the electrical output flagged with duration. The machine showed no sign of doing so – partly, he suspected, due to Jean's anxiety toward the testing (a normal reaction in any human being) – but remained deep within the beta range. Finally, he switched off, faced Jean with a grandfatherly smile, and removed the pads.

"The first test is complete. Now, relax while I prepare for the next test."

"What did you find out?" she asked nervously.

"Simply that you are an emotional dynamo. Your levels of brain activity are very high and easily triggered."

"*Humph!* I coulda told you *that*!"

"*Nye somnyenno.* But scientific verification is very necessary. How else are we to believe anything otherwise?"

"So, what's the next test about?"

"I will examine your amygdala" – a look of alarm passed across her face – "that part of your brain that responds to emotional attitudes. If the EEG readings corroborate the previous readings, then we will have a base to work from in developing your ability and controlling it for useful purposes."

"You make it sound so easy, Doctor. But I ain't convinced yet."

"I will endeavor to convince you, dear lady. Now, excuse me while I re-set the EEG."

He would have done so too, had not Eve, Stan, and Freddie chosen that particular moment to amble into the laboratory. All three had

Cheshire-cat smiles on their faces. The old man took one look at them and frowned. What were they up to now, with their ridiculous grins? he wondered.

"*Shto eto?*"

"We have good news for you, Doctor," Eve replied. "The En – uh, the gestalt is back."

"*Pravda?*" he asked breathlessly.

"Yeah," Stan said. "We don't know why it left us or why it came back. But it's back, an' we're ready to experiment some more."

"*Khorosho.* This is as good a time as any to introduce our newest member to it."

"I've heard some talk about this…gestalt," Jean remarked. "What is it?"

"You shall see, dear lady, and you will be amazed. Eve, Stan, Freddie, prepare yourselves."

The Triad found chairs and formed their usual triangular setting. Dr. Razumov took a seat next to Jean. Still pleased, Eve and Stan clasped hands.

As before, the black sphere appeared instantaneously as if it had been waiting in the wings for its cue to make its entrance. It shimmered slightly in the bright light of the laboratory, something it had never done before. Eve and Stan regarded it with what could only be described as "parental pride."

Its effect on the newest member was quite the opposite. Having never seen the phenomenon before, Jean jumped to her feet, full of anxiety and fear; despite the calm demeanor of the pair who had summoned it into existence, she reacted as most humans would have in the face of the Unknown and inched away from the thing. Then, what she feared even more took hold of her. The tingling which started in her brain and coursed throughout her body built up in intensity, and she clutched her abdomen in a futile effort to hold the powerful electrical charge within her in check.

"Oh, no!" she shrieked. "It's happening again, and I can't stop it. Make it go away! *Please!* Before I hurt someone!"

While she uttered that plea, something weird occurred on/around/ in the sphere...

* * *

Alert!

Investigate! Analyze! Protect!

Investigation: unknown entity with [undecipherable] **appendages, directly before this One. It radiates in the** [undecipherable] **frequency, creating heat energy of modest proportions. A mass of dangerous electrical energy is building up in the entity's body. Electrical energy is harmless to this One, but it may be harmful to others, including the Summoners.**

Analysis: This One has resumed contact with the Summoners for both the purpose of continued information exchange and the possible recruitment of them to serve the Communion. Research of the past [undecipherable] [undecipherable] **of the Summoners' space-time continuum reveals that they have bonded with the unknown entity but are unaware of its potential for harm.**

The danger to the Summoners now involves this One. Consequence: loss of information exchange and recruitment possibility and a permanent return of this One to the [undecipherable] **Zone, an unacceptable condition. Disruption and termination is imminent unless a counter-action is taken. Conclusion: neutralization of the unknown entity's electrical build-up will restore the previous balance.**

Protection: based upon the nature of the energy flow from the unknown entity, this One will generate [undecipherable] [undecipherable] **in the** [undecipherable] **range.**

Initiating containment field.

* * *

...and it became mottled with pink splotches which rotated and zigzagged in kaleidoscopic fashion.

"*Bozhu moyu!*" the Doctor cried out. "The gestalt has changed coloration, just as George said it did before it destroyed Mr. Jones. But why Miss Fulton? She is not evil." He turned to the Triad. "Eve, Stan, break off! *Beestro* [quickly], *beestro!*"

The pair complied at once and stared in amazement and horror as the cessation of contact failed to cause the disappearance of the gestalt. The sphere remained in place, its mottling rotating faster and faster. Jean screamed in sheer terror as she believed she was going to die a horrible death.

She did not die, however. To everyone's astonishment, the pink mottling separated itself from the parent body, drifted over to the panicky woman, and enveloped her. She stopped screaming as she realized that, instead of the discharge of electrical energy she expected, the charge was dissipating harmlessly into the pink envelope. She felt warm and cuddly all over, relaxed and perplexed.

Once the danger was neutralized, the envelope faded away, and the gestalt returned to its normal black color. Then it too disappeared, leaving behind general consternation.

Jean stood in place, completely mesmerized by what had just occurred. The others rushed to her side; concern for her well-being was evident in everyone, and particularly in the Director who had precipitated the event.

"Are you well, Miss Fulton?" he asked solicitously.

"Yeah. Far out! I was frightened by that – 'gestalt,' you called it – but then, when it surrounded me with – whatever it was – I felt like I had been wrapped up in a big fuzzy blanket." She stared off in space to where the gestalt had been. "And that thing took away my electrical charge. How'd it do that?"

"I have no idea," the Russian replied. "The gestalt has been a mystery from the first moment it appeared. Well, you are excused from any further testing for today. I must ponder this latest development."

"Great," Freddie piped up. "I need my assistant back. Come along, Jeanie. Break time's over, and we got a ton of work to do."

"OK, Chief. After what I just went through, work will be a welcome relief."

A few seconds later, Eve and Stan were alone in the laboratory. Each eyed the other and somehow knew what (s)he was thinking. Stan moved to put their thoughts into words.

"The Entity di'n't go away when we broke off. That never happened before."

"No, it didn't. It sensed danger and remained until the danger was past. Do you think it needs our contact to come into our world but can stay as long as it wants without it?"

"Dunno. But, there's only one way to find out."

"Right. The next time it speaks to us, we have a lot more questions for it."

* * *

Larkin hated to turn away potential clients. For one thing, his expenses were fairly high – rent on the office space, the electricity to run all of his electronic equipment, employee salaries (including stipends for his "special operatives"), upkeep and maintenance on everything, on-line subscriptions, and so forth – and he'd like a little something for himself in order to brag about being in the "middle class." For another thing, his reputation for solving mysteries was fast outstripping his ability to handle a large workload (even with Sheena's assistance), and he was in danger of over-extending himself, physically and mentally. And for a third thing, there were certain requests he didn't care to take on but which he was increasingly asked to handle.

A case in point: already this morning, he had turned down two would-be clients whose requests he thought were beneath his considerable talents. One was the ever-popular spying-on-a-cheating-spouse case whereby one had to follow the spouse all day long to learn (if possible) whether (s)he had had any assignations and how many – and would you please get some photographs? Larkin had had plenty of those cases when he first hung up his shingle (when he was not on assignment with the Chicago Police Department), and he had hated every one of them. Once his practice was up and running, he believed he could pick and choose his clients. The other one involved finding some missing jewelry. He had flatly refused on the grounds that he specialized in finding missing *persons* (which was true enough).

Turning away business was always risky. Those turned away were potential sources of bad publicity. While his sterling reputation was sufficient to carry him extremely well, that could change at any moment, and then where would he be? He'd be reduced to taking on those damned spying-on-a-cheating-spouse cases!

Now, a fourth thing had reared its ugly head. With the threat of an alien invasion from outer space looming over the Earth, he had had to devote an ever-increasing amount of time and resources to counter-act that threat. He and DEDEP – and the gestalt (if it co-operated) – could deal with just about anything the Swarm threw at them, but only as long as they remained diligent. He had "recruited" the Disciples by means of a ruse; but religious fanatics were unpredictable and therefore unmanageable, and he could not always count on them to play along, no matter how grave he made the threat out to be. This was purely *his* show – like it or not – and he had to deal with it as he could. The cheating spouses were free to cheat away, as far as he was concerned!

He was hoping to hear from the Quintessential Quark this morning. Since the initial contact, the UFO-conspiracy-freak had sent him daily messages – most of them quite incoherent but the rest somewhat useful. Usually, the Quark sent his messages at a certain time of the day – before or after he took his medication? – but he was late today. Had he finally OD'ed from whatever he was on? Or had he stumbled onto something he was too frightened to report? It was hard to tell with that sort of "informant."

At the moment, Larkin was standing in the cupola attached to his office and watching the traffic, vehicular and foot, on the streets below. He observed the usual mix of the casual and the urgent, the mundane and the important. The unwashed masses were going through their paces in complete ignorance of what was happening in the wider world.

How would those people down there react if he were to tell them of the imminent danger of an alien invasion from outer space? Would they look at him oddly and silently measure him up for a strait jacket? Would they tell him he was nuttier than a fruitcake and he could go to

Hell? But, what if they actually believed him, no matter how impossible-sounding his warning was? Would they ask him what they should do to prevent such an invasion? Or would they behave like typical human beings, screaming at the top of their voices and running this way and that out of sheer panic?

"Ignorance is bliss," the old saying went. And, in this particular case, it was especially so. George Larkin and DEDEP were on their own, come what may. Deal with it, George old buddy.

As he studied the human condition below weaving ever changing threads, he spotted a familiar vehicle – a white sedan with a dent on the right front fender – pulling up to the curb on River Street and grimaced. He didn't need any visitors from old man Fogarty's bunch just now, thank you very much! He had to plan a counter-move to what Lacey had reported on when she peeped the Swarm on Ridgeway, and he was discarding one useless idea after another. Some days, it just didn't pay to get out of bed.

The door on the driver's side opened, and "Brother" Kincaid eased himself out of the sedan. He slammed the door shut and walked slowly and deliberately to the entrance of Larkin's building. Three minutes later, Mrs. Watson was on the phone, announcing his arrival. The detective braced himself. His office door opened, and the Archdeacon's right-hand man glided in.

"Brother Kincaid." Larkin said as cheerily as he could, "how good to see you again."

"Brother Larkin," the other responded tonelessly. "The Archdeacon wants to see you."

"So soon? It must be urgent."

"It is. He sent me to pick you up."

Now, that sounded ominous!

The detective nodded and followed Kincaid out of the office without hesitation. He stopped long enough to tell Mrs. Watson that he was going to look at some property – code words which meant he was going on a dangerous assignment – if Sheena asked about his whereabouts. The two men descended to the street level, exited the building, and climbed into the sedan. Neither said a word to each other. Kincaid pulled away from the curb with barely a glance at oncoming traffic; he made a right turn and headed west on Main Street rather than continuing south on River Street. Larkin felt butterflies fluttering in his stomach.

"We're not going to headquarters?" he inquired artlessly.

"No. We're going to the Mayor's residence. His Worship is a temporary guest there."

The number two Disciple offered no further information, and Larkin did not press the issue. He glanced surreptitiously at his traveling companion. He had always prided himself on being a good judge of character. It had helped a great deal in his line of work to know how clients and interviewees behaved and responded to his questions; their responses usually gave him clues as to what sort of resources he might need to work the cases (if he worked them at all). He could count on one hand the number of individuals he hadn't been able to figure out.

He now added Kincaid to that short list. The man was a complete enigma. He spoke very little; and, when he did speak, he chose his words very carefully. He stood/sat in a rigid position and never offered any body language to read. His face was as stony as a statue. But, it was his eyes which gave Larkin the shivers; they were cold and expressionless, and they looked at a person in the manner of a vivisectionist. The more one studied him, the less one believed he really was a Disciple. He struck one, instead, as much of a "hell-spawn" as the fanatics purported to oppose.

Kincaid drove to the far west of the City, to one of the trendier neighborhoods, made a left turn at the entrance to the Cherry Valley subdivision, and continued to the southernmost street. He pulled up in front of a white stucco, Victorian-style semi-mansion and cut the engine. The detective gazed at the luxurious house and marveled that the City's chief executive could afford such a residence. On the other hand, he was not surprised that the Archdeacon was a "guest" here; knowing Fogarty as he did, he knew the old man was attracted to wealth. It was well-known that, before he had become a "man of the cloth," he had led a simple life with few of the amenities many of his peers enjoyed. Larkin surmised that this sort of a background had been the driving force in the Archdeacon's choice of profession; without too much effort on his part to be a respected authority figure, he could be sought out and fawned over by the rich and poor alike and therefore enjoy a life-style he never could have afforded otherwise.

If the exterior of the Mayor's house bespoke of luxury, the interior bespoke of opulence. As soon as Larkin stepped inside, he was greeted by a scenario fit for royalty. A thick, plush, wall-to-wall carpet adorned the entryway and continued on into the adjoining rooms. Filmy lace curtains covered all of the windows. Potted plants stood in every corner. Glass chandeliers hung from every ceiling. In the living room, several stuffed, leather sofas and chairs were strategically placed to allow easy conversation no matter where one sat. In the dining room, table and chairs carved from logs of mahogany accommodated twenty-four diners. What the other rooms looked like, he was never to know, for Kincaid waved him to one of the leather chairs, ending the unguided tour. The Disciple then mounted a stairway (also carpeted) to the upper story.

How long the detective waited was anybody's guess – too long, in his estimation. He was never comfortable in the presence of the Archdeacon, no matter how luxurious the environment. He felt as trapped here as he had been in the apartment of the late Mr. Jones and wished he was somewhere else. Yet, he had chosen to engage Fogarty in his Grand Plan, and he had to take the bad with the good (although it seemed like the one outweighed the other).

Presently, Kincaid returned, followed by the old man and another man Larkin had seen before. The latter was the same large grinning idiot Sheena had identified as Farquhar in one of his many guises. What in the hell was *he* doing here? And was he visible to only him? This situation was getting hairier by the second!

Nevertheless, he dutifully rose to his feet at Fogarty's entrance and waited until the man sat down on one of the sofas before resuming his own seat. Kincaid took a chair opposite that of the detective and maintained a steady scrutiny of him. The grinning idiot plopped down on the same sofa as the Archdeacon had. Neither Disciple seemed to be aware of him. The scene was much too bizarre for Larkin's taste, and he *really* wished he was somewhere else. But he was stuck here.

"I'm pleased that you were able to meet with me on such short notice, Brother Larkin," the City's foremost "moral compass" said disingenuously. "You're here because what I wish to discuss with you requires a more private environment."

"Thank you for your…invitation, Your Worship," Larkin responded just as disingenuously. "I am greatly honored. How may I be of service this time?"

"Well, it's embarrassing for me to say so, but I have need of your professional abilities."

"You need a detective?" Larkin asked, genuinely astonished by the admission.

"Yes, indeed. Ordinarily, I'd employ one of my own people – Brother Kincaid for one – but the matter is so delicate that I'd rather not involve anyone within the organization."

"I…see. Which of my abilities do you need?"

"I want you to find someone for me -- one of my own people in fact. He seems to have…disappeared. I trust you'll be discreet in this matter?" The detective nodded in acquiescence. "Fine. This Disciple has strayed from the Light of Purity, I'm afraid. He has claimed to have received a 'message' from the Lord to the effect that the Light of Purity is a hoax and that all of us should turn away from it."

"Excuse me, sir, but I thought the…Lord spoke to all of you."

"Indeed He does, as needed. You see my dilemma, Brother Larkin. I believe that this unfortunate soul has received a *false* message – not from the Lord, as he claims, but from the Devil himself (who is also driving those whom you have pointed out). I see a massive conspiracy of evil at work here. If only I could speak to this lost soul, I'm sure I could bring him back to the Light of Purity."

"Well, I'll see what I can do, Your Worship."

"Thank you, Brother Larkin. Brother Kincaid will take you back to your office and provide you with a photo of the wayward Disciple. Good-bye."

As the detective got up to leave, he glanced at the grinning idiot who winked at him. He shook his head in disbelief and hurried to the front door.

Later, after Kincaid had dropped him off, he pondered the Archdeacon's "dilemma" and request. The implications were astounding. From its inception, the Return-to-Purity movement had presented itself as a formidable monolith, a rock-solid organization single-mindedly pursuing a specific goal, i.e. the complete domination of the entire Earth heralding the Age of the Light. All those in the organization – from the Archbishop-*cum*-President of the United States, Hadley Richardson, to the newest convert – had no other purpose in life but to work tirelessly and selflessly toward that goal. Those who failed to do so were as persecuted as those who resisted the movement.

When the movement took off in the closing years of the twentieth century, the Christian Coalition had decided to manage it as a separate entity. Their rationale was two-fold: first, they wanted to give Hadley Richardson a vehicle of his own so that his new popularity could draw more people to The Cause; and, second, they wanted to keep the new organization's base separate in case the idea proved to be a flash in the pan and fizzle out, thus tainting the main organization. Richardson was pleasantly surprised when he was told of the plan – the first part of it, however – and immediately drew up a platform and recruited a number of people closely allied to him to implement the planks of that platform.

Richardson divided the United States into twelve parts – "provinces" – centered around the major metropolitan areas of the country in order to facilitate the implementation. He grandiosely named himself as the "Archbishop" and "ordained" twelve of his closest allies as "Senior Bishops" to take charge of the "provinces." Each province was subsequently divided into twelve "parishes," and each "parish" was the bailiwick of a "Junior Bishop." It was a grand conceit on the part of "Archbishop" Richardson, one which could have easily backfired on him; yet, such was his popularity and the disgust of the general population over the direction the country was going that he pulled the scheme off admirably. Dissenters abounded, of course – there were always dissenters to one philosophy or another – but they were sidelined by a wave of religious fervor.

On their own, but tacitly approved by the Archbishop, the provincial leaders created new subordinate groupings on the local level – Archdeaconates, Deaconates, and Fellowships. The first held sway over whole states, the second took charge of municipalities, and the third operated in neighborhoods. Very little was left to chance when it came to proselytizing and converting. And the fact that, as the twenty-first century dawned, the ranks of the movement swelled immensely, justified the organization's activities.

And in all the twenty years that the Return-to-Purity movement had been in existence, its membership had stood shoulder-to-shoulder in pursuit of its goal. Not once had anyone questioned either the goal or the methods by which that goal was pursued.

Until now.

How had it been possible, given the thorough indoctrination each convert received? Larkin knew how, and he was immensely pleased. The Archdeacon had said that the wayward Disciple claimed to have heard God speaking to him, although he hadn't elaborated on the circumstances of that "revelation." Somehow, someone had planted a seed of doubt in the man's mind; and, in his confusion, he had believed he was receiving a message from on high. And the detective knew who that "someone" was – one Paddington Smythe, prankster. Larkin would locate this Disciple all right, but not for the reason given by Fogarty. Rather, he hoped to protect the fellow from the sort of "interrogation" the Archdeacon had in mind and to recruit him to the "other side."

* * *

Browsing Unlimited was nearly empty at the time Larkin entered it. Usually, there was a crowd from the time the store opened until it closed; usually, there were potential customers waiting outside for the doors to open and actual customers hurried out the door at the close. For some unknown reason, today was different.

The detective noted that only three people were browsing. One was the *hausfrau* he had seen before; she had returned to find more cookbooks by which to dazzle her friends and neighbors with her culinary skills. From the shaking of her head and the frown on her face, he deduced that she was frustrated in her explorations. As she pushed aside one book after another, a few fell on the floor, but she was too focused on her search to retrieve them and put them back where she had found them.

The second potential customer was a short, balding man who perspired heavily and frequently mopped his face and neck with an oversized maroon handkerchief. Curiously, he was not passing through the stacks but stood rooted to one spot and turned his head this way and that as if to spot what he wanted by some form of mental osmosis. If he possessed *psi*-talent, then he was very bold about using it in public. Larkin doubted he was a candidate for DEDEP, however; the fellow was simply displaying uncertainty, unaware that he was making a spectacle of himself.

The third would-be buyer was another of that rare breed in a bookstore, a Disciple who read something other than the latest propaganda from Fogarty's printing press. The detective made a point of wandering his way in order to learn why the man was here. He pushed past the white-suit, reached around him, and mumbled an insincere "Excuse me." As he did so, he quickly glanced at the selection the other had just made and was shocked to see that it was a tattered copy of Emil Razumov's *Radiopsychology: The New Science of the Future*, which was standard reading for all of DEDEP. But why was this Disciple so interested in Emil's "bible"? Was it simple curiosity, or was it something more sinister?

This fellow bore closer inspection. Larkin scanned his face as he turned to go toward the check-out counter and received another shock. He had seen that face before and not too long ago either. Surreptitiously, he pulled the photo Kincaid had given him as he was exiting the sedan, the photo of the "lost sheep" he had been "commissioned" to find. The photo was hardly professional in nature, but it matched the Disciple not six feet away from him. He had come here to enlist the Twins' abilities to find an unknown person, and he had found him by accident!

Neither Kenny nor Paddy was at the counter (whosever turn it was to be on duty) – a further surprise. It meant that both were in the back room. Nonchalantly, he maneuvered his way in that direction and, after checking to assure himself that he was not being paid any attention, gently rapped on the door.

"Come on in, George."

Larkin stepped inside and discovered the Twins engaged in a chess match. Neither player seemed to have an advantage, but that was no surprise.

"How can you two play chess?" he had to ask. "Each of you would always know what the other's moves would be."

"This is one of those rare times, old darling, when…"

"…we 'turn off' our minds and act as if we…"

"…were ordinary mortals. Granted, it's sometimes…"

"…difficult, but we usually muddle through."

"Huh! I wouldn't have believed it if I hadn't seen it with my own eyes." He paused, then shook his head. "I still don't believe it."

"What might we do for you, George?" Kenny asked as he moved one of his pawns forward to threaten one of Paddy's knights.

"First of all, who's minding the store?"

"I am," Paddy replied as he moved his knight laterally out of harm's way. "If those blokes out there need anything, they can bloody well ring the bell."

"Seems like a slow day today."

"Indeed it does," said Kenny as he moved his queen's bishop across the board to dominate Paddy's king's side. "That's why we can have a jolly good game of chess."

"Well, I had a task for you, but it seems I don't need you."

"Marvelous," Paddy murmured as he castled on his king's side. "What's changed your mind?"

The detective withdrew the photo from his coat pocket and handed it over. The Twins both scanned it briefly in turn. At Paddy's turn, his eyes went wide with surprise.

"Bloody hell!" he exclaimed and broke into a grin.

"What is it, dear heart?"

"This is the bloke I pulled that prank on the other day. What's this all about, old darling?"

"It seems like your little prank may be paying dividends. The Archdeacon wants me to find this character, because he's suspected of preaching heresy. Since religious fanatics are always paranoid, Fogarty is scared that this 'heretic' will infect others. Best case scenario: the Return-to-Purity movement will split into factions and lose its credibility."

"What a delicious thought! To see…"

"…those buggers fighting amongst themselves…"

"…would warm the cockles of our hearts. Would…"

"…you like us to play some more 'pranks'? We…"

"…have several tricks up our sleeves we'd like to play."

"Let's run with this ball for a while."

"As you wish," Paddy acquiesced. "But what did you mean you didn't need us to find him for you?"

"I don't. He's outside, browsing. And he's got a copy of Emil's book in his hands."

"Good God!" the Twins exclaimed in unison.

"Right. Keep an eye on him, hmmm?"

"Will do, George. Ta-ta!"

The detective exited the back room as discreetly as he had entered it and made a show of wandering through the stacks again. The Disciple was still absorbed by the DEDEP "bible."

Yes, we'll all keep an eye on that one.

UF⊕'S

"UFO BUZZES CITY," screamed the main headline of the City's daily newspaper, the *Sentinel-News*.

And the secondary headline read: "AERIAL PHENOMENON SIGHTED FOR SEVERAL HOURS."

The first sighting occurred about an hour before sunset. Four patrons of Woody's Tavern at the corner of Ridgeway Avenue and Elmwood Drive were the first to spot it. They were chatting outside prior to entering the establishment when one of them happened to glance eastward and saw what he described later as a "cigar-shaped" object rising into the sky. He then alerted his companions who reacted with varying degrees of alarm; two of them confirmed their companion's description, while the third claimed to have seen a "saucer-shaped" object. All agreed that the UFO's color was black and that there were several flashing white lights fore and aft of the thing. One of them subsequently ran into the tavern, first, to alert those inside and, second, to call the police.

Soon, a sizeable crowd gathered outside the tavern, consisting of not only patrons and its bartender but also a number of residents in the neighborhood who were drawn out by the hub-bub taking place. Several more varying descriptions were reported, and two or three minor arguments concerning the nature of the UFO broke out. A police squad arrived before matters got out of hand; the officers spent nearly an hour alternately taking statements, eyeballing the UFO themselves, and cooling tempers. Meanwhile, the thing circled the area several times before ascending further into the sky and flying off westward at "jet speed," according to one witness.

The crowd did not break up until very late at night but speculated endlessly about what they had seen. Some thought it had been an experimental aircraft being tested by the U.S. Air Force (which, later, denied any such activity). Others believed it had been a conventional aircraft, but they were immediately hooted down. A few claimed it was an alien spaceship and "men from Mars" had finally arrived; they too were debunked in often obscene terms. A few others concluded it had all been a hallucination, and they had to be rescued by the police from those who resented the implication that they were "crazy." All in all, it was a night none of them would ever forget, even if none of them knew exactly what they had seen.

The next sighting occurred fifteen minutes after the UFO had departed the Ridgeway area. It was spotted by a group of shoppers at a mall on the City's far west side. Here, it took time out to perform some rather complex aerial maneuvers – some witnesses said that "no ordinary aircraft could do what that thing could do" – before speeding off westward. Again, descriptions of the object varied, as did the speculations on its origin, and more arguments accompanied them.

The City's police department was kept busy all night fielding calls from panicky residents who wanted to know what was going on. Unfortunately for their peace of mind, the 9-1-1 operator provided only the standard bland statement authorities everywhere issued in cases like this. Curiously, the Mayor was on the phone with the Archdeacon rather than with some higher government official, asking the same questions and getting the same answers. One local pundit likened the event to the infamous 1938 radio broadcast of H.G. Wells' *War of the Worlds*, but he quickly disallowed any danger to America and added that he was as puzzled by the sightings as anyone else.

The most notable statement on the subject was provided the next day by Archdeacon Fogarty, who was interviewed by the *Sentinel-News* at Disciple headquarters. The City's "spiritual leader" averred, in his considered opinion, that "we are witnessing the signs and wonders as described in the Book of Revelations" and that "these are the End Times, when the Lord will make His Second Coming, as it was prophesized, and set forth divine judgment upon all the Earth." Predictably, his pronouncements did nothing to soothe the panicky residents but made them even more despondent.

The last official sighting of the UFO occurred around 3 a.m. in the southwest by late-night revelers. Due to their low level of sobriety, no one took them seriously, and no one saw the thing descend toward the horizon and disappear from view at the Ridgeway area.

The *Sentinel-News*, always ready with a clever retort, thereafter referred to the night's "festivities" as "the day the City stood still." The retort outraged thousands of residents, and the newspaper's telephone lines were inundated by calls by irate people (many of whom cancelled their subscriptions); and, for two weeks, a solid stream of letters-to-the-editor arrived, but only the most coherent were printed (including more requests for cancellation).

* * *

The day after the UFO flap, Larkin read the articles on it in the *Sentinel-News* three times. Since he possessed an eidetic memory, there was little need to; a quick scan was all he required, and he could recall whatever he read years later. The only reason for repeated reading (he told himself) was to savor each word and chuckle over the folly of the local press.

Two things in particular amused him. The first was the number of witnesses who had concluded that the Earth was being visited by beings from another world. This number divided up into two distinct camps: those who believed that the visitors were benevolent and wished to make contact in order to share their knowledge and wisdom; and those who believed that the visitors were hostile and wished to conquer Earth and enslave humankind. Both camps would have been greatly shocked to learn the truth of the matter, and neither would have been pleased by the implications.

The second was Archdeacon Fogarty's take on the UFO phenomenon. The old man had spectacularly put an apocalyptic spin on the incident and played it up for all it was worth. His views fell somewhere in between the "benevolents" and the "hostiles" in that the visitors were here to pass judgment upon a "sinful" people and to take the "righteous," i.e. his group, up to Heaven. He too would have been shocked to learn the truth of the matter and would not be pleased by the implications. It was Larkin's job to convince him that the "signs" and "wonders" had more to do with the "satanic" creatures the Disciples purported to oppose and less to do with their salvation.

Historically, humankind had been puzzled by aerial phenomena, ascribing a wide range of explanations for their existence. Mostly, superstitious explanations reigned supreme (and still did in the twenty-first century) whereby it was claimed that "gods" or "demons" visited the Earth to work their will upon powerless mortals. As the centuries passed and more knowledge of the natural world accumulated, many UFO's could be explained away as planets, optical illusions, or mass hysteria; as technological skills grew, many more UFO's could be explained away as misidentified aircraft, balloons, or hoaxes. People had seen something beyond their understanding and they wanted an explanation they could believe and tell them what it meant for the future of the species.

Truth to tell, neither George Larkin nor Emil Razumov had not put much stock in the possibility of intelligent life on other planets whose own sense of curiosity had been piqued by what might be "out there." The detective thought the UFO phenomenon was "interesting but had no immediate relevance"; the parapsychologist had briefly studied the question as an adjunct to the psychic and occult phenomena he was working into a theory of radiopsychology but had dismissed it also as irrelevant.

Now, however, reality was staring both of them in the face, and they had had to re-evaluate their views on the subject. Now, both knew that there was indeed intelligent life on other worlds and that some of it had visited the Earth in times past and was visiting it in the present. And the prospects deriving from the latter did not bode well for humankind.

As he read and re-read the news reports, Larkin recalled hearing one elderly gentleman in the City propound an alternative theory on the existence of intelligent life elsewhere. This gentleman claimed that the laws of probability dictated the fact. Furthermore, he claimed that all intelligent life wherever it was found occupied specific places on a spectrum of technological and social development parallel to the spectrum which existed on Earth, i.e. from the primitive societies in the southern hemisphere to the highly technological ones in the north. It was quite obvious to him that more advanced beings had visited Earth in the past, not out of benevolence or malevolence but out of simple curiosity, and that they had no interest in either sharing wisdom or enslaving the indigenous population. The detective wondered how this gentleman would react if he learned about the Swarm and their *raison d'etre*.

He then went online and called up other newspapers in the Mid-West, from Ohio to Nebraska, from Minnesota to Kentucky. North, south, and east, reports on UFO's appeared on page three and were sketchy; taken verbatim from the newswire, one article read like another. Westward, however, it was a different story altogether. In western Illinois, Iowa, and Nebraska, the sightings were legion and made the front page; they were very detailed, and extensive quotations from eyewitnesses peppered every article. The further west one went, the greater the number of sightings. In Omaha, the headlines were as bold as those which had appeared in the *Sentinel-News*; thousands had seen a light show like no other, and the same sense of alarm filled every page.

Larkin could track the UFO by matching newspaper articles to points on a map. It had made a straight line from the City to Omaha and wreaked fear and loathing at all points on the line. He could picture in his mind's eye the Swarm craft making some initial maneuvers in order to ascertain how well it functioned after take-off and then dashing off to report to the base in Nebraska. Eventually, it would return to the City and wait for the order to perform its awful purpose. The thought sent a shiver up his spine.

He turned next to his e-mail account, expecting to hear from the Quintessential Quark very shortly. He had no doubt that his "informant" would be all over the map on this one.

He was not disappointed. The second message posted for the day contained the familiar long, rambling "update" he had come to know and love. From his vantage point near the Swarm base – did he camp out there? – the Quark had spotted the craft as it approached from the east at a rapid velocity and made one circle around the base before landing. He reported that two "Martians" disembarked and were greeted by the chief "Martian"; the three spoke briefly to one another and entered the smallest structure. The Quark had remained where he was in order to monitor the base further, and he was glad (he said) he had brought some "uppers" with him or else he would have been "totally freaked out, man!" Nothing out of the (relative) ordinary occurred until shortly before 3 a.m. The three "Martians" re-emerged from the small structure and spoke briefly to each other; the pilots embarked and took off again, making another complete circle before flying eastward. The Quark ended with his "signature" statement.

The detective could have told him, but he was afraid his reply would have sent the fellow into a spiral of psychosis. He really would have been "freaked out."

As Larkin re-read the Quark's message, he was aware of the creak of the door to the "snoop room" being opened, followed by the scrape of a stool across the floor, and the warmth of Sheena's breath on his cheek as she looked over his shoulder. He felt another shudder along his spine, but this one was altogether pleasurable. He sighed deeply without realizing that he was doing so.

"Did you get any sleep last night?" he inquired without turning around.

"Hardly. Everybody in my apartment building was running up and down the hallways and running in circles around the yard, making nervous comments about the UFO. It was *gruesome*! How about you?"

"Same here. Since I already suspected what caused the commotion, I spent part of the night observing the behavior of everyone else. And you're right: it *was* gruesome. Speaking of which, check this out."

He reached over to his master control panel, switched on the voice synthesizer, and replayed the Quark's message. A soft, feminine voice repeated every sentence exactly. It was a most incongruous sound – the informant's disjointed sentence structure (especially the concluding comment) in dulcet tones. The detectives had to work hard to keep a straight face. At the completion of the message, Sheena grunted in amazement.

"You weren't kidding, George. This *is* frightening. If the Quark is right, then we should expect to have more sightings."

"Uh-huh. Lacey should have her hands full on this one. She'll --"

He was interrupted by the telephone when it rang, momentarily startling him. He relaxed when the caller ID identified a Washington, D.C., number, and that meant only one person. He activated the speaker-phone function.

"Gordy!" he boomed. "What's up?"

"Besides my Irish?" The ex-F.B.I. agent launched into a highly sarcastic account of the latest actions of President (Archbishop) Hadley Richardson's Administration, liberally laced with choice obscenities. At the end, he heaved a sigh of frustration and added: "Does that answer your question, old buddy?"

"Quite. But I suppose you didn't call to share the latest gossip."

"For sure. I caught the news on the *Today* show about the UFO flap in your neck of the woods. Most people around here are treating the reports with the usual grain of salt. But, from what you've told me, I suspect this is the real thing."

"And you'd be right, chum." The detective brought his friend up to speed on the Swarm's activities which elicited a long, loud whistle at the other end. "The best case scenario is that the Swarm is preparing for some sort of military operation."

"The *best* case? What's the *worst* case?"

"Oh, invasion. Utter destruction. Genocide. That sort of thing."

"You're freaking me out, old buddy."

"I'm just stating the possibilities. Relax. We've got a couple of aces up our sleeves."

"I should hope so. I plan to live to a ripe old age."

"We all do, Gordy," Sheena interjected.

"Sheena. How're you doing, gorgeous?"

"Just fine, thank you, handsome sir. How's yourself?"

"Wel-l-l, I could use some female companionship in my ripe old age. Will you marry me?"

"I'll take your proposal under consideration. However, you should know that I've had several other offers."

"I'll just bet you have. Anyone I know?"

"Nope. I'll have to get back to you on that."

All during this little repartee, Larkin frowned deeply. Even though his head told him that Gordy and Sheena were just joking around, his heart told him he could lose Sheena to some other suitor if he continued to avoid expressing his feelings for her. Yet, he still could not overcome the barrier his physical disabilities presented to him. Listening to his best friend and his heart's desire jousting with each other in a playful manner did nothing to lower his level of frustration.

"Well, if you've got nothing more to add, old buddy, I'll be signing off."

"Eh? Oh, no, no. That's all I have for now. Be talking to you later."

Larkin disconnected and regarded his partner for a long moment, wondering if this was the right time to declare himself. His hesitation defeated him. Sheena regarded *him* for a long moment, then brushed his cheek lightly with her fingertips and departed. He cursed himself for his indecisiveness.

* * *

When Larkin and Sheena returned from lunch, Mrs. Watson handed the former a message slip. It was from Mr. Smith, who had been there not fifteen minutes ago. Short and to the point, it read: "Urgent I speak with you."

The message raised hopes that maybe, with the UFO flap, the Coalition had changed its stance concerning providing DEDEP some advanced weaponry. One could always hope. In the meantime, Larkin busied himself with updating files and billing clients. Though Mr. Smith had said "urgent," he needed time to return to his base. Sheena asked to accompany him, a request which took him by surprise since she had had such a difficult time coping with the EMF in the abandoned supermarket on her previous visit. She would not go inside, however, but wait for him in the station wagon as before. Still, her company was welcome for more than one reason.

When he arrived at the alien's base, the detective made a rapid (though still agonizing) passage through the "back of the house" and spied Mr. Smith engaged in conversation with one of his fellow agents on Earth. Larkin came to that conclusion by noting that one of the ten lesser towers – instead of the taller one – was glowing brightly. Where this particular agent was located, he had no clue – not that it made any difference in the greater scheme of things; but wherever the agent was, he represented yet another alien species.

He had a round face, or so the detective assumed, because he could not see all of the face. The new alien had a huge mop of black hair which completely covered the upper part of his skull; and he wore a large bushy, black beard which covered up most of the lower part. His skin was swarthy, and his eyes were two black beads set deep into their sockets. A pug nose and thick lips protruded from the beard.

Larkin again made no effort to conceal himself – what was the point? he was an ally of the Coalition, wasn't he? – but ambled in as if he had every right to be there. As soon as Mr. Smith's colleague spied them, he stopped speaking in an even tone and barked something sharply. Mr. Smith turned, recognized his visitor, and gave him a brief smile. He addressed his colleague again and said something apparently mollifying while gesturing at the human, and the "black beard" returned to his even tone of voice.

Eventually, the conversation drew to a close, and the smaller monitor darkened. Mr. Smith switched off the array and greeted his visitor more formally.

"Hhhello…again…Mr.…Largin.   Thhang…you…for… responding …so…quigly."

"Your message said 'urgent,' Mr. Smith. I, uh, took it to heart. We have much to discuss."

"Yes...we...do. I...hhhave...been...monitoring...thhhe...reports... about...thhe...'UFO's'...of...last...night. Whhhat...gan...you...tell... me... about...them?"

"What I have to say will shock you."

Larkin recounted everything he knew about recent Swarm activities, beginning with a carefully edited version of the monitoring of the abandoned factory and finishing with the Quark's report on the happenings in Nebraska. With each sentence, the alien's face registered ever-increasing distress, and he stroked his nose repeatedly. Oily perspiration beaded his face.

"My feeling," the detective concluded, "is that the Swarm have stepped up their timetable due to the unexplained loss of their agent, Mr. Jones, and that they are testing their war machine in preparation for an assault on the City."

Mr. Smith did not respond immediately but continued to regard empty space with horror and to abuse his nose. Was he recalling the events on his own world? Did he foresee the same fate for this world? In the Coaliton agent's place, Larkin might have reacted in a similar fashion. Presently, the other faced his human ally with sadness in his eyes.

"It...is...as...I...feared...Mr....Largin. Thhhe...'UFO's'...gould... not... hhhave...been...a...goincidence. You...hhhave...certainly... gome...to... thhhe...gorregt...gonglusion. I...must...gontagt... thhhe...Goalition... right...away...and...inform...thhhem...of... thhhese...new... developments."

"Of course." Larkin paused momentarily, then: "Um, in light of this new development, could you renew my request for some *defensive* weaponry?"

"I...will...do...so...but...I...am...not...optimistig. You...will... egsguse... me...now."

Larkin departed as quickly as he had arrived. As soon as he clambered into the station wagon, he brought Sheena up to speed. Alarm was written large across her face.

"It sounds like he was on the verge of a nervous break-down."

"Huh! Would you have blamed him, after what he had been through personally? I don't know much about alien psychology myself, but I think it's imperative that we do what we can to keep Mr. Smith on an even keel. There's no telling what he might do otherwise."

Sheena was about to comment on that point, but Larkin held up a hand for silence. He had just felt a buzzing in his head which could mean only one thing: the Twins were contacting him.

*George, old darling [Paddy's voice sounded], I've been tracking the bloke you wanted us to find.

*Great. Where is he now?

*On the corner of New York and Union. And he's spouting all sorts of 'heretical' things.

*That's not too far from where I'm at. I'll buzz by there and see what's what. Thanks, Paddy.

*Glad to be of service. Toodle-oo!

* * *

The segment of Union Street between Main and New York was an island of commerce in a sea of single- and multi-family residences. The major business in the area was one of several in the City of the Golden Arches chain of hamburger purveyors; it took up the entire southeast corner, replete with gaudy signage and parking space for a dozen or more vehicles. Next to it, on the northeast corner of Union and Main, a handful of retail shops. Across New York, on the northeast corner, a mini-strip mall boasted half a dozen more shops, chief of which was a pizza parlor. Across the street from the Golden Arches, on the northwest corner, one could visit a medical clinic if one spoke Spanish; all of the signage was in that language. On the northwest corner of Union and New York, also for the Spanish-speaking, was a supermarket with a butcher shop and a bakery for added features. To round out the variety of businesses, a small used-car dealership hunkered on the northeast corner of Union and Main; and across the street, on the southwest corner, stood a bilingual auto-repair shop.

Changing demographics resulted in this area of the City being heavily Hispanic in nature. Most of the residences surrounding this miniature business "district" were occupied by immigrants from "south of the border," who had replaced a largely Caucasian population after the latter removed themselves to the new subdivisions on the fringes of the City. One supposed the several businesses would cater to all ethnic groups – money was money after all, regardless of who possessed it – but most of the clientele were the locals, and some businesses were blatant about whom they would serve.

One would also suppose that this would not be a likely place for Disciples to be proselytizing. One would be wrong, for it was an area heavily targeted by the Archdeacon's army.

On this particular day, a large number of Disciples were in the neighborhood, but none of them were proselytizing. Rather, they were gathered around one of their own, listening intently to what he had to say. This individual of medium height and build with brown hair and eyes was holding court (as it were) as he had done for the dozenth time in the past few days. His "sermon" followed a pattern: first, he recounted how he had been recruited into the Return-to-Purity movement, what his personal goals had been, and what some of his "good works" had been; second, he described the events surrounding his "conversion" and his subsequent meditations on them; third, he spoke about how he had re-examined all he had been taught as a Disciple in light of the Lord's admonition to follow a different path; and fourth, he admitted to an "inner struggle" to know the Truth and concluded that he had been chosen to preach a new "gospel." During this discourse, he remained calm and spoke quietly but forcefully, knowing full well (as he mentioned repeatedly) that many – even in this audience – would not receive his message with enthusiasm.

His assessment of his fellow Disciples' reception of his preaching was quite correct, as he had learned the hard way. He told of the times he had been set upon by the more extreme members; they had shouted out epithets like "backslider," "heretic," and "apostate," and they had countered his statements with rote from Disciple propaganda. And, when they had failed to convince him of the error of his ways, they had resorted to pushing and shoving. He told how he had been spared more physical violence by some few who were more thoughtful – but no less skeptical – and counseled against it in the name of the Light of Purity. Nevertheless, the "convert" remained adamant that all Disciplehood should hear what the Lord was telling him to say.

Some few in his audience asked him questions, asked for elaboration of his views, and, more importantly, asked for proof of his allegations. Most, however, were skeptical and muttered to each other in derogatory terms. The scene was beginning to turn ugly as Larkin and Sheena pulled up to the curb. They exited the station wagon and walked slowly toward the crowd. A young male noticed them, detached himself from the group, and hurried over to meet them. By no mean co-incidence, he was the same pockmarked youth whom they had encountered downtown and who had warned them of the Swarm presence. He greeted them breathlessly.

"Brother Larkin, Sister Whitley, do you remember me?"

"Yes, of course. That little fracas on Main Street. You were in the right place at the right time. Your actions were most commendable."

"Thank you," the young man gushed. "How may I help you now?"

"You should know that we're not here by accident. His Worship sent us to locate that…lost soul who's created a big stir. We mean to escort him back to HQ."

"I see. Well, we'd better hurry before something terrible happens."

The young Disciple turned and hurried off to announce the arrival of the Archdeacon's personal "emissary." Sheena chuckled throatily.

"How does it feel to be a VIP in the Return-to-Purity movement?"

"Ha-ha. Very funny. But I'll play the part as long as it gets results." He paused. "Ordinarily, I'd let those clowns beat each other up. It would serve that 'heretic' right if he got a taste of his own medicine."

"But?"

"*But*, it's in DEDEP's best interest to keep him healthy – and talking. So, it's off to the rescue, partner."

"I'm sensing rising hostility, George. They're on the verge of rage. How are you going to convince them to hand the 'heretic' over to you?"

"I've got an idea. Hold on a minute."

Larkin retrieved his cell phone and tapped out a number. After the second ring, a familiar tinny voice responded.

"Hello, world."

"Hello, Chris, it's George."

"Hello, George. What's up?"

"Are you busy right now?"

"Nothing I can't put aside for a while. What do you need?"

"I need your 'angel' again. I've got a pack of Disciples I want to be put into line. I'll leave my cell phone open so you can listen in. Just wait for my cue, then ad-lib. OK?"

"OK. I love playing an 'angel.'"

Sheena shook her head and grinned.

"You are *so* devious!"

"Aren't I though?"

The detectives continued closing the gap between them and the angry crowd. The closer they came, the more distinct were individual voices. With few exceptions, they were angry voices, rising in pitch. Several Disciples began to move toward the 'heretic' to silence him once and for all. One male voice in particular began the cruel litany Larkin had heard too many times before when the Disciples intended to "cast out" someone. It was interrupted by the young Disciple who directed attention toward the Archdeacon's "emissary."

All heads now regarded the newcomers with interest. Larkin felt his stomach knotting up. He had to conduct this little role-playing very carefully, or his scheming would come to naught. Like all of their kind, these Disciples had been so thoroughly indoctrinated by RPP propaganda that they could not think further than the ends of their noses. Only a "miracle" would turn them aside from the course they had been taught to follow. The detective intended to provide that "miracle."

A couple of Disciples recognized him from previous encounters and regarded him expectantly. The rest remained suspicious. For his part, he exuded cordiality toward everyone with whom he made eye contact. When he neared his "herald," he took his hand and shook it vigorously. The young man responded with enthusiasm, pleased to be in the presence of a RPP VIP. Larkin turned to address the crowd.

"Be careful, George," Sheena whispered. "Some of these characters have murder on their minds."

"I hear you," he whispered back. To the Disciples, he declared: "You've been told that I represent Archdeacon Fogarty. While I am not formally one of you, I have chosen to ally myself with His Worship. There is an evil abroad, one which threatens the whole world, and His Worship has called upon my skills as a private detective to fight the Good Fight in the name of the Light of Purity."

More mutterings issued from the crowd, but less intense and murderous than before. Larkin felt he was pushing the right buttons by invoking the "Light of Purity" and began to take advantage of it.

"Now," he continued, "evil takes many forms. This man" – he gestured at the "heretic" who by now was more resolute in his efforts despite the danger to his person – "has been judged by some of you as 'evil.' It is true he brings a message seemingly – *seemingly*, I say – contrary to what you have been taught. Whether he is evil is not for us to say. That is why His Worship instructed me to bring this man to him. He is imminently qualified to judge who is evil and who is not, and he will determine the truth of the matter."

"But can we trust *you* to deliver him up?" the voice of the Disciple who had begun the vicious litany called out.

"Call the Archdeacon then, if you doubt me. He is, after all, God's emissary, is he not? He will say what is true and what is not."

More mutterings were heard, and they were filled with confusion and indecision. Suddenly, a female voice cried out in shock.

"Oh, my God! Look!"

All heads turned toward the direction to which she was pointing. As one person, the entire group registered consternation; many, both male and female, began to cry, and all fell to their knees in abject fear. Neither Larkin nor Sheena had to look at what the Disciples were witnessing, the one because he had called up the phenomenon, the other because she had sensed the familiar vibration of a psycho-projection.

Christopher Wredling had picked up his cue and put in an appearance!

His appearance was the same as that which he had assumed only days before when he "led" some Disciples to attack the late Mr. Jones and his henchmen – a pile of blonde curls cascading to his shoulders and a long white robe suitable for church choirs, no wings or a halo but a "celestial aura" about him. What really astounded the Disciples was *where* the "angel" appeared. Chris had improvised in a manner which matched George's own deviousness by situating his projected image behind and slightly above the "heretic," giving the faithful the impression that the wayward Disciple had "divine blessing."

This gesture had not been lost on anyone, especially the object of the exercise. Once he got over his own shock, he too went to his knees – not out of fear, however, but out of adoration.

Larkin now gazed on Chris' image and feigned surprise, though he really wanted to laugh out loud at his collaborator's audaciousness. Though sightless, Sheena followed his lead, using her biometrical abilities.

"A messenger from the Lord!" the detective hammed it up. "We've been blessed!"

The "angel" placed its "hands" above the head of the "heretic" and smiled beatifically, a smile which was reciprocated. Abruptly, the "angel's" smile was replaced by a stern demeanor as the image regarded the quailing Disciples.

"THOU SHALT TROUBLE THIS MAN NO FURTHER," Chris declared in his best stentorious voice, "FOR HE IS AN INSTRUMENT OF THE LORD THY GOD. GO NOW, AND SEEK FORGIVENESS!"

With that pronouncement, the image blinked out of existence.

Instantly, a clamor erupted among the Disciples as confusion overtook them. Murmurs of regret and contriteness mingled with disbelief. The skeptics were decidedly in the minority, and they were quickly subdued by the majority. Larkin's "herald" seized the moment and admonished his cohorts to heed the advice of the "Lord's messenger." He was aided and abetted by the "heretic" who was relieved and pleased to learn that his "ministry" had not been in vain. One by one, the crowd dissipated, each individual lost in his/her own thoughts. Only the "heretic" remained behind, and he now regarded the detective with concern.

"Are you really going to turn me over to the Archdeacon?" he asked tremulously.

"I'm obliged to, much as I find it distasteful. You may recall that I was there when His Worship admonished you. He wasn't happy that you disobeyed him. Nevertheless, you seem to have received…God's 'stamp of approval,' as it were, and I for one would not like to be on the wrong side of this matter."

"So, what do I say to him?"

"You say exactly what you've been saying all along, and let him sort things out – if he can. You see that station wagon over there? Get in it and wait for us. 'Sister' Whitley and I need a moment to collect our thoughts."

"It was all I could do to keep from laughing out loud," Sheena remarked as soon as the "heretic" was out of earshot. "You and Chris put on quite a show."

"Thank you, Sheena," the tinny voice responded. "Do I get an Oscar?"

"I'd certainly nominate you for one," Larkin added. "That was a brilliant – if brief – piece of work."

"I thought so too. Well, I'm off to Nebraska. Talk to you later."

"And we're off to see the Archdeacon."

* * *

From the diary of Christopher Wredling:

It was great fun, pulling the wool over the eyes of Disciples. They're a heartless bunch for the most part, so dead serious about their beliefs and their "calling" to proselytize 24/7. Anytime anyone can get their goat is well worth the effort.

I have to admit that George's plan was especially brilliant – even for him, the 'master strategist.' The idea was to convince the more gullible among the Disciples that what they had been taught to believe was wrong and that they should be following a different 'gospel.' They would then tell others, and by that means, spread dissension throughout the Archdeaconate – and perhaps even beyond. Old man Fogarty would have his hands full trying to perform damage control before his whole organization fell apart.

No one knows that I love to play-act. I've watched any number of movies and studied the actors as they performed. Some of them have had great skill in convincing their audiences that their lines and gestures were genuine. If I had been born a mobile, I should like to have been an actor. George thought I deserved an Oscar for my 'performance' as an 'angel.' If only he knew how much I desired such a goal. If only…

The euphoria of that moment quickly wore off by the return trip to Nebraska. George needs regular reports from now on on the Swarm's activities; and, much as I found my previous visits extremely distasteful, I have to play another part, as a spy. I had been so lost in thought concerning the trick we played on the Disciples that I nearly collided with an EMF just outside of St. Louis, and my lack of attention almost cost me. My hitting an EMF is equivalent to a mobile running into a brick wall; even touching one causes severe pain. George and Emil thought my encounter with Mr. Jones' EMF was an isolated incident. It wasn't. I've experienced more similar incidents than I care to remember during the times when I was just learning to perfect my psycho-projectionism, and I've got the equivalent of what the mobiles call 'scar tissue' to show for it.

When I arrived at the Swarm base, I noticed one significant change in its appearance. The aliens had constructed a tower near one of their buildings; and, although I'm not familiar with alien architecture, the thing looked like a broadcasting antenna – and a fairly powerful one at that. If that is what it is, I can only speculate that they are preparing to contact their main fleet (wherever it is). And, if they are, it can only mean one thing: they're about to advise their 'high command' that the time is ripe for an invasion. It's crunch time, folks!

Otherwise, the soldiers were still in training mode. They had gotten their hands on a fresh supply of Disciples for 'target practice.' I tried to ignore that as much as I could, but it was hard to do what with the screams of terror filling the air.

To my great surprise, I learned that I wasn't the only spy in the area. As I was maneuvering around to get a closer look at that tower without being *detected myself, I spotted a furtive figure crouched behind a tree at the edge of the part of the clearing where the 'training' was taking place. I moved in to get a better look at him. Happily, he was so focused on the Swarm that he wasn't aware of my presence.*

He was a scrawny-looking fellow with a lean face and sunken cheeks. His eyes were set deep in their sockets, and they seemed…haunted. He hadn't shaved in days, and maybe he hadn't bathed for as long as well (I don't have a sense of smell, so I can't testify to that). His clothes were shabby, unkempt, and perhaps unwashed. All in all, he was a pitiful sight. Occasionally, he would pop something into his mouth and swallow it with difficulty. I can only surmise that he was doing drugs.

It didn't take a rocket scientist to determine who he was – George's weird informant who calls himself the 'Quintessential Quark' – and why he was there. He was snooping out the Swarm for the same reason I was. He had a pair of binoculars, a notepad, and a pencil, and was scribbling away like mad.

Abruptly, he stopped scribbling and peered about him in alarm. He couldn't have spotted me as I was high above him. Something else must've spooked him. Or else, he was hallucinating from the drugs he was taking. Whatever the reason, he departed in a crouching position.

I decided I'd seen enough too. George needed to be updated on the tower. He wasn't going to like what I had to report. And who could blame him? Things were starting to get hairy around here!

PROGRESS REPORT

OF ALL THE psi-*talents, psycho-occulism, a.k.a. "clairvoyance," is the most passive and therefore the most benign. In this regard, it is one step below its "cousin," psycho-oraculism, a.k.a. "precognition" (the subject of the next chapter). Psycho-occulism requires very little effort; it comes to one whose mind is at rest and receptive to various frequencies and fills that mind with wondrous images.*

In ancient times, this ability was known as "seeing visions." More often than not, the images appeared unbidden and took the form of scenes the psychic had never seen before or of current events (s)he could not have known about. Predictably, the arrival of such images caused much confusion and fear, and the one who had these visions may well have believed that (s)he was going mad. And, if (s)he had in all innocence told others about these visions, more than likely they also would have believed that insanity was at the heart of the matter; in the more extreme cases, (s)he would have been accused of "witchcraft," "possessed" by the Devil, and persecuted and/or tortured until such time as (s)he recanted

In rare cases, the psycho-occulist, having realized that (s)he possessed such talent, made a conscious effort to acquire the images and so learn of things no one else could. This sort of person was often called a "prophet." The motives for desiring such conscious efforts varied from psychic to psychic:

gaining new knowledge for its own sake; making money by selling one's "services"; gaining power over others whose ignorance could be exploited. Whatever the motive, however, the psychic had to exercise caution in whom (s)he confided, for (s)he could be denounced and put to death. The whole history of humankind is replete with gruesome tales of this sort....

...If then, psycho-occulism is the most passive and benign, it is also the most difficult to explain in terms of radiopyschology. Scenes and events which are perceived by the psycho-occulist are actually two different phenomena, and each must be explained separately. Furthermore, in the case of scenic views, there are two separate categories. Personal memories can trigger one category; by focusing on those memories, one may bring psycho-occulism into play. The second category, however, must be explained in the same manner as events are. This is because non-mnemonic scenes and current events are not ordinarily the progenitor of radio energy (which is at the core of radiopsychology) – at least, not directly.

The creation of radio energy in these cases must therefore be an indirect one, a "by-product" of a natural cause, if you will. We have already established that the human brain is an electro-chemical generator of radio energy and that this energy acts as a carrier for one's thoughts and memories which then can be picked up by another person who "operates" on or near the same frequency. Thus, what the psycho-occulist "sees" is actually an impression of a non-mnemonic scene or current event as viewed by someone else....

Joyce set the book aside and sighed deeply. The chapter on clairvoyance may have been the shortest one in Dr. Razumov's seminal work, but it was no less confusing than anything else she had read in it. She found the same technical jargon, the same dizzying concepts, and the same convoluted explanations, and it was all enough to make one want to throw the damned thing into the wastebasket. Yet, she was expected (more or less) to read it through so that she could be on a par with the rest of DEDEP. She certainly did not want to be viewed as being deficient in the eyes of her fellow "inmates" in this "looney bin."

Still, she had to admit, it would be useful to possess a *psi*-talent like clairvoyance. For one thing, it would help her keep an eye on her rascal of a son. Stan might not get into trouble all the time if he knew his mother was watching him, even at a distance. For another thing, she could have been more alert as to the whereabouts of those damned Disciples who were determined to punish him for being different and her for birthing him, as if it had been *her* fault that he was different.

It hadn't been her fault, she kept telling herself. Her family did not, as far as she knew, have a history of psychic abilities and/or strange behavior; at least, no one spoke openly of possessing the same for fear of inviting unwanted attention and/or vicious rumors and accusations.

No, the fault had to have been Stan's father. What had she known about him? Very little, it seemed. She had met him at a party shortly after she graduated from high school. He was good-looking and charming and had a winning smile, and he had swept her off her feet – quite literally, eventually. After a few routine dates where they acted like normal young people in love, there came the fateful tryst in the forest preserve which resulted in Stan's conception. And, as soon as his future father learned of the pregnancy, the rat deserted the ship, leaving her to sink or swim.

Did Stan's father possess a *psi*-talent and pass that gene which pre-disposed one to it on to his son? Joyce was sure she'd never know the answer. Still, it was the only logical explanation – if you could call the whole business of radiopsychology logical. She sighed again and wondered what to do next. She wasn't due at her work station for another two hours.

A gentle rapping at the door made the decision for her. When she opened the door, Jean Fulton was standing there with a tentative smile on her face.

"Jean! Hello. What a pleasant surprise."

"Hi, Joyce. Did I catch you at a bad time?"

"No, no. Come in." She waved the younger woman to the sofa and sat next to her. "What's on your mind?"

"Well, you said we could get together and have a talk. So, here I am. Freddie gave me a half-hour break, and I figured this was as good a time as any."

"OK. What'll we talk about?"

"I wanna know how long it took you to get used to this place."

"Ha! You're talking to the wrong person, Jean. I've only been here two weeks, and I'm still trying to adjust."

"No kidding? I thought you were an 'old hand.' You seemed so sure of yourself when we first met."

"Did I? I was shaking in my boots, hoping I wouldn't scare you off."

"So, we're both 'newbies,' huh? Well, we can commiserate with each other then."

"Fine by me. I could use being around someone who's not so intimidating."

"Is that how you see this place? Then we got another thing in common."

"Tell me about yourself. How'd you get to be an…'eel'?"

Jean leaned back against the sofa and stared at the ceiling for a moment. Where to begin? she wondered. Start from the first time she knew she was different? Earlier than that?

Jean remembered how, at the age of four, she started giving everyone in her family a small shock when she touched them. Her parents ascribed the phenomenon to her deliberately shuffling her feet when she walked and building up a charge of static electricity as a childish prank. Several times a day, she was admonished to walk "normally." She felt hurt by the constant scolding, because she thought she had been walking normally; and, since she couldn't explain why she was shocking everyone, she began to build a wall about herself. That only made things worse. Her parents wondered out loud if she were autistic.

After several years of odd behavior, they sought professional help. But a doctor who specialized in autism examined her thoroughly (and received several shocks himself in the process) and found no symptoms of the disorder, a pronouncement which further unsettled her parents. In the meantime, they received numerous complaints from one school administrator after another who fielded reports from teachers and students alike concerning electrical shocks. The consensus was that Jean was doing it deliberately to keep people away from her; the notion wasn't true, of course, but people tended to keep their distance after the third or fourth shock. The problem grew worse in her teenage years when most girls became interested in boys and dating. Her hormones were telling her one thing, but the rumors spreading about her were telling her another.

Eventually, she was "discovered" by the Psi Squad, who turned her over to Emil Razumov. Despite the frightening nature of the world of psychic phenomena – which she had always thought was the stuff of science fiction – she too wanted answers and so made the trip to the City.

A long silence followed the conclusion of Jean's tale of woe. Reactively, Joyce squeezed Jean's hands.

"Oh, Jean, you poor thing! And I thought *I* had it bad."

"I suppose it could have been worse. I could have been chased after by the Disciples."

"Well, I *was* chased by them – until George found me and Stan and brought us here."

"Hmmm. Another thing we got in common."

The two women gazed at each other for another long moment, communicating with that secret language women use amongst themselves.

* * *

Two years after Emil Razumov was smuggled out of the Soviet Union before he could be charged and prosecuted for "sedition," the Cold War between the USSR and the USA came to an abrupt end. The presence of the former in Afghanistan, intended to prop up a friendly government, had been a total disaster and brought the country to the brink of bankruptcy. Few Afghani cared for a government which tried to replace traditional values with Western ones, and various guerrilla groups (funded by the American CIA) made life miserable for the Soviets. The loss of so many Russian soldiers was an added point of contention; in a way, the average Russian viewed the war in Afghanistan in the same manner as the average American had viewed the war in Vietnam, and they staged their own protests. Premier Mikhail Gorbachev saw the handwriting on the wall and began withdrawing troops.

Gorbachev also announced the introduction of a new paradigm which he termed *perestroika* – in essence, an olive branch to the West. By this time, however, Washington was in the hands of staunch conservatives, anti-Communists all, and they saw an opportunity to destroy the Soviet Union once and for all. They needn't have bothered, as Premier Gorbachev had already had that in mind. Piece by piece, he dismantled the Soviet state and replaced it with a parliamentary system. The process was completed in 1991; and, under a new constitution, Gorbachev stood for election and won as the first President of the new Russia. Once in office, he completed what he had set out to do by spending more on social services and less on military matters, thus alienating a few powerful hold-overs from the previous regime. The combination of American machinations and domestic obstructionism led to his decision not to run for a second term.

The obstructionists backed the demagogue, Boris Yeltsin, as their candidate, seeing in him a return to more comfortable (and profitable) policies. But they did not foresee a grassroots upwelling by the general populace which had had enough of austerity and Cold War politics and which desired to perpetuate the new Russia. To this end, they turned to a most unlikely candidate, the scholar-turned-anti-war-protester, Andrei Sakharov. Dr. Sakharov was at first reluctant to enter the political arena on the grounds that he was not qualified, but daily rallies by his devotees finally persuaded him to accept the nomination. And so, in 1996, he became the second President of the new Russia, for better or for worse.

As it happened, it turned out for the better – for him at least. By this time, John F. Kennedy, Jr. was on his way to securing his re-election as President of the United States. The two men participated in a summit in early 1997 in which they pledged mutual friendship, entered into negotiations to reduce their nuclear arsenals, and signed a free-trade agreement between the former Soviet bloc and the former NATO bloc. The reduction of the arsenals proved to be a thorny issue – on both sides – but was eventually ratified by both national legislatures. Many joint ventures followed, including the Shackleton Lunar Base and the Antarctica Biological Preserve.

One of the programs abandoned with the end of the Cold War was that of energy preparedness in case of an all-war between the USA and the USSR. There were four principle facilities -- collectively known as the Department of Energy, Division of Energy Preparedness (DEDEP) – engaged in research and development which were located in the East, the South, the Mid-West, and the West, each staffed by fifty scientists and their families. The order to close down and abandon the facilities was received with a sigh of relief, as no one wanted to live in a hole in the ground on a permanent basis. Due a minor snafu, however, funding for only three of the facilities was eliminated; the Mid-West location continued to receive funds to support a caretaker staff of ten, but eventually that number dwindled to two.

The Mid-West facility lay underneath the yard of a farm, purchased by the government from a long-time farmer who had retired from the business and who had no children willing to continue farming. The two caretakers lived in the farmhouse and did no work other than maintaining the property and keeping up appearances. Only the steel fence surrounding the property and the officious-looking sign on the entrance gate suggested that DEDEP was still functional. Delivery of food and supplies arrived on a regular basis, and no one questioned the truck traffic which disturbed an otherwise placid environment.

In the basement of this farmhouse, one of the two caretakers stood, pondering a puzzle of large dimensions. Monk came down to the basement when time allowed to tinker which was his avocation and his delight. The basement contained as complete a workshop as any repairman could ever hope for; and, thanks to the continued funding of the facility, nothing mechanical or electronic was beyond its scope. Monk had personally ordered most (if not all) of the equipment and tools – both George and Emil had accused him of extravagance but nonetheless had given him his head – and he found uses for all of it.

Monk was a tinkerer from a long line of tinkerers, beginning at the age of eight. He had started out by taking apart and putting back together again all of the household appliances – much to the chagrin of his mother – and learned what made them tick. His father's automobile and pick-up truck had received the same treatment at the age of eleven – much to the older man's amusement – and the two of them often collaborated in practical repairs. Young Monk earned money doing work for others; and, after graduation from high school, he was hired by the school as a maintenance man. When an opening for a maintenance man at the Mid-West (official) DEDEP facility caught his attention, he jumped at the chance to move up in the world and, eventually, he worked his way up to Chief Maintenance Supervisor.

The glory ended along with the Cold War and the close of the energy-preparedness program. But, thanks to the bureaucratic oversight, the *job* did not end. Monk as Chief Maintenance Supervisor stayed on as a caretaker, but there was little for him to do in the way of tinkering. He and Ted sent in monthly (fake) reports about the "progress" toward energy preparedness and submitted an annual budget for future expenses – monies which paid *official* DEDEP's bills (but any surplus funds were handed over to the *unofficial* DEDEP). They also drew paychecks and donated a portion of them to the secret facility. Occasionally, he lent Freddie Hamilton a hand when a particular task was beyond the dwarf's physical or intellectual ability. For the most part, however, he kept his distance from what he didn't understand and busied himself however he could in the world above.

Now, to his great relief and pleasure, George Larkin had thrown him a bone – a *large* bone – which challenged everything he knew about things mechanical and electronic: alien technology. And the detective wanted answers yesterday! Monk was in his glory again!

The modules he and Larkin had spirited away from the late alien spy, "Mr. Jones" -- right under the noses of the Disciples, no less! – squatted in front of him, and he was pondering hard about how to pry their secrets out of them. He had to be very cautious, of course, as one misstep could either alert the other aliens to the whereabouts of their missing equipment or turn the whole of DEDEP into a very large hole in the ground. George had indicated that the one module was a communications device which linked to the aliens' base (and elsewhere as far as he knew). He certainly didn't want to play around with that piece until he had examined the rest of the array and learned how it functioned individually and collectively.

Therefore, he selected another module at random and studied it for a long time. He had already established that each module possessed a built-in power pack and a transmission antenna. He didn't know how large a charge the power pack contained, and so he had to operate the units sparingly at first. But, first things first: he had to learn how to power up the damned thing!

The surface of the selected module was covered with a multitude of symbols, grouped in sixes so that each group formed a hexagram. There were twelve groups altogether arranged in four rows. Monk deduced that each symbol was pressure-sensitive – even if he didn't know just yet what it might represent – and that each group performed a specific set of commands. One symbol, resembling a lower-case "h" laying on its side, stood alone at the right-hand edge of the panel. His repairman's intuition told him that it might be the power switch. Suddenly, his palms were sweaty with anticipation.

He wiped his sweaty palms on his trousers, took a deep breath, and pressed the symbol lightly with a trembling finger. With contact, the symbol turned a brilliant orange, followed by a humming sound from deep within the module; and, one by one, each group of symbols lit up in different colors. The whole looked like a neon sign in Las Vegas. Monk released the breath he was holding, pleased with himself for having started off on the right foot.

Now what?

He studied the array of symbols further and noted that in all twelve groupings the top symbol of each hexagram was the same. The only difference was the color. That suggested to him that that particular symbol had to be pressed first in any sequence -- which implied the existence of an "owner's manual" or a "code book." Since he had no idea where such a book might be (although it might be built into the module's computer), he would have to experiment with various combinations and see what happened. He hoped that one of those combinations would *not* be a self-destruct code!

Then, he noticed an interesting thing. Some of the symbols were pulsing, one flash per second; but not all of the groupings were represented, and three of the groupings showed more than one flashing symbol. He counted a total of nine flashing symbols. Did that mean a program was active? He took another deep breath and began pressing the glowing symbols one by one, from left to right, top to bottom. Nothing happened. He pondered some more. On a hunch, he pressed the symbols top to bottom, left to right. As soon as the final symbol had been pressed, he got results – and the biggest surprise of his life.

A transparent screen had now appeared above the module in holographic fashion. He could still see objects in the background but only dimly. What was displayed on the screen took center stage – an image of Planet Earth as seen from outer space. Monk had found an alien atlas!

* * *

The battered old station wagon pulled up at the rear entrance to Browsing Unlimited five minutes before closing time, clanking and rattling as it ground to a halt. Larkin clenched his teeth, fearing the worst. Why hadn't he invested in decent transportation before now? He could have afforded it; the agency's business was, if not booming, well off. *I put all my spare money into my electronic gizmos*, he answered his own question. Well, as soon as this business with the Swarm was over – if he survived, of course – this junk-heap was heading for the scrap yard, no ifs, ands, or buts!

Sheena sat behind the wheel this trip. She glanced surreptitiously at her partner and smirked. She could guess what he was thinking, simply because she was thinking the same thing. She didn't want to operate this pile of junk any more than he did. She had thought to hint at buying a newer vehicle any number of times in the past, but George had always made some excuse not to follow up on her suggestions. That wasn't going to deter her from nagging him some more, of course.

The minutes passed slowly. Presently, the rear entrance opened, and the Twins ambled out and piled into the back seat.

"Good evening, George, Sheena. How was your…"

"…day? Ours was grueling. For some reason, business…"

"…was especially brisk, from mid-morning all the…"

"...way until closing. We're glad it's behind us."

"Our day was eventful as well, guys." The detective brought them up to speed, sparing no details. "Things are getting hairy around here."

"What's on the agenda tonight?" Kenny asked.

"Emil says that Monk has made a breakthrough on the Swarm equipment. Lacey, Chris, and I will update on recent developments. I don't know what Emil has in mind. He's said he's been experimenting with our 'eel,' so that may be on the agenda. We'll just have to wait and see. Let's go, Sheena."

She put the station wagon in gear and creeped away from the shopping complex. Once out of the parking lot, she headed west across the river, then south to Main Street. No sooner had she turned onto Main Street and headed west again than Kenny cried out in alarm.

"Bloody hell!"

"What's wrong?" Larkin asked, equally alarmed.

"We 'troll' as a matter of course, old darling..."

"...just to keep our hand in, monitoring specific signals..."

"...and we just picked up signals nearby which are..."

"...definitely Swarmish. Take a look, won't you?"

The detective did, scanning both sides of the street. He spotted two figures up ahead, walking slowly and casting glances left and right. He couldn't make out any facial features at this distance, but the body build and the posture were unmistakable. The Swarm were again on patrol on the streets of the City!

Even though she was concentrating on her driving (using visual images from Paddy), Sheena dared to open up her hyperesthetic senses a couple of notches. Heartbeat, respiration, body odor – all matched the alien patterns she had first detected in the late Mr. Jones. She moaned softly.

"They must still be looking for the 'eel,'" Larkin observed. They're doomed to disappointment, of course, but I'm afraid we won't be rid of them any time soon."

"Bloody hell!" the Twins muttered in unison.

The remainder of the trip was made without incident and with silence. When they arrived at DEDEP, they encountered a beehive of activity. The two caretakers and several volunteers from the residential sector were busily setting up folding chairs in the barn. Other volunteers were installing portable lamps at strategic points and connecting them to a portable generator. A dais had been set up before the arrangement of chairs, and an intercom for Chris sat on it. Larkin was mildly surprised to see one of the alien modules squatting next to the dais. He *humph*ed to himself at the sight; it must've been all Monk and Ted could do to drag that thing up from the basement to the barn. Beyond that, he hadn't witnessed so much hustle and bustle since DEDEP took over the underground facility.

Monk caught his eye and waved him over. He headed in that direction but had to dodge several volunteers along the way. The latter greeted him cheerily but did not stop.

"Good timing, Georgie!" Monk boomed. "The work's almost done."

"Sorry. I had to wait on the Twins."

"Just kiddin'. We're gonna have a bang-up session tonight."

"I see that. I'll be all ears."

The detective wandered away and began helping with the chair set-up. Sheena and the Twins had already disappeared below. Not fifteen minutes later, they re-appeared with Emil in tow. And they were not alone; the remainder of the residents were right behind them, clambering up the ladder in a steady stream and chattering at each other over this change in routine. To a man and woman and child, they all stared in fascination at the set-up as if they were tourists in a strange country. Once they had gotten their fill of the unusual surroundings, they hastened to find seats. Among the last arrivals were Eve, Stan, Freddie, and Lacey, who took seats on chairs near the dais opposite the module. Monk joined them and took the last chair in the group. Two empty chairs behind the dais were reserved for DEDEP's leadership.

When all had been seated and quiet settled in, Dr. Razumov stepped up to the dais. Larkin noted that he seemed to be his old self again. The re-appearance of the gestalt – and possibly the presence of the alien technology sitting nearby – obviously had everything to do with it. That was certainly a relief; the Doctor's expertise and guidance were sorely needed at this juncture.

"*Dobry vyecher, druzhy moyee,*" the Director greeted the assembly. "I am pleased to announce that the rumors you have heard are true. The gestalt is back with us." A murmur of surprise and anticipation rippled through the crowd. "You will see another demonstration of it later in the evening. Also, I have recovered my equipoise, and I apologize for any discomfort you may have felt by my previous behavior. We have several reports tonight, and most of them will undoubtedly cause some alarm. But we will persevere. George?"

The detective changed places with the Director and regarded the audience for a moment while he collected his thoughts. Then he launched into an account of his recent experiences – the presence of members of the Swarm who were searching for Jean Fulton (at the mention of her name, she blanched and clutched Joyce's arm), the transfer of Swarm technology to DEDEP, the Archdeacon's strange request and the reason for it, the UFO flap, and the latest conversation with Mr. Smith – leaving out no detail. The alarm Emil had foreseen manifested itself almost immediately and grew with each sentence. By the time he had finished, most of the group were talking in hushed tones amongst themselves.

"I'm sure you have questions," Larkin stated the obvious. "Fire away!"

Predictably, Henry Rawlins was on his feet at once. His face seemed redder than usual, and his jowls shook like sails in the wind.

"You've certainly painted a pretty picture, George," the fat man grumbled. "What I – we – want to know is what this 'Coalition' is doing about the Swarm. This is *their* war, not ours."

"You know as much as I do, Henry. I've asked them several times for some of their weaponry, but they've got a 'policy' – they say – about arming us 'primitives.' I'll keep after them, of course, but I'm nothing if not realistic. We're on our own. And, by the way, as I've said before, it *is* our war now, whether we like it or not. Let's not fool ourselves."

"Damn!" the "sleeping prophet" muttered and sat down.

Bill Perkins stood up next, and he looked as haunted as "Fat Henry" had.

"George, I already know most of what the Swarm has been doing from what Lacey has told me, and I won't steal her thunder by pre-empting her. I'd like to know how reliable an ally the Disciples will be when the time comes."

"It's like this, Bill, the Disciples will fight their 'holy war' against the 'legions of Satan' as long as I can feed their fantasies about the 'end times.' They aren't any sort of match for a ruthless bunch like the Swarm, but they'll fight to the last man if the Archdeacon orders them to. They'll buy us time to develop our own forces. Anyone else?" No one responded. "No? Back to you, Emil."

He and the Doctor traded places again. The latter pursed his lips in thought.

"I think we shall hear from Christopher now. His report will corroborate some of what George has reported. Christopher, if you please?"

In response, a familiar shimmering in the air near the dais took shape, coalesced into human form, and revealed itself in Chris' preferred image – a young man casually dressed. The image smiled and waved awkwardly at the assembly.

"Hello, world," his tinny voice issued from the intercom.

"That's...*awesome!*" Jean whispered to Joyce. "How does he do it?"

"I'll tell you later," Joyce whispered back, "but you may not believe me. I'm still trying to believe it myself."

"George assigned me," the psycho-projectionist was saying, "to spy out the Swarm's main base in Nebraska. What I'm about to say will alarm you even more than what he had to say."

He then related the aliens' continuing military exercises, including their use of local Disciples as "target practice," the construction of what may be an interstellar transmitter, and the arrival and departure of the war machine which had caused the UFO flap in the City and elsewhere. The level of worry rose a few notches here and there, and a number of residents could not sit still in their seats. Chris' image turned to the Doctor (who nodded) and faded away in the reverse process of its appearance.

"It is a terrible thing," Dr. Razumov stated with sorrow, "to have to listen to such disturbing remarks, and I am afraid there is more to come. However, we must have all the available information out in the open if we are to successfully combat the Swarm. Lacey will now add her piece of the story."

The psycho-occulist traded places with the Director and faced the audience with trepidation. She bit her lip before speaking.

"My 'piece of the story' isn't any happier, folks. Sorry. In fact, it may be even worse than what you've already heard – if that's possible. I've had the job of monitoring the Swarm at their local base on Ridgeway Avenue. I watched them build that damned spaceship that caused the UFO sightings. I watched it fly out of the building, maneuver around, and fly off to Nebraska. And I watched it as it returned.

"This morning, I – I watched the Swarm make alterations to their ship. It looked like – it looked like they were adding" – she suddenly licked dry lips -- "adding weapons, the same weapons Eve 'saw' in her vision. My God! *They're planning to attack the City!*"

She buried her head in her hands and sobbed. More DEDEP'ers joined her; the rest were too stunned to do anything. Larkin and the Doctor exchanged worried looks. The latter rose quickly, embraced her in a consoling manner, and led her back to her chair. The detective now stood to fill the vacuum.

"Folks," he said in his best authoritative voice, "I know we're all upset by what we've just heard. But, I want you to know that DEDEP now has the means to stop the Swarm in their tracks and keep the City from harm."

"What means are those, George?" asked Bill Perkins as he made his way toward his distraught wife.

"We've got our dangerous weapon back, haven't we?" He paused briefly. "But I think we should all take a break now in order to collect ourselves. We'll finish the meeting in, say, thirty minutes from now."

As the residents moved off toward the ladder which connected the world above to the world below, Larkin drew the Director aside.

"I hope you didn't mind if I called a 'recess,' Emil. I thought it was necessary."

"*Konyechno*. You did the right thing, George. There was entirely too much *angst* in the air. Some…'down-time,' as you Americans call it, was assuredly in order."

"Let's hope the remainder of the meeting is more uplifting. It won't do to have a panic on our hands."

"*Da, oo tyebya pravdy*. I – yes, William?"

They were joined by the elder Perkins, who with his sons had stayed behind to comfort Lacey, still in an overwrought state. At the moment, she was locked in an embrace with the boys. Out of the corner of his eye, Larkin noticed that Sheena had also remained. She stood as close to him as she dared under the circumstances. He also noticed that Joyce and Jean were engaged in an animated discussion with the gestalt-makers.

"That was a fine pep talk, George," Perkins remarked. "I hope it did some good."

"So do I, Bill. And I trust I have your support?"

"Huh! I've got a wife and kids who have abilities I'll never have, but I still love them very much. Like it or not, I'm here for the long haul. You can count on me. Now, you'll excuse me. I have to return to the Missus."

Thirty minutes passed by much too slowly to suit the leadership of DEDEP. Emil Razumov kept consulting his watch every few minutes and nervously examining the module within arm's reach. Larkin spoke privately with Sheena and wished he had the nerve to hold her close; he could have used some consoling himself at that moment. He also knew she wouldn't resist his initiative.

Thirty minutes passed by quickly, and there was no sign of returning residents. The DEDEP leadership became very concerned, worried that everyone was so distraught that they didn't want to expose themselves to any more bad news. Neither man could have blamed them, however; if they hadn't been who they were, they might have been in a state of shock and fear as well. Still, it was important that the residents participate in these meetings fully, since the well-being of the organization depended upon their being well-informed. It was a hoary old cliché that "in union, there is strength"; but, in this case, it was absolutely true. DEDEP needed to stay organized; otherwise, their enemies would pick them off, one by one.

The detective reluctantly broke away from Sheena and wandered off toward the ladder to see what was delaying everybody. Sheena did not follow him though she wanted to. When he peered down the shaft, he saw emptiness and frowned. He hated to have to go down and cajole the residents into returning. Happily, he did not have to. Five seconds later, the emergency door below swung open, and Paddy popped into view. The psycho-communicator gazed upward, spotted his "fearless leader," and grinned.

"Hello, old darling. Looking for someone?"

"As a matter of fact, I'm looking for a lot of 'someones.' What's keeping everyone?"

"We had a bit of a debate. Some of the chaps had had their fill of troubling information and just wanted to go hide under their beds. Kenny and I gave them a jolly good dressing down and told them exactly what was at stake here. Chris showed up unexpectedly and put in his two cents' worth, as you Yanks would say. That turned the tide, by Jove! I've got the lot of them right behind me."

"Great. I'll go tell Emil."

Ten minutes later, all chairs were filled. Worry, concern, anxiety, apprehension, and not a little fear still hung over the assembly like an invisible shroud. But each person who was most affected by those emotions was comforted by neighbors who were not – such was the resilience of the human spirit – and soon all gave their attention to Dr. Razumov.

"*Spaceebo, druzhy moyee*," he greeted them cordially. "I had planned, for the next segment of this meeting, another demonstration of the gestalt. Instead, I want everyone to connect to the gestalt in order to ease his/her concerns. Eve, Stan, Freddie?"

The Triad rose, re-arranged their chairs in the familiar pattern, and sat down. Eve and Stan regarded each other solemnly for a few seconds and then clasped hands. Freddie slumped forward with his chin resting on his chest.

Instantly, the black sphere appeared above them, vibrating slightly. It elicited even more awe and apprehension than it had always done, and its current size had everything to do with it. Dr. Razumov had determined that its size was in direct proportion to the number of persons in its vicinity from whom it drew energy. But the number of persons in the barn had increased by only one, and the sphere now measured over two meters in diameter.

"That thing is larger than ever," Larkin whispered to the Director.

"*Da*, and I think I know why. Look at Miss Fulton."

The newest member of DEDEP had reacted to the *psi*-gestalt as she had before – fearfully – and she was hugging herself intensely in an effort to calm herself down. Beside her, Joyce threw her arm about her shoulders.

"I see what you mean, Emil. Our 'eel' is charging up due to an emotional overload, and the gestalt is drawing extra energy."

"*Tochno*. And now I must defuse the situation." He turned to the assembly. "*Pozhalsto*, everyone, line up and take what wonders the gestalt has to offer."

Fortunately, the residents had had prior experience to guide them and, one by one, they came forward and touched the clasped hands of Eve and Stan. The awe they had felt before remained (and perhaps increased) but the apprehension dissipated in the face of fantastic images in their minds as dew before the Sun. Only Joyce and Jean held back, the latter refusing to budge, the former offering encouragement.

"What is that thing doing to them?" Jean whined.

"It's like a movie, Jean. You see scene after scene in a panorama. I was also scared at first – until I experienced it. Look, we'll go together, and we'll both touch Stan and Eve's hands at the same time."

"Wel-l-l, all right, if you think it's safe."

"It is. Trust me."

The two women slowly approached the gestalt and cautiously placed their hands on those of Eve and Stan. Instantly, Jean's eyes went wide with surprise as a host of unbelievable images flooded her mind and filled her entire being. She turned to Joyce with shining eyes.

"*Far freaking out!*"

Once the mind-show had run its course, the Doctor signaled to the Triad to cease. The black sphere vanished into nothingness.

"Now that we are all refreshed, we come to the 'main event,' so to speak. Our friend Monk has been experimenting with the Swarm technology he and George 'liberated' from Mr. Jones' apartment, and he has made a most interesting discovery. Monk?"

The short, stocky DOE man, unofficially the "front" for DEDEP, rose from his seat and walked over to the module. He then put on his best face. This was the very first time he had met the whole of DEDEP *en masse*, and he was understandably nervous; he hardly knew how he should behave in the presence of these people with unusual – and often frightening – abilities.

Monk's nervousness reflected that of the general populace where *psi* was concerned. That portion of humankind which actually accepted the reality of psychic powers was divided into two distinct factions. The minority faction regarded *psi*-talent as another step in the evolution of the species, but the majority faction regarded it as a threat to society. The fear of the Unknown played a large part in the latter's thinking, and it was unlikely that that reaction would completely disappear. It represented what DEDEP had most to fear. Monk, having worked (albeit at a distance) with these gifted people and therefore had come to know them (somewhat), probably would have placed himself in the minority faction. Nevertheless, he did feel a certain awe in their presence. And now he found himself in a whole roomful of them, and a lot of them, never having seen him before or rarely, were staring at him and perhaps wondering what he was doing here – which increased his nervousness exponentially.

"Hi, everybody. I ain't much of a public speaker, so bear with me. George and me hijacked this little gizmo here, so to speak, and I been workin' with it since. What I've found I think will amaze you. It amazed *me*, that's for sure.

"This here symbol all by itself" – he pointed at the symbol in question – "is the power switch. Now watch."

He touched the symbol lightly, and the module lit up as before. Many "ooh's" and "ahh's" issued from the crowd.

"Pretty nifty, huh? Well, you ain't seen nothin' yet. You'll notice that some of the lighted symbols are flashin'. As far as I can tell, they are a recent sequence as a result of data input. How the data was entered, I have yet to determine. Now, watch what happens when I press those flashing symbols."

He did so, and the transparent screen with the image of the Earth appeared. More "ooh's" and "ahh's" resulted. Monk smiled to himself. He had this bunch in the palm of his hand.

"You can tell that this gizmo is an atlas of sorts. The aliens have collected data about our world and entered it into the memory banks so that visualizations can be created. Now, you'll see that some symbols are flashin' with this visualization."

He then pressed those symbols. The image of the Earth was replaced by an image of the United States of America. The "oooh's" and "ahh's" were joined by a few gasps and mutters.

"I should point out before I ferget it that there are twelve groups of six symbols each. That means there are six –to-the-twelfth-power possible combinations, or – lessee – um, 362,797,056 altogether. Whether or not the Swarm use all o' them is anybody's guess, but they're available. I got yet to find a code book. Now, again, some symbols are flashin'."

The image of the USA gave way to one of a representation of the Lake Michigan region. "Ooh's" and "ahh's" yielded to more gasps and mutters. The audience's initial reaction of wonder had changed to one of unease.

"You all can see what is pictured here. I'll direct yer attention to the symbols on the image itself. They're all the same, and they're placed in strategic places, some of which I recognize from my own training. What's pinpointed are potential targets." Monk paused for dramatic effect. "What we got here, ladies and gentlemen, is where the Swarm will attack when the time comes."

The uproar over this impromptu analysis was deafening. DEDEP was now on the verge of panic.

CHAPTER THIRTEEN

A CL⊕SE ENC⊕UNTER

LARKIN STARED AT a blank screen in the "snoop room" for a long while, mulling over the uproar at DEDEP the previous evening. He hadn't counted on Monk's being so melodramatic about his presentation, and he wished that the DOE man had briefed him prior to the meeting so as to coach him on what to say – and what *not* to say. What Monk did say had thrown the residents – with a few exceptions – into a sheer funk, and quick action on his and Emil's part had to be taken before hysteria set in. Soothing speech had taken a while before the crowd settled down (aided by Monk's hasty departure). And, in the back of his mind, the detective could see his Grand Plan falling to pieces – along with DEDEP itself.

"'Forewarned is forearmed'" he had told them. "However bluntly it may have happened, we've just been forewarned. Now that we know where the Swarm will strike first, we can take steps to counter their attack."

Of course, leave it to "Fat Henry" Rawlins to be his usual skeptical self. He had wanted details. In a way, he was only putting into words what everyone else was thinking, but the Grand Plan had already been thrashed out. Had Henry forgotten already?

"We follow the plan I've devised," he had answered wearily. "We dupe the Disciples into thinking the Swarm is the real enemy – which they are – and we dupe the Swarm into thinking the Disciples are a resistance group – which they are – they must eliminate before they can conquer Earth."

"George is right," Bill Perkins (one of the cooler heads) had come to his aid. "We're the only ones – well, some of us anyway – who can do what whole armies can't. And, besides, we've got the gestalt that'll blast those SOB's right out of the galaxy!"

There it was in a nutshell: the fact that *psi*-talent was a more potent force than mere physical weaponry. The combined abilities of all of DEDEP would be more than a match for whatever the Swarm could come up with. The demise of Mr. Jones had been a small case in point; his downfall had been at the hands of just a few members. Think what could be accomplished by everyone working in tandem!

Larkin had played the "cheerleader" in bringing this point home, and that had done the trick. The residents had returned to their quarters with a renewed sense of purpose and a readiness to press the attack against the Swarm. Later, in Emil's office, he and the old man had expressed relief at being able to defuse a potentially dangerous situation. It may or may not have been a premature reaction, but their own self-confidence had also been renewed. Only time would tell.

One other piece of information had come to light before the detective returned to the City. Chris had contacted them in the office and apologized for forgetting to mention in his report the fact that he had seen George's unintentional informant lurking about the Nebraska site. Chris' description of the fellow fitted what Larkin had surmised from the sort of messages he sent. This information had also reminded him that he hadn't provoked the Quark for a few days and that he was overdue for some provoking.

With his mind swirling with conflicting thoughts, that "provoking" was being hard to come by – hence the blank screen. His "composing process" was interrupted by the opening of the door.

"What're you doing right now?" Sheena inquired.

"Oh, just some heavy-duty thinking. Why?"

"I thought I smelled smoke in here."

He whirled around and regarded the smirk on her face.

"You made a joke! That's a first!"

"Our kind of business doesn't call for making jokes, George."

"No, it doesn't. Especially now, it doesn't."

"Did you sleep at all last night?"

"Not much. You?"

"Same here." She paused for the space of a heartbeat. "Although I understand that having sex is a good soporific."

Larkin grimaced and was glad that Sheena could not see the look of annoyance on his face. Not that it made any difference that she was blind – she could use her other senses to "read" his mood whenever she wanted. Still, he couldn't help being annoyed. What she had just said was meant to let him know – subtly or otherwise – what she wanted from him and what she knew he wanted to give to her. Annoyance gave way to a pained expression, and he turned back to a blank screen.

"Actually," he said casually, "I was just about to contact the Quark and give him some new 'instructions.'"

The sound of a chair being dragged across the floor told him that Sheena was going to sit in on this session. He switched on the voice synthesizer and checked his e-mail in case there was already a message from the Quark. There was, and it was long and rambling as usual. Everything Chris had reported on concerning the arrival and departure of the Swarm craft was corroborated here (more or less); but, whereas Chris had been calm and reserved in his delivery, the Quark punctuated his with a lot more profanity than usual. The detectives had to read between the lines more often than not.

One observation near the end of the report made Larkin sit up and take notice. The Quark claimed to have seen a Disciple "hobnobbing" (his word) with the commander of the Swarm unit rather than being used for target practice, and he wanted to know "WHAT THE FUCK'S GOIN' ON, MAN?" What the fuck, indeed, the detective wondered. And how had Chris missed that little *tete-a-tete*? Possibly, the Quark had had a different vantage point and therefore seen more than Chris had.

This new development raised more than one red flag in Larkin's mind. And the gasp of shock from his partner indicated that she had a few red flags of her own. A collaborator working with the Enemy? How many more might there be? Would one of them be in the City, acting as a spy? The notion was, on the face of it, allegedly beyond the realm of belief, but not beyond the realm of possibility. In any war, there had always been collaborators, fearful and/or unscrupulous persons who curried favor from the would-be conqueror, even if – or, more to the point, especially if – that conqueror intended to destroy everything in sight. The collaborator hoped to be spared the slaughter and/or share in the spoils. He was the worst kind of traitor because he did what he did for personal gain and not for ideological reasons.

"Your thoughts?" the detective asked as soon as he closed the message.

"That...*bastard*!" she spat out. "How can he sell out all of humanity and still sleep at night?"

"It boggles the mind, doesn't it?"

"What are you going to tell the Quark?"

"First, I'll congratulate him on a job well done. That'll encourage him to stay on the job. Next, I'll 'suggest' he keep an eye on that Disciple and find out what he's doing for the Swarm. We just might get some useful intel out of this."

"If you say so, George. Excuse me, please. I have to go somewhere and *scream*! Loudly! More than once!"

* * *

After he had completed his "paperwork" and sent out final reports to some of his clients (and their bills!), Larkin set out to visit the Archdeacon. He had two reasons. The first was his curiosity about the "heretic" he had turned over to Fogarty. He wanted to learn the man's fate and to use the incident on Union Street as additional ammunition to keep the Disciple leader on a string. The more he spun his web of deceit, the happier he was about dealing with religious fanatics. The second was along a similar bent involving the presence of a Disciple at a

Swarm base but not as a prisoner. If he could induce in the Archdeacon a greater sense of paranoia than the man already had and have him question the loyalty of his own "troops," it might just tear the whole organization apart. At least, that was the plan; implementation would require many more plausible lies.

As soon as he exited his office building, he braced himself for the walk down the street. Even though Disciple HQ was only three blocks away, it was still a slow and awkward journey. Add to that the fact the temperature was pushing into the nineties – and it was only mid-morning! – and the short walk became more difficult to navigate. He'd have preferred to remain in his office working crossword puzzles!

He noted that a great number of Disciples were on the street. That was a good sign, as the Archdeacon had instructed his people to be on the look-out for the Enemy; the more they were occupied in wild-goose chases, the less time they had to harass innocent people with their inane and overbearing methods of proselytization. He also noted that they recognized him as an "ally"; when they caught his eye, they gave him a quick smile and a friendly nod of the head. That too was a good sign, for it justified his tactics.

When he arrived at Disciple HQ, he discovered yet another young woman at the receptionist's desk, and he idly wondered if the position was a rotating one and why. Still, the new receptionist had a familiar face: the mousy little brunette with narrow facial features and close-set eyes who had with "Brother" Connolly been monitoring his building the previous week. He introduced himself and stated his purpose here. The introduction was not necessary, since the woman recognized him immediately and greeted him as "Brother" Larkin. She dialed the Archdeacon's extension, spoke briefly to whoever answered, hung up, and sent him off toward the stairs.

What? he mused. *No escort by the redoubtable 'Sister' Hedberg? Am I to be spared from the machinations of that female shark today?*

Upstairs he rapped gently on the door. The voice of the Archdeacon bade him enter. He did so and spotted "Brother" Connolly himself standing stiffly before Fogarty's desk. The ever-present "Brother" Kincaid was in his usual place, but Hedberg was surprisingly absent.

"Good morning, Brother Larkin," Fogarty greeted him cheerfully. "I've been meaning to contact you. Now, here you are."

"Good morning, Your Worship. I came to report on some recent developments."

"Yes, yes, the very reason I wanted to talk to you." He gestured at the young man. "I believe you've met Brother Connolly?"

"Of course. He's been of great assistance to me on a couple of occasions." Connolly actually blushed at the compliment. "As a matter of fact, he actually saved my life and that of Sister Whitley a couple of days ago when we were almost captured by some of those evil creatures on Main Street. He assessed the situation right away and contacted Brother Horton, who brought a 'rescue party.'"

"Well, I'm pleased to hear that, Brother Larkin. His indoctrination hasn't been lost on him."

"Far be it from me to tell you your business, sir, but I'd recommend that you give him more responsibility. We need quick-thinking fellows like him if we're to win the war against the Enemy."

"I'll take your recommendation under advisement. Right now, I'd like your account of the incident on Union Street."

"Yes, sir. That was one of the reasons I'm here." The detective proceeded to deliver a carefully crafted version of the events in question, up to and including the appearance of the "angel." He left nothing to the imagination but still put a spin on every sentence for maximum effect. All the while, the Archdeacon nodded in agreement. "I have to admit," Larkin concluded, "that it was an extraordinary experience."

"I daresay," Fogarty remarked. "Well, Brother Larkin, in your own fashion, you've validated everything Brother Connolly has reported, and I thank you. What was your other reason for being here?"

"Um, what I have to tell you must be made in the strictest confidence. It's a rather delicate matter."

"I...see." The old man eyed Connolly. "That'll be all, Brother Connolly. I'll speak to you later about a possible re-assignment."

The young man thanked Fogarty profusely, gave the detective a nod, and hastily departed. Both the Archdeacon and "Brother" Kincaid regarded Larkin expectantly.

Now for another Oscar-winning performance, the latter smirked to himself.

"This has not been verified, mind you, but one of my informants claimed to have seen a Disciple in league with the Enemy."

Neither of the Disciple leadership could have expressed more shock if they had been slapped by Hadley Richardson himself. They gazed at each other with genuine astonishment, then at Larkin with deep suspicion.

"I see you're skeptical," the detective remarked, "and I don't blame you. I'd be skeptical too. As I said, this information has not been verified, but I felt that you should be alerted to the possibility."

"Someone here in the City?" the Archdeacon murmured.

"My informant wasn't specific. He just said 'a Disciple' and let me draw my own conclusions. Frankly, Your Worship, my informant could have been mistaken. These are strange times."

"Indeed they are. You've raised a serious point, and you were correct to maintain confidentiality. If this were to be made public, an uproar of tremendous proportions might result." He turned to his lieutenant. "Brother Kincaid, I'd like you to put out some feelers and get to the bottom of this."

Kincaid nodded, rose, and departed. His whole demeanor was filled with grim determination. Fogarty stared at his desk for a long moment and tapped his fingers together nervously. Larkin exulted – the Plan was proceeding as he had hoped.

"Two disturbing reports in one day," the old man muttered.

"Sir?"

"Brother Larkin, I see no need to keep you out of the loop inasmuch as the work you've done for us has been invaluable. Now, I will tell *you* in the strictest confidence that there have been…repercussions concerning the Disciple who has been causing dissension in the ranks. Despite my pleas to him to reconsider his position, he continues to defy me. Now I hear that those who listened to him on Union Street have taken his words to heart – the appearance of the Lord's messenger was a convincing factor – and are spreading those words throughout the City. It's like a cancer."

"You may be right, Your Worship. Is there anything I can do to defuse the situation?"

"Perhaps. I'll have to meditate on the matter a bit. I'll get back to you."

He waved his hand in dismissal, and the detective turned to leave. As he did so, he looked over his shoulder and observed the old man staring pensively out the window. He grinned wickedly and marched out of the office.

Downstairs, he spotted "Brother" Connolly at the reception desk, holding hands with the receptionist. They were speaking in hushed tones, prompting him to raise an eyebrow. At his approach, the couple disengaged; Connolly straightened his tie, and the young woman smoothed her skirt. Both regarded him with guilty expressions.

"Still here, Brother Connolly?" he asked disingenuously.

"Uh, yes, Brother Larkin," was the nervous response. "I was, uh, telling Sister Smithers about the, uh, possibility of getting a promotion. I, uh, told her that you recommended it to His Worship."

"I meant what I said up there. You're a bright lad. You should go far, whatever the future holds."

Hah! George, you old smoothie you!

"Well, thank you again."

"Carry on," Larkin said by way of farewell and gave the pair a knowing wink.

Outside, he congratulated himself for a job well done and began the slow, arduous walk back to his office. He hadn't gone a block before he was aware of someone tagging along side of him. He turned to face the stranger and winced. The other was a rail-thin man with unkempt hair and a five o'clock shadow; his pale blue eyes were rheumy and Basset-hound-like. His clothes were shabby, rumpled, and smelly. All in all, he was the saddest sack Larkin had seen in a long time.

"Can I help you, friend?" he asked the sack.

"Ya got any spare change fer a veteran, buddy?"

"I haven't got any change." The sack looked even sadder. The detective reached into his pants pocket, pulled out some currency, and handed over a five-dollar-bill. "Here you go. Get something to eat."

"Thanks, Georgie," the sack hooted and displayed a mouthful of crooked, yellow teeth as a grin. "Yer a real soft touch."

Larkin goggled at the familiarity and was about to question the sack's audacity. Then it dawned on him who was in front of him.

"Farquhar! I should've guessed."

"Yer favorite uncle, in the flesh."

"That remains to be seen. What have you got for me?"

"I got a question, same question I asked before. What's DEDEP?"

"DEDEP again? What's your interest anyway?"

"It sounds like a group I'd like to join. I'm guessing they and I have a lot in common."

"And you think I'd know something about it."

"Yes. As I said before, I overheard the name in a conversation, and you were mentioned as well."

"Huh! Now you've piqued my curiosity. I'll look into it and let you know what I find out."

"Sure thing, nephew. You want your fiver back?"

"What? Oh, no, you can keep it. It's only money, don't you know?"

Larkin walked away as quickly as he was able, his mind awhirl with a host of dire thoughts. He hadn't the least idea of what Farquhar would do with any "knowledge" he learned about DEDEP. He did know that he'd have to concoct something plausible in order to throw the informant off the trail – if that were possible. What did he really know about the fellow, beyond the fact that he was a reliable source of information? Reliability did not automatically translate into trustworthiness; and, even if it did, outsiders still had to be kept in the dark for the sake of DEDEP's safety.

When he returned to the agency, Mrs. Watson had a verbal message for him.

"That strange Mr. Smith came by not five minutes ago. He wanted to see you ASAP."

"Hmmm. I hope he has good news for me. Is Sheena in?"

"Yes. She came in as he was leaving. She looked upset when she saw him."

"Mr. Smith seems to have that effect on everybody. Thanks, Madge."

He tapped on Sheena's office door and stepped inside. She was busy typing a response to a client, using a voice-activated typewriter, and tossed a "hello" over her shoulder. He took a seat and waited her out. At the conclusion of the typing, she spun around and flashed a big smile.

"And how has your day been so far?"

"Mixed up, as usual." He related his meeting with the Archdeacon and his plot to unnerve the old man. Sheena grinned wickedly. "Then I encountered Farquhar again."

"Oh?" Glee turned to worry. "What did *he* want?"

He told her, and she sagged in her chair.

"What're we going to do about him, George? His abilities are frightening, to say the least. And, to be fair about it, we could put those abilities to good use. I'm sure Emil would love to get his hands on him and run him through the hoops. But he's still a loose cannon that needs to be muzzled."

"You've hit the nail square on the head. It seems I'll have to move him further up on my list of priorities – not that my list is that long in the first place." He sighed. "Well, first things first. Mr. Smith desires an audience. That's where I'll be the rest of the morning. Hold down the fort."

* * *

It was probably his imagination, but Larkin could have sworn that the abandoned supermarket was sagging more than it had at his previous visit (which hadn't been all that long ago). The western side seemed to be on the verge of collapse, and a sharp blow against the wall or a clap of thunder would be sufficient to send it crashing to the ground. Mr. Smith's operation would be exposed for all the world – and the Swarm – to see. How he would recover from such a calamity was problematic. There was too much heavy, bulky equipment in the building to be removed at a moment's notice, and it might have to be destroyed rather than allowing it to fall into the wrong hands and compromising the Coalition's mission here.

That was the least of the detective's worries just then, and he could not be bothered with "what if?" scenarios. Besides, he had to believe that the alien group had contingency plans to meet any and all possible "what if's." If they didn't, then they weren't as advanced as they wanted others to think they were.

When he entered the central section of the building, Mr. Smith was nowhere to be seen. Either he was still trudging along the City's streets or he was inside the large silver-gray cube which housed the cold-fusion generator, making whatever adjustments one made to such things. Wherever he was, however, he had just afforded his "guest" an opportunity to snoop around a bit; in particular, Larkin wanted to examine the broadcasting tower which linked this base to the Coalition's base in the Oort Cloud.

He never got the chance. As he passed by the base's power source, the door slid open, and Mr. Smith emerged. On seeing the human, the alien shifted from surprise to resignation to welcoming in a matter of two seconds.

"Ah...Mr....Largin. You...are...your...usual...prompt...self."

"Matters that concern both of us are rapidly coming to a head. More frequent conferences seem to be in order."

"I...agree. I...hhhave...shust...received...a...gommunigation... from...thhhe...Goalition...informing...me...thhhat...a... messashe... from...thhhe...Swarm...base...on...thhhis...world...to... thhheir...fleet ...hhhas...been...intercepted...and...degoded. Thhhe... Goalition's... alert...level...hhhas...been...elevated...as...a...result."

"That doesn't sound good. Will you share that message with me?"

"Of...gourse. You...are...our...ally...now. You...are...entitled... to... hhhave...information...goncerning...thhhe...fate...of...your... world.

The...messashe...was...a...report...from...a...'Gommandant... Yowg' ...to...'Great...Leader...Wash.' Yowg...says...thhhat...hhhis... tasg... force...hhhas...gompleted...all...necessary...preparations... and...stands ...ready...to...launch...a...pre-emptive...strigue... against...specific... targets."

"That confirms information I received from my own sources. Was there a reply from this…'Great Leader Waj'?"

"Not…at…thhhis…time.   Begause…of…thhhe…distances… involved…messashing…is…necessarily…slow. Now…my…orishinal… reason… for…asging…you…hhhere…was…to…put…you…into… gontagt…withhh …Frommar. Hhhe…hhhas…important…news… for…you."

"Wonderful. And I have news for both of you."

Mr. Smith moved toward his control console with Larkin right behind him. The detective watched carefully as the alien pressed the necessary sequence of symbols; he noted that the sequence was the same one used when he first met the Coalition's sector commander. And he filed it away in his memory for future reference. Presently, the image of the bulbous-headed, hairless alien appeared on the large monitor. Mr. Smith spoke briefly with his superior, then activated the program for translating English into Frommar's language, and vice versa.

"La-kin," the ululating voice issued from the speaker, "we pleased to you one-more speak."

"And I'm pleased as well, Mr. -- uh, Frommar. I have a report to make."

"Excellent. Supplying it to us."

Larkin then related what DEDEP had learned about the Swarm's activities in the area in the recent past without, of course, mentioning DEDEP by name. He spoke slowly and deliberately, since he was not sure how well the translation program could pick up on the nuances of the English language (if at all). When he had finished, he waited anxiously for the response. The response was also slow in coming. Frommar kept looking left and right and back again, and part of his face wrinkled. Presently:

"La-kin, we not understanding what you meaning by 'oo-eff-oh.' Please elaborating."

"Ah, I apologize, Frommar. That expression is what my kind calls vessels from space – in this case, the Swarm warship."

"We understanding now. We appreciating this information. It corresponding to reports our own agents reported-have. Thanking you."

"You're welcome. Um, Mr. Smi – uh, Mabel-choo-choo said you had news for me."

"Yes. This new information causing a change in our attitudes. We believing you needing equipment-add to your efforts assist."

"Excellent. Weaponry?"

"No. We give-will you devices for defending. Mabel-choo-choo instruct-will their operation. We send-will them in the next cycle of your planet. Farewell, La-kin, and good fortune."

"Good fortune to you, Frommar."

The monitor went blank, and Mr. Smith shut down his console.

"Not what I was hoping for, of course, but it's a step in the right direction."

"Perhhhaps. Our...weaponry...is...very...powerful...as...you... might...imashine. In...thhhe...hhhands...of...one...whhho...hhhas...

no...understanding...of...thhhem...thhhey...gould...gause... mush... unintentional...damashe."

"I'm capable of understanding a lot of things, Mr. Smith. I wouldn't be standing here if I didn't."

"True. But...you...must...be...patient. Evenshually...you... will ...earn...our...gomplete...trust."

"I hope so. Um, what Frommar said about delivery of these new devices reminds me of something I've been meaning to ask you."

"Whhhat...do...you...want...to...know?"

"How did you get all of this equipment in here without attracting attention from people in the neighborhood? This is not ordinary Tellurian furniture by any stretch of the imagination."

"Mashig...Mr....Largin."

"'Magic'? You're joking."

"I...am...not...shoking. I...say...'mashig'...because... thhhat... is... whhhat...it...seems...to...me. Before...thhhe...Swarm... destroyed...

my...world...my...people...were...simple...farmers. We... hhhad ...an ...industrial...strugshure...but...it...was...not...as... advanced...as... yours...is. Whhhen...I...was...resgued...by...thhhe... Goalition...and ...saw...hhhow...mush...more...advanced...thhheir...

worlds...were ...thhheir...machines...seemed...ligue...'mashig'...
to...me."

"Yes. I can see that it might. It took my people several centuries to
evolve to what you see now. So, what is the delivery system?"

"I...do...not...know...thhhe...word...for...it. Thhhere...is...a...
flash ...of...light...and...thhhe...eguipment...appears."

"Ah, I know what it is. It's a concept used in our science fiction
stories. We call it 'teleportation.' Matter is converted to electrical
impulses, sent to a distant point on a carrier wave, and re-converted into
matter again. Over short distances, the process is almost instantaneous."

"If...you...say...so...Mr....Largin.   It...is...still...'mashig'...
to...me.

Frommar...said...hhhe...would...deliver...thhhe...devices...
tomorrow.

I... will... egspegt... you... thhhen."

"I'll be here without delay, Mr. Smith. Good-bye for now."

* * *

After leaving Mr. Smith, Larkin's next "port of call" was the
restaurant at Main and Broadway in order to have a leisurely lunch. He
needed some space and some time away from the "rat race" (mostly of
his own making) to relax and to mull over recent events. Those events
were moving at a quicker pace than he cared for, and they needed to
be evaluated in depth before proceeding to the next phase of his Grand
Plan. The restaurant was crowded as usual at this hour, and the noise
level was accordingly elevated; but the notion that he was in a non-work
environment surrounded by ordinary people appealed to his sense of
well-being, and he could lose himself in the mundane for a while.

He placed an order for soup *du jour* and a salad. He would have
preferred a ham sandwich on rye bread with mustard, lettuce, tomato,
and cheese with a side of breaded onion rings; but that would have
meant taking off his gloves so as not to soil them and thus exposing his
artificial hands to everybody around him. He had learned, right from
the beginning, people with real flesh-and-blood limbs tended to be

uncomfortable in the presence of one who had none. Therefore, eating out became a rare occasion for him. In this respect, he was no different than anyone in DEDEP; even though he had no *psi*-talent to speak of, he was just as much a "freak" as they were.

While he waited for his order, he relaxed and let his mind go into free-association, a technique which had served him well in the past when he was creating psychological profiles for the Chicago Police Department. He had learned the hard way that forcing his mind to come up with an identity for a violent criminal was counter-productive; it had taken him longer than it should have to pinpoint the suspects in his first half dozen cases, and it had almost cost him his employment there. While he didn't know to this day why or how free-association came to him, he had discovered that the clues to solving violent crimes were easier to come by, and he had several commendations to prove it. Those commendations had led to his being assigned as liaison to the FBI's kidnapping unit and his friendship with Gordon Sommers – and to more commendations from the Bureau.

His reverie did not last long. Just as the waitress was setting down his soup and salad, he spotted an all-too-familiar sight outside. Passing by the restaurant were two members of the Swarm, and one of them was the scarred individual who was the only one of his kind (other than the late Mr. Jones) to have seen his face. If the aliens came inside, that one would surely recognize him and attempt to apprehend him with possible unfortunate consequences to the innocent humans around him. He eyed the Swarm members studiously. They stopped at the street corner and looked about as if waiting for someone. The detective went into "high alert" status.

While he was plotting his escape route in a worst-case scenario, another familiar but more welcome face came into view: the City's Vice Mayor and Larkin's other long-term friend, Jack Torres. The latter entered the restaurant, and the detective quickly waved him over. The Vice Mayor broke out into a huge grin, marched over to Larkin's table, and took a seat.

"Well, old son," the City official remarked, "I've been wondering where you had got to. I've missed our little chats."

"So have I, Jack. I've been rather busy lately, and I haven't had much spare time."

"And what have you been up to – if you don't mind me asking? It's been rumored that you're working with the Archdeacon, of all people. Care to fill me in?"

"I'm going to tell you a story, old friend, one you're going to find hard to believe. But it's all true."

And, for what seemed like the hundredth time, Larkin recounted the events of the past two weeks, beginning with his introduction to Mr. Smith and followed by the tracking down of Mr. Jones. He continued with his dealings with both aliens and included the conversation with the sector leader of the Coalition. Next came his plan to dupe the Disciples into battling the Swarm and the demise of Mr. Jones (*excluding* the involvement of DEDEP). He finished with the current activities of the Swarm – their search for the person(s) responsible for killing one of their number (without being too specific) and the UFO flap – and his further enlistment of the Disciples. All the while, the expression of Torres' face alternated between surprise, incredulity, amusement, and horror in no discernible pattern. The detective leaned back in his chair, sighed deeply, and regarded his friend with a there-you-have-it look.

Torres did not speak for several moments. Larkin could just picture the mental gears shifting as the man tried to absorb the most incredible story he would ever hear. The Vice Mayor was actually sweating! Finally, he found his tongue.

"You're right, old son, I do find that story hard to believe. And, if anyone but you had told me it, I'd've made a reservation for him at the State Hospital." He *humph*ed. "Y'know, on the other hand, this could explain those strange reports I've been getting from Police Chief Barnwell. He's got two bodies in the City morgue that has the coroner stumped." He rubbed his jaw. "So, we're not alone after all."

"Nope. And we're caught in the middle of an interstellar war, one that could spell the end of civilization – and the planet – as we know it. It sounds like hyperbole, Jack, but it's not. Really."

"OK, George. What can I do for the Good Cause?"

"Did you happen to notice the two bruisers standing on the corner as you came in?"

"Yeah, now that you mention it. Weird-looking dudes – gave me the shivers."

"And well they should. They're part of the Swarm."

"*No shit!?!*" Torres exclaimed uncharacteristically, swinging around in his chair, staring out the window, and upsetting the restaurant patrons nearby. "Be damned!"

"No shit, Jack. And we all may be damned before this is over. Tell Barnwell to have his people keep an eye out for anyone who looks like them and report their whereabouts. But, *under no circumstances* are they to approach those bozos. They're dangerous, and they'll kill you as soon as look at you."

"It's hard to believe there's someone my boys can't handle, but I'll pass the word. Anything else?"

"Isn't that enough? Look, Jack, I need information, not false heroics. My Grand Plan depends on it."

"All right. We'll play it your way, for now. Just keep me posted." He peered at Larkin's soup and pursed his lips. "I think your soup is getting cold, old son. Let me buy you some more."

* * *

After lunch and an inquiry about the Torres family, the detective decided to pay a visit to Browsing Unlimited. Although he had enlisted the aid of the Disciples and now the police department to monitor the streets, he couldn't rely on either organization one hundred per cent; the former was limited to a physical description of the Swarm which it might misinterpret to the detriment of innocent humans, while the latter had higher priorities, i.e. law enforcement, than searching for faces on the street. Kenny and Paddy, however, had a much more reliable method of searching, and they could perform far faster. The Disciples and the police would act as red herrings to throw the Swarm off the scent of the real threat to their plans of conquest.

The bookshop was again crowded. Although Larkin was a criminal psychologist rather than a social psychologist, he was beginning to understand that people browsed/shopped as the spirit moved them, and they became random factors in the world of commerce. Madison Avenue could pump out all the advertising it wanted to, as fast as it could, but it could not ever hope to persuade as many browsers/shoppers it wanted for its clients when and where the clients desired. People heeded the ads – or not – as the spirit moved them.

Larkin preferred large crowds. More people in a given area spent a considerable amount of time jostling each other and therefore paid little attention to someone with a disability – unless they were jostled by that someone. He could lose himself in a crowd and perform his detecting uninterrupted by those who had other things on their minds. That was the theory anyway and, most of the time, the theory played true.

This day, it didn't.

As he wended his way through the mob, handing out perfunctory apologies as he jostled, he felt a tap on his shoulder. He slowly spun around and gazed into the face of the one person he'd rather not have encountered: Dorothea Hedberg. He had completely forgotten about her desire to meet him here today, and he had no way out of the assignation. Instead of her usual Disciple garb, she was wearing a powder-blue matching skirt and jacket and a pink blouse which complemented her straw-blond hair. She was also wearing her best smile. He smiled back – insincerely -- and shook her hand perfunctorily.

"I was in His Worship's office this morning," he said by way of misleading her, "but you weren't there."

"I was running errands for him. My loss for having missed you. Really, George, if I didn't know better, I'd swear you were avoiding me."

And you'd be right, sister!

"I'm not avoiding you, Dorothea. It's just that I've been very busy lately. Not only do I have my own business to run, but the Archdeacon has me running some errands for him as well."

A browser pushed past them, and "Sister" Hedberg used the occasion as an excuse to press herself against him. Larkin groaned inwardly at the touch of her warm, soft body and the aroma of her cheap perfume. She had just ratcheted up her seduction tactics a few notches and, under the present circumstances, he was unable to resist the contact. She picked a piece of lint off his coat and gazed into his eyes with unabashed desire.

"If I didn't know better, *Sister* Hedberg, I'd swear you were trying to seduce me. What would His Worship say about that?"

"What he would say is irrelevant, George. Don't you find me attractive?"

"I do. I certainly do." He took a deep breath and concocted his biggest lie yet. "Look, when we have finally defeated those hell-spawn and the world is safe for God-fearing people again, we'll both have plenty of time for…more pleasurable activities."

"Promise?"

"I promise."

I'm glad Sheena isn't here. She'd be arrested for two counts of manslaughter right about now!

"All right, I guess I'll have to be patient a little while longer. But we can still meet here for more private conversation, can't we?"

"Of course – as time permits. I wouldn't have it any other way. Now, you must excuse me. I'm here researching a matter for one of my clients."

"Very well." On an impulse, she leaned forward and kissed him on the lips. "Bye-bye, George."

Larkin disappeared into the stacks and breathed a heavy sigh of relief. "Sister" Hedberg was getting out of control; and, if he weren't careful, she could ruin his Grand Plan by spreading vicious rumors about him throughout the Disciple organization. "Hell hath no fury like a woman scorned," would be absolutely true in his case. He'd be on the run then, spending more time protecting himself than protecting humankind. What to do, what to do? as Emil often said.

He waited until Hedberg had exited the bookstore before approaching Paddy, whose turn it was to man the check-out counter. The psycho-communicator finished his transaction with a customer – the *hausfrau* again with another armload of cookbooks – and regarded the detective with a smirk on his face. Larkin shook his head.

"I suppose you saw what happened."

"*Everybody* saw what happened, old darling. When's the wedding?"

"Very funny. Don't hold your breath waiting for that 'happy' day. I'd hoped to speak to both you and Kenny, but it looks like I'm out of luck."

"P'rhaps not. Kenny can open a channel, so to speak, and I can 'listen' in."

Assured of a three-way conversation, the detective surreptitiously made his way toward the back room. He had gone not halfway when, out of the corner of his eye, he spied a very chilling sight. The same two Swarm members he had seen outside of the restaurant had just entered the bookshop and were glancing left and right and examining each face in a most blatant fashion. As each face was scrutinized, the face's owner frowned or scowled as the mood took him/her. One or two examinees made remarks reflecting their displeasure at the unwarranted and unwanted scrutiny; this reaction netted them an even deeper scowl from the scar-faced Leader of the task force which was sufficient to intimidate the foolhardy humans into silence.

Larkin glanced at Paddy. If the Englishman could have been more pale than usual, he was then. Undoubtedly, his memory of Kenny's recent kidnapping by the late Mr. Jones was running wild through his brain; equally undoubtedly, the images Paddy was transmitting to his brother were producing the same sort of alarm in the other Smythe. The detective had his own concerns; if the Swarm decided to make a circuit throughout the Store, he was not safe. The Leader would recognize him and seize him without a moment's hesitation. His disability would prevent him from resisting, and he could not count on any assistance from any of the customers, by now too cowed by the menacing appearance and behavior of the aliens to move against them even though the humans outnumbered them. He had to get into the back room ASAP.

His route had to be carefully planned. He had to maneuver through and around the stacks without exposing himself to anyone in the front section of the store. That was easier said than done, given the arrangement – or the lack thereof – of the shelving. Thus, he inched along one aisle – all the while peeking through (if possible) the rows of books to pinpoint the exact location of the Swarm – painstakingly slid around the end of a stack, and entered the next aisle. By this circuitous route, he managed to reach the door to the back room. He made one last scan to avoid the possibility of the Swarms' noticing the door opening, waited anxiously until both aliens were looking in other directions, quickly opened the door, and slipped through. Once inside, he released the breath he had been holding.

He glanced around the combination "office"/storeroom and saw no one immediately. Where was Kenny? Had he left the building when Paddy relayed the frightful images to him? He wouldn't have blamed the psycho-communicator one bit for running for his life, not after the brutal treatment he had already received. But, would he leave his brother in the lurch to face the Enemy alone? The Twins' relationship to one another was such that the notion that one would desert the other was unthinkable. They had once been linked together physically; they were now inexorably linked together psychically. So, where *was* Kenny?

"George," a whisper issued from his left.

The detective pivoted and spied the errant brother huddled in the far corner of the room, a broomstick held tightly in his hand. If he too could have been more pale than usual, he was then. Larkin hurried over to him and gripped the man's thin shoulders. Tears were streaming down the other's face, and he trembled all over.

"Thank God it's you, old darling," Kenny murmured tremulously. "I don't know what I would've done if it had been those bloody barstards coming through the door."

"Well, now there's two of us. Together, we'll knock them about a bit, eh?"

Kenny laughed in spite of himself and wiped the tears from his face.

"Good old George. You do love to play the cheerleader, don't you?"

"Of course. How else am I to keep the troops in line? I –"

"Hold on! I'm getting a message from Paddy." Two seconds later: "Ah, the all-clear. The bloody barstards have departed at last."

"Hoorah! You should know that I was as scared as you were. One of those jokers knows my face. If he had spotted me, I'd've been disappeared."

"And we can't have that, can we? We'd be lost without you, old darling. Um, I'm sure you had a reason for being here, yes?"

"Yes. I've a got a new assignment for you two – or rather I've got an update of your old assignment. Open a channel to Paddy, will you?"

SPIES

IT WAS AN ambitious plan, even for the "master strategist" of DEDEP: to locate every single member of the Swarm in the United States and to place colored pins on a map to mark those locations. George Larkin was concerned that the Twins' formidable mental powers might have their limitations; but they assured him that, although they had never actually tested their powers for any limitations, they didn't think they had any on Earth and the assignment would be "a walk in the park" (their words). The detective then asked if they would access the mind of a Swarm member, preferably one in a leadership position. The answer was a qualified "yes"; Kenny and Paddy allowed that, since an alien mind was involved, accessing it and understanding how it functioned would take more time than it took to do the same with a human mind. Larkin gave them *carte blanche* to carry out the task and departed the bookshop.

The Smythes started with "ground zero," i.e. the City. From there, they would expand their search in concentric circles until all sections of the country had been covered. Once the Swarm locations had been discovered, they would focus on the base in Nebraska, determine which member was the "Commandant," and scan him.

It was easier said than done, as they were about to find out.

* * *

The infinite blackness, peppered with points of pulsating lights.

The pulsating lights are the "stars" in the metaphysical universe, created by the energies generated by extant minds. The brightness of the "stars" is in direct proportion to the strength of the signals, but each radiates at a unique frequency and therefore can accurately identify any given mind.

Into this universe enter two more points of light. They are very bright, and they pulse rapidly, marks of a high signal strength. These two lights are so close together that they almost appear to be a single point. The surrounding blackness shows many other points of light, but they are very dim in comparison with the newcomers.

The Twins now stretch forth their combined consciousnesses into this universe. They ignore most of the dimmer lights. They know the frequency on which the minds of the Swarm operate, and that is the focus of their concentration. Carefully and methodically, they scan.

The members of the Swarm present in the City soon come into focus. Their energies are concentrated in two groups; the first consists of two units, one of which is infinitesimally brighter than its companion, and the second numbers eleven units. The first group causes the searchers alarm for it is not far from their own location.

*Bloody *hell*! [Paddy exclaims]. Those are the blighters who were in the shop. They're still in the neighborhood.

*The one might be the local leader [Kenny observes]. Our dear George said that a high-ranking officer was in the City. I'll make a note of his location, dear heart. He's a likely candidate for scanning.

In the physical universe, any number of tools exist for pinpointing a given object, ranging from a simple measurement of distance between the object and a prominent landmark to a sophisticated radar scan. In the metaphysical universe where no such landmarks are available, one is limited to a sort of "mental radar." The searcher designates a point as "ground zero" and creates a new system of measurement of distances. Since the searcher is now at the center of an imaginary sphere, (s)he necessarily denotes the location of the target by use of three units of the new system – one for distance from him/her, one for distance above or below the horizontal plane of the center of the sphere, and one for distance left or right of the vertical plane of the center of the sphere. The names of the units of distance are completely arbitrary, but they must be consistent throughout the process of location.

As they developed their mental powers over the years, the Twins had discovered that Kenny's "radar" was more accurate than Paddy's, and so he has taken it upon himself to create the mental "map."

The immediate members of the Swarm are duly "registered" on the "map." They begin the expansion of the search.

As the tedious work continues, they are surprised that the targets are few and far between. They are not surprised, however, to learn that, when they do come upon a likely location, a large number of the Swarm are concentrated there; for example, the base in Nebraska numbers thirty-plus individuals, one of which is obviously the "Commandant." They surmise that the Swarm has concentrated its spy operations to only a few select locations on the planet, locations which present the highest threat of resistance to any assault launched against the inhabitants of Earth.

Eventually, the task is completed. Kenny now has a complete "picture" of Swarm activity on the planet. When the Twins return to the physical universe, they will transfer the "data" to George Larkin's mind and let him play with them as he will.

With Phase One of the task behind them, they prepare themselves for Phase Two: the scanning of an alien mind. But, first, they decide to rest and gather their strength.

* * *

(Paddy announces that, as part of his relaxation, he'd like to go for a walk and sort things out.)

*Don't be too long about it, dear heart [Kenny admonishes him]. We've got to report to our dear George before the day is out. And scanning a Swarm mind will take a while.

*Oh, I'll be back before you know it. I wouldn't want to keep our end down, don't you know?

(He takes his derby – the one with the bright orange band above the brim – off the coat rack in the back room and places it on his head at a jaunty angle. With a two-fingered salute to his brother, he exits out the rear entrance and ambles toward the southern end of the row of small businesses, humming softly as he goes.)

ah me it's a good thing i remembered to wear my topper bloody hell it must be hotter than ever today oh yes it is can't wait for winter to come it'll be a welcome relief hum the little exercise in the zone tuckered me out i'm afraid i ain't got the stamina for that sort of thing that kenny has if i had had to do the exercise alone i'd be a bloody nervous wreck by now oh yes i would we told our dear george that we didn't have limits to our powers a little white lie that was we do get tuckered out now and again and our range is limited to this planet but the old darling doesn't press us too much bless him

the real task is ahead of us i for one am not looking forward to scanning an alien mind you never know what you'd find in there human minds are mostly cesspools full of lies misconceptions devious thoughts schemes and other such rubbish it's a wonder they don't all collapse from the sheer burden of all that garbage but at least they're familiar an alien brain is another beast altogether don't you know it's like a forest you've never been in before you don't know what to expect worse you're liable to get lost and never find your way out br-r-r-r what a chilling thought that is

and kenny has the same fears oh he puts on a brave face in the presence of the mundanes but i can tell when he's afraid as much as he can tell in me

well, we'll muddle through for george's sake lord knows he's got a greater burden to bear than either of us all that planning and scheming i don't see how he can manage it all i guess that's his particular psi-talent even if emil doesn't classify it as such i should mention it to the old boy yes i should

ah there are a couple of familiar faces jolly good

(As Paddy approaches the nearby bus stop, he spies the visually-impaired gentleman and his seeing-eye dog whom he had chanced to meet a week-and-a-half ago. The dog turns its head upon hearing the tread of human footsteps; its ears perk up as it recognizes the human, and it wags its tail in friendly greeting.)

*Why, it's Paddy! [the dog says]. Hello. I haven't seen you for some time.

*Hello, Meredith. How've you been?

*Very fine, thank you. And you?

*Couldn't be better. I do wish it were a bit cooler though.

*Yes, I agree. It's a good thing my master doesn't require my services too often. I think if I had to spend all day in the hot sun, I'd be completely exhausted.

*You and I both. Have you had any more problems with the white-covered [humans]?

*No, nothing serious. But the noises they make frighten me.

*They frighten me as well, lad.

*I shouldn't wonder, since you can speak. If you don't mind me saying so, we [dogs] must stick together.

*I'm pleased that you regard me as a [dog]. Makes me feel I'm good company.

*You *are* good company, Paddy. We should try to meet more often.

*I'd like that, Meredith.

*Oh, before I forget. I've got some interesting news for you. Two days ago, I met a female [human] who could speak.

*Did ye now? Tell me about her.

*Her name is Melissa. She's tall and slender and wears the raggediest coverings I've ever seen. I've seen her before several times, but I thought she was just another [human] who couldn't speak. So, I didn't pay much attention to her.

*How did you learn she could speak?

*Well, that's the oddest thing. I saw her rummaging through a trash barrel. She pulled out a brown paper bag that had some [human] food in it and started eating the food. I thought it was disgusting and before

I could stop myself, I told her so. I didn't care if she could speak or not. I just had to say something.

*And she heard you?

*Yes, she did. She looked at me, and her face turned red when your kind is embarrassed. That's when she spoke. She said, 'You'd eat anything too if you were hungry enough.' Then she hurried off before I could speak with her some more.

*Hm-m-m. I'd dearly like to meet that [human]. If you see her again, would you mention my name to her? I'd really appreciate it.

*I certainly will. Um, here comes the vehicle my master is waiting for. Good-bye, Paddy.

*Good-bye, Meredith.

(The City bus comes to a stop, and the driver opens the door. The dog clambers in first, then waits patiently as its master struggles to board the bus. When both are aboard, the door closes, and the bus speeds off. Paddy watches it go, lost in thought.)

good god a female *telepath who can speak to animals too kenny will be thrilled george will be thrilled and emil will be delirious and will you be thrilled as well paddy old sock wouldn't it be loverly to have some female companionship oh yes it would*

*Kenny, dear heart. You'll never guess what I've just learned.

* * *

The Twins return to the infinite blackness of the metaphysical universe. They make their way unerringly to the group of lights generated by the minds of alien invaders located, in the physical universe, in Nebraska. All but one of these lights are in a tight formation; based upon previous reports by Christopher Wredling, Kenny and Paddy deduce that the Swarm is engaged in military maneuvers. They ignore these and seek out the solitary light which is brighter (comparatively speaking) than the others. This one has been identified as "Commandant Yowk," and his mind is to be scanned for any useful information (if possible). Any information gleaned will be relayed to DEDEP's Director of Operations who will then devise a defense against any Swarm attack and perhaps an offense to send them packing.

The scan will be tricky, however, and may entail a high level of risk. While the Smythes have tracked the aliens on several occasions, neither has had the desire to access their minds. Such an invasion might expose them to defensive mechanisms designed to snare an unwary probe and/ or to cause extensive damage to the prober's mind. A human analogy is a labyrinth or a maze; it must be entered cautiously and navigated one slow step at a time.

*How do we proceed, dear heart? [Paddy inquires].

*Let's access the sensory regions first, shall we? We'll have a fair idea of what the blighter is doing at the moment.

As they have surmised, finding the sensory regions in this alien brain takes some time. For one thing, these regions are located in a different portion of a Swarm brain than the human counterparts are. For another, the Swarm optical apparatus operates at a different frequency, and they must decode that frequency before they can access any sensory input. After much effort – and not a few "wrong turns" – they achieve one of their goals -- images received from the alien's optical nerve -- and now "see" what Commandant Yowk sees.

This individual is in an enclosed space, presumably his "command post." He seems to be seated at a console similar to the ones George and Monk had purloined from the apartment of the late Mr. Jones. This console also has a holographic monitor displaying the image of another Swarm member in an unknown location. Apparently, the Commandant is reporting to his own superior officer on whatever progress – or lack thereof – his unit has made in the prosecution of the Swarm's war plans. The Twins cannot hear what is being said as they have yet to find the auditory region of the alien brain – not that doing so would be helpful as they would not have been able to understand the Swarm's language. It is clear, however, that the "superior officer" is not pleased by what is being reported to him, judging from the fierce scowl on his face. Kenny and Paddy can imagine any number of reasons for displeasure, and none of them is comforting.

Abruptly, the monitor disappears, and a partial view of the enclosure greets the observers. This view shows a doorway. On either side of the doorway, on the walls, are plaques with alien script engraved upon them. Prominent above the script is a representation of a winged creature; it is clutching a circular object with strange markings on it.

*Bloody hell! [Paddy grumbles]. I'll wager that thing is the barstards' symbol of identification, similar to the one the Nazis used when they tried to conquer Europe.

*I agree wholeheartedly, dear heart. That image is quite militaristic. It fairly screams 'Conquest!'

A moment of silence passes. The doorway opens suddenly, and a lesser-ranking soldier enters. He approaches Commandant Yowk, stiffens, and slaps his forehead in a parody of a salute. He shows signs of nervousness at being here. There is a brief conversation as the soldier makes his report. He slaps his forehead again, pivots, and hastily exits the command post.

*I'd give any amount of money [Kenny remarks] to know what just transpired. But I'm not likely to.

*A pity. It could have been useful information for our dear George.

*Ah, well, let's proceed to the next task, shall we?

*Could we rest a bit? Doing an alien brain has used up a lot of energy.

*Very well. A *brief* respite, though. This brain makes me ill at ease, and I'd rather not stay in it any longer than I have to.

*I agree. A hundred count then?

During the count, the Twins "rest" by reviewing what they have learned so far. One, there is a rigid pecking order which dominates the Swarm – not too surprising, given its militaristic organization – and it seems to be governed by fear. Two, the Swarm credo has its parallel in fascist organizations on Earth. Three, it thrives on cruelty, torture, and sadism. And four, it exists solely to conquer for the sake of conquest which is inexplicable to the human mind; conquest without the desire for plunder, territorial gain, or enslavement – the essence of a large part of human history – has no terrestrial equivalent. And perhaps this is why the Swarm is more dangerous than "run-of-the-mill" conquerors;

bloodlust which cannot be sated ends only when there is nothing left to conquer. The very idea chills the blood of the Smythes. Having grown up listening to accounts of world war and utter destruction and having witnessed first-hand the mind-set that produces war is not a legacy to be wished on anyone.

They are happy when the hundred count is concluded, for they can put aside such unnerving thoughts and focus on the daunting task ahead. That task, the searching of the Commandant's memories will be very exacting and require extreme concentration. One misstep may alert the alien to a potential threat to his well-being; and, given his advanced technology, he may have a device which will counter and/or destroy the originator of that threat.

After long moments of searching, Kenny and Paddy locate the region where Swarm memories are stored. They promise themselves that they will limit the scan to only the top layers, i.e. the most recent memories. A deeper probe would require more time than they want to expend. Byte by byte, they examine first the very top layer, and they almost regret having undertaken the project.

*Bloody hell! [Paddy cries out]. I thought human minds were sewers full of dark thoughts and negative emotions. This blighter positively reeks of evil!

*Steady on, lad [Kenny responds soothingly]. I know it's like a sewer in here, and I'd like nothing better than to run away as fast and as far as I can. But we've got a job to do. George is depending on us.

Despite their misgivings, they continue the search. They pick their way through memories of the Swarm's most recent ruination of an inhabited world: the attack without warning, the use of fearful weapons of destruction, cities vaporized in a matter of minutes, millions upon millions of innocent beings slaughtered without surcease or mercy, whole landscapes scorched beyond recognition. Worse: the soldiers of the Swarm laughing riotously as they raze city after city, pick off fleeing refugees one by one, rape and torture as the mood suits them, and lay waste to the entire planet. Commandant Yowk is apparently the equivalent to a company commander whose duty it is to hunt down stragglers among the doomed population who attempt to hide from the invaders and to execute them summarily (often barbarously). It takes all the resolve the Twins can muster to complete their mission.

Despite the horror of it all, they finally find the useful information they have been looking for. It is a detailed plan for the upcoming assault on Planet Earth – where the Swarm will strike first, what weapons it will deploy, how it will proceed during successive phases of the invasion, what it will do to apply the *coup de grace*, and how it will deal with resistance from the indigenous population. These thoughts are as sickening as the previous ones, but Kenny and Paddy file them away for future retrieval when they report back to the Director of Operations.

*Good God! [Kenny heaves a mental sigh of relief]. I'm happy to have that behind us. I don't think I could've endured a single second more of that bloody awful mind!

*You won't get any argument from me on that score, dear heart. Let's go home.

As carefully as they entered the alien mind, they withdraw from it and pull back until the point of light which represents it is just one of many. They are now in the comforting confines of the empty spaces of the metaphysical universe. The search has depleted much of their energies and disturbed them greatly, and they decide to take a moment or two to contemplate on the peace and quiet which surrounds them before returning to the physical universe. It is a blissful interlude.

Or so they think.

Kenny spots a very bright point of light far off and alerts his brother. This point of light is not stationary but is moving toward them at a steady pace. Neither has ever seen the like, and they are naturally concerned. Nevertheless, they remain where they are because they wish to discover what this strange new phenomenon is.

The mobile point of light halts before them and vibrates slightly for the space of a few heartbeats. Then, in a thundering tone, a Voice fills their minds.

*WHO ARE YOU?

*We are travelers and explorers [Kenny replies with feigned self-confidence]. Who are *you*?

*I AM THE MONITOR FOR THIS DIMENSION. I WISH TO KNOW YOUR POINT OF ORIGIN AND YOUR PURPOSE HERE.

*I've already told you why we're here. And our origin is in a physical reality, a planet called 'Earth,' if that's any help to you.

*'EARTH'? I HAVE HEARD THAT DESIGNATION BEFORE. ARE YOU THEN 'HUMANS'?

*We are.

*I HAVE MADE CONTACT WITH OTHERS OF YOUR SPECIES. BUT YOU ARE THE FIRST I HAVE ENCOUNTERED IN THE [indecipherable] ZONE.

*Really? And where is *your* point of origin, if I may ask?

*I HAVE ALWAYS EXISTED IN THE [indecipherable] ZONE SINCE THE BEGINNING.

*The beginning of what?

*THE BEGINNING OF ALL. I HAVE BEEN ASSIGNED AS THE MONITOR OF THIS DIMENSION.

*'Assigned'? By whom?

*I AM NOT PERMITTED TO SAY. I BID YOU FAREWELL, HUMANS. WE SHALL MEET AGAIN.

The bright point of light retreats until it fades from view. The metaphysical universe becomes very still once more. A long moment passes before either brother dares to speak.

*Bloody hell! [Paddy exclaims, shaken to his core]. That was an astounding…revelation!

*Indeed. A 'monitor' of this 'dimension.' Who or what is it monitoring? And why? And, more importantly, for whom? Here's a great mystery, dear heart, one that may change everything about — about *everything.*

* * *

"OK, Jeanie, I'm ready for the big wrench now."

"Right, Chief," the young woman responded and rummaged through Freddie's tool box for the requested implement.

In the short time she had been assigned to assist DEDEP's "Mr. Fix-it," Jean Fulton had (she believed) found a kindred spirit. Not only did the dwarf have an amazing knowledge of repair work – in some ways, he reminded her of her father from whom she had learned *her* own skills – but he also recognized his own limitations and deferred to her for some of the more difficult tasks. She appreciated this and was encouraged to suggest new ways of repairing things. Sometimes Freddie heeded her advice, and sometimes he didn't; but he always explained why he didn't, and she acquiesced in light of his greater expertise.

They made a great team (she believed), and they were seldom apart. To the rest of DEDEP, they were an "odd couple" – the diminutive man and the tall, lithe woman – but she and he ignored the whispered comments and went about their business. Whenever Stan was not in "school," he joined the "Fix-it Team" and used his psycho-kinetic ability to great effect. Jean's absence from the Team occurred only when Dr. Razumov summoned the "eel" to his laboratory for further testing.

Not long afterwards, she and Freddie began to confide in each other about their respective pasts. Far into the night, they told "war stories" of their abuses and indignities at the hands of so-called "normal" people which had led to their isolationism. These sessions also contributed to the whispered comments. Despite initial reservations, she and Freddie both agreed that their acceptance for *who* they were, and not for *what* they were, by DEDEP had been the best thing to happen in their short lives. The one thing they did not talk about was the handy man's involvement in the gestalt, mainly because neither of them really understood the thing at all.

At the moment, both were in "Fat Henry" Rawlins' apartment replacing a burst water pipe in the bathroom. The task was made more irksome by the "dreaming prophet's" incessant whining over the loss of his conveniences and his useless "suggestions" for repairing the same. Ordinarily, Freddie might have deferred to his assistant in the use of the large wrench; but the problem pipe lay in a tight space, and his smaller size made the job easier to perform. By working with each other and contributing their respective skills, the repairs went faster, and they accomplished more in a day's labor than either could have alone.

"Here ya go, Chief," Jean said cheerfully as she handed over the wrench.

"Huh! Ain't nobody ever called me 'Chief' before. Kinda like it though. Just don't go crazy with it."

"Right, Chief," she said and giggled.

The dwarf was about to make a piquant comment when he was prevented by an announcement over the PA system.

"Attention, please," the voice of the Director came muffled through the walls of the apartment. "Miss Fulton, please report to Laboratory #2. Miss Fulton, come to Laboratory #2, *pozhalsto*."

"Damn!" Freddie swore. "The Doc is takin' away my #1 assistant again!"

"I don't like it any more than you do. But, in the short time I've been here, I've come to realize that we all have certain…obligations."

"Yeah, yer right about that, kiddo. Well, off ya go. Give my regards to the Doc."

"Sure thing, Chief."

When she entered Laboratory #2, the Doctor was busily puttering away (as he often did) with some piece of equipment, examining it with a careful eye as if he were looking for signs of damage or wear. All the while, he hummed tunelessly. The sound of the door opening and closing caused him to look up in surprise, but he relaxed when he saw who it was.

"*Spaceebo*, Miss Fulton, for being so prompt. I shall not take too much of your time. Today, I will hook you up to the EEG again to examine your amygdala. We were interrupted before, as you will recall."

He wheeled a cart in front of her. The EEG on it appeared similar to the one she had seen previously, except it was larger and had more control knobs. Carefully he attached four sensor pads to her skull, two at the left and right of the top, and two at the left and right of the base. He then fiddled with each of the control knobs, turning them to pre-determined settings.

"You may feel a slight tingling in your head, and I apologize in advance. The region I will be testing is deep within your brain, and therefore I must apply additional power."

"What if it gets too much to handle?"

"Say so, and I will disengage. Are you ready?"

She sighed, nodded, and braced herself for the alleged tingling. Dr. Razumov activated the EEG. At first, the "pens" quivered in place as the machine sought out the specific electrical impulses coursing through the amygdala; after ten seconds, the "pens" began to move back and forth but very slowly and in short arcs. He adjusted several of the controls to increase the power. The "pens" now moved in a more pronounced manner, although whether it was due to naturally strong impulses in Jean's brain or to her rising anxiety – or both – was a matter for conjecture. The old man made another adjustment, and the "pens" became quite animated. He nodded with satisfaction.

Jean started to become animated herself. The tingling in her head she had been warned about was now manifesting itself. It started out as a tickle, and she thought she was imagining things. But, as the Doctor made new adjustments to the EEG, the tickle gave way to a definite tingle, beginning at the back of her brain and radiating outwardly. It wasn't harming her, but it was annoying. She screwed up her courage in order to ride the sensation out and took a few deep breaths for good measure.

After what seemed like hours, the Doctor switched the EEG off. The tingling in Jean's head lingered on for several seconds, then dissipated altogether.

"Are you all right?" he asked solicitously.

"Yeah. It wasn't as bad as I thought it might be. Of course, I wouldn't want a steady diet of it."

"I may have to make further tests at a later date. The readings I have taken today will require some evaluation. Now, for the second phase."

"Second phase?" she asked anxiously. "What's that for?"

"I am going to measure your electrical potential in a resting state. I wish to see just how strong you actually are."

"Oh, brother!" she murmured.

The Director bent down and retrieved a black, metallic, rectangular box with two wires protruding from it. At the end of the wires were miniature, serrated clamps. He attached the clamps to her forefingers.

"This is called a voltmeter," he said by way of explanation. "It measures voltage in an electrical circuit. The human body contains a complex circuitry of neural pathways, and each individual registers a specific operating voltage in accordance with a number of biological factors. *Your* body, however, is much different than most, as I am sure you will agree. I hope to learn how much different."

"Far out!"

He activated the device and watched the gauge with no little amazement. The needle advanced steadily through numbered gradations until it halted at the maximum reading and quivered. Again, whether the output was due to her natural voltage or to her anxiety – or both – was a matter of conjecture. At the moment, he was quite impressed – not to say pleased – with what he had discovered. He de-activated the voltmeter and removed the clamps.

"I may have to employ a voltmeter with a higher range. To use one of your American expressions, you have 'maxed out' this one. The average human would have registered slightly more than half this scale."

"And that's just when I'm at rest?"

"Indeed. You are a biological dynamo, Miss Fulton. I should like to measure you when you are in an emotional state." Her eyes went wide with apprehension. "That is merely a hypothetical notion, however. I assure you that I am not the 'mad scientist' everyone thinks I am."

"Are we through here then?"

"We are. You may return to your normal duties. *Do sveedanye.*"

* * *

From the diary of Christopher Wredling:

I botched it! No doubt about it – I screwed up!

George's weird informant, the 'Quintessential Quark,' saw something I didn't. We were both at the Swarm base, and I missed the presence of a Disciple collaborating with the aliens. After the last conference, George spoke to me in private about it. He wasn't angry or disappointed or anything. He just wanted to know how I could have missed an important development in the war against the Swarm. I didn't have an answer for him, and I apologized for my failure.

I had been riding high after my last performance as an 'angel' in the presence of a group of Disciples. George's plan to sow dissension among the fanatics was to plant doubt in their tiny little minds about their supposed 'mission' to 'bring everyone to the Light of Purity.' If they thought that that doubt came from a 'messenger of the Lord,' so much the better.

I admit I hammed it up. Those characters deserved to have the wool pulled over their eyes. And it worked! They ate up everything I said. You could see it in their faces – the acceptance of a message from God, the self-doubt and confusion, and the need to re-evaluate their current beliefs. It felt good to sow dissension.

Well, the high didn't last long, did it? George counted on me to get the job done that he assigned me, and I let him down.

It won't happen again....

...The next time I scouted the Swarm base, I was determined to make a more thorough search of the area – no matter how long it took me – and leave no stone unturned. I wasn't going to let some wild-eyed, drug-besotted conspiracy freak get the best of me.

I've just returned from my latest foray in Nebraska, and I'm glad to be home. This trip was the most harrowing experience I've ever had, including being zapped by Mr. Jones.

When I first arrived, I already had a plan in mind. First, I'd search the perimeter of the base in order to (1) see if the Quark was back on the job and (2) keep an eye out for any Disciple collaborators. I don't think the Quark is a threat to anyone but himself, but I like to keep track of all the 'players' in the 'game.' Second, barring no outward sign of either (1) or (2), I'd penetrate the interior of the base and snoop all of the structures for any inward signs.

I started the search where I last spotted the Quark. He wasn't there. The SOB was falling down on the job! Well, perhaps he was elsewhere on the perimeter. I moved on.

It was a slow, tedious process, I want to tell you. I peered left and right, keeping an eye out for the least sign of movement, either in the wooded area that surrounds the base or inside the base itself. The only movement I was seeing was that of the birds and small mammals I disturbed by my approach. (Emil says that the 'lower orders' are more sensitive to radio energy than we humans — a survival mechanism, apparently — and that they bolt at the first sign of an unusual amount of it. I guess that includes snooping psycho-projectionists! I'll have to take Emil's word for it.)

About halfway around the perimeter, I finally spotted a major movement — a Swarm soldier in the woods. I had no idea why he was there, and so I moved in closer to investigate. I was sorry I did. The bugger was relieving himself! Sad to say, that's an image that will stay with me the rest of my life. The Swarm behave like animals in more ways than one.

I hurried on and finished the circuit. For some unfathomable reason, the interior of the base seemed deserted. One would think that a militaristic bunch like the Swarm would be like a beehive, training and preparing for battle. Maybe it was lunch-time and they were in their version of the 'mess hall.' Or maybe they were being given a lecture by their commandant, reminding them of the 'glorious victories' they had already scored and promising them more of the same in the days to come. One must keep the troops' morale up, mustn't one?

To my pleasant surprise, when I returned to my starting point, the Quark was at his 'post' again. I moved closer and 'looked' over his shoulder, as it were.

I'll give the Quark this: he may be a whacked-out conspiracy freak, but he knew enough to make notes of his findings. He had a pair of binoculars and was scanning the base from one end to the other. Every so often, he'd scribble something on a dog-eared notepad with a stub of a pencil — just what any diligent observer should do.

(I had to laugh to myself at that point. If the Quark ever learned that he himself was being spied upon by an 'invisible man,' he'd probably lose it then and there.)

What the Quark was writing was as disjointed as his mind probably was. There were few complete sentences — mostly phrases and single words. Obviously, he was under the influence of some drug as well as his paranoia. His scribbling — and that's the best way to describe his 'literary' output — spoke more about the impact on him by what he was observing than about what he was observing from an objective point of view. After a minute of trying to make sense of it all, I gave up and left him to his own devices.

It was time to go to Phase Two of The Plan.

I blew the Quark an invisible kiss and moved to the interior of the base. My first 'port of call' was the Swarm warship, as I have never seen a real spaceship up close before (and who has?). Lacey had described the ship in the abandoned factory on Ridgeway, but second-hand reports seldom do justice to first-hand observations; only by getting up close can one get a real feel for a thing.

This ship was four times as large as the one Lacey saw. I suppose that was because she saw an actual attack craft whereas I was looking at a troop/cargo carrier. Otherwise, the shape and coloring were the same. There were no 'portholes,' which meant that I couldn't peek in (not that I'd understand what I might see), but the outer hatch was clearly visible. I didn't see any rocket tubes at the rear; whatever motive power drove this ship was something beyond what we humans had come up with so far.

I circled the ship and examined every square inch of it, but nothing else distinguished it from Lacey's craft. I left it and started for the structures a short distance away.

And that's when I spied what I fear most: an EMF generator in the exact center of the base. The sight chilled my blood, and I thought briefly of getting out of there – fast! Obviously, the device was not in operation at the time; otherwise, I would not have been able to access the base.

As I have stated before, an EMF to me is equivalent to a brick wall to mobiles. I have to detour around it in order to get where I'm going and, more often than not, it takes me longer – and uses up considerable energy – to get there. What really puts the fear in me is what would happen to me if I was caught inside an EMF when it was activated. Would I be trapped like a fly in a spider's web? Or would my own energy field be disrupted and I die? Horrible scenarios to contemplate.

DEDEP has acquired an EMF generator which George and Monk pilfered from the apartment of Mr. Jones, and Emil activates it at certain times of the day when I am not out wandering about. It is on the upper level and its effects do not extend to the lower level where my body resides.

I am relatively safe; yet, I do 'hear' it when it is on – a faint pulsing hum, reaching out to seize me in its grip.

From that moment on, I walked on eggshells, hoping that the Swarm would not activate the generator while I was still there. I wondered idly why they needed it in the first place. The base was located in the middle of a woods, and only a sturdy hiker could have trekked in and spotted it. Maybe it was SOP for the security of Swarm bases, no matter where they were. In any event, I kept a close eye on it, though in the back of my mind, I knew that no alertness on my part would save me if the unthinkable occurred.

The three structures on the base looked like cardboard boxes. The smallest one was maybe five meters wide, five meters long, and three meters high. I assumed it was the 'command post,' although it could have been anything. The other two were twice as large, ten by ten by six. One of them had to be a barracks for the soldiers, but the purpose of the third one was anybody's guess. None of the structures had any windows, but doorways were in evidence.

While I contemplated the possibility of going inside one or all of the structures and snooping around, the entrance to one of the large ones flew open, and the soldiers filed out at a brisk pace. They numbered thirty-six altogether, and they all looked like Mr. Jones. Were they a clone race then? Once outside, they formed up into six ranks of six each – squads? – and stood stiff as statues. Another Swarmer followed them, but his pace was slow and deliberate. He marched to the front of the formation.

This person was undoubtedly the Commandant – 'Yowk' was his name, George informed me – and his uniform bore several markings that the others lacked, suggesting a chain of command. He appeared more vicious and sadistic than his troops, and he carried more scars than they did. Plus, he wore an eyepatch. Apparently, that was how a Swarm soldier advanced in rank – by being more cruel than anybody else.

The Commandant addressed his troops, and they broke formation. Four of the squads took up positions at the four major compass points and spread out at six-foot intervals, while the other two formed a circle around the EMF generator. All of them drew side arms attached to their belts and stood at the ready awaiting further orders. Yowk then marched over to the generator.

That's when I panicked for real. If he was going to switch that thing on, I wanted to be somewhere else. Immediately, I headed for the Quark's position. I should say his former position, because the moment the troops deployed, he was off and running. And who could blame him? I was 'running' too, but for a very different reason.

Thankfully, I made it to the woods in time (I might not be here composing this journal entry otherwise). I felt a gentle push as the EMF expanded and encompassed the entire base. It had been much too close for comfort, I can tell you! On the other hand, I now knew what might have happened if I had been within range of the generator; I would have been sent flying, out of control, to God-knows-where.

After gathering my wits about me, I made one final observation. The Swarm troops began firing their side arms into the woods. Where their fire struck an object, that object burst into flames. They kept up the fire for five minutes, then returned to their original formation. Commandant Yowk spoke to them again and dismissed them whereupon they returned to the structure they had occupied. Yowk de-activated the generator, scanned the area with a wicked grin on his face, and headed for the command post.

I had seen enough for one day and returned home.

* * *

*Can this situation get any more complicated? [Larkin grumbled as soon as the Twins reported back to him].

*One would hope not, old darling. We...

*...have enough to worry about as it is.

*Still, you must agree that this 'Monitor' bloke...

*...represents a force to be reckoned with.

*That goes without saying. Did you get the impression that it was hostile?

*No. It seemed to be simply curious about...

*...us, because our presence took it by surprise.

*On the other hand, its reluctance to share information...

*...about itself or the alleged beings behind it may...

*...constitute hostility. But we can't be sure on that...

*...point until we have further contact with it.

*I agree. There's no telling what its intentions are, now that it's aware of our existence and can travel in its alleged territory. You two have to be extra careful when you're in the 'zone' from now on.

*Right you are, guv [Kenny responded mischievously].

Larkin leaned back in his chair and stared at the ceiling for a minute or two, mostly to clear his head. He'd already received Chris' latest report on the doings in Nebraska, and he had yet to consider its implications. The notion that there was an extra-dimensional creature wandering about was making his head spin, and he had to place the creature somewhere on his mental "map."

The idea of beings existing outside the normal space-time continuum – what humankind called "reality" – for the most part belonged to the realm of science fiction, and the writers of the same had used that idea as an additional tool to make a point. There was, however, a small band of scientists, calling themselves the "Borderland Science Associates," who took the idea (among others just as fantastic) seriously and discussed/investigated the possibility of actuality just as they might in the appearance of a new biological species or a new astrophysical phenomenon. The Borderlanders kept pretty much to themselves and seldom informed the general public of either their investigations or their findings (if any). The detective had learned of their existence quite by accident when he was familiarizing himself with psychic phenomena (another of the Borderlanders' interests), although he had never followed up on the discovery.

Now, he needed to follow up – if he could. A group of mysterious beings existing extra-dimensionally and purporting to "monitor" the dimension humans lived in was something not to be taken lightly. Just what were they monitoring? And why? There were too many unknowns here, and his analytical mind hated unknowns. He had to know -- if not to determine that these beings posed a threat to humankind, then to satisfy his own curiosity about them. Learning about their philosophy, political and social organizations, economic system, and history was a worthwhile endeavor.

It occurred to him then that they might have some connection to the gestalt which had suddenly appeared in the human dimension. The gestalt seemed to have originated from either another dimension or extra-dimensionality. Eve and Stan, who were responsible for bringing it into human reality, hadn't provided any clues. And, now that he thought about it, he had observed a subtle change in their attitudes – especially Eve's attitude. And then there was the way the two of them looked at each other whenever someone mentioned the gestalt. What did they know (if anything)? If they did know something, why hadn't they shared that knowledge with him and Emil? Why were they keeping it a secret?

Too many mysteries here, George old buddy. You let them pile up on you, and your brain will explode!

SECRETS

STAN JANKOWSKY WAITED half an hour after his mother retired to her bedroom before making his move. Quickly, he slid out of bed, slipped on his clothes, and tiptoed into the living room. He went to the door of his mother's bedroom and put his ear to it; he heard no sounds of activity and deduced that she was sound asleep. Psycho-kinetically, he opened the door to the apartment, tiptoed out, and closed the door in the same manner. This was a routine he had followed for the past two years, ever since he discovered that he had psycho-kinesis. Because the things he could do with his mind disturbed his mother greatly, he had elected to do them without her knowledge. For the most part, that meant sneaking out at night and practicing moving various objects he came across in the neighborhood. Sticks, stones, discarded cardboard boxes, garbage cans, beer bottles – whatever came to his attention was fair game to him – and his imaginary friend, the giant, blue-skinned "Mr. Whosis." For an hour each night that he could get away with it, he gradually increased his abilities to the point where he could maneuver multiple objects all at once and move them around in more sophisticated patterns. There were times when he wanted to stay out all night to practice, but the risk of falling asleep during the daytime was one he had learned the hard way to avoid. He did not want to add to his mother's suspicions.

During his short time at DEDEP, Stan had not had to sneak out at night as much as he had before. When he was not in a classroom seeing to his formal education under the tutelage of Christopher Wredling, he was in a laboratory performing for Emil Razumov. The Russian gave him his head, and he performed a variety of mental juggling acts, much to the surprise and delight of the Director. And, when he and Eve discovered that they could create a psychic gestalt, the time in the laboratory became even more intense.

That was the routine – until the mysterious extra-dimensional being he and Eve called the "Entity" came into their lives and changed them forever. Now, they wished to maintain contact with their new "friend," but they had to do so in secret until a time they deemed right to inform the DEDEP leadership. They needed to learn more about the Entity and its environment before revealing its existence to anyone else. Perhaps, if they felt obliged to do so, they would keep the secret as long as possible – perhaps forever.

Thus, Stan was on his way to the lower level – the maintenance area which was Freddie Hamilton's domain – where he and Eve and the handyman had agreed to meet and bring the gestalt into being for their own purposes. He moved as stealthily as a ten-year-old could, always looking over his shoulder to spot any other wanderers in the corridors, always listening for footsteps coming his way. By this means, he descended into the bowels of DEDEP.

* * *

Eve Pelletier had no need of stealth. She was considered an adult capable of making her own decisions about what to do or not to do. That she had succumbed to mental illness in the recent past might have precluded her from making any momentous decisions; yet, she had begun the long, painful road to recovery under the counseling of Emil Razumov. Her experience with the gestalt, she believed, was a major stepping stone toward recovery, although she still couldn't tell anyone about it.

She too slipped on her clothes – finding pieces quite at random, a habit she hadn't quit as yet – and exited her apartment cautiously. While it wasn't anyone's business why she might choose to wander down a darkened corridor, she would rather not encounter any other resident of DEDEP and have to explain why she was wandering and risk having others report her activities to the Director. Therefore, her movements were just as furtive as Stan's.

As she was about to exit her level and descend to the next one down (Stan's level, she thought idly), a sudden movement further down the corridor caught her eye. It was difficult to distinguish the real from the unreal in this silent, gloomy world where fantasy took on any shape one cared to give it and where creakings and rustlings became the *lingua franca*. She took one more cautious step. One of the shadows did move, and she shrank against the wall as a precaution. She hadn't imagined anything at all; someone else was out and about as well. Worse: the other was the one resident who had never seemed real to her from the beginning, not only because of his ethereal appearance but also because of his unearthly manner of traveling. Though she never would dare to speak the epithet aloud, she fully concurred with the ever-audacious Freddie Hamilton in labeling this person the "Spook."

Eve swallowed the lump forming in her throat. Ever since she had become aware of Christopher Wredling's existence and his awesome *psi*-talent, he had made her uneasy – an irrational reaction, as Dr. Razumov might have said – but she could not help herself. Her paternal grandmother, a lover of ghost stories, had tried – and succeeded – to turn her into a believer of the supernatural; and, from childhood on, young Eve had absorbed everything the old lady spoke on the subjects of ghosts and hauntings and communicating with the dead. The Church hadn't offered any counterpoint either; the priests and nuns simply passed off the idea of ghosts as a "divine mystery." Of course, she had never actually *seen* a ghost – under any circumstances – until she had encountered the "Spook," a creature who fit the classical description but who was treated by the DEDEP leadership as a "normal" person with unusual abilities.

The irony of her attitude toward Christopher Wredling (if she had chosen to examine the matter objectively) lie in the fact that she had not so long ago accepted the existence of a creature wholly out of her space-time continuum. Moreover, she (with Stan) had engaged this creature – whom they called the "Entity" – in a fantastic adventure. The Entity had promised and had delivered freedom to observe all there was to observe and to travel wherever she wished to go, and all she had to do was to open her mind to extreme possibilities. The Entity would take her away from the state of affairs which had made her life up to this point a living hell and brought her to this place deep in the Earth; it would take her away from Father Driscoll, from Dr. Razumov, from the whole world if she had the desire. And she had the desire.

If Christopher took notice of her presence in the corridor, he did not give any sign. He merely moved off in his own inimitable fashion. Eve breathed a sigh of relief and hurriedly opened the stairwell door and scrambled down to the maintenance level.

* * *

"Dunno why I let you two talk me into this," Freddie groused. He took a long drag on the stub of his cigar and blew the smoke out slowly. "Ain't bad enough I got to put in long hours tryin' to keep this place runnin' right. Now I hafta spend my nights doin' crazy stunts."

"It's only for an hour, Freddie," Eve tried to placate him, "until we get our bearings. Then we can shorten our sessions."

"Besides," Stan added, "it'll be cool."

"*Humph!* What I did in the circus was cool too, and it was a lot safer." He took another drag on his cigar. "Aw right, let's get started."

Eve and Stan started to clasp hands, but the dwarf held up a stubby hand.

"Hold on there! You ain't gonna bring that thing into my room, are ya? There ain't enough space here."

"Where then?"

"Come with me. I got just the place fer these experiments of yours."

He waddled out of his workroom-*cum*-"apartment" and down the corridor toward the area allegedly off limits to all but designated personnel. At the end of the corridor stood a large, olive-drab metal locker which nearly reached the ceiling; it possessed double doors secured by a heavy chain and padlock. Freddie pulled a ring of keys out of his tool pouch, selected a long, thick, brass-colored key, and fitted it to the padlock. The lock opened, and the chain fell away to the floor. He opened the double doors to reveal an empty space. Curiously, at the rear of the locker, a light fixture had been mounted. The handyman reached inside and flicked a switch on the side wall; a bright white light flooded both the locker and the corridor.

All the while, Eve and Stan stared in amazement. Then they noticed that the locker had no bottom. In fact, it stood over a hole in the corridor floor; and, in the hole, a ladder led down into stygian darkness. Freddie grinned at his friends' incomprehension.

"Nobody knows about this hidey-hole but me. I discovered it by accident – damn near fell down it, I did. The people who built this place wanted an extra level in case of attack. What's down there is an air-raid shelter which'll hold up to two hundred people fer a year, if it comes to that. Watch yer step."

He grasped the top rung of the ladder, swung himself onto it, and disappeared into the darkness. Stan, ever the adventurer, followed suit. Eve hesitated for a long moment, wondering what she had gotten herself into, but decided she had nothing to lose and clambered onto the ladder.

At the bottom of the shaft, another door beckoned. Freddie had already opened it and was flicking switch after switch on a panel on the inside wall. Beyond the door, overhead lights illuminated the secret place, section by section. The dwarf entered the interior with Eve and Stan hot on his heels.

It was a cave of steel, clearly the size of a football field, with a high ceiling, overhead light fixtures, and gray steel partitions every five meters. A central aisle divided the cave in two. Each partition contained eight aluminum-and-canvas cots, four on each side; each cot was accompanied by a paperboard wardrobe. At the far end of the cave, two banks of vending machines (now empty) hunkered on either side of yet another door. This door was marked with the symbols for men's and women's rest rooms; opposing arrows showed which way each gender was to go. The cave was devoid of any decorations but was strictly functional in nature, meant to be a temporary retreat in case of emergency. A heavy musty odor permeated the air; it had been a long time since anyone had been down there.

"Jeez," Stan remarked in his ten-year-old manner of observation, "what a dump!"

"I'll say," Eve agreed. "I hope they had ventilation."

"They did," Freddie informed them. "But, it takes time to kick it in at full power. Be patient. Meanwhile, pick one of these 'sleepin' rooms,' and we can get started on yer little fun 'n' games."

Eve and Stan plopped down on the nearest cot and leaned against the partition bordering it. Freddie took the opposite cot and sat cross-legged on it. The gestalt-makers clasped hands, and instantly the black sphere popped into existence. It was its original size of a softball. The woman and the boy gazed at it rapturously.

"Eve 'n' me talked about what kinda experiments we ought to do. We wasn't sure if we could pull it off, but we're gonna try."

"But first, Freddie, we want to show you more of the wonders the gestalt has to offer." Eve stretched out her hand and gently touched the sphere's surface. Her eyes went wide with delight as fantastic images flooded her mind. Stan's facial expression echoed hers. "Join hands with us, and you'll see what we're seeing."

The dwarf shook his head in disbelief but slid off the cot and moved closer to them.

"Man, it's weird how you two are the only ones who can touch that thing."

"The Entity has given us that ability," she replied simply.

Freddie stared at her incredulously. This was the first time he had ever heard the gestalt given a name – and what a name it was! Neither the woman nor the boy showed the least sign of embarrassment at speaking the name aloud; rather, they seemed like it had been the natural thing to do when one introduced a stranger to an old friend.

"Is that what you call it?" the handyman asked.

"Yeah," Stan replied. "We don't know if it's got a name where it comes from, but we decided to call it the 'Entity.'"

"Yeah? I'm thinkin' you two been holdin' out on me. When were you gonna interduce me to this...'Entity'?"

"Someday," Eve declared. "We'll ask it if it will accept you. Now, join hands with us."

The handyman took a deep breath and placed his hand on top of theirs. His eyes too went wide with wonder. He saw:

A solar flare in slow motion shoot out into space from the surface of the Sun;

A rock rolling down the side of a mountain, striking other rocks and sending them cascading downward in a long chain reaction;

A fetus in its womb shifting slightly to a more comfortable position;

A hare leading a snow leopard a merry chase across a wintry field;

A sunrise, deep orange in color, inching above the horizon and dispelling the blackness of the sky.

"Damn!" Freddie swore as he broke contact. "I seen stuff like that on the Internet, taken by photographers. But this was like actually *bein'* there in person."

"We knew you'd like it."

"An' there's lots more like it. I could watch it all day long."

"Uh-huh. So, what's next on the agenda?"

"Well," Eve answered, "we know that the Entity sends us those images in order to open up our minds. What we don't know if it can, or wants to, *receive* images from us. So, I will attempt to send an image, and you and Stan can tell me if you see it."

The young woman touched the sphere again and concentrated. The image she hoped to transmit had to be unique to her and her alone. No ordinary image would do; otherwise, one could claim that the Entity, and not her, was sending it. It occurred to her that the Entity might not allow transmission after all it had said to her and Stan about working together; it had disappeared when they had broached the subject before. But she'd soon find out, wouldn't she?

She sorted through a few recent memories – those of her life at DEDEP – and rejected them as being not very unique. She dug deeper into her past, before DEDEP, and analyzed them. Most of them were horrible: images of her family berating her for acting "odd" and/or "sinful"; images of the nuns, and the monstrous Father Driscoll, attempting to "save her soul" and punishing her for her "willfulness" when her *psi*-talent manifested itself time and again; images of her life on the streets after she had run away from home and the dirty-minded people she'd encountered there. Finally, she selected one which was less ugly than the others. It *was* unique to her, wasn't it?

She was twelve at that time and, to her utter shock and dismay, she was undergoing puberty and menstruation. One of the nuns was lecturing her about the evils of the flesh and about lustful boys; and, all the while, Sister was rubbing her own belly and working herself into a lather. Eve hadn't known whether to laugh or to cry. Either action would have been misconstrued as "willful behavior," i.e. "sinfulness."

Eve brought this image to the fore, focused on it, and *willed* it to enter the gestalt. Simultaneously, she signaled to Stan and Freddie to make contact again. The boy gasped audibly when he did so, then started to laugh at the comical behavior of the nun. Freddie chuckled and muttered something about "typical human behavior." Eve relaxed, and the image returned to the depths from which it had sprung. She was pleased that the experiment had gone so well on the first try. That meant that the Entity was willing to accommodate external sources of imagery; more importantly, it meant that it was willing to accept her and Stan as worthy collaborators in whatever venture it had in mind.

"That was a hoot!" the handyman exclaimed. "I'd sure like to know what was runnin' through that nun's mind at the time. Betcha it wasn't 'spiritual' at all. Heh-heh-heh."

"I guess I'd hafta be an adult to understand what that was all about," Stan observed. "But it sure was funny anyways. That was *cool*, Eve!"

"Thank you, gentlemen. Now, it's your turn, Stan. Think of something that was special to you and to no one else."

For Stan, that was a tall order. A ten-year-old boy hadn't as many memories as a twenty-three-year-old woman, and he was hard-pressed to think of anything "special" which had happened to him in his short life – other than the discovery that he could move things around with his mind. That had happened when an apple had fallen off the table and fallen to the floor; he had wished it would get back on the table again and, for good measure, he had pointed at it and then at the spot where he wanted it to go. He was amazed beyond belief when the apple had obeyed his wish.

Afterwards, he had wanted to know if he could repeat that stunt. He pointed at the apple and directed it to the counter next to the sink; without fail, the apple whisked away to the very spot like a trained animal. He then focused on a flower vase on the kitchen table and wished it to go next to the apple. Other objects obeyed his will as well.

In the days and weeks and months which followed, Stan experimented extensively until his abilities became second nature. Always, however, he kept those abilities a secret from his mother because he didn't want to alarm her. She had too much on her mind already – a single mother working a menial job so that he had food to eat, clothes to wear, and a roof over his head – and usually came home so tired that she often snapped at him when he displeased her. She later apologized for snapping at him, hugged him, and told him that she loved him, and that made the hurt go away. He tried to repay her love by doing little things around the apartment with his mind when she wasn't looking, and he'd smile to himself when she wondered how it had happened.

Ten-year-old boys could hardly be expected to understand what psycho-kinesis was or how it worked. To Stan, it was akin to magic, and he rationalized his abilities away to an "invisible helper" he named "Mr. Whosis." He imagined his helper to be a blue-skinned giant who laughed a lot and loved to play games. Mr. Whosis was kept secret from all around Stan, because he didn't want anybody to think he was crazy.

In the real world, secrets do not stay secret forever. One day, two months after his ninth birthday, he and Mr. Whosis were playing a game in which Stan sat on a chair and the giant would pick both up and spin them around the room. Stan thought his mother was outside at the time and that it was safe to play the game. Imagine his surprise when she walked in unexpectedly and saw what was occurring. She, of course, had been at a loss for words. Stan had to confess then and there about what he could do and, for good measure, demonstrated by "lifting" the sofa six inches above the floor. Thereafter, she always watched him warily. He took care not to upset her more than he had to, but life was not the same from then on.

So, what *special* memory could he send to the Entity that Eve and Freddie would know that it was his and not someone else's? The only thing he could think of was that terrible night two weeks ago when he and his mother were waiting for the detective George Larkin to meet them and the Disciples discovered them and started chasing them. One of the white-suited men had grabbed his mother and hurt her, and he in desperation "threw" a bunch of trash at him and hurt him back. He had rescued his mother, and that was certainly *special.*

Stan now touched the gestalt and concentrated on the memory of that incident. After a few seconds, Eve asked him if he were focusing, and he nodded his head.

"Sorry, Stan. I'm not receiving anything."

"Me neither, kid. Ya sure you concentrated on just one memory?"

"Yeah!" He relaxed and stared at his co-conspirators. "Jeez. How come you couldn't see what I was sendin'?"

Freddie fished another half-smoked cigar out of his tool pouch, lit up, and took a drag. As the smoke curled around his head, he gazed at the ceiling in deep thought. Eve eyed him anxiously.

"It seems to me," the handyman said at last, "that mebbe you got to be an adult before this…Entity character can get the signal."

"That's absurd," Eve objected. "The Entity accepted Stan easily enough when we created the gestalt. It showed us both the same wonders you saw a few minutes ago. There has to be some other explanation."

"What then?"

"I think – I think it has to do with the *nature* of our powers." Freddie raised an eyebrow. "Look, Dr. Razumov has always said that *psi*-talent could be grouped into two categories – passive and active. Passives cause people to *see* things happening, and actives cause people to *make* things happen. I'm a 'passive'; I get these visions when I touch objects. However, Stan is an 'active'; he moves objects around. Do you follow me so far?"

"Uh-huh," the dwarf replied dubiously and flicked some ash into his pouch. "Go on."

"Well, Stan and I created this" – she nodded at the black sphere – "because – I think – it required both a 'passive' and an 'active' to do so."

"Wait a minute! Didn't the Doc experiment with a bunch of DEDEP'ers in various combinations? And couldn't he find no other combination than you two who could bring the gestalt into being?"

"That's true. Apparently, Stan and I have a higher level of ability than those others. I don't know. Anyway, getting back to 'passives' and 'actives,' perhaps it has to do with imaging. Perhaps only people with image-creation can send them to the Entity so it can feed them back to others with different abilities."

"Hmmm. Possible, possible. If someone like Lacey (who 'sees' distant places) was hooked up with the gestalt, mebbe she might be able to do the trick."

"An' so would Chris," Stan interjected. "He's a psycho-pro –pro-projectionist."

"Right you are, kid. But, he can't hook up."

"Oh, yeah. I fergot."

"Why can't he?" Eve asked.

"I'll tell ya later, kiddo. Time here is runnin' short. You got more experimentin' to do?"

"Yes. Stan came up with an idea of his own, using his ability."

"Whatcha gonna do, kid?"

"I'm gonna try to send the gestalt to wherever *I* want it to go – like upstairs, outdoors, the City, you know."

"Hey, you already done that. You sent it outside when Mr. Jones came callin', and it wasted him."

"We were unconscious at the time," Eve retorted, "or so we were told. The Entity acted on its own initiative to protect us."

"Yeah. Now, *I* wanna be in control."

"Well, then, have at it, my man."

Stan placed his hand on the sphere again and concentrated. He wished it to go to Dr. Razumov's office and then return. The gestalt shimmered and vibrated more intensely for the space of five seconds. Abruptly, it winked out of existence. Eve, Stan, and Freddie held their collective breaths, each of them lost in their own private thoughts. The woman and the boy hoped for success; the handyman imagined the look on the Director's face if he suddenly had the gestalt appear before him where he least expected it. Half a minute passed, even though it seemed longer. As quickly as it had disappeared, the sphere re-appeared in its original position, still shimmering and vibrating. Eve and Stan smiled broadly, but Freddie looked doubtful.

"It worked!" the boy exulted.

"Yeah?" the dwarf questioned. "How do ya know it went to the Doc's office? For all we know, it just went home or somethin'."

"Well, it went somewhere outa my sight. We'll hafta ask Dr. Razumov if he saw it." He yawned hugely. "But, it'll hafta wait until tomorrow. I'm awfully tired now."

He let go of Eve's hand and headed for the exit. The others trailed him in full agreement.

* * *

Mid-morning the next day, the Director rapped gently on the door to the Jankowskys' apartment. He was the picture of calm and collectedness as if he were paying a mere social visit. Inwardly, however, his mind was abuzz with several dozen questions, speculations, and half-formed theories. Presently, the door opened, and Joyce peered at him in surprise and a little bit of apprehension.

"*Dobroye ootro*, Miss Yankofsky."

"Good morning, Doctor. What can I do for you?"

"I would like to speak with Stan, if I may."

"What's he done now?" came the suspicious response.

"I am not sure. That is why I must speak with him."

The woman directed him to the sofa and headed toward Stan's room. He heard her knock and call Stan's name. The boy's voice was muffled through the door, but it became clearer when the door opened psycho-kinetically. Joyce announced the presence of the Doctor. Stan's reaction was one of expectation. He padded into the living room, barefoot, still in his pajamas.

"*Dobroye ootro*, Stan."

"Mornin', Doctor. I guess I know why yer here."

"Do you indeed? Come sit by me."

Stan complied. His mother took a seat on a nearby chair, worry lines forming by the second. In the short time she had known the psychic researcher, he had never paid a personal visit to any of the residents. If he was here now, it must be for a serious reason – and her son was in the middle of it.

The old man regarded the boy for a long moment as if attempting to read his mind. Then:

"I had a…'visitor' last night in my office, a visitor I had not expected to have. As you might guess, I was quite startled. Are you able to enlighten me?"

"Stan," Joyce said accusingly, "what have you done?"

"I *was* gonna tell ya, Dr. Razumov, as soon as I had breakfast. Really, I was."

"*Oo myenya vyereetsye oh tyebye* [I believe you]. I am not angry with you, Stan. I only want an explanation that I think you can give me."

"Well, last night, me 'n' Eve 'n' Freddie did a little experimentin' on our own. We wanted to know what else we could do with the gestalt."

"You snuck out of the apartment, young man?" his mother cried out indignantly. "If we weren't where we are now, I'd give you a good spanking."

"I'm sorry, Mom. I won't do it again."

"Indeed you will not, *ryebyonok*. I will not tolerate any sneaking about, and I give your mother permission to spank as she will. If you choose to experiment – and I believe you do – you will do so in my presence so that I may monitor the proceedings. Everything we do at DEDEP must be scientifically correct. Do you understand?"

"Yes, sir."

"*Khorosho*. Now, tell me what you hoped to accomplish."

The boy related all that had occurred the night before and included the whereabouts of the secret area down below – information which greatly surprised the Director. At the end of the account, the latter gazed at the ceiling. Presently:

"*Spaceebo*, Stan. You and Eve have shown great initiative and reached a milestone in your development. After lunch, you and she will report to Laboratory #2, and we will do some real experimenting, *da?*"

"You betcha!"

"You have a fine son, Miss Yankofsky. You should be proud of him."

"I am – most of the time." She gave Stan a steely glare. "When he behaves himself."

* * *

Eve and Stan had lunch together, and he told her of the Doctor's visit that morning. Eve then related how she had had a similar visit and that she was pleased that the Director was not angry but rather happy about the whole affair. They discussed other possibilities they could suggest and looked forward to exploring those possibilities.

Half an hour later, they walked into Laboratory #2, hand in hand. As expected, the Russian was puttering around and re-arranging the equipment he planned on using during this research session. Unexpectedly, however, they noted that Lacey Perkins was also present; the psycho-occulist greeted them warmly and informed them that she was going to be part of the session. On the other hand, the third member of the Triad was nowhere to be seen. Dr. Razumov assured them that he would be along shortly as soon as he and Jean finished checking some electrical circuitry in the infirmary.

Another half hour passed before Freddie made his appearance. He waddled in as if he had all the time in the world -- an attitude he knew would irk the punctilious Emil Razumov – and was secretly gleeful when he spied a look of annoyance flash briefly across the latter's face. He grinned toothily at all the others.

"The wiring is all back in order, Doc," he reported. "You need to order some more fuses, though."

"I shall make a note of it. *Spaceebo*, Freddie. Now to the business at hand. I have invited Lacey to this session on the strength of Eve's supposition that those who deal in images can transmit them to others via the gestalt. If you will be seated, we will begin."

The Triad assumed their usual formation while the psycho-occulist and the Doctor sat in front of them. Eve and Stan joined hands, and the black sphere materialized. Its size was half again as large as when only its summoners were present, now that another high-level *psi*-talent was in the lab.

"First of all," the Director intoned, "we will all make contact with Eve and Stan, and she will repeat what she did last night. By this means, we will establish that the phenomenon is repeatable and not merely a 'flash in the pan,' as you Americans are fond of saying."

He and Lacey and Freddie touched either Eve's or Stan's hand. Eve concentrated on another of her memories. This one she chose, not because she wanted to but because it was strong in her mind, and she feared it would never leave her. The image was of Father Driscoll as she always saw him: fierce, condemnatory, and bullying with a touch of perverseness as he anticipated the "punishment" he was about to inflict upon her. As the image flowed through the gestalt and into the minds of the others, gasps and mutters of shock and indignity distinguished their reactions to it. Contact lasted only a few seconds as it was more than sufficient to outrage the compassionate individual.

The only one not given to shock and indignity was the Doctor. Instead, he maintained a scientific detachment and only marveled at Eve's resolve in providing this particular memory to be viewed by outsiders. He was well aware that the rapes she had endured at the hands of an immoral and predatory priest was the reason behind her mental disorder; and, up until her experiences with the gestalt, they had threatened to throw her into total insanity. By furnishing this memory, he deduced that she was well on the road to recovery and that soon she would be made whole again. What had happened while she was in contact with the gestalt was still a mystery, and one he would dearly love to solve; but she and Stan were being close-mouthed where the sphere was concerned, and he dared not press them too vigorously lest they retreat into absolute recalcitrance.

"*Ochen khorosho*, Eve. The phenomenon is repeatable. Now, Lacey will have her turn."

"I'm just full of memories," the older woman said, "and a lot of them are way more pleasant than what we've just seen."

She concentrated and, as promised, a happy moment in her life formed in the minds of her cohorts. A younger Lacey Perkins held an infant in her arms whom she lovingly identified as her new-born son, William Junior, the day she left the hospital. Next to her was the proud father. The reaction from the others was appropriately positive (although Stan wrinkled his nose a bit). Even the ever-cynical Freddie was touched.

"*Choodyesny*, Lacey. Now, for the real test. I want you to use your psycho-occulist ability to pull in a distant scene for all of us to view."

"Any scene?"

"*Konyechno.*"

"Well, then, here's another pleasant image – or it used to be."

The image she produced was one of a white stucco, two-story house. A spacious lawn surrounded it on all sides, and hedges lined up along the sidewalk in front of it. Ringing the house itself were bush after bush of bright yellow marigolds and pink peonies. Against one side of the house stood an ivy-covered trellis. A scattering of dandelions dotted the lawn. In one corner of the lot, a regal-looking oak tree, fully mature, brooded; a couple of squirrels could be seen scampering over its branches. A cardinal occupied a branch and watched the squirrels guardedly.

"That was our house on Garfield Avenue in the City – until the Disciples hounded us out of it and we were forced to join DEDEP."

"*Spaceebo*, Lacey. I think we are making excellent progress, although I regret that we cannot utilize anyone who does not possess a visual-oriented *psi*-talent. Otherwise, we might have had a marvelous gallery of images – an organic gallery, as it were." He sighed deeply. "Ah, well, we must move on. Stan will now show us his new ability."

"Oh, boy!" the boy enthused. "There's lotsa places I can send the En – uh, the gestalt."

"Of that I am sure. But it must be a location which we can verify by contacting someone there. Let me see. Ah, we will surprise George by having the gestalt appear in his office."

"OK." Stan placed his hand on the sphere. "Go to George Larkin's office."

The sphere hummed and vibrated as before but remained in place. Both Stan and the Doctor furrowed their brows in perplexity. The former repeated his command, and still the thing did not de-materialize.

"*Shto eto?* Why has it not moved?"

"Stan," Eve spoke up, "have you ever been in George's office?"

"No. What's that got to do with it?"

"*Konyechno!*" Dr. Razumov exclaimed. "I should have foreseen it. Just as he cannot send an image because his psycho-kinesis does not involve images, so he cannot send the gestalt a place he has never seen before."

"Jeez! What a bummer!" He thought a bit. "How about my school? The kids there was always pickin' on me after they found out about my power. Sendin' the gestalt there will be a blast!"

"Hey, kid," Freddie cautioned him, though his voice was weak, "you start thinkin' about 'pay-back,' the next thing you know, you'll be walkin' down the wrong road."

"Freddie is correct," the Doctor allowed. "You must not use your *psi*-talent for vengeful purposes. DEDEP was set up to accentuate the *positive* uses of psychic abilities. Send the gestalt to the dining room. We shall soon learn if you have succeeded."

The boy complied, and the black sphere disappeared as expected. The Director strolled over to the door, opened it, and peered down the corridor. Shortly, he observed several DEDEP'ers – the post-luncheon clean-up crew, including Joyce Jankowsky – hastily exiting the targeted area, babbling incoherently. The old man smiled to himself and returned to his test subjects.

"Perhaps it was a mean thing to do," he confessed, "but we have verified Stan's ability. For the next round of tests, I shall attach each of you to an EEG so that I may learn how much energy is being expended for each task."

* * *

Lacey Perkins hadn't felt this exhausted since her initial examination by Dr. Razumov the day after she and her family took refuge in DEDEP. There had been frequent tests in the weeks following; but, as she became accustomed to the regimen, she had had an easier time of it with each succeeding session.

This latest session, however, was – as her teenager might have said –a 'corker." The Doctor seemed to have wanted to get as much "mileage" out of his test subjects as he could; and, in his enthusiasm, he pushed them all to their limits. The idea that the gestalt could be used as a conduit for radiopsychological abilities fascinated him, and he had conducted several different types of tests, first with Eve; then with Stan, then with her, and finally with all three in combination. And, all the while, he studied three separate EEG's carefully, making periodic utterances – in Russian! – every step of the way. He was literally and figuratively a man possessed, possessed by the search for new knowledge and hopefully new understanding of the world of *psi*.

New knowledge and understanding aside, all Lacey wanted to do was to return to her apartment, kick her shoes off, and lie down on the floor. But first, she decided, she had better look in on her "patient" in the infirmary. In her pre-DEDEP existence, she had been a practical nurse at a hospital on the far east side of the City; in fact, she had been Chief Nurse in the emergency room and therefore the "second-in-command" to the doctor on her shift. As such, she surreptitiously utilized her psycho-occulist ability to "monitor" the actions of the emergency medical teams as they performed their first-responder duties and to give them critical advice on what to do in a particular case, a feat which astonished them no end. In time, she acquired a reputation as a *wunderkind* and was consulted by the EMT's on a regular basis.

Her downfall came, as it often did with persons with *psi*-talent, as a result of suspicions raised in the mind of one of the staff who was a Deacon in the Disciple organization. Thereafter, she was watched carefully by this individual who subsequently reported her suspicions to the Archdeacon, triggering a campaign of persecution against her whole family.

The targeting by the Disciples soon came to the attention of George Larkin. He asked the Twins to scan her, and they verified that she did indeed have *psi*-talent. He made contact and made the pitch about DEDEP. If it had only been her who had been persecuted (she told him), she would have declined the offer and taken her chances by moving away from the City. But, she had two young children to consider – one of whom had the same ability she did and the other of whom was a certified mathematical genius – and they didn't deserve to be hounded by religious fanatics. After much discussion with her family, she and they had yielded to the inevitable and went into exile in a hole in the ground.

Like most of the residents of DEDEP, the Perkinses were uncomfortable with their new environment and tolerated it only because the alternative was infinitely worse. But now they had a purpose: the war against the Swarm.

As she was about to open the door to the infirmary, a vision came to her. She stood very still and let it form and play out in her mind. Her ability was such that she could "see" scenes from an external source or from her own personal knowledge. (Her son Billy could "see" only from personal knowledge.) The scene was from personal knowledge: images of the Swarm base on Ridgeway which had been implanted in her memory by Kenny Smythe.

She now "saw" what the aliens were up to, and the sight disturbed her greatly. The soldiers were having target practice inside the building, first using pistol-like weapons, then rifle-like weapons. Each discharge produce a flame which burnt the targets – effigies of humanoid figures – to a blackened crisp. She couldn't hear what the soldiers were saying, of course, but their facial expressions and their gesticulations spoke volumes of a perverse camaraderie amongst creatures who thrived on cruelty and brutality. She shuddered at the thought that these blood-thirsty monsters were looking forward to exterminating the entire human population as sport.

One part of the scene which both fascinated and horrified her was the Leader of this group. She recognized him from George's description as the one who had been leading the search for Jean Fulton. The cruel face, the steely eyes, the wicked scar along one cheek – these were the marks of a ruthless and amoral person devoid of a conscience, a dedicated killer who took pleasure in the killing. He stood apart from his "command" and observed the exercise with obvious satisfaction.

Lacey had "seen" enough, and she willed the vision away. It left her as quickly as it had appeared. She leaned against the infirmary door to steady herself. She had to report this incident, of course, so that George and Emil could determine a proper counter-action. She was thankful she was not in their shoes; making plans in the face of total destruction was not her cup of tea. Rather, she would have curled up in a ball and cried interminably.

As soon as she had regained a modicum of equilibrium, she entered the infirmary to check on her patient, a girl approximately six-years-old who required absolute privacy until such time as she could cope with the presence of others. The youngster had been discovered by Larkin several months ago walking the streets of the City in a trance-like state; even though he was not an expert in mental disorders, he clearly understood that she had been traumatized by unknown causes and was unaware of her surroundings. He also clearly understood that she was not a normal child physically; the webbing between her fingers and toes, giving her a duck-like appearance, hinted at a genetic mutation. Under ordinary circumstances, the detective would have bundled her up and taken her to the nearest hospital. But ordinary circumstances did not prevail in the United States of America in the year 2018; the Disciples of Purity held sway over all of civil society, including the medical profession. The latter, in order to save their own skins, would have reported the girl's physical abnormalities, and she would have disappeared at the hands of unforgiving religious fanatics.

Larkin took the only humane option open to him and delivered the child to DEDEP, where she could be properly examined and possibly treated by a sympathetic person, i.e. Emil Razumov. Sadly, the girl had remained unresponsive all these months; whatever traumatic experience she had suffered was deeply rooted, and only a long and patient attendance on her immediate needs seemed best until her mind refocused on the external world again.

Enter Lacey Perkins, the former practical nurse who had knowledge of such things. Lacey took charge of the girl as if she were the daughter she never had. The psycho-occulist fed (intravenously as the child refused solid food) and bathed her and disposed of her wastes. And she spent two or more hours a day simply talking to her and reading her children's books in the hopes of getting some response. Nothing had worked so far, but Lacey wasn't about to give up just yet.

She checked her "daughter" for any signs of recognition of her surroundings and made sure she was comfortable. Before leaving the infirmary, she kissed the girl lightly on the cheek, whispered words of encouragement, and gave her a loving farewell.

ALIEN TECHNOLOGY

THE CALL CAME in on Larkin's private line. He glanced at the caller ID and frowned. The information was not recognizable, and he feared the line had been compromised.

The private line was a throw-back to the days when telephonic conversations were the chief form of communication between individuals, long before the Internet and e-mail. Private lines were for the purpose of communicating with certain individuals who wished to remain anonymous; the nature of the business of the owner of a private line dictated who had access to it. In the case of a private detective, the private line was reserved for informants (who, if they were discovered transmitting sensitive information, were in danger of losing their lives) and close friends. Even in the Electronic Age, when the World Wide Web had largely replaced telephones, some business persons still retained their private channels. George Larkin was one such. He really didn't need a private line, since he seldom dealt with sensitive information in the course of his ordinary work; but he felt he had to carry on a tradition in his profession and therefore maintained his private line as a personal affectation.

He could count on one hand the number of persons who had access – Sheena, Emil, Jack, and Gordy – and the caller ID displayed didn't belong to any of them. Undoubtedly, it was someone who had misdialed and got his line by mistake. He *hoped* it was a misdial; if so, he would set the caller straight. Also quite possibly, it was a "robo-call" placed by some tele-marketer who wanted to sell something; if so, he would definitely set the caller straight.

"Hello?" he answered the phone cautiously.

"How ya doin', old buddy?" a familiar voice sounded.

"Gordy?"

"None other."

"I didn't recognize the caller ID. I thought someone had dialed by mistake."

"Ah, well, I'm calling you from a different phone, one that's not likely to be tapped."

"You think your phone is tapped?"

"I know it is, George. You know the signs of a phone tap. You and I did a lot of them in our day. Well, I heard the signs a couple days ago, and now I'm taking no chances when I call certain people – like you."

"Why would anyone want to tap your phone?"

"It stems from being called on the carpet by the Assistant Director after I snooped in the Bureau's files. The AD is a 'bishop' in the Disciple structure, and he's paranoid as hell. He'd like to get some dirt on me."

"It's come to that, has it?"

"You know it, old buddy."

"So, what do you have for me that requires all the secrecy?"

"It's the Quark. He called the local police in Omaha about 'men from Mars' planning an invasion. He told them he saw the 'aliens' loading up their spaceship with weapons and practicing invasion tactics. Of course, he didn't say all this as eloquently as I just did. The local boys thought he was whacko and threatened to lock him up.

"The detective-in-charge didn't want to be bothered with the guy, so he called the local SAC and kicked the matter over to him. The SAC is an old friend, and he knew about my interest in 'men from Mars' – and my run-in with the AD. He gave me a jingle and filled me in – strictly on the QT, of course – and I'm passing it on to you, my friend."

"So, the Quark is going public, is he? I can tell you for a fact that he's absolutely right."

"How d'ya know that?"

"I have other, more reliable sources, chum. They've corroborated everything the Quark has reported."

"Then an attack by the Swarm is imminent?"

"We don't know their exact timetable – yet. But, they're gearing up for it."

"Holy shit!"

"Amen!"

"Well, keep me posted, old buddy, so I can pack my bags."

"Will do."

After the ex-FBI agent hung up, Larkin thought long and hard about the implications of this newest development. Apparently, the Quintessential Quark had been so rattled by what he had recently witnessed – the same scenario that Chris had reported on – that he had seen fit to "spread the word" to whoever would listen. He had to be quite frustrated by now, if the local police thought he was a crackpot and refused to take him seriously – not that anyone could be blamed for discounting such a wild tale told by a wild man. The detective might have been one of the discounters himself if the enormity of the situation hadn't fallen into his lap two weeks ago and if he hadn't had to deal with flesh-and-blood extraterrestrials who intended to use Planet Earth as their next battleground.

He decided to check his e-mail to see if the Quark had a new message for him. He hoped so, because it would give him an excuse to tell the "whacko" to be more careful about going public. He would tell him that the aliens might have spies and that, if they reported what he was doing, his life would be in danger. The damnable thing about that little white lie was that it wasn't a lie at all. There was paranoia, and there was paranoia, and it behooved the cautious person to know whom to trust. Even the Quintessential Quark needed to be protected.

There wasn't any new messages from the "whacko," so the detective spent the next two hours tending to business: writing reports, billing clients, answering queries, and updating files. When the nuts and bolts of private investigation had been dealt with, he left the office to keep his appointment with Mr. Smith. He was anxious to learn what sort of alien technology the Coalition was going to give him, although he was quite certain that it would not include weaponry, even strictly defensive weaponry. He was still determined to press his "allies" to relent in light of what he knew the Swarm possessed; as it stood, it was akin to attacking someone with a machine gun with a club.

The drive eastward on Main Street proved to be very enlightening for a change, and it heartened him somewhat. He observed the usual number of Disciples here and there, but they were engaged in heated conversations; some of the exchanges bordered on physical confrontation in the form of arm-waving and offensive and defensive posturing. Larkin could make a shrewd guess concerning the nature of those confrontations, and it pleased him that the Disciples were minding their own business and not someone else's.

His passing did not go unnoticed. By now, most of the Disciples recognized him on sight and regarded him with something approaching awe as a "confidante" of the Archdeacon himself. They ceased their discussions with each other as some few gestured in his direction to call the attention of their companions to him.

As he crossed Broadway, he spotted two familiar faces walking eastward: "Brother" Connolly and "Sister" Smithers. They were holding hands again and giving each other loving glances. He pulled over to the curb, honked his horn, and waved at them. Immediately, they disengaged from each other and assumed expressions of chagrin. Larkin rolled down the window on the passenger side.

"Hey, you two! D'ya want a lift?"

The pair approached cautiously, and Connolly gave the station wagon the once-over in undisguised disgust.

"Good morning, Brother Larkin," the young man greeted him. "We appreciate the offer, but – well, you'll excuse me for saying so, your car doesn't look too safe."

"Probably not," the detective responded, chuckling, "but it's held up so far. Do you want a ride or not?"

"Sure. The Lord will keep us safe."

Smithers slid in first and was careful not to make physical contact with their benefactor either out of piety or of awe. In point of fact, she used the opportunity to snuggle up against her companion without being too obvious about it. Larkin smirked at the gesture and resumed driving.

"How far are you going?" he inquired.

"Union and Second Avenue. That's where Henrietta – uh, Sister Smithers' aunt lives. We're looking in on her because she's bedridden."

"Well, that's a co-incidence. It's right on my way." He cast them a side-long glance. "Um, it's obvious that you two are interested in each other beyond a, um, *spiritual* bond. You don't have to hide it from me. I'm not going to tell anyone, least of all the Archdeacon."

"Thank you, Brother Larkin. Sometimes, we forget appropriate behavior when in public. His Worship lectures all of us on that point."

"And he's right to do so. Nevertheless, your relationship is your business, and I'll keep it a secret, if you want."

"Thank you again. At the appropriate time, we'll make an announcement."

"I noticed something odd just before I picked you up. Maybe you can enlighten me."

"I'll try. What do you want to know?"

Many of the…brothers and sisters seem…distracted for some reason. What's going on?"

Connolly did not answer right away. Instead, he worked his jaw muscles considerably. The detective could just picture his mental gears shifting as he struggled to formulate the correct response. Smithers bowed her head and wrung her hands. Presently:

"Well, it's like this, Brother Larkin. The word is out about the… 'revelation' on Union Street. It's spreading throughout the rank-and-file, and some of us are wondering how it will affect our organization. Those of us who actually witnessed the event – you especially – are being seen as greatly blessed by the Lord, and you are being regarded as – as a *prophet*."

Larkin wanted to laugh out loud, but he restrained himself. The idea that he could be a "prophet" in the eyes of the Disciples was ludicrous in the extreme, and he would have dismissed it out of hand if not for a sudden idea which popped into his head. He could use this new "revelation" to his – and DEDEP's – advantage as they sought to drive a wedge into the ranks of the Disciples, break up the whole rotten lot of them, and put an end to their evil influence over decent folk and the nation as a whole.

The remainder of the trip was spent in silence. At Union and Second Avenue, the detective pulled over to the curb and parked.

"Before you go," he said, "I'd like you to do me a favor."

"I'll be glad to, Brother Larkin."

"It may involve some risk on your part."

"As I said before, the Lord will keep us safe."

"Uh-huh. One of my informants has told me that some of these evil creatures we've been fighting are hanging out in an abandoned factory on Ridgeway. I'd like you to investigate and report back to me." He noted the look of concern on both faces. "Don't worry. I'll clear it with the Archdeacon. I just need some extra eyes over there, and you strike me as being worthy of the job."

"Of course, I'll do it," Connolly said with forced determination. "I have to do my part in the battle against the enemies of the Light."

"*We* have to do our part," Smithers spoke up for the first time and gave her companion a fierce scowl. "You're not doing this alone, Brother Connolly. After all, as Brother Larkin has already pointed out, we're committed to each other."

"You can't argue with that, Brother Connolly," the detective chuckled. The young man smiled and shook his head in resignation. "You can approach this assignment however you want. Use your own discretion. But, do be careful. The Enemy is exceedingly cruel."

As he continued on to Mr. Smith's base, Larkin somewhat regretted drafting the young lovers as he had. Lacey Perkins had the Ridgeway location covered in her own inimitable fashion, but his request would pull the Disciples deeper into his plan to pit them against the Swarm and neutralize them both. For the safety of Planet Earth – and DEDEP – he would do anything and everything necessary. In a chess match, pawns had their place and their purpose. And he, the self-styled "master strategist" aimed to use them as he willed.

* * *

When Larkin entered the abandoned supermarket, he received the shock of his life. The pasty-faced alien was lying on the floor, flat on his back, and he was very still. The detective hurried over and bent down to examine the body. If he had been looking at a human being, he might have believed he was viewing a corpse. Yet, one could not be that positive where extraterrestrials were concerned; physiological and biological differences had to be taken into account, even if one did not know what they were. As it happened, Mr. Smith was not dead; his respiration had slowed to four per minute, a phenomenon Larkin had witnessed once before.

What he should do in the present circumstance was a mystery. The Coalition agent might be taking a nap for all he knew – even if it was on the floor! – and might not wish to be disturbed. At the other end of the spectrum, he might be quite distressed and in need of medical attention, whatever that might be. He now remembered that Mr. Smith had twice ingested a small, pink capsule in his presence. At the time, he had had other matters on his mind and had taken little notice of it. Were those capsules medication the alien needed in order to survive on Earth? Or did he have a condition peculiar to his species which the capsules ameliorated? Did the alien need one now before he actually expired? It was a damned-if-you-do-and-damned-if-you-don't situation, and Larkin found himself in a king-sized dilemma.

Better to err on the side of commission rather than omission.

The pink capsules, he remembered, were to be found in the alien's jacket pocket. He searched first one outside pocket, then the other, and came up empty. He checked the jacket's inside pocket – still nothing. He would have to search the pants pockets. He cautiously slip his hand into the right-front pocket – feeling quite embarrassed about doing so – and found it also empty.

He was about to search the left-front pocket when Mr. Smith's eyes popped open, startling him. The Coalition agent stared at him in bewilderment.

"Hhhello…Mr.…Largin. Whhhat…are…you…doing?"

"Uh, I, uh, found you lying here, and I, uh, thought something had happened to you. I, uh, thought you might need one of those pink capsules you carry with you."

"Thhhang…you…for…your…goncern…but…I…am…not…in… need …of…one…of…thhhose…shust…yet.

"Why are you on the floor then?"

"Ah…as…you…may…hhhave…observed…I…hhhave… diffigulty… moving…about. Your…world's…gravity…is…mush… greater…thhhan …it…is…on…my…world. Egcessive…movement… puts…undue…stress …on…my…body…and…I…must…rest… freguently."

"You rest on the floor?"

"Yes. Thhhe…pull…of…your…world's…gravity…is…lessened… in…thhhat…position."

"I see. Well, I'm glad to see you still among the living."

"A…gondition…I…hhhope…to…maintain…for…a…good… long …whhhile. Would…you…mind…hhhelping…me…to…my… feet?"

"Not at all."

Gently, the detective lifted the frail alien up until the latter was firmly on his feet. Mr. Smith smiled broadly, exposing his yellow teeth.

"I…feel…guite…refreshed… now. Thang…you…again…Mr.… Largin."

"You're welcome. Um, if I may ask, why *do* you take those capsules?"

"Thhhey…hhhelp…to…purify…my…blood. My…species… breathhhes…hhhelium…to…a…great…degree. Thhhere…is… hhhelium …in…your…atmosphere…but…not…enough…to… sustain…me. Thhhe …hhhigh…ogsyshen…gontent…is…togsig… to…me…and…I…must…egspel …it…from…my…bloodstream… or…die."

"Knowing this, you still accepted this assignment."

"It…was…for…thhhe…greater…good…Mr.…Largin." He sighed briefly. "Now…to…our…business. Wait…hhhere…whhhile…I… obtain…thhhe…eguipment…you…were…promised."

Mr. Smith turned slowly and shuffled off toward the large silver-gray cube and disappeared inside. Two minutes passed before he re-appeared holding three small disparate objects in his hand. None of them looked like what a human would call a "weapon." On the other hand, one *was* dealing with alien technology.

"Thhhese…devices…should…prove…useful…to…you…Mr.… Largin."

The alien handed over first a sphere fifteen centimeters in diameter. It differed in appearance from the tracker the detective had been given earlier only in its coloring; whereas the tracker had been brass, this object was silver. Moreover, it had only two depressions in it, both of which were side by side. Larkin examined it minutely and regarded Mr. Smith expectantly.

"Thhhis…will…shenerate…an…elegtromagnetig…shield… around… thhhe…user. It…operates…on…a…similar…principle… to…thhhe… shenetator…whhhish…protegs…thhhis…station. Face… thhhe…two… depressions…toward…you…whhhen…operating…it. Press…thhhe… right-hhhand…depression…to…agtivate…or.…to… de-agtivate. It… will…automatigally…proshegt…a…field…one… meter…in…radius… around…you. Press…thhhe…left-hhhand… depression…to…ingrease …thhhe…radius. Eash…pressing…will… double…thhhe…radius…up… to…a…magsimum…of…sigsteen… meters."

"And what will it protect me against?"

"Thhhe…enershy…weapons…of…thhhe…Swarm. Thhhe…field… reflegts…thhhe…enershy…bag…towards…its…point…of…orishin."

"The Swarm gets a taste of its own medicine?"

"I…am…not…familiar…withhh…thhhat…egspression…but… if…I…gash…your…meaning…thhhen…yes."

"That's almost as good as a weapon. What's next?"

Mr. Smith next handed over a golden bracelet-like metallic object upon which was attached a disc ten centimeters in diameter and five millimeters thick. Whatever the metal was, it glimmered with the colors of the rainbow when turned a certain way.

"Thhhis…is…a…prototype…of…a…portable…universal… translator.

It…hhhas…been….programmed…to…translate…all…of… thhhe… languashes…of…thhhe…Goalition…and…of…thhhe… Swarm…into… your…own…languashe. I… regret… to… say… thhhat…for…obvious… reasons…it…does… not… translate… precisely…but…well…enough… to…enable…you…to…learn… thhheir…intentions."

"That'll certainly come in handy. How do I activate it?"

"It…is…voice-agtivated. You…say…'agtivate'…and…it…will… produce…a…beep…to…indigate…it…is…operating. Say…'mute'… to…lower…thhhe…volume…or…'ingrease'…to…raise…thhhe… volume.

You…wear…it…on…your…wrist…ligue…so." He placed the device around Larkin's right wrist and squeezed the arms of the "bracelet" for a secure fit. He then pulled back the sleeve of his jacket to reveal a similar device on his own wrist. "My…translator…hhhas…been… programmed…withhh…your…languashe. Thhhat…is…hhhow…I… am…able…to…speag…it…as…well…as…I…do."

"I'll be damned! And I thought you had taken lessons."

"I…gould…hhhave…but…thhhis…is…guiguer. Thhhis…last… device …will…be…of…special…interest…to…you…as…someone… whhho… deals…in…information."

The object was a silver cube ten centimeters to a side. Its surface was mirror-like, and Larkin was amazed to see his image reflected back at him. If he turned it at different angles, he could see various parts of the base.

"Thhhis…is…a…portable…universal…encyclopedia…by… whhhish …you…may…learn…all…thhhere…is…to…know…about… thhhe…member…worlds…of…thhhe…Goalition."

"*Fantastic!* How does it work?"

"It…also…operates…by…voice…gommand." Mr. Smith pulled another piece of the metal-like "paper" from his jacket pocket and handed it over along with the cube. The detective peered at it as if it were a precious jewel. "Thhhis...is...a...list...of...thhhe...member... worlds. Asg...thhhe...gube...anythhhing...you...wish...to...know... about...any....world...and...it...will...provide...an...answer. It... hhhas ...also...been...programmed...to...translate...into...your... languashe."

Larkin could hardly wait to test-run his new toys. After a hasty "Thank you," he took his leave of Mr. Smith and walked as fast as he was able out of the building. If his alien ally was put out by the sudden departure, the detective failed to notice; and, if truth be told, the alien's mental state was the least of his concerns. He hadn't been this excited over innovative technology since he had been fitted with his state-of-the-art prostheses six years before.

As he walked to the station wagon parked across the street, he scanned the "membership list" Mr. Smith had given him. He saw that the names of the worlds listed had been transcribed into Roman letters; even so, the names seemed quite unpronounceable, and he further assumed that native speakers would not pronounce them as the average human would. For instance, the name at the top of the list was written as "Blstad." A human would, in his/her ignorance, might pronounce it "blasted" or "bullstad" and have a good chuckle over the implications of the gaffe. Larkin hoped that, when he called up for information on that planet, the correct pronunciation would be included.

As it happened, "Blstad" was Mr. Smith's home world. In a moment of nationalist pride and/or memorialization for a dead world, he had listed it first. And, now that the detective thought about it, perhaps "Blasted" was an appropriate way of saying the name after all. Before the name, there was a mark in the shape of an upside down "U." Other world names had the same marking as well. Were these the worlds devastated by the Swarm? If so, why would they be included on a "membership list"? There had to be a different explanation, and he'd have to ask Mr. Smith about it when he had a chance.

As soon as he began the return downtown, he set the silver cube on the dashboard and formulated his first request for information. That request, quite naturally, would concern "Blstad" before the Swarm "visited" it, but he had to be precise in the wording lest the encyclopedia misinterpret the request and give him information he didn't want – or, worse, fail to respond at all.

"Describe the environment of Blstad prior to the invasion by the Swarm."

He waited patiently while the cube's mini-computer sorted through its memory core for the desired information. The seconds ticked by, and no response was forthcoming. What had he done wrong that the gadget failed to function? He thought back to the Coalition agent's instructions for operating it and slapped his forehead in self-chastisement. The alien had said "ask the cube" in order to extract information. He had been quite literal; a request had to be in the form of a question.

"What was the environment of Blstad prior to the invasion by the Swarm?"

Three seconds later, the cube glowed with a reddish-orange light and emitted a tinkling sound in the manner of chimes. A heavily-accented baritone voice followed.

"The planet Blstad [it was pronounced "Billstad"] be a world of lush vegetation. Its soil be very fertile and be capable of produce a wide variety of crops for consume and export. The atmosphere be compose of [untranslatable] and [untranslatable] and result in frequent falls of rain which assist in the fertility of the soil."

To Larkin's pleasant surprise, the cube also generated a "slide show" of holographic images of Blstad before its ruination. He viewed scenes of croplands containing tall bluish-yellow stalks undulating in a gentle breeze which may or may have been the local equivalent of grain. Other cultivated vegetation consisted of low-lying bushes with large orange spheres, row after row of purple vines with long yellow pods suspended from them, and short, slender trees loaded with green fruits. Mr. Smith had stated that his world had been largely agrarian; if these scenes were typical of the whole planet, then Blstad must have been a farmer's paradise.

And now it was all destroyed, perhaps never to bloom again.

The detective cursed the Swarm for the thousandth time for its wanton destruction for no other reason than they enjoyed doing it.

As the "slide show" drew to a close and the cube's glow died away, he vowed for the thousandth time to avenge the Blstadians and the billions of other victims of the Swarm by whatever means it required, up to and including the sacrifice of some lives – his included, if necessary.

Instead of returning to his office, he wended his way through town southwesterly. He had hatched a daring plan even before he left Mr. Smith's base, and he now pursued it. He intended to sneak into the Swarm's base and test-run his other new toys – the translator and the protective shield (although he hoped he wouldn't need the latter). Additionally, he wanted to get some first-hand information on the Swarm's method of attack. The whole idea was risky in the extreme – the capture by Mr. Jones and his henchmen was still fresh in his memory – but, theoretically, the risk would be lessened by Coalition technology. Nothing ventured, nothing gained, as the old saying went.

Upon arrival, he drove past the abandoned factory and parked the station wagon just west of the freight spur which serviced various factories in the western part of the City. He walked back, heading for the rear entrance of the building. The going was particularly rough for him as the area was strewn with debris accumulated over years of disuse; he had to pick his way through the trash and watch his step to avoid tripping and falling down. Getting to his feet from a prone position was always a problem – worse than driving an automobile.

The loading docks were still occupied by the three black semis. How had the Swarm gotten their hands on them? he wondered idly. No one just walked into a dealership and bought brand new trucks off the showroom floor; they had to be ordered specially, and that took time. Undoubtedly, the semis had been stolen. That would be in keeping with Swarm methodology.

Larkin climbed a short stairway which led to the rear entrance. He was not surprised to find that the lock had been burned out and the door ajar. The Swarm never did anything with finesse; brute force was their only method. He slipped inside and cautiously picked his way toward the front end of the building. Presently, he spotted the warship. A chill ran up his spine at the thought of what that thing was capable of doing. The City could end up like Dresden after World War II in short order.

As he drew closer to that engine of destruction, he kept an eye out for its operators. When he reached a point he deemed to be the minimal safe distance, he hunkered down behind a stack of empty crates and peered around it. What he saw fascinated him no end. Six members of the Swarm were lying flat on their backs on the floor; transparent masks covered their faces. All of the masks were hooked by thin tubes to a machine which looked for all the world like an old-fashioned residential radiator. A whooshing sound issued from the machine every four seconds. As the detective puzzled over the purpose of the machine, he was reminded of what the Quark had said in one of his early reports of Swarm activity in Nebraska. Those aliens were having deadly oxygen flushed from their lungs and replaced by whatever gas they could breathe. A seventh Swarm soldier stood by the machine and monitored its progress.

Larkin grimaced at the sight of this latter individual. He was the scar-faced Leader of this bunch – the only one of the Swarm who knew his face. Extra precaution was now needed.

He removed the universal translator from his coat pocket and slipped it onto his wrist. He then said "activate." One second later, the device beeped in what for it was a "normal" tone, but it seemed too loud for human ears. He said "mute," and the translator beeped again, an octave lower; he muted it twice more and was satisfied that it would not inadvertently alert the Swarm to his presence. The minutes passed by in a slow procession, but it seemed like ages before anything happened. Eventually, the Leader flicked a switch on the "radiator's" control panel and uttered a single word in his own language. The translator on Larkin's wrist duly spoke a single word – "up" in a whispery voice. One by one, the aliens lying on the floor removed their masks and scrambled to their feet.

"Ahhh," one of the soldiers said to the Leader in a rumbling voice, feel I like new man."

The Leader stared a hole in him in undisguised disgust.

"Say you that always, Kruf. Can think you not of something original?"

Kruf merely laughed. His comrades joined in the merriment.

"Attention!" the Leader ordered. The others became serious and obeyed. "Will relieve you those on patrol. Go now!"

The six wordlessly pivoted and marched toward the rear of the building. Larkin crouched down as best he could so as not to be seen. The Swarm soldiers passed by him, looking neither left nor right, unaware that a spy was observing their every move, and exited the building. He waited a few minutes until the aliens had cleared the area before taking his own leave. Meanwhile, he kept an eye on the Leader. The latter busied himself by gathering up the masks and tubes and storing them in a cabinet nearby. He then picked up a slender brass-colored rod, twenty centimeters long and one in diameter, and spoke at it.

"Processed Squad One at [*untranslatable*]. Sent them on patrol on [*untranslatable*]. Will request I now Commandant Yowk to arm my team."

The hairs on the back of Larkin's neck stood up upon hearing that message. He did not like the sound of it. Were the Swarm ready to attack the City? If so, how soon? There was no time to waste; this base had to be neutralized ASAP before the Swarm had a chance to launch any sort of assault. He would have to convince the Archdeacon to mobilize his special task force and use any weapon at hand to counter the threat.

He would also have to put DEDEP on high alert. Specifically, he had to select particular *psi*-talents with the potential to inflict substantial damage on the Swarm. The Twins, of course, were at the top of his list. There was another, but he would have to consult with Emil and the "candidate's" mother and convince them of the necessity of his participation.

The risky business had just gotten riskier!

* * *

Dr. Emil Razumov gazed forlornly at the latest EEG readings of his "eel" and shook his head in frustration. The readings showed no improvement – as he understood improvement – and he was at a loss as to how to improve them.

It had been so very different in his native Russia. First, as a graduate student and doctoral candidate, then as a full-fledged professor of parapsychology, he had had many potential *psi*-talents with which to experiment. The government of the Union of Soviet Socialist Republics had been quite serious in its approach to parapsychology; it had funded the program without question, had advertised for volunteers who believed that they possessed psychic abilities to be tested, and had used its secret police to be on the look-out for such individuals who were reluctant to volunteer. And all it asked for in return was results.

Anyone with half a brain knew why Moscow took such a great interest in those would-be paranormals and those programs. The Communist Party wanted unique weapons to use against the hated capitalist powers of the West; with an army of *psi*-talents, the Soviets could accomplish any goal they could conceive. They could deploy telepaths to read and influence the minds of key government and military leaders, telekinetics and pyrokinetics to sabotage key facilities and to assassinate key figures, and clairvoyants to spy on the West without risk to themselves. And the West would be defenseless against such attacks by the powers of the mind – indeed, it could not even comprehend the *nature* of the attacks until it was too late.

The young Dr. Razumov at first turned a blind eye toward the politics of testing for *psi*-talent. He was in his glory as the steady stream of "volunteers" showed up at his laboratory and underwent the bank of tests he and others had designed, first to determine the nature of the paranormal abilities an individual possessed, second to measure the strength of those abilities, and third to train the volunteers in the use of their abilities. The latter task had led the Doctor to doubt the efficacy of his work and motivated him to conduct secret experiments of his own devising, experiments which would ultimately be the foundation of his General and Special Theories of Radiopsychology. He worked for the State by day and for himself – and true science – by night until the State grew suspicious of his *official* reports. He then put aside his private work and concentrated on being smuggled out of the country and finding a safe haven where he could carry out his experiments in peace and to announce to his colleagues in the West the new science of the future.

What he found instead was a nation of skeptics. The Soviet Union had believed in parapsychology but only for its own sinister purposes. America, on the other hand, viewed the subject as one would witchcraft. The few parapsychologists which existed (and he had met and talked with all of them) were quite reserved; they published papers now and then, but their results were couched in scientific gobbledygook. They taught classes on the subject, but their budgets were minimal, reluctantly approved by administrations who had the least idea of the need for such classes. They met in annual conferences; but the publicity for the meetings was for their own edification, and the general public had little knowledge and smaller interest. The more mature Dr. Razumov railed futilely against the irrationality of it all until he learned that he was talking only to himself.

Little wonder that Jean Fulton and others at DEDEP proved to be reluctant test subjects. Having been indoctrinated with the notion that *psi* was an aberration – and in some circles, akin to "witchcraft" – Americans shied away from the subject and refused to take it seriously, even when psychic abilities stared them in the face. The only test subject the Doctor had who was eager to demonstrate his power, Stan Jankowsky the psycho-kinetic, had to be restrained at times lest he become reckless. Everyone else humored their leader and went through the motions.

Hence the Director's frustration. How in the world, he asked himself almost daily, could they hold such attitudes in the face of persecution in the outside world at the hands of religious fanatics? They all should be willing to develop their paranormal abilities and stand shoulder-to-shoulder against the common enemy.

He regarded Jean's readings once more and sighed heavily. If only he could break through her reserve....

His musings were interrupted by a gentle rap at the door, followed by the entrance of Larkin and Sheena. He registered surprise at the unannounced arrival but had the good grace to accept it with magnanimity.

"*Dobry dyen*, George, Sheena. I had not expected to see you again so soon."

"New developments, Emil. I'd like to call an emergency conference to bring everyone up to speed."

"Another emergency conference? They seem to be more and more frequent these days. However, I should not be too surprised, given our current circumstances, *nye pravdy*?"

"Absolutely. Events are rushing headlong toward some unknown conclusion, and we must keep up or lose the race."

"May I ask about the new developments?"

In response, the detective pulled the three gadgets Mr. Smith had given him out of his jacket pocket and laid them on the Doctor's desk. The latter picked up each one in turn, examined them from different angles, carefully placed them back on the desk, and regarded Larkin expectantly. The other identified each one and explained its function; he emphasized in particular the value of the translator.

"I tested this baby personally by sneaking into the Swarm's base" – here, Sheena bit her lip – "and overheard some of their conversation. What I learned is the reason for this conference."

"Which is?"

"The Swarm soldiers are planning to carry arms while on patrol."

"*Bozhu moyu*! This is most distressing!"

"You know it, Emil. I want to propose the formation of a quasi- 'defense team' of our own in case we're ever attacked again."

"You would use our people to commit violent acts? I cannot permit that, George. That is not what this facility was designed to do."

"I know, and I wouldn't have suggested it if I didn't think it was necessary. Would it soothe your conscience if I asked for volunteers? If no one volunteers, I'll forget the whole thing. In any event, everyone needs to be informed of this new danger."

"*Konyechno*. Very well, I will call the conference. But I caution you not to press your proposal too vigorously."

A half hour later, Larkin sat in the dining room near the serving line and watched the residents straggle in. From the expressions on their faces, he could tell that they were not pleased by this "emergency conference" inasmuch as it had been extremely impromptu and disruptive of what passed for a normal routine in a hole in the ground.

It couldn't be helped, though; the exigency was real enough. He just had to convince them of that.

Not everyone chose a table at random to sit at, and the exceptions were interesting. Eve, the former wallflower, sat at the table nearest the detective along with Stan and Freddie; next to Stan was his mother and Jean. The Twins, Sheena, and the Perkinses occupied the adjacent table. Larkin considered them his "core group" in the project he had in mind, and he hoped they would volunteer and force Dr. Razumov's hand.

When all had been seated, the Director stood up and apologized for the short notification. He then nodded to the detective. Larkin stood, displayed the alien technology recently obtained, and described their functions. Murmurs of wonder and awe greeted each description, and he promised to demonstrate each one after the meeting. He proceeded to relate his experience at the Swarm base, overhearing an actual conversation and learning the intent of the Swarm. He paused to let this new information sink in. Some of DEDEP moaned in fear; others simply bowed their heads. When he had their attention again, he laid out his proposal.

"Emil has his reservations about this plan," he stated forthrightly, "and he has every right to be concerned. I've 'recruited' some of you in the past to do some spy work for me (for which I'm very grateful), but I made sure there was very little risk to you. But, now, what I'm proposing may be dangerous. I won't mince words. Some of us may die before this conflict is over. Therefore, at Emil's insistence, I'm asking for volunteers."

The silence which ensued was the silence of the tomb. The members of DEDEP sat stunned by the enormity of the proposal, and no one dared to be the first to raise his/her hand. Larkin couldn't blame them for being reticent; if he had been one of them, he'd have had reservations himself. He glanced at Sheena instinctively for support; she was lost in her own thoughts and remained silent. He was not prepared for what happened next.

"Damn it, George!" Henry Rawlins was on his feet as soon as the implications of the detective's proposal had sunk in. "We're not soldiers. We can't fight a war. What you're asking is – is – is *suicide!*"

"I'm not asking you to go into the City looking for trouble, Henry. I'm asking you to form a *defense* team in case trouble comes looking for us. Remember, we have the example of Mr. Jones fresh in our minds. We defeated him using only a few of our resources."

The "dreaming prophet" *humph*ed and sat down. Out of the corner of his eye, Larkin spotted Eve leaning over and whispering in Stan's ear. The boy gazed at her for a moment, then whispered in *her* ear. To everyone's surprise – including both the Director of Research and the Director of Operations – the psycho-imagist stood up in determined fashion. Half a second later, the psycho-kinetic was on his feet as well. His mother looked at him in shock.

"George, Stan and I are volunteering," Eve said in a steady voice.

"Are you sure you want to?" Larkin asked, secretly thrilled by the prospect.

"No, Stan!" Joyce wailed and tugged at him to get him to sit down. "You mustn't do this, baby."

"It's OK, Mom. The gestalt will protect us – just like it did when Mr. Jones attacked us."

He nodded at Eve and clasped her hand. Instantly, the black sphere appeared above their heads. Since there were more sources of energy present, it was necessarily larger; and, since Jean Fulton was also present (and feeling uneasy), it was larger than anyone had seen it to date, measuring nearly two meters-and-a-half in diameter. Even though the assembly had witnessed its appearance several times before, the huge size startled them and filled them with anxiety.

"Damn!" Freddie muttered. "I wasn't gonna volunteer at all. But it looks like the kids 'volunteered' me anyways."

"We're ready, George," Eve said with a grin.

"And so are we, old darling. We've got scores…"

"…to settle with those Swarm blighters."

"Count me in too, George," a tinny voice issued from the PA system.

"Thanks, guys," the detective responded with pride. "Anyone else? I could use one more person."

"That'll be me." Sheena was on her feet, although she hadn't jumped up as Eve and Stan had. "You'll need my hyperesthesia."

"And you'll need a 'spotter,'" Lacey declared suddenly.

"And an illusionist to confuse the enemy," her son Billy added. "Wait'll you see what I can do."

"Well, this is more than I had hoped for. It's good to have you all on board." He scanned his volunteers briefly while his analytical brain kicked into high gear. "I'll divide you into two teams in order to utilize your talents to maximum effect. I'll be back tomorrow with a plan of action and each one's part in it. Emil?"

The old man rose, appearing even older than usual. Worry lines criss-crossed his face.

"*Druzhy moyee*," he spoke in a tired voice, "the world has turned upside down, and I am at a loss for words to comprehend it. That I should live to see a day like this is more than I can endure. All I ever wanted to do was to conduct a few experiments in order to provide a firmer foundation for my theories on radiopsychology. Now my theories are going to war. *Soomasshedshiye!* Mnogo *soomasshedshiye!*

"Still, I shall do my part, if only to listen to your hopes and fears. Good luck to all of you." He smiled wanly. "Kick ass, as you Americans say."

CHAPTER SEVENTEEN

A RUDE AWAKENING

IN THE BEGINNING, Stan Jankowsky created "Mr. Whosis."

He did so as a survival mechanism. A small boy who had no real friends because his *psi*-talent set him apart, who was afraid to interact with his peers because he might get angry and do unthinkable things, who could not show off because others might become afraid of him and hurt him and/or inform the authorities – that small boy needed a very special friend who would never desert him, never say nasty things to him, never hurt him and/or turn him over to the authorities, and never, ever make him unhappy. He had imagined this special friend as a blue-skinned, very powerful giant who liked to play games and pull pranks. In the back of his mind, Stan knew "Mr. Whosis" was an imaginary being, but it was easier to put a form to the being rather than to keep it invisible.

Now, Stan had a new "friend," and this one was far from being imaginary. The Entity was real, and it was powerful – even more powerful than "Mr. Whosis" ever was. Where it came from, he did not know – yet – but he intended to find out. In his reality, the Entity appeared as a black sphere; in its own reality, it appeared as a shiny silver ball. So far, it had shown him and Eve wondrous scenes with promises of even more to come.

In the beginning, encountering and dealing with the Entity had not been much fun for either him or Eve. Stan's youthfulness gravitated more toward doing what he wanted to do rather than what others wanted him to do. And, though she was an adult, Eve shared that sentiment inasmuch as she had been robbed of her childhood by those who could not – would not – understand her own *psi*-talent. Had they both been independent agents, they might have amused themselves in any of a thousand ways. There were activities which were merely glimmerings in the mind's eye that they wanted to explore if only they had had the freedom to do so. The fact of the matter, however, was that neither of them was wholly independent – the one because of his age, the other because of her fears – and therefore neither could actuate the schemes they had in mind nor could they foresee the possibility of being in such a position.

In the first place, activating the gestalt was a *co-operative* venture. Eve and Stan were only two-thirds of the ability to bring the Entity into their reality; they were forced to "share" their new "friend" with another and hope that his stamina held up. In the second place – and perhaps this galled them more than anything else – ultimate control lay in the hands of yet a fourth person. Far from being independent agents, Eve and Stan were inmates in DEDEP; in exchange for food, shelter, and protection from the horrors of the outside world, they had to obey the dictates of Dr. Emil Razumov, whose experimenting took precedence over all else. Whatever the Doctor decided to do, whether it fit into their own plans or not, that was what they must do. They might "suggest" a few things; but, in the end, whatever they did was whatever he approved.

For his part, the Director had no intention of just sitting around and staring at the gestalt while Eve and Stan "played" with it. He theorized that it had come into this reality from some other dimension for a purpose. What that purpose was, he had no clue; but he had seen an opportunity to use it for his own purpose, i.e. to advance his theories of radiopsychology. The gestalt was an *active* phenomenon in his theories' scheme of things and, as such, its strengths and weaknesses needed to be tested. How long it could remain in this reality and how much it could be controlled were important questions.

So far, he had been encouraged by his results and just recently formed two working hypotheses. The first was elementary; the gestalt was more affected by an *active psi*-talent than a *passive* one. He had thought as much from the beginning; the logic was impeccable, and now he had evidence to support the idea. Throughout his testing, he had noted that the difference in duration between Eve's activity and Stan's was a multiple of two-and-a-half minutes. That figure never varied and led to the notion that, like physical phenomena, *psychic* phenomena obeyed a set of natural laws. The description of these laws had yet to be achieved, but now there was a quantitative factor with which to begin.

The second was problematical because the gestalt had been created by both an active and a passive *psi*-talent. In Emil Razumov's mind, it made perfect sense that this should be so; actives and passives were merely opposing sides of the radiopsychological coin, and both in conjunction were required. The fact could be tested by selecting other pairs of *psi*-talents, but he believed that the results would be a foregone conclusion. The real question was what sorts of gestalts would other pairs create. Eve and Stan had been the most proficient. Would their gestalt be more powerful than someone else's? And, if so, how much more?

The Doctor could not be faulted if these hypotheses induced in him a bit of euphoria. He had, in effect, taken a giant leap in the formulation of his "grand unified theory" of radiopsychology, a goal he had dedicated his life and career to discovering. Those fools in the American Psychological Association would rue the day they had booted him out of their ranks!

Having established the groundwork for this "grand unified theory," Dr. Razumov had turned his attention to the *nature* of the gestalt. Question: were all gestalts – assuming others existed – uniform, or did they have individual parameters? The black sphere appeared to be a solid object – smooth, firm, and cool, like a miniature bowling ball. Yet, since Einstein had demonstrated over a century ago that matter and energy were interchangeable, one's sensory apparatus could be deceived. One application of radio energy was the projection of a force field which when touched seemed as solid as a brick wall; logic therefore dictated that it could take on the semblance of solidity under the proper circumstances. And it was reasonable to assume that the strength of this field was quite high. How high had been determined by hooking the gestalt to an EEG.

To his chagrin, he had learned first-hand that he could not touch this phenomenon directly. Nor could anyone else – except Eve and Stan, the co-creators. He would have to content himself to place the electrodes in close proximity. He had attached first one, then another, across Eve and Stan's clasped hands (the assumed "nexus") and discerned a slight vibration as they received the output of the spheroid. This too was as it should be; the gestalt had its own frequency and amplitude as measured by the EEG. Without further thought on the matter, he switched the machine on and was hugely – but not unpleasantly – surprised. The "pens" immediately arced to the edges of the oscilloscope *and remained there for the duration of the experiment.* Rather than the usual "spikes" of the typical encephalogram, two parallel lines were traced out. Had he more sophisticated gear, he might possibly have seen the limits of the gestalt's energy output. This development had been both revealing and frustrating – revealing because it proved beyond a doubt that a gestalt *is* greater than the sum of its parts, frustrating because any exact quantification had to be deferred to some future date.

Would that his inspiration, T.C. Lethbridge, were still alive to witness this moment. The Englishman would have marveled at the sight of an energy field which far surpassed any he had ever encountered and/or speculated about. The gestalt possessed a potential beyond mere dowsing and recording "ghostly" images; it had the power to unlock all of the mysteries of the Universe and to reveal them as an interconnected whole for the benefit of humankind. He, Emil Razumov, was climbing a mountain, and soon he hoped to stand on its peak!

* * *

The Doctor's concerns were not those of Eve and Stan. Now that they had interacted with the Entity on a higher level, more than ever they wished to be independent of his wishes and explore the multiverse. For now, however, they had to act in secret, late at night, risking suspicion, despite the Director's admonitions. And, while it had been a sudden impulse on Eve's part to volunteer her and Stan's "services" to George Larkin, they both viewed the action as part of their agenda. They knew that the detective (unlike Dr. Razumov) would not put any restrictions on how they would carry out their part of his plan. As yet, they had not been informed of their part of the plan, but they intended to do it their way.

"It ain't bad enough," Freddie was grumbling, "I hafta do my work and let the Doc use me in his experiments. But you two go and volunteer me in this war against the Swarm. I'll never get anything done around here."

The Triad had departed the emergency conference and were walking down the stairs to the lower levels. The handyman and the boy were side by side, and the young woman tagged along behind them. Freddie, without any special provocation, was working himself into a lengthy diatribe by claiming "old age" and longer familiarity with DEDEP's environment gave him the right to criticize and that Eve and Stan would "hafta eat an extra bowl of cereal to keep up with me." As always, Eve giggled at his verbal mannerisms.

"Oh, pooh, Freddie," she chastised him. "Now that you've got Jean as an assistant, you've got plenty of time."

"Yeah, Freddie," Stan chipped in. "An' besides, we're doin' sumpin important."

The dwarf ignored them and kept on grousing.

"Also, I got to look in on the Spook more often since his run-in with Mr. Jones. He says he doesn't need the extra attention, but the Doc says otherwise."

The interjection of Christopher Wredling's nickname into the conversation stirred up a forgotten idea in Stan's mind. He had practically memorized the nameplates on all the doors in DEDEP – including those of the function rooms – but not one of them had Chris' name on it. He had always meant to ask where the psycho-projectionist resided, but some other business usually sidetracked him. It was a minor puzzle, but one which nagged at him. And, in a ten-year-old boy – one of the truly irresistible forces in Nature – the "itch factor" was exponential; finding a solution became an all-consuming passion. Everything else – even playing with the gestalt – was inconsequential. Freddie knew the answer to the puzzle but, on this matter, was uncharacteristically close-mouthed.

"Sure wish we could visit him," Stan remarked nonchalantly. "I bet he'd 'preciate some company."

"Outa the question, kid. The Doc's real strict about people seein' the Spook."

"Why?"

"That's hush-hush too. *I* know why, and George knows why; that's 'cause we need to know in order to do our jobs. The Doc decided long ago that nobody else needs to know."

"Jeez, what a bummer!"

"Live with it, Stan. That's how it is, here in Wonderland. Ya follow the rules, or yer out!"

Long after the Triad had gone their separate ways, Stan pondered Freddie's last remark. And the more he thought about it, the more it rankled his ten-year-old's perception of the world. To a child, rules were necessary evils, the price one paid for the benefits society provided; one obeyed in order to obtain treats, favors, gifts, or privileges. What galled him, however, was the fact that most rules were *adults'* rules, that kids had no say in either their formation or their implementation. Even if obeying the rules led to rewards, it was still an adult's idea of the way things should be. And, when it came to rules that made no sense at all (in terms of obtaining rewards), resentment ran higher. Given his own preferences, a child would have made his own rules, *simple* rules that everyone could understand.

Making Christopher Wredling's whereabouts a secret was one of those stupid rules. Even if he was crippled and bound to a wheelchair, that was no reason to hide him away. Stan had seen people in wheelchairs before – people with no legs, people paralyzed from the neck down – and he had not been particularly frightened by them. They just couldn't do things the way other people could, and they needed extra help. What could Chris' problem be that he was reduced to a projected image, appearing and disappearing like, well, a "spook"? Like all children, he hated mysteries. There shouldn't be any mysteries at all; there should be only honesty and openness. Unfortunately, the rules – the *adult* rules – got in the way, and kids ended up being regarded as "nuisances" if they asked too many questions. Adults didn't like to answer questions they thought were embarrassing and/or irritating. And so, they made up rules.

Stan was determined to find Chris' room and talk to him face to face, even if it meant getting kicked out of DEDEP. He already had a fairly good idea of where to begin his search. In the short time he had been in DEDEP, he had examined –surreptitiously, of course – all of the function rooms except one; that one he had almost entered during his first foray into Freddie's "domain" when the handyman had taken him by surprise and foiled his efforts. The door was marked "NO ADMITTANCE. AUTHORIZED PERSONNEL ONLY." Until now, he hadn't given that door much thought, but now it was time to explore that last "frontier."

After his mother had gone to bed, the boy slipped quietly out of their apartment, padded down the corridor, and eased into the emergency stairwell. Before entering the corridor of the maintenance level, he peeked out to make sure no one else was down here. Because only one person inhabited this region, it might have been seen as an unnecessary precaution; yet, Freddie could be very sneaky when he wanted to be. The corridor appeared to be empty. Apparently, the dwarf was as tired as he had claimed to be and was not prowling around. Stan slipped in and tip-toed toward the forbidden door. At one point, he heard a creaking sound and froze in his tracks. When he determined that the noise had been just the shifting of the foundation, he continued on. After what seemed like hours, he halted in front of the heavy steel door with its red, white, and black warning sign.

Working the lock presented no great obstacle, even without Freddie's help as a "psychic battery." The job might require more concentration, but he had all the time in the world. He gently pushed the door open and entered. His immediate impression was the unmistakable odor of chlorinated water as one would have found in a swimming pool. His second impression was the *sound* of water lapping against a wall, plus the gurgling noise when air is forced through water. His third impression was the sight of a large dark object in front of him, three meters high and six meters long. Stan wondered why there was a pool down here where no one could use it.

He mentally reached out for the light switch and flicked it on.

He instantly regretted his action.

* * *

It floats upon the waters of an artificial womb and dreams.

Tubes of all colors and diameters protrude from Its body. From some of these, It takes oxygen and nutrients; others cleanse Its blood and expels Its wastes. A tether holds It stationary so that It will not collide against the walls of Its artificial womb. A fiber-optic cable implanted at the base of Its skull links Its cerebral cortex to a communications network; through this, It sends and receives sounds and images to and from the outside world.

Communication, however, is limited. The Outside is content to speak to It only when Its services are needed.

Mostly, It dreams.

It dreams of what is and what might have been, of what was and what can never be.

Its dreams are all that separate It from despair and the madness that despair produces. The dreams hold back Eternal Night which oozes around It and sings out a siren song.

Surrender to the siren song would be easy, but It refuses to surrender. It prefers to defy the odds. It has defied the odds from the very beginning.

The doctors never thought It had any chance for survival, even when It had been in a biological womb. They told Its mother that she ought to abort It, despite her religious beliefs which strictly forbade such practices. She did not disobey her religion and so brought It to term.

The doctors never thought the delivery would produce a live birth. Rather, they believed that It would rupture Its mother's uterus and kill both her and Itself. They were nearly correct. Its mother died on the table because of the difficult birth, but It miraculously survived.

The doctor in charge of the delivery swore furiously in order to keep from crying when It emerged from the birth canal. Two nurses fainted when they saw It. Others in the delivery room paled and crossed themselves repeatedly.

They called It a "macroencephalic," a creature whose skull was twice as large as it should have been, and someone suggested that It ought to be terminated (surreptitiously, of course) and listed as a "still-birth." The doctor in charge feared lawsuits and criminal charges and moral censure and overruled the suggestion. It was put on emergency life-support.

Early on, the doctors determined that It could achieve maximum viability in an artificial environment, a pool of saline solution in imitation of a real womb. They also determined that It would never develop physically but remain fetus-sized for however long It lived – a misshapen and grotesque caricature of a human being.

The doctors blamed Its misfortune on Its mother's being exposed to toxic chemicals in the factory where she had worked. Though she was now beyond help, they hoped to use It as an "example" to other would-be mothers. They believed that this would be Its only useful function.

They were wrong.

While Its body never developed, Its mind did. The extra-large cranium possessed an extra-large brain which contained double the normal number of brain cells. It discovered at an early age that these extra cells enabled It to compensate for Its loss of physical development. It learned how to communicate with the Outside by means of projecting images of Its own design and having these images pantomime Its desires. From there, It was able to obtain mechanical and electronic aids in communication.

Its ability to bilocate both fascinated and horrified Its attendants. One faction wanted to study It and make practical use of Its abilities. Another faction simply wanted to destroy It on the grounds that Its abilities had been "spawned by the Devil" and that It was an instrument for evil. The former faction prevailed, and It lived on.

It was unaware of these political intrigues as It floated in Its artificial womb and dreamed a thousand dreams. And, even had It been aware, It could have done nothing about them. Though mentally agile, It was physically weak and at the mercy of others. Its formidable mental powers were next to useless in this regard; bilocation helped It to see the Outside but not to be a part of it.

The years passed, and the tides of fortune eventually reversed themselves. A new social force was on the rise, one which was wholly dominated by self-righteous individuals who would have nothing to do with "deviants" and "aberrations," either the physical or psychological kind. These persons found sympathetic ears everywhere, even in hospitals. In the facility where It resided, the pressures to terminate It grew in intensity. Humanitarian-minded staff, fearing for Its well-being, took a desperate gamble; under the cover of darkness, risking their own lives and reputations, they spirited It away and delivered It to a place and a person they knew would be a safe haven.

It has fared well in this place, protected from evil-minded people by infinitely more sympathetic people. Here, It may dream without interruption, without impediment, without fear.

Today, however, all that may change.

It senses the presence of another in Its "room." It cannot move Its head to see the intruder; the jumble of tubes and tether and fiber-optic cable hinders all movement. The gesture would have been useless in any event, as Its eyes have long since atrophied and are now formless lumps imbedded in Its over-sized cranium. It "sees" only through bilocation.

"Who's there?" It calls out in a tinny voice.

Silence is Its only reply. It calls out again. Silence still.

It now bilocates into Its "room" and sees a small, dark, silhouetted figure near the door. It moves Itself closer. The dim shape becomes a boy whom It recognizes. The boy is staring straight ahead at Its womb – at Its body. He is wide-eyed, paralyzed with – terror? No, not terror, but with morbid fascination. It has seen that look many times before – too many times before – and regrets seeing it on the face of one so young.

Immediately, It projects Its familiar image of a smiling young man, the creature It might have been if not for a cruel twist of fate. The image appears to one side so that the boy has to turn away from the monstrosity he sees before him.

"Stan," It asks softly, "what are you doing here?"

Reluctantly, the boy tears his gaze away from the water-filled tank and stares uncomprehendingly at the projection. He swallows the large lump that has formed in his throat and attempts to speak. Only gibberish issues from his lips.

"You shouldn't be here, Stan. It's a...rule -- for your protection as well as mine. I – I'm not a pretty sight."

"Chris?" Stan whispers at last. "Is that...is that the *real* you?"

"I'm afraid so. I'm sorry you had to see this."

"Jeez, it ain't yer fault you was...born that way. Just like Freddie can't help bein' a dwarf. Just like I can't help bein' a psycho-kinetic. It just happens. Dr. Razumov can explain it better'n me."

"I wish others had your level of tolerance. My life, such as it is, would have been a lot happier."

"Yeah, I know whatcha mean. Mom tells me what I can do don't scare her, but I see the fear in her eyes whenever she catches me doin' it. Sometimes, I wish I di'n't have this power."

"But you do have it, and you must live with it, just as I have had to live with" -- the image's "arm" arced toward the tank – "*this*."

Stan glances at the tank again. He is not as wide-eyed as before, but he licks dry lips before speaking again.

"Uh, Chris? Do you wish you, uh, you wasn't, uh, you wasn't –"

"Yes, often. But wishes don't come true, and there's no use in wasting one's time with them."

Chris is about to speak further but is interrupted by the opening of the door to his "room." Standing in the doorway is Freddie, and he wears a fierce scowl on his face.

"I thought I heard voices down here." He peers at Stan with sharp disapproval. "Damn, kid, ya knew this place was off-limits, but ya had to come anyways, didn't ya?"

"Stan didn't mean any harm, Freddie. He's just a curious little boy, despite his *psi*-talent. *You* were a curious little boy once, weren't you?"

The handyman grimaces at the pointed remark. A long-time rule-breaker himself, he doesn't want to be in the position of a rule-*maker*. To cover his embarrassment, he fishes a stump of a cigar out of his tool pouch and lights up. He eyes both Chris and Stan.

"OK. I'll back off. *But*" – he jabs the cigar at Stan – "you don't wanna make a habit of comin' in here. The Doc'll have both our butts in a sling if he ever finds out."

"Sure, Freddie," Stan murmurs, happy to be off the hook. "I don't wanna get you into trouble. I was just curious 'bout Chris, is all. Now I know."

"You won't tell anyone else?" Chris asks anxiously.

"Heck, no! I don't wanna get *myself* into trouble either!"

"We can still be friends, can't we?"

"Yeah. People like us – you 'n' me 'n' Freddie 'n' Eve – we need all the friends we can get." He breaks into a huge smile. "I know! We can be the 'Fabulous Five,' defendin' the world 'gainst the forces of Evil."

"I'd like that, Stan. Thank you for visiting me."

"C'mon, kid. Time to go."

The boy and the dwarf depart, leaving It alone again. It relaxes immeasurably. It has survived yet another crisis and hopes that Its future privacy is assured.

It floats upon the waters of Its artificial womb. And It dreams.

PDF

To a lesser degree – but only slightly lesser – the occult phenomenon known as "near-death experience" or "out-of-the-body experience" is as misunderstood as "re-incarnation." The difference between the two is that NDE is an internal phenomenon, while re-incarnation is an external one.

We have seen that re-incarnation stems from a transference of life energies from a deceased person to a living person, both of whose brains operated at nearly the same frequency. Thus, seemingly, the living person believed (s)he had existed in a previous life, a wholly false assumption....

I hasten to point out that NDE should not be confused with psycho-projection, a.k.a. "bilocation." Although it is true that, in both cases, the consciousness leaves the physical body, psycho-projection involves a conscious, voluntary act whereas NDE is a subconscious, involuntary act.

What happens when NDE occurs?

The medical literature is replete with anecdotes, and most of them follow a pattern. The individual – often a hospital patient on the brink of dying – experiences a sensation of "floating" above his/her physical body and observing doctors and nurses attempting to revive him/her. After a short period of time, (s)he is aware of a bright white light and is drawn to it. (S)he enters the light and observes various figures, some of whom are previously deceased family members and friends and some of whom are "authority" persons, i.e. "angels," "saints," etc. (S)he is led to believe that the light is the portal to "Heaven" and that the observed personages are there to welcome him/her. At which point, when the doctors and nurses succeed in resuscitating the patient, (s)he finds him/herself back in his/her physical body.

What has actually happened here is that the brain of the individual in these situations had suffered damage to the left posterior insula, that region in which the body's states seem to be represented; the damage gives rise to a perception of a bodily self which is external to the actual body. The brain must then choose which image to anchor upon; due to the damage, it often chooses the external image and thus 'looks' down on the actual body. The individual who experiences NDE/OBE in reality hallucinates and draws a false conclusion upon recovery....

Joyce was having more than her usual difficult time in grasping Dr. Razumov's explanations of radiopsychological phenomena. In the first place, she knew two people who had spoken about their own NDE experiences; one of them was her uncle on her mother's side, and the other was a friend of a friend. Her uncle had had a heart attack and had been in the emergency room of a hospital in the City for half an hour as a cadre of doctors and nurses worked feverishly to resuscitate him. All seemed hopeless, and eventually the lead physician pronounced him dead. But, moments later, life signs were detected, and her uncle regained consciousness. Afterwards, he couldn't stop talking about what he had experienced while "dead" and called his revival "God's will" and a "miracle." The friend of a friend spoke of a similar experience when she underwent emergency surgery after an automobile accident.

The Doctor had claimed that NDE/OBE was some form of psycho-projection – similar to what Christopher Wredling was capable of – but yet, he also said that the people who experienced this phenomenon had simply been hallucinating and really did not leave their bodies nor see their loved ones or a glimpse of Heaven. He was practically calling them liars at worst and simpletons at best. But all of them had been sincere and believed their experiences to be real. How could the phenomenon be both a *psi*-event and a hallucination? Joyce shook her head in disbelief.

What really made reading this short chapter so frustrating to follow was that she couldn't concentrate on the material but found her mind drifting off toward maternal concerns. She was worried about Stan's safety in light of the previous night's activity. What had possessed him to volunteer for a "defensive team"? Didn't he realize how dangerous that could be? George had claimed that no one would go looking for trouble but act if trouble came their way. But she knew from personal experience that sometimes things got out of hand and took a direction nobody anticipated.

She didn't want harm to come to her son, but she felt powerless to do anything about it. As she had already learned, parental rights took a back seat to DEDEP's mission – Dr. Razumov's mission, actually – which was paramount to all else, and the residents were subtly reminded day in and day out that this was the price they paid for sanctuary from the religious fanatics. She understood that as well, but her helplessness still sat in her craw.

Stan had changed in the short time he had been in DEDEP, and it had everything to do with that gestalt thing. While it existed, he was less of a ten-year-old and more of a – what? She didn't have the words to describe what he had become; she knew only that he was drifting away from her and that, if he continued to do so, she would lose him altogether.

And he wasn't the only one who had changed, and here again the gestalt was involved. Even a dope like herself could tell that Eve, once the near psychotic wallflower at DEDEP, had become more self-confident and self-assured. Why else would she have volunteered herself (and Stan) for this defensive team? When she and Stan were together in public, they spoke in hushed tones and gave each other knowing looks. Their relationship wasn't exactly sinister, but it was definitely disturbing. If both of them had been adults, one might have believed they were lovers. Joyce would have given her right arm to learn what they did and said in private. Ignorance was not always bliss. Sometimes it led to curiosity and then to knowledge. But, did she really want to learn the truth of this relationship? Would it do any good if she did?

A knock at the door dispelled those unsettling questions, and Joyce was more than happy to put them on hold. When she opened the door, she confronted Jean with a look of concern on her face.

"Hi, Joyce. Got a minute?"

"Hi, Jean. Sure. I've got the afternoon shift today. Come on in."

The two women settled themselves on the sofa. Neither spoke for a few seconds. Jean seemed troubled by something, and Joyce gave her time to sort things out.

"What did you think of last night's meeting?" the "eel" said presently.

"Well, it was full of surprises, that's for sure. But all of the meetings I've been to have been like that. Life here is like a rollercoaster. Why do you ask?"

"I thought sure that George wanted me to volunteer for his so-called 'defensive team.' I can do a lot of damage with my 'talent.' And I'd've been a likely candidate."

"George said he wouldn't send anybody out to look for trouble."

"Uh-huh. But, if trouble came looking for us, George would want someone to knock it on its butt."

"We've got the gestalt to do that. It's already got one mark on its 'scorecard.' Did you want to volunteer?"

"Oh, hell, no!" Jean gripped Joyce's forearm in consternation. "I just want to live a normal life, that's all."

"Huh! You won't as long as you're here. You better get used to it."

"I suppose I'm really concerned about Freddie." Joyce raised an eyebrow. "I'm getting to like the little guy. He treats me like a kid sister. I wouldn't want anything to happen to him, and that's what's bothering me. If I were to volunteer, I could protect him."

"You do have a problem, Jean. I'm afraid I haven't any answers for you. I'm still having trouble coping with all of this myself."

"'S okay. Just hearing me out helps a little. Thanks."

"Any time, 'little sister.'"

Both of them giggled like schoolgirls at the joke and turned to some "girl talk."

* * *

Larkin had "requisitioned" Laboratory #1 for his orientation of his new defensive team. He was now sitting at the desk that Emil Razumov used to conduct his Zener-card tests and waiting for the residential contingent of his "troops" to show up.

He had spent about two hours after he returned to the City working up the table of organization and equipment, much like a general would at the Hexagon, and assigning specific members of the team to perform specific tasks. The "equipment" part was simple enough inasmuch as DEDEP had at its disposal only five pieces with which to work: the gestalt, first and foremost; the universal translator; the force-field generator; the tracker; and the universal encyclopedia. How effective a tool the latter piece would be had yet to be determined, according to changing circumstances.

For the "organization" part, he had already made some preliminary judgments by grouping specific *psi*-talents into two distinct "squads." "Alpha Squad," an extension of his original task force after he had learned about the presence of extraterrestrials on Earth, would be the actual defensive part of the team, called upon to meet any attack head on and repel it. "Beta Squad" would be the "espionage" wing, called upon to gather intelligence that Alpha could use to blunt any attack more efficiently. What he intended to do today involved creating hypothetical scenarios and instruct individual members how to respond to each scenario. Given what little he knew about Swarm tactics, he realized that any real-time scenarios would probably be radically different from his imaginary ones. But that was what Beta was for – to observe Swarm tactics and report back.

He marveled at how quickly events had progressed in the past two weeks. From being a simple private investigator plying his trade and avoiding attention by religious fanatics to being the "savior" of Planet Earth was a giant leap for one man, one which he would have gladly foregone given a choice. Circumstances had dictated otherwise, and he was stuck with the job. His one major counter-offensive to date had been to pit the Swarm against the Disciples by means of elaborate ruses.

Now, however, he was going to commit DEDEP to the front lines and use its paranormal abilities in a master strategy. He hoped against hope he wasn't sacrificing his friends needlessly.

He had wanted volunteers for the defensive team, and he had hoped certain individuals would step forward. When Henry Rawlins voiced the obvious concerns, no one had stepped forward immediately, and he had envisioned his plan going down in flames. Then, to his great surprise, the last person he thought would volunteer jumped to her feet; her action stirred others to show themselves, and quickly he had his team – the very ones he wanted in the first place!

The gestalt-makers were the "wild card" in all of this. Not only had Eve Pelletier morphed from a wallflower to a self-confident, mature person, but she had also caused her "partner-in-crime" to morph from a ten-year-old who regarded the gestalt as a new toy to an "adult" who made life-and-death decisions. Did what had gotten into Eve get into Stan as well? Was that why their relationship resembled two mature individuals working on a project mutually beneficial to both? There was much to meet the eye, and he was damned if he could fathom it by simple observation.

As he pondered the question, the objects of his pondering sauntered in, chatting amiably. The pair looked for all the world like tourists visiting a museum; they spoke quietly and gesticulated broadly, and yet Larkin noted an air of conspiracy in their movements. That notion was re-enforced when they spotted him eyeing them and immediately assumed an air of neutrality. Both took adjacent seats in a semi-circular arrangement the detective had previously set up. Eve exhibited a Mona-Lisa smile while Stan stared aimlessly at the ceiling.

The Twins and Sheena arrived a minute later. Although they had made the trip out to the farm with Larkin, they had gone off to the dining area to see if they could snatch a late breakfast. Kenny and Paddy were cheerfully munching on doughnuts, and Sheena had a cup of coffee and a saucer with two slices of toast. They took seats one chair away from the "co-conspirators." The Smythes instantly assumed blank expressions as was their habit when they were in mental communication with each other. Sheena seemed nervous and had been so all the way to DEDEP. Larkin had had other matters on his mind at the time and so paid her little heed, but he intended to correct that little oversight as soon as the meeting was concluded.

The next person through the door was Freddie, stretching and yawning every step of the way. The detective was put in mind of the old saw, "look what the cat dragged in and dragged right back out again." The handyman appeared to have slept with his clothes on; they were quite bedraggled, rumpled, and disheveled, giving their wearer the epitome of how *not* to dress in the morning. Freddie ambled over, sat down on the empty chair next to Stan, and yawned prodigiously. When he spied Larkin with a bemused expression, he countered with a "so what?"

Finally, the Perkinses made their entrance. And they were not alone. Preceding them was a green troll with purplish splotches all over its body; it shuffled and snorted its way to the semi-circle, glaring at the assembly with rheumy yellow eyes. Following the mother-son duo was yet another troll; this one was blue with green splotches and had only one huge red eye in the middle of its forehead. It also shuffled and snorted – and drooled. As Lacey and Billy passed by Eve and Stan, the boy grinned and gave the teenager the "OK" sign. The Perkinses took the remaining two seats. The trolls stood behind them, snorting and drooling. Larkin gaped unabashedly at the procession and smiled in spite of himself at Billy's imagination.

"Would you mind dismissing your…friends?" he addressed the teen. "I haven't yet any part for them to play."

"Sure thing, Mr. Larkin."

Billy took a deep breath, let it out slowly, and waved a hand at the trolls. Instantly, the trolls disappeared.

"That was cool, Billy!" Stan enthused.

"Thanks, Stan. It was something I threw together on the spur of the moment to show you what I could do."

"Very enterprising, Billy," Larkin said dryly.

"'Enterprising' isn't the word *I* would use," Lacey retorted. "How would you like something like that sitting across from you at the dinner table? It gets to be rather unnerving after a while."

"I'm sure," the detective murmured. He switched on the intercom. "Chris? We're all here."

"Hello, world," the tinny voice responded. "I'll be there as quick as a flash."

And he was. The "Spook" materialized next to Larkin. He had elected to assume his "angelic" persona for this meeting, and his "eyes" gleamed mischievously.

"Damn!" Freddie muttered. "First, two monsters. Now an angel. What the hell's next? Darth Vader?"

"I'm sure Billy could accommodate you, Freddie – later. Right now, I want to give all of you your assignments. Then we'll do some exercises using hypothetical situations."

"Excuse me, George," Chris piped up. "I think we need a name for this team."

"Oh? And what do you suggest?"

"Um, how about the 'DEDEP Dappers'?"

A ripple of laughter passed through the group. The detective reflexively looked askance at the apparition next to him.

"Really, Chris!"

"I got a better one," Freddie chimed in. "'Larkin's Lackeys.'"

More laughter.

"We rather fancy something more sophisticated…"

"…like 'George's Jokers' or even 'Larkin's Layabouts.'"

The laughter became more raucous. Larkin smiled in spite of himself.

"Very funny, you guys. Can we get serious now?"

"Ok, George," Chris replied. "How about, instead, the 'Paranormal Defense Force,' or "PDF'?"

"Well, that makes more sense. Any objections to that?"

No one spoke up with a better suggestion.

"All right. We're the PDF, and we're here to bring law and order to the Galaxy."

That elicited another round of laughter. The detective immediately switched to his serious mode.

"For the purposes of utilizing your talents to maximum efficiency, I've organized you into two squads. Each squad will have a specific role in dealing with the Swarm. Alpha Squad – Sheena, Kenny, Eve, Stan, and Freddie – will act as the actual defense against any attack on DEDEP. From our experience with Mr. Jones, we know that the gestalt will counter an attack on itself; I'm hoping that it will include us in its protective function if we're in its vicinity. Sheena will act as Alpha Squad Leader.

"The rest of you will be Beta Squad, our 'espionage unit,' and Lacey will act as Squad Leader. You'll spy out the Swarm, monitor their activity, and update your reports for analysis.

"Kenny and Paddy will be our 'communications network.' They'll relay messages to and from each squad and to and from me. Also, they'll do double duty as back-up defense. Any questions so far?"

Billy raised his hand. Larkin nodded in his direction.

"Do I get to use my illusion-casting?"

"Absolutely. Most of the time, you'll use your psycho-occulism to scan the Swarm. But, in the case of an actual attack, you can cast illusions to confuse and misdirect them. That'll give Alpha Squad time to set up its defensive shield. Anyone else?"

"You can't be too sure about the gestalt, Georgie," Freddie grumbled. "What'll we do if the damned thing goes and hides?"

"Then we go and hide. That's what we've been doing the last eight years."

"What about the Disciples, old darling? Do…"

"…you still intend to use them as shock troops? And…"

"…are you going to invite them to DEDEP and…"

"…introduce them to their good and faithful allies?"

"You should know better than to ask those questions. The formation of the PDF won't change anything where the Disciples are concerned. In fact, I'll use the intelligence Beta Squad will gather to direct the Disciples' activities – without their knowledge, of course. Any more questions?"

There were none, for which Larkin was thankful. His Grand Plan entailed enough risks to cause even the most stout-hearted individual to quail. He needed DEDEP on board to stand four-square for the risk-taking. So far, so good. But time would tell if his faith in his "troops" was well-founded.

"OK. Since our base of operations against any possible attack will be in the farmyard, we'll go upstairs and do a bit of conflict resolution."

The newly-formed PDF marched to the shaft which led up to the barn. Larkin and Sheena were the first to clamber up the ladder. As usual, it was a hard slog for the former, but he made a brave showing of it. Eve and Stan were next. Then it was Freddie's turn. He peered upward and grimaced.

"Man, oh, man! 'S a good thing I don't hafta climb this thing every day."

"Hang on, Freddie," Stan called out to him. "I wanna try sumpin."

The boy pointed his finger at the dwarf who stiffened in shock at the sudden sensation of being gripped in a vise and tried to squirm loose.

"Hold still," Stan admonished. "Don't fight me."

He raised his finger toward the ceiling of the barn. Abruptly, Freddie was lifted off his feet and began to rise up the shaft. He cried out in terror and flailed his arms in all directions. In less than five seconds, he was at the top of the shaft, and Stan set him gently on the floor of the barn. The boy smiled grandly at him. The handyman stared back at him in wonder.

"Damnedest elevator *I* ever rode," he murmured. "Don't do that again, huh?"

When the group had all assembled in the barn, Larkin led them toward the barn door. They did not go far before they spotted Monk and Ted on the premises; both were tinkering with the Swarm's map module – Ted with the display screen, Monk with the power pack. Out of curiosity, the detective made a detour.

"Hiya, George," Monk and Ted greeted him simultaneously.

"Hi, guys. What's up?"

"Got somethin' really interesting to show you," Monk replied. He turned toward Ted. "Ted, call up A2."

The tall, lanky, horse-faced man pressed a long sequence of the touch-sensitive hexagons. The map of the United States Monk had originally accessed appeared once more on the holographic display;

yet, it was not exactly the same map. This rendition had extra points of reference, red in color; from these points, heavy black lines radiated in all directions, connecting them to the original points which represented the Swarm's primary targets.

"This is different," the detective stated the obvious.

"Yeah. There's an 'A' series and a 'B' series – so far. You already saw the 'A1' part the other day. 'A2' here shows the location of all the Swarm bases in the U.S. and the targets each is responsible for." He pointed to a red dot in the center of the map. "This'n's that base in Nebraska you been monitoring. Then you'll see two other bases, one each on the east and west coasts. Altogether, they got the whole country covered. Ted, let's see 'A12.'"

Ted completed a shorter sequence. One of the regional maps appeared. No one had to be told which region it was; the markings clearly identified it as the metropolitan area of Chicago. A black dot at the western-most edge of the display could be only one specific target: the City. A gasp of horror passed through the PDF as the reality of the situation sank in deeper than it had before.

"Pretty grim, all right," the government man commented. "But, you ain't seen nothin' yet. Let's have 'B12,' Ted."

A new map replaced the previous one. It displayed an enlarged view of the metropolitan area but was altered slightly. Whereas before the black lines between Swarm bases and targets had been singletons, on this display the lines were differentiated into thick, medium, and thin representations. The City merited a medium-sized line. Larkin studied the display briefly, then glanced at Monk.

"Is this what I think it is?"

"Uh-huh. Primary, secondary, and tertiary targets, respectively. Those Swarmers are ruthless bastards, but they know how to plan." A second gasp of horror arose from Monk's "audience." "Sorry to be so blunt, folks, but now you know exactly what you're up against."

"Thanks for the 'tutorial,' Monk. What're you working on now?"

The short man gazed at the module and sighed.

"I'm tryin' to open the power pack and see what makes it tick. I ain't had much success yet. I'll keep at it though." He now regarded the others. "What's up here?"

"Ah, well, meet the brand-new Paranormal Defense Force – PDF for short – DEDEP's new 'army.'"

"Be damned! Our own little army, eh? This your idea?"

"You got it, chum. I'm taking them out for their first drill session. See you later."

Once outside, Larkin positioned his "troops" into their "battle formations." Alpha Squad lined up with the Triad in their usual triangular formation; Kenny stood behind them, and Sheena took her place behind *him*. Beta Squad had Lacey and Billy in front with Paddy behind them; because of his particular *psi*-talent, Chris hovered above his squad-mates but in actuality was a roving member of the PDF. The detective positioned himself between the two squads.

"Ordinarily," he observed, "we'd all be sitting comfortably – or as comfortably as we could get in the event of an attack – in the barn. But, if an attack should occur when we are off the premises, these are the positions I want you to assume. Naturally, I don't expect any of you to take unnecessary chances. Cover for each other, if you can – run like hell, if you can't. Any questions?"

"Yeah," Freddie piped up. "I don't run so fast any more. What're *my* options?"

"Not to worry, chum. What I just said applies to those instances when we get separated. When we're together like now, we'll have this for added protection."

He reached into his jacket pocket, pulled out the force-field generator, and activated it. A low-level hum filled the air for a second or two; then a light-blue haze formed around him. Instantly, he felt the same tingling sensation he had experienced in Mr. Jones' apartment; happily, it was not as severe, and he adjusted to it quickly. Some of the group "oohhed" and "ahhed" in amazement. The rest showed apprehension.

Sheena squirmed as the EMF interacted with her hypersenses. But rather than voice her discomfort, she simply wrapped her arms around herself and bore the sensations as best she could.

"That gadget isn't doing any wonders for me, George," Chris' voice issued from the detective's cell phone. "I'm blocked out."

"Sorry about that, chum. What happens if you're caught inside an EMF?"

"It's never happened yet, but it's something I don't like to dwell on."

"Then you'll be on your own in a pinch."

"I've survived worse."

"Kenny, Paddy, what about you?"

"Like Chris, we've always avoided EMF's for…"

"…much the same reason, old darling."

"Are you willing to take a chance?"

"We'll give it a go just for you. Who…"

"…knows? Maybe we'll learn a new trick."

Larkin touched the left-hand depression, and the blue haze extended to a four-meter radius, enveloping both squads. The Twins went silent. The only indication that they were in a psycho-communicative mode was the blank look on their faces. After a second or two, they faced each other with sad expressions.

The next reaction came from Sheena, who shook uncontrollably as the force-field overwhelmed her senses. She staggered backwards until she was clear of the haze, sat down on the ground, and sobbed loudly. Lacey quickly went to her side to comfort her. Her partner reduced the force-field's range to its original setting.

"So much for that idea. Kenny, Paddy, what about you?"

"No such luck, George. All we got was…"

"…'static,' similar to radio and television signals…"

"…when interfered with by solar storms. We'd…"

"…both have to be outside the field to use our powers."

"And I can assume that you couldn't 'talk' if only one of you was inside it. Freddie, I'm entrusting you with this device since your squad will require the maximum protection."

He passed over the device and the instruction sheet. Freddie grimaced but said nothing (uncharacteristic for him). The force-field automatically shifted its position to center on the new operator. Larkin retrieved the universal encyclopedia.

"Billy, I'm giving this to you to play with. Teens these days have grown up with electronics and can understand them better than us 'old folks.' Our espionage unit will need to know what other intelligent life-forms did – if anything – about the Swarm."

The teenager beamed with pride at the honor bestowed on him as he accepted the device (and its accompanying instruction sheet). The detective went silent, deep in thought. Then he turned to Freddie.

"Extend the range of the force-field to the last setting."

The dwarf studied the instruction sheet for a moment, then pressed the appropriate depression. The blue haze once again blanketed both squads.

"Billy, cast some illusions, will you?"

Billy concentrated, and his facial expressions suggested difficulty. After half a minute, he wrinkled his nose in frustration.

"I can't do it, Mr. Larkin. Like the Smythes, I'm getting 'static' too."

"I thought as much. Mr. Smith told me that this gadget would protect against energy weapons. It's obvious that the EMF interferes with mental energy as much as it does with other forms of energy."

"What about the gestalt, George?" Eve asked. "It's a force beyond your, uh, *our* understanding. Maybe it can function where we can't."

"It's worth a try. Call it up."

Eve and Stan joined hands. The black sphere appeared...

* * *

Alert!

This One has entered an unacceptable environment!

Investigate! Analyze! Protect!

Investigation: this One finds itself surrounded by an electromagnetic force-field radiating in the [*undecipherable*] range. The nature of this environment is not harmful to this One, but it prevents this One from functioning normally.

Analysis: the Summoners called this One into their dimension for the purpose of information exchange. They were also inside the electromagnetic force-field but appeared not to be harmed. They are unaware of the effect this unacceptable environment has on this One. Consequence: loss of information exchange. Conclusion: closure of the portal to this dimension will restore the balance.

Protection: this One will initiate closure of the portal.

Initiating.

* * *

...and disappeared again.

"Eve! Stan!" Larkin called out. "What happened? Where did it go?"

"We don't know, George," the psycho-imager replied. "We felt a warmth only for a second or two – the same warmth we feel when the gestalt is activated – then it was gone."

"Yeah," Stan added. "That's the second time that's happened."

"Hmmm. This is the third time it's acted unpredictably if you count the destruction of Mr. Jones. I'd hazard to guess that being inside an EMF doesn't agree with it any more than Chris or Kenny or Paddy or Sheena. Which means that we can't use the generator except under specific circumstances. Freddie, shut it down."

"With pleasure," the dwarf muttered and complied.

"OK, gang, that's enough for one day. Tomorrow, we'll work on some defensive tactics."

When the DEDEP contingent had returned to the barn to resume their underground life and the City contingent was alone, Larkin regarded Sheena a moment. She was still feeling the effects of being caught inside an EMF, hugging herself and breathing shallowly. He had never seen her in this state before; on the other hand, he'd never subjected her to an EMF before.

"Sheena, are you all right?" he asked artlessly.

"No, I'm not all right!" she retorted. "How could you do this to me?"

"I guess I just got caught up in the moment. I'm sorry. It won't happen again."

"'Got caught up in the moment'? George, you need to step back and look at what this whole crazy business in doing to you. This... paranormal defense force is a huge gamble, and we may not win. We shouldn't be confronting the Swarm at all. We should be hiding, as we've been hiding from the Disciples."

"And how long do we hide? Until we run out of food and water? What then? The Swarm won't leave this planet until they've completely destroyed it. How will we survive? Mr. Smith is alive today only because his Coalition rescued him, but he lost his home and is dependent on the charity of others. Is that what you want for DEDEP?"

"It's better than getting ourselves killed."

"Is that what's really bothering you?"

"Oh, God, George, I don't know what I'd do if I lost you." She bit her lip. "I love you more than Life itself. I know you know that. I want you to hold me and kiss me and make mad passionate love to me. I – I want to have your children if at all possible." She took a deep breath and released it slowly. "There, I said it. No more dancing around the issue. If you die at the hands of the Swarm, my life won't have any meaning."

Larkin was stunned into momentary silence by Sheena's outburst. He didn't know whether he should be shocked or surprised by her sudden candor. Neither reaction would have had any foundation in logic, given the subtle and not-so-subtle hints she had dropped since becoming a junior partner in the agency. Despite his reluctance to reciprocate her feelings for him, she had persisted in an effort to wear him down and force him to admit that he loved her as much as she loved him.

He did, of course, but his disability worked against him – at least in his eyes. If he had believed he was a whole man, he would have made advances toward Sheena long ago, and they may have had the sort of relationship that she had just stated she wanted. And there was the added factor of being caught up in an impending alien invasion wholly without warning and wholly not to his liking. He was using this as an additional excuse not to express his true feelings, but he was sure that it would be equally as hollow to her as the other excuse. It was a matter of reality slamming head-on against self-deception, and he was caught in between.

"I don't intend to die any time soon," he responded finally, "especially at the hands of the Swarm. That's exactly why I came up with the idea of a PDF in the first place. We've already had one brush with the aliens because I was careless; and, if it hadn't been for the gestalt, I – and the rest of DEDEP – would have become very dead. I won't make that mistake again.

"Right now, the Swarm is pre-occupied with locating Jean Fulton so they can avenge the killing of one of their own. Also, they're busy making war preparations. Sooner or later, however, they're going to resume looking for the person or persons responsible for the death of their advance scout. They have one suspect – me – and the leader of their vanguard is the only other Swarm member to have seen my face. If Mr. Jones reported what he planned to do before following me here, then we're likely to have the whole vanguard at our doorstep. We'll need the PDF in reality as well as in principle.

"I don't want to lose you either, Sheena. Your being around has… enriched my otherwise drab life immensely, and I hope that we can continue to be close. Look, as soon as this alien business is over, we'll talk about the future – *our* future – and see what happens. Is that agreeable?"

"I won't wait forever, George – if we do survive the Swarm."

"I know. But I promise we'll talk."

The Twins rejoined them. Having sensed that their leaders wanted to engage in a private conversation, they had discreetly withdrawn to the barn door and waited patiently. Now, having sensed that the conversation was at an end, they ambled over and regarded their leaders with unfeigned impatience.

"We haven't had a proper breakfast, old darling…"

"…and now it's time for lunch. We're famished."

"Well, we can't have you famished, can we? I'll spring for lunch at an eatery of your choice when we get back to the City."

"Jolly good!" the Twins said in unison.

* * *

From the diary of Christopher Wredling:

Who can fathom the curiosity of children?

Not I, because I never had a childhood in the normal sense of the word. My mother died giving birth to me, and my father – whoever he was – shunned me shortly afterwards. I was placed under the care of an ever-changing cadre of physicians, nurses, biologists, physiologists, neurologists, and psychologists. They all poked and prodded me almost every day.

I was educated – after a fashion – by specialists in the field of education for 'abnormal' children, and I read a lot on my own. That was the limit of my curiosity – reading about human activity and culture but never experiencing it as the mobiles do – until I discovered my psi-talent. *As a consequence, I transitioned into 'adulthood' at a relatively early age; I knew more, intellectually speaking, than most adults could ever know, but less, practically speaking, than all children.*

Do I miss having a childhood? I have been told by any number of psychologists that one does not miss what one never had, and I suppose it is true in my case. Still, I would like to have had the opportunity, if only to satisfy my own curiosity. I can do what no mobile can do, as Emil keeps re-assuring me. But, given a choice, I would have opted to be a mobile too. I've never told anyone this – not even Emil Razumov – and I don't intend to. Only posthumously will anyone ever learn about my fondest wish.

There is, however, the possibility that my...condition will become known to others beyond Emil, George, and Freddie. It all depends on how well Stan Jankowsky can keep a secret. I have been told that children can keep secrets under certain circumstances, but I have no personal experience of that observation and so cannot take any comfort in it. I must trust Stan to keep his word. I fear I will have to keep a close eye on him (so to speak), a proposition I don't relish. Having been the object of close observation myself most of my existence, I can't picture myself turning the tables and spying on others close to me – especially other psi-*talents who are the closest I will ever come to having friends.*

On a more positive note, George has come up with a highly imaginative scheme. I suggested calling it a 'paranormal defense force (PDF).' Ironically, it means I'll have to a lot more spying on the Swarm than I have been doing. George hasn't given us any specific assignments – yet – our first 'training session' consisted only of how to co-ordinate our abilities with each other. One would not have thought that George Larkin could behave like a drill sergeant until one had seen him put us through our paces. He is quite the task-master when he puts his mind to it!

The emphasis is, of course, on defense, not offense. If anyone attacks DEDEP – its members and/or its base – we will mobilize en masse and counterattack. George assures us that, if we do go on the offense, it only will be to rescue a DEDEP member from harm or abduction. We will not go looking for trouble.

The core of the PDF is the gestalt – our so-called 'dangerous weapon' – controlled by Stan, Eve, and Freddie. Yet, we can't really count on it to protect us from danger, since we know so little about it and since it has disappeared on us a couple of times without warning. It vaporized Mr. Jones because he attacked it. Whether that is the extent of its ability – or willingness – no one knows – maybe not even its 'controllers.' We won't know unless we are attacked. And there's a strong possibility that that will be the last thing we know. Br-r-r! what a thought!

Speaking of the gestalt, has anyone else noticed the change in Eve and Stan – especially Eve? In the beginning, she was reluctant to bring the black sphere into existence and had to be coaxed to get her co-operation. Now, she has no problem with it; and, when George asked for volunteers for his PDF, she actually volunteered to be a part of it. Something has happened to her and Stan – something very interesting.

BTW, I should point out that I'm probably the only member of DEDEP who hasn't interfaced with the gestalt. It's not that I won't interface with it; it's because I can't. The thing is akin to an EMF which protects it from physical contact (except for Stan and Eve). Emil and Freddie found that out the hard way. To me, it's just another barrier when I psycho-project. So, whatever the others have experienced when they interfaced is one more experience denied to me.

What a 'life'!

* * *

In the VOID, five points of light appear in a circle. After a brief moment/eon, a sixth point appears in the center of the circle.

One of the points in the circle brightens slightly.

-- REPORT.

The point in the center of the circle now brightens slightly.

-- This One informs the Inner Ring that the candidates in the [undecipherable] Zone and their allies now possess an electromagnetic force-field generator. This One was nearly entrapped by it.

A second point of light in the circle brightens slightly.

-- Are you unharmed?

-- Yes. This One recognized the danger immediately and closed the portal to that Zone.

A third point of light in the circle brightens slightly.

-- Why do they possess such a device?

-- Investigation and analysis show that the candidates and their allies face imminent attack by a hostile race of beings which originate in another part of their Zone. This One recently encountered one of these hostiles and destroyed it when it attempted an attack on this One. The candidates believe that their device will protect them.

A fourth point of light in the circle brightens slightly.

-- Do the candidates require assistance?

-- This One believes so. Their species is young and unsophisticated. The candidates stand out like a beacon.

The final point of light in the circle brightens slightly.

-- The Inner Ring will analyze your report and advise. You are dismissed.

The point of light in the center of the circle winks out of existence. After a brief moment/eon, the remaining points of light are extinguished.

Only the VOID remains.

THE SWARM IN COMBAT MODE

LARKIN WAS WRITING up battle plans for the PDF and hoping he hadn't left out any possible contingency when his private phone rang. He checked the caller ID and was surprised to see that the caller was Gordy because this was the second time in less than a week that he was calling. Which meant that the ex-FBI agent had some serious business to discuss. He pushed the speakerphone button.

"Hi, Gordy. What's up?"

"Hi, George. Got an interesting piece of news for you."

"Let's have it."

"My contact at the Bureau apparently sent the word out to all of the regional offices that I was into UFO sightings all of a sudden. As a result, I've gotten a ton of e-mails and newspaper clippings about sightings. Even got a couple of clippings from your local paper."

"Huh! Looks like the Swarm is mobilizing everywhere."

"I thought they only had a base in Nebraska."

"Nope. My sources say they've got bases on both coasts where the greatest population is. That's why there're so many sightings being reported."

"Be damned! You still have the Disciples working for you?"

"Yeah. As long as I can feed their paranoia, they'll be loyal shock troops."

"You always were the devious sort, old buddy. I just hope you don't trip over your own tongue."

"I've always got you to keep me on the straight and narrow, don't I?"

"Right. Hang in there. See ya."

"So long, chum."

Gordy's news was disturbing, to say the least. Not only was the local Swarm base flexing their muscles, but wherever they were in America (and perhaps the whole planet) they were making serious preparations for the inevitable strike. And, worse, they were doing so without any concern that their presence might be compromised. The Swarm was so confident that Earth's defenses were no match for their assault capabilities that they were behaving impudently and recklessly. That attitude made them all the more dangerous. The detective hadn't formed the PDF any too soon. In fact, there was the real possibility that his group would get some OJT sooner than expected.

His office phone rang insistently.

"Yes, Madge?"

"I've got a Brother Connolly on the line. Do you want to take the call?"

"Yes. Patch him through." The phone went silent for two seconds; a click indicated life again. "Hello, Brother Connolly. What can I do for you?"

"Hello, Brother Larkin. I'm glad I caught you in. I've got an important message for you."

"I'm all ears."

"His Worship has appointed me to be the liaison between you and Brother Horton's task force. That's so you don't have to spend time coming to his office when you're needed in the field."

"Hmmm. That was thoughtful of him. As you know, it's hard for me to get around. So, what's the message?"

"At your suggestion, we posted a monitor at that abandoned factory you told us was the Enemy's base of operations. Less than an hour ago, the monitor reported that a large group of those creatures left their base, on foot, and were headed downtown."

"How a large a group?"

"Maybe a dozen – no more than that."

"This sounds like trouble to me. Can you gather up Brother Horton and his people on short notice?"

"Not a problem, Brother Larkin. They're all primed and ready for the word to move out."

"Great. Have them meet me at the corner where my office is." He paused dramatically. "Thanks for keeping me posted, Brother Connolly."

"You're welcome, Brother Larkin. I'll see you in half an hour."

And thanks for being my 'go-fer,' 'Brother' Connolly, he added after he had hung up. *You're icing on the cake.*

Now he slumped in his chair and opened his mind.

*Kenny, Paddy.

*Hello, old darling [Kenny responded]. What's the good word?

The detective filled him in on what the young Disciple had reported.

*This does not bode well, George.

*I agree. It's time Beta Squad got its feet wet. I want all hands on deck on this one. Contact Lacey and Chris and get them moving. Put Paddy and Billy on stand-by.

*Aye, aye, Captain. Anything else?

*Not at the moment. Stay alert though.

*Right you are, guv.

Larkin exited his office, stepped over to Sheena's, and rapped gently. There was no answer. He rapped again, a bit louder. Still no answer. He opened the door and entered an empty office. He turned and headed for the outer office. Mrs. Watson regarded him cheerfully at first, saw the frown on his face, and switched to "Office Neutral."

"Madge, has Sheena been in?"

"No, George. And she hasn't called in either."

"Strange. That's not like her. Well, I've got an appointment. I don't know when I'll be back. If she does come in, have her call me."

"Will do."

The detective left the office and took the elevator down to street level. His mind was awhirl with concern. What was behind Sheena's uncharacteristic absence? Did it have to do with yesterday's emotional outburst?

The changing circumstances caused by the threat of alien invasion and the possible destruction of the Earth had apparently forced a change in his partner's approach to their relationship. No longer did she drop subtle and not-so-subtle hints of wanting something more than simple friendship; instead, she had been straightforward and blunt about it.

And what had been his response? He had attempted to be objective about their relationship. He had assured her in oh-so-neutral terms that he would "re-evaluate" the relationship once the clear and present danger was over – *if they survived*. He had not mentioned one word about how much he loved her. No, his hang-up over his disability – his *perceived* disability – would not allow him to express his true feelings, much as he so desperately wanted to do.

Sheena had said she would not wait forever. If she quit the agency, if she left him because he could not be a man and love her back, then he had no one to blame but himself. His life would be empty, devoid of the one thing which mattered the most to him. His life wouldn't be worth living without her. Somehow, he had to break down the psychological barriers he had erected which threatened to deny him happiness. But how? When?

* * *

Lacey Perkins was clearly alarmed. She sat on her sofa with fists clenched.

Since she had volunteered her services to the PDF, she was operating on an enhanced schedule. Every ten minutes, she scanned the abandoned factory on Ridgeway Avenue, noted any new activity taking place within, and wrote down on a notepad what she had just "seen." She would then call Paddy (her assigned go-between) and read her notes to him in accordance with the established "chain of command." Presumably, Paddy would pass the information on to George Larkin.

This morning, the activity took on a more ominous note. After the Swarm were lined up in formation, the Leader paced back and forth in front of them and silently (to her) harangued them, emphasizing whatever he said with wild gesticulations. Once he had finished his harangue, he pointed toward the rear of the building; his command pivoted and marched in that direction. Lacey then focused her attention to the exterior of the building as it was obvious (to her) that the Swarm were about to exit it. Outside, the Swarm with the Leader at the head broke formation and began moving northward by pairs toward downtown. She had known about the patrols previously, but they had been one or two at a time. Now, however, the entire unit was being ordered out.

There was no time to follow "protocol." She had to notify George directly right away. As she reached for the telephone, she felt a low-level buzzing in her head.

*Hello, love [Kenny greeted her].

She looked around for the source of the "voice." She saw no one and cried out:

"Who's there? Where are you?"

*It's I, Lacey, Kenny Smythe. I'm 'speaking' to you telepathically.

"But I don't have any telepathic abilities. How can I 'hear' you?"

*I gave you the ability to send and receive the day I showed you how to scan the Swarm. I opened up a few neural pathways that aren't normally used. Now you can contact Paddy or myself anytime just by thinking about it. Try it.

She concentrated.

*Are you 'hearing' me? [she asked tremulously].

*Loud and clear, love. Soon, it'll be old hat to you. I did the same for George and Sheena, because they needed the ability in their work. And, before you ask, no, you can't contact either of them in the same fashion; it only works with Paddy and me.

*OK. Well, I'm glad you 'called.' I've got some really big news to pass on. [She related what she had just witnessed]. George needs to hear about this right away.

*I can tell you that our dear George already knows about it from other sources. You just corroborated it. Now he wants you and Chris to step up the pace.

*How can I do that? I'm only limited to specific locations.

*Not to worry. I'll simply open up a few more neural pathways. Just relax while I do it.

Ten seconds passed, and Lacey fidgeted.

*When are you going to do it? [she asked].

*It's already done, love. Now, I'll send you the signal unique to the Swarm, and then you'll be able to track them wherever they go.

*I never knew just how awesome your mental powers were, Kenny. They can be…frightening at times.

*I know. If the general public – and especially your government – were aware of what Paddy and I are capable of, our lives wouldn't be worth a tuppence. Well, I'm off. Ta-ta.

*Bye-bye.

Lacey remained seated quietly for a long while. The experience she had just undergone was too overwhelming to allow any movement. She just wanted to sit still and play it again and again in order to convince herself that it had all been real. It seemed too fantastic to be real. And, yet, how less real was telepathy than her own *psi*-talent? She was a clairvoyant – a psycho-occulist, in Emil Razumov's lexicon – simply by accessing some anomalous part of her brain. A spin of the genetic roulette wheel had put that part there and allowed her to "see" what most people could not. It shouldn't have been all that great a leap that she now could communicate by mind alone.

Wait'll I tell Will and the boys! They'll be floored! Now, I should give this new ability a test run.

She searched her mind, found the signal Kenny had placed in it, and focused on it. Instantly, the images filled her mind. It was like watching a number of television screens all at once. She could "see" each pair of Swarm soldiers and the Leader as they wended their way across city block after city block in their inexorable march to the business district of the City. Immediately, she grabbed her notepad and began writing brief descriptions of each scene and identifying whole neighborhoods by the occasional sight of a street sign.

And, in the back of her mind, she would have to thank Kenny for this marvelous gift.

* * *

Sheena did not get a good night's sleep. Instead, she had tossed and turned, nodded off, awoke, and tossed and turned some more.

And, during the tossing and turning, she replayed in her mind the last conversation she had had with her partner. She hadn't spoken at all during lunch, except when ordering, but kept mum while George and the Twins yammered on about one thing or another. Once or twice, he had glanced at her but turned away in embarrassment. Mentally, she had kicked herself for having had that conversation. What had she been thinking, blurting out her feelings for him like that? Frustration? Exasperation? Despair? All of the above? She supposed that years of dropping hints hadn't advanced their relationship to where she wanted it to go and so she had taken the bull by the horn and confronted George directly.

And still he hid behind the excuse that he was only "half a man." Yes, he did say that, after the war with the Swarm had concluded – assuming, of course, that they both survived the battle – he would "re-evaluate" their relationship. But, she could read his biometric signals, and she had seen doubt and fear in them. George was still gripped by his disability, and he couldn't let go. He was more of a man in her estimation than most fully-formed human males. Couldn't he see that?

She had finally fallen into a semi-deep sleep, but it had been short-lived. The alarm woke her at the usual time, but she laid in bed hiding in her own thoughts. When she finally did rouse herself, she puttered around the apartment for several hours, trying to keep busy and not return to the previous day's conversation. She didn't want to go to the office in her present state of mind. She needed some peace and quiet in order to re-evaluate her own feelings. She didn't succeed.

Why, oh, why, had she fallen in love with a man like George Larkin? He was only the most fabulous person she'd ever met, everything she'd looked for in a possible mate. Except he had this psychological hang-up.

When she finally did leave the apartment to wander the streets, changing directions as the spirit moved her, all she encountered were passersby who felt pity for the "poor blind girl" whom she could "read" as clearly as if they had uttered a blunt verbalization. If they only knew how much she despised their phony feelings…

"Sister Whitley!"

The salutation that only a Disciple would make snapped her out of her self-imposed zone of silence like a slap in the face. She turned in the direction of the voice (a young voice), "read" the caller's biometrics in an instant, and recognized them as belonging to "Brother" Connolly, George's new "informant."

"Brother Connolly," she greeted him in a neutral voice. "Good morning."

"Good morning. Running into you is a piece of luck."

"Oh?"

The young man explained the mission Larkin had set him on. Though she could not see them, she sensed four other Disciples – all male, all exuding primitive life-signs – in a parked car four feet away. What Connolly had to say alarmed her no end. George was actually gathering up an "army" to confront the Swarm! He could be killed! Then where would she be? All alone, that's where.

"You'd better take me to him. He'll…need my assistance."

"Sure thing, Sister Whitley." He turned to his cohorts. "Make room for the lady, guys, and let's roll!"

In the back of her mind, Sheena marveled at how someone as young as Connolly could take command so easily and how easily he could take charge of four bruisers without question. How had that happened? The answer was sure to be very interesting.

* * *

Lacey contacted Kenny again. She had wondered briefly how to do so, then decided she'd just "call" his name. It worked like a charm.

*Hello, love.

*Hello yourself. This is just too easy!

*Paddy and I think so. And speaking of him, you really ought to follow George's protocol from now on and report to Paddy. He'll relay your report to our fearless leader.

*Yes, sir! How do I make my report?

*How are you recording what you 'see'?

*I write everything down on a notepad.

*Ah, excellent. What I will do now – and what Paddy will do from now on – is to enter your mind and access your visual center. When I – and he – say 'Go!', you look at the pages of your notepad one by one, and we'll store the images in our minds for subsequent transfer to George. Is that clear?

*As clear as glass, as Chris might say. I'm getting out my notepad now.

Five seconds passed.

*Go!

Lacey peered at the first page of her notes, flipped to the second, and continued until the last page came into view.

*Did you get everything, Kenny?

*I did. You've done excellent work, love. The Swarm will never make a move but we will know about it. We'll meet them at the pass, as you Yanks say.

*It's too bad George is restricting us to only defensive actions. I think we could defeat them with the PDF's combined abilities.

*The old darling has his reasons, Lacey. Yet, it may come to that in the end. Toodle-oo!

*Bye-bye.

* * *

*George.

*Go ahead, Kenny.

*I've just been in contact with Lacey. She can now track the Swarm as easily as Paddy and myself can.

*That's great. We'll be able to fine-tune our tactics almost minute by minute.

*Glad to be of service. Ta-ta.

Larkin was standing at the entrance to his building and waiting for "Brother" Horton and his task force to show up. He hoped to get at least a three-to-one advantage (more if possible) over the Swarm, because the aliens were proven ruthless combat troops and were likely to win any one-on-one conflict. He was sure they'd be armed with whatever alien weapons they had at hand, so countering them with overwhelming numbers would definitely even the odds. The Archdeacon might not approve of sacrificing so many of his people; on the other hand, the old man hadn't been overly concerned about the loss of those Disciples by Mr. Jones' weapon. And, if even a small victory were achieved, he might consider any losses "necessary expenditures" in the "service of the Lord."

Meanwhile, the detective needed to issue some more orders. He called Chris on his cell phone.

"Hello, George," came the tinny voice.

"Hi, Chris. Got a job for you."

"I wish I could say I'm all ears, but I haven't got any. What's the job?"

"The Swarm is on the move, heading downtown. Lacey is tracking them, even as we speak. I want a bird's-eye view from you."

"Not a problem."

"Great. Do you have Lacey's cell-phone number?"

"I'm not sure. Let me check my directory." A pause. "Sorry, no."

"I'll give it to you then." Another pause as he texted the phone number. "Call her and get the exact location of the Swarm."

"Check."

Larkin was about to call Sheena, who was nominally Alpha Squad Leader, to update her when a solid white sedan pulled up to the curb and halted with a lurch. Upon seeing it, he grimaced. The vehicle was the very same one which had been involved in the hit-and-run murder he had witnessed two weeks ago. He could still see the dent in the fender where contact had been made.

"Brother" Connolly and four bruisers piled out. One of the bruisers in a moment of gentlemanly courtesy assisted Sheena as she wriggled out of the car. The detective was taken aback at the sight of her in those circumstances, but he was also relieved to find her safe and sound. She and Connolly approached, one confidently, the other sheepishly. The bruisers remained near the sedan with appropriately grim looks on their faces.

"Are these all you could find, Brother Connolly?" he asked desultorily.

"Oh, no! not by a long shot, Brother Larkin. Brother Horton will be along shortly with the rest of the guys. Sister Whitley said it was urgent that she hook up with you, so I rushed over here."

The young Disciple re-joined his part of the task force. Larkin regarded his wayward partner with a mixture of worry and accusation.

"I was worried about you," he began placatingly. "I thought maybe you had, um…"

"*I* was worried about me. I spent a lot of time sorting things out."

"And did you sort them out?"

"It's still a…work-in-progress. Right now, I'm ready to go back to work. What do you want me to do?"

"What you do best: monitor people. Let me know if you pick up any unusual signals."

"All right. I – oh, God! *George, I'm picking up Farquhar!*"

"You have got to be kidding!"

The detective scanned the area but saw no one close by except Connolly and the four bruisers. Connolly was keeping an eye out for "Brother" Horton. Two of the bruisers were engaged in a whispered conversation. Another was picking his teeth with a fingernail. The fourth stood like a statue with a glazed look in his eyes. If the so-called "psychic chameleon" was in the vicinity, he had to be invisible.

"I don't see anyone but you and the Disciples."

"I never thought to scan them. I forgot that Farquhar assumed a Disciple disguise twice before." She faced the quintet and focused. "His signal is coming from the second from the left."

Larkin regarded the group again. The second from the left was the tooth-picker. He cleared his throat to get the Disciples' attention. When he had it, he motioned to the picker to join him. The latter strutted over and looked at the detective stupidly.

"Farquhar," Larkin spoke in a low voice, "what are you doing here?"

The picker grinned hugely.

"I thought I'd give you a hand, Georgie. There's trouble in River City from what I've heard."

"There is, but I don't know what you can do to help. You have no idea what we're up against."

"Aliens from outer space?"

Larkin stared a hole in the still grinning "Disciple." He didn't know whether he should be angry or frightened by this admission – or both. If Farquhar were spying on the Disciples as a matter of routine, he could not have learned about aliens from that quarter. The religious fanatics did not know about the true origin of the Swarm but believed they were battling demons from Hell. Therefore, the "psychic chameleon" could have learned the truth of the matter from only one source – DEDEP. He had used his *psi*-talent to listen in on his and Sheena's conversations and caught wind of the alien invasion from them. Which raised the question: just exactly how much did he know?

Other questions instantly slipped into place, and they sent a chill up the detective's spine. Was Farquhar's eavesdropping the reason he had asked about DEDEP earlier? How much did he know about it? More to the point: what was he planning to do with the information? And what could he (Larkin) do to send him off on a wild-goose chase?

"You know about that?" he asked in as neutral a voice as he could manage.

"Like I said, I hear things. At first, I thought it was wild talk. But the more I listened, the more I realized that the talk was serious. Look here, Georgie, this planet is my home too. If there's anything I can do to protect it, I'm volunteering for duty."

Larkin made a snap decision. Actually, it was the only decision he could make under the circumstances.

"All right, you're in. Continue to monitor the Disciples. I need to know what they're doing at all times so that I can point them in the right direction."

"You *are* a devious sort, nephew. That's why I like you so much."

"Thanks -- I think. You'd better re-join your 'friends.'"

"Can you trust him, George?" Sheena inquired as soon as Farquhar was out of earshot. "He knows too much for our own good."

"I can't see that we have much choice at the moment, given his abilities. We'll just have to play it by ear for a while."

* * *

They move with a precise and deliberate pace. Three pairs of soldiers walk on either side of the street. Five meters separate each pair.

They move fully alert for any sudden and/or hostile action. Their training has provided them with the protocols necessary for patrolling in an unsecured urban environment, particularly one which has not been "softened" by a massive barrage of missiles. With the latter absent, hostile forces may be lurking anywhere, ready to fire their weapons in a deadly ambush. The soldiers have had enough experience to know what carelessness and inattention on their part will bring.

With a precise and deliberate pace, they examine each building they pass, watching for sudden movements and listening for telltale sounds of activated weapons. Their own weapons are holstered, but they are not far from hands; at the first sign of enemy attack, the weapons will be brought to the ready, activated, aimed, and fired, all in the space of a single heartbeat. Their training has been such that combat readiness is second nature to them. The soldiers have had enough experience to know what hesitation and confusion on their part will bring.

The soldiers' current orders are clear. Their Commander (who walks at the head of one squad) has drummed their mission into their heads incessantly during the previous axial rotation of this world (which they call "Telluria"), and they have been required to memorize their orders and repeat them when ordered to do so. The orders are to apprehend any and all of the white-clothed Tellurians who apparently are a local militia, interrogate them, and then terminate them. In particular, they seek the leader of this militia, he who was responsible for the murder of one of their agents in this region of the planet. The Commander wants very much to interrogate personally this Tellurian and then to terminate him in the most excruciatingly painful method he can think of. Nothing else matters for the time being. Once this troublesome fellow has been dealt with, then and only then will the invasion and conquest of this primitive world be implemented.

The street along which the soldiers march has not so far presented any problems. For the most part, they pass small retail shops and light manufacturing facilities, but vehicular and foot traffic seem extremely sparse for a city this size. This circumstance will make difficult the location of any of the white-clothed Tellurians. If they are the local militia, they are extremely lax and/or inefficient. It may be necessary to root them out at considerable cost of time and/or manpower.

The Commander raises his hand to call a halt. He has spotted one of the white-clothed Tellurians emerging from one of the retail shops. He makes several hand gestures, directing the lead pair of soldiers nearest the target to close in and apprehend. The designated soldiers break into a trot and approach the target. The target spies them and attempts to escape, but he is not quick enough and is caught and slammed to the ground. One of the soldiers presses his boot against the target's neck and grins in triumph at his comrades.

The Commander speaks to the soldiers in his guttural tongue. They seize the Tellurian by the arms and yank him to his feet. The Tellurian fears the worst since he has been told that these creatures are the Devil's own and they delight in torture and murder. The Commander pulls a sheet of paper-like material from his tunic and pushes it up to the Tellurian's face. The sheet contains an image of another Tellurian.

"Tell me," the Commander orders his captive in a heavily-accented English, "where I may find this person."

The captive blanches. He recognizes the image on the sheet. Though that person is not a true Disciple of Purity, he is the Archdeacon's trusted ally, and the word has spread that he is to be rendered all possible assistance at all costs. The captive knows that he must refuse the demand made of him, even if it means his martyrdom. He shakes his head resolutely.

"Away with you, devil spawn!" he utters with false bravado. "The Light of Purity will protect me and destroy you."

The Commander's face becomes a grotesque mask of fury, hatred, and contempt. He speaks to the soldiers again, and they tighten their grip on the Tellurian. The Commander returns the sheet to his tunic and draws his ceremonial knife, a wicked-looking, serrated blade twenty-five centimeters in length. He holds it up to the Tellurian's face.

"Tell me, or die," he growls.

The Tellurian whispers a brief prayer and shakes his head again.

Without warning, the Commander rams his knife into the captive's abdomen nearly up to the hilt and twists it viciously. A gout of blood spurts from the captive's body and splatters all over his white suit. He screams loudly in agony. The Commander pulls the blade out, opening the wound further. Blood pours out in a steady stream, and the screams grow louder. At the Commander's next utterance, the soldiers release their grip, and the captive falls to the sidewalk to lie in a pool of his blood.

The Commander signals to his soldiers. They begin the march again toward the central city, leaving the Tellurian to bleed to death.

* * *

Lacey could not remember if she had ever been this sick to her stomach. After witnessing the murder of the Disciple in cold blood, she had rushed to the bathroom and vomited for a full five minutes. Emptying the stomach had left her woozy, and she remained motionless over the toilet bowl for another ten minutes, just in case.

It would have been safe to say that she had never before witnessed an act of violence. She had read/heard about violent acts, had seen images of the aftermath of violence, and had as a nurse witnessed the aftermath of violence. But actually to *see* violence *as it occurred* was beyond her experience. In a split second, that had all changed and overwhelmed her senses.

When she felt reasonably calm again, she returned to the living room and slumped on the sofa. She gathered up her mental strength and made a "call."

*Paddy?

*Right here, love. What have you to report?

She described the incident of murder in a halting voice and struggled to keep from gagging again.

*Bloody hell! [Paddy murmured]. Those barstards have raised the stakes.

*Amen! It was...*gruesome*!

*I sense fear in your mind. If you like, I can take it away.

*No, no. I have to deal with it in my own way. Thank you for your concern anyway.

*As you wish. I will make it a standing offer, though.

*There is one thing you can do, if you can.

*And that is?

*I'm seeing multiple images of the Swarm. It's like seeing with a fly's eyes. Is there a way I can select just one image at a time?

*Indeed there is. Simply think 'top left,' 'second row, right end,' or however you care to phrase it. To return to the multiplex, think 'full scan,' or some such phrase.

*Ah, that sounds easy enough. Thank you, Paddy.

*My pleasure, love. Cheery-bye!

Lacey felt the disturbing image of murder creeping back into her consciousness and tried to dispel it by performing some mundane task, but she feared that she would have to live with the awful memory for the rest of her life.

* * *

*George, Sheena. Paddy here.

*Go ahead, Paddy.

*Lacey reports the Swarm contingent now at River Street and Second Street. They've just murdered a Disciple.

*Damn! [Larkin cursed]. In broad daylight too. The pace is picking up.

*Paddy, did she say how many? [Sheena asked].

*Around a dozen, I believe. Why?

*Their signal will be that much stronger, and I can track them better.

*Thanks, Paddy.

The detective turned to his partner. She was staring off into the distance in the direction of the reported location of the Swarm. Abruptly, she clenched her teeth as a massive wave of radio energy filled with obscenity and cruelty engulfed her mind. Instinctively, she pressed against Larkin for comfort. He put a tentative arm around her shoulder.

"I'll have to bring the Archdeacon up to speed. Are you all right?"

"I'll manage. Let's go."

The detective motioned for the bruisers to join them. Three of them he posted at the intersections of Main Street and Lake Street, Main Street and River Street, and Main Street and Island Avenue. The fourth – the disguised Farquhar – was directed to accompany them to Disciples HQ. As soon as they reached the building, Larkin turned to the hugely grinning informant.

"This is your 'guard post,' Farquhar, although I suspect you'll do as you please."

"You suspect right, Georgie. I'll stick around here for a while. Then I'll keep the aliens company – in my own inimitable fashion, of course."

"Be careful. They mean business."

"You care about me? How touching. Don't worry about me, nephew. I can take care of myself."

Larkin grunted at the bravado, and he and Sheena entered the lion's den again. To their surprise, yet another teen-aged girl was sitting at the reception desk. The detective wondered idly if there were a pool of them on a rotational basis or if old man Fogarty just wanted to try out each one in his "flock" until he found the right one for the job. The new girl, a rosy-cheeked, red-haired, overweight person wearing Coke-glass spectacles burst into an oversized smile and greeted them in a throaty voice. Larkin stated his business and was told to have a seat.

Half a minute later, to his chagrin, "Sister" Hedberg came bounding down the stairs and rushed over to greet them. Sheena hissed imperceptibly as the Disciple female positively radiated sexual desire. Larkin didn't need to be a biometrist to know what was on Hedberg's mind; he *was* disturbed that she wasn't bothering to maintain a professional demeanor in public. Nevertheless, he smiled at her approach.

"George, Sheena," Hedberg gushed, not bothering to use the honorific as outlined in Disciple protocol. "How good to see you again. His Worship is anxious to hear the latest."

"Hello, Dorothea," was the response as long as no one was being formal. "I'm afraid the latest is not very good. Things may be getting out of hand."

When they entered the *sanctum sanctorum*, they discovered the Archdeacon in an unusual mode – shuffling papers around, trying to arrange them in some sort of legible order, and muttering all the while. On the left-hand sofa, the ever-stolid "Brother" Kincaid sat quietly and watched him with bemusement. He did turn his head long enough to acknowledge the newcomers with a nod of the head. Larkin returned the gesture. Without looking up, Fogarty waved them to the right-hand sofa. Sheena had hoped to wedge herself between her partner and Hedberg, but the latter beat her to the punch and boldly snuggled up against the detective. Sheena seethed while Larkin squirmed.

Presently, the Archdeacon finished his paper-shuffling, looked up, and gave his visitors his best professional smile.

"Good morning, Brother Larkin, Sister Whitley. What news do you have for me today?"

"Not very happy news, I'm afraid, Your Worship." He then gave a carefully edited version of the latest developments, up to and including the recent murder. "Even as we speak, Brother Connolly is collecting Brother Horton and his group and bringing them to my office building. If I've exceeded my authority, I apologize. I thought quick action was necessary, under the circumstances."

The old man regarded him for a moment. He shifted his gaze toward Kincaid without moving his head. The number-two simply shrugged.

"Perhaps you're right," the Archdeacon said at last. "We are witnessing the End Times for certain. As long as you keep me informed on a regular basis, I'll back you up."

"I will. Thank you, sir."

"I won't detain you any longer. You have work to do."

Larkin took that as a dismissal for which he was utterly thankful. Being in the presence of this individual was upsetting enough; being in the presence of this individual and concocting plausible stories for his edification was becoming more and more difficult, and he was afraid of being tripped up at any given moment. Old man Fogarty may have been a religious fanatic, but he was no fool. And Kincaid was the sort who suspected everyone and everything. And then there was the matter of the warm body next to him!

He and Sheena rose and departed as expeditiously as possible with Hedberg still attached to him. At the bottom of the stairs, the "shark" placed her hand on his arm and searched his face with undisguised longing.

"Be careful out there, George," she said softly. "I – we need you in one piece."

"You can count on me on that score, Dorothea," he replied noncommittally and left the building.

Outside, Sheena laid her own hand on his arm but not in the same fashion as her new rival.

"I'm going to strangle that bitch before too much time passes," she growled. "I swear –"

She was interrupted by a distant sound picked up by her hypersenses and faced southeast. Larkin also peered in that direction but saw nothing out of the ordinary.

"George, did you hear that?"

"No. What is it?"

"Somebody is screaming bloody murder over on River and Cross Streets."

"River and Cross? Then that means the Swarm is close by."

He retrieved his cell phone and punched up a number.

"Hello, George," the tinny voice answered.

"Chris, I need you to scan River Street near Cross Street and report back to me."

"On my way."

"Meanwhile," the detective told his partner, "we return to base and hope that 'Brother' Horton has shown up with his bunch."

* * *

They move closer toward the central city and, accordingly, slow their pace in order to search more diligently. They observe more Tellurians, both on the street and inside the buildings. Those Tellurians who spot them gawk curiously at the spectacle of strangely-garbed, strangely-appearing beings; yet, they do not linger long but go about their business. This pleases the Commander, for he does not wish to be intruded upon by the peasantry. He seeks only the white-clothed individuals for interrogation.

He regards his soldiers. They are edgy and crave action. They want to draw blood and revel in the victory over this primitive world. Still, they remain disciplined. Lack of discipline will net them a punishment too awful to contemplate. This is the way of the Swarm.

For untold generations, the Swarm had scoured their galaxy, seeking inhabited worlds to ravish. They had gone from one planet to another for so long that the present generation has no idea from whence they originated. Records exist if they are curious; but the lower echelons are not curious, and the upper echelons do not encourage curiosity. Soldiers have but one purpose: to fight and to conquer.

Having thoroughly scoured their own galaxy, the Swarm had then migrated to the nearest one (this one) and found hundreds more worlds to ravish. Here, they followed established procedure: reconnaissance, intelligence-gathering, battle preparations, and attack. What little resistance that was offered had been overcome easily, and the Swarm had counted coup after coup. They look forward to another one.

Except –

This world possesses a force the Swarm has never before encountered – or, if they have, it had been too weak to be effective. This force poses an unknown variable; and, if they are to conquer, they must neutralize it. The key lies in the white-clothed individuals – or so they believe.

The Commander halts his soldiers. He has seen – or thinks he has seen – one such creature inside one of the buildings (one which smells of grease and oil). The nearest pair of soldiers is dispatched to investigate. They enter the building, only to re-appear a few moments later. They report that the individual the Commander had seen did indeed wear white clothing (smeared with grease and oil), but the clothing did not match that of the designated targets. The Commander frowns, then signals the soldiers to move out again.

The Swarm are now very close to the central city, and their alertness level rises proportionately. Their pace slows to that of a small child, and they peer in all directions in preparation for sudden attack. It is standard operating procedure – to assume the worst-case scenario and deal with it in an appropriate manner. This is the way of the Swarm.

As luck would have it, a white-clothed creature exits a building containing a number of ground vehicles. This person seems to be distracted – he is gazing into the sky and moving his lips – and he does not notice the Swarm. The Commander signals the advance pair to apprehend the Tellurian fool. The soldiers rush forward, seize the Tellurian by the arms, and drag him before their Commander. He scowls fiercely at his captive. The latter swallows a large lump in his throat; he knows about these strange creatures and fears the worst.

The Commander pulls out the sheet with the image on it and shows it to the captive.

"Tell me," he growls, "where I will find this person."

Like the previous captive, this Tellurian recognizes the image, and he too understands that he must not betray the Archdeacon's ally to anyone – or any*thing*. Unlike the previous captive, however, this Tellurian has the presence of mind to perpetrate a ruse whereby he can cause these evil beings to drop their guard long enough for him to escape their clutches, flee, and sound an alarm.

"Yes, yes," the captive responds with trepidation, half feigned, half unfeigned. "I know where he is. I can take you to him."

"Then do so, fool. But try no tricks."

The Commander barks an order, and his soldiers release their grip on the Tellurian. The Commander signals the captive to move out. The Tellurian turns and takes a few steps forward. When he thinks that he is far enough ahead of the evil creatures, he breaks out in a fast trot and shouts for help as he goes.

Infuriated, the Commander barks another order. The soldiers who had had the captive in their grasp give chase and, because their strong leg muscles in this world's lower gravity gives them extra speed, run the Tellurian down easily. They throw him to the ground, and one of them places a boot on his neck. The Commander approaches and towers over him.

"I have told you to do no tricks," he says menacingly. "Now, you will pay for your trickery."

He signals to the soldiers to deal with the Tellurian as they see fit. Both soldiers grin wickedly, kneel beside their captive, and begin pummeling him with solid, vicious blows of their fists. The captive screams loudly and begs them to stop, but they pay him no heed and continue to pound him until his face is a bloody mess. And still they beat him until he loses consciousness.

The Commander looks down on the fool in disgust and draws his ceremonial knife again. A quick slash opens the Tellurian's jugular vein, and his blood pours out in a steady stream. The Commander fears that the captive's screams may have alerted others to the Swarm's presence. He orders his unit to take shelter inside the building with the ground vehicles and stand by while he assesses the situation.

THE THIRD BATTLE

"GEORGE."

"Go ahead, Chris."

"I've got an update. The Swarm is near the corner of River and Benton. They've just murdered another Disciple, and now they're holing up in the auto dealership nearby."

"That must've been the screaming Sheena heard a moment ago. How many are there?"

"Thirteen. Looks like a full platoon, by our standards."

"Uh-huh. How about civilians on the premises?"

"One minute. I'll check." The minute passed agonizingly slowly. "I see four altogether – two men and one woman in the sales section and one man in the repair section. Um, just a second. Correction: the guy in the repair section is being herded to the front of the building. We may have a hostage situation here."

"Could be. Stand by."

When he and Sheena had returned to their office building, "Brothers" Connolly and Horton were waiting patiently for them. Horton was still wearing the cuts and bruises he had received from his previous encounter with the Swarm. With them were a dozen and a half white-suited, stocky males; meaner-looking individuals the detective was not likely to meet in this lifetime. And, from the facial scars and bent noses, they obviously had seen their unfair share of fist fights. They wore grim and resolute expressions, and their eyes hinted at a willingness to do great harm at the drop of a hat. Larkin had been glad they would be at his back instead of his front. When he laid out the situation for them, they had reacted with curled lips and squinting eyes.

"One of my…informants is across the street from the dealership, monitoring the demons. He'll keep us posted if anything changes." He regarded the burly group again. "Brothers, I know you're ready to do battle with these creatures. But there are innocents in that building as well, so we proceed with caution."

Nods and murmurs of acquiescence were pleasing responses. The detective turned to his partner.

"Sheena, you and Brother Connolly go get those sentries I posted down the street and send them over to the dealership. Then stand by."

"Don't you want me with you?" she whined.

"No. I don't want you to have any part of what we're going to do."

"Be careful then."

"Of course. Gentlemen, let's move out."

* * *

From the diary of Christopher Wredling:

I now know what it's like to be a fly on the wall. That was what I was after the Swarm entered the auto dealership. More precisely, I was 'perched' above the sales-office door where I had a clear view of the entire showroom.

The first thing the aliens did was to round up the employees — two salesmen, the secretary-bookkeeper, and a mechanic — and herd them into the sales office. If the appearance of the Swarm wasn't enough to frighten those four out of their wits, then the display of knives certainly was. The secretary-bookkeeper was crying her eyes out. The mechanic was waving his arms in anger and scowling like a bulldog in a show of false bravado until a knife pointed at his face shut him up. What the salesmen were thinking was anybody's guess; they were trying to remain calm and re-assure the others.

The Swarm's mood was such that they'd sooner slaughter the humans than look at them.

The leader was particularly menacing. He directed his people like a traffic cop, and they moved quickly to obey. Two of them pushed the employees into the sales office – none too gently, I might add – then stood guard at the door. Two others took up positions leading to the maintenance area, and the rest stationed themselves around the showroom. Once the soldiers were in position, the leader peered out the window, looking for God-knows-what. Signs of awareness of the Swarm's presence? An attack force? He didn't know it then – but he soon would – that the presence of the Swarm was known and an attack force was on the way.

I reported the situation to George as I saw it, and I alerted him to the possibility that the employees might be used as hostages and/or killed if the aliens felt threatened. George agreed but launched the attack anyway. I assumed he had a plan to deal with the situation. George always has a plan!

Even though he had told me to stand by, I felt I should be doing more than acting as a spectator. I thought of distracting the Swarm's attention so that they would not notice George's bunch until it was too late. And I knew just the trick to pull it off – the same trick I'd pulled twice on Mr. Jones' henchmen.

I re-created my 'angel' character, white robe and all, and added a new feature – a flaming sword. I would be an avenging *'angel'!*

I appeared in the middle of the showroom, shining brightly and waving the sword menacingly. I didn't speak because I had no connection to an audio outlet and because I was sure they wouldn't understand a word I said. I had to rely on gestures alone. As it happened, gestures were sufficient to produce the desired effect.

My sudden appearance caused the maximum confusion and fright in the soldiers. I first focused my attention on the pair guarding the office; if I could scare them off, perhaps I could allow the humans to escape – assuming, of course, they would not be as frightened by me as by the Swarm. The expressions of fear on the guards' faces were priceless; both were so overwrought that they dropped their weapons and cringed against the wall.

I next turned to the rest of the aliens. They too were alarmed by my appearance and looking for a means to get as far away from me as possible.

I spotted George and his bunch out of the corner of my 'eye' across the street. I had to change tactics now and maneuver all of the Swarm so that their backs were to the street. That would give our side the advantage of surprise. I started to circle around the showroom, menacing first one soldier, then another. The ploy worked; like frightened children, they all gathered around their leader with their backs to the street.

Ah, their leader. He was made of sterner stuff, it seems, and perhaps that was why he was the leader. My appearance had taken him by surprise as well, but he had quickly recovered and did not succumb to abject fear. He followed my every movement with narrow, calculating eyes, and I could well imagine that he was analyzing the amount of threat I posed. Like any good leader, he gave orders to his soldiers and emphasized them with threatening gestures. That seemed to calm his people down, although some of them still fidgeted.

What the leader did next frightened me. *He reached inside his tunic and pulled out an all-too-familiar black cube, the same sort of black cube the late Mr. Jones had used on me. Were those things standard issue for command cadre? Well, I could ponder the question later. I had to get out of there before I was zapped again. Once was enough!*

In the instant before I bilocated, I looked out the window and saw George and his bunch nearing the door. I disappeared just as they…

* * *

…crashed through the door with bats, clubs, lead pipes, and steel rods at the ready.

Per Larkin's instructions, each of the Disciples selected a target and engaged it with ferocity. In a matter of seconds, the Swarm were dancing about the showroom in an effort to avoid being bludgeoned. The Leader shouted orders, but his soldiers were too busy shielding themselves to pay him any heed; he stood close to the window, cube in hand, and muttered impotently to himself.

The Disciples scored the first coup when a swing of a bat caught one of the soldiers on his knee. The latter groaned in pain, lost his balance, and fell to the floor. His opponent was on him in an instant and delivered a crushing blow to the skull. The victor moved away to look for another target.

The Swarm evened the score when a soldier was able to put a couple of feet of space between him and his attacker whereupon he fired his weapon. A burst of energy caught the Disciple square in the chest; he screamed in agony as the discharge burned away clothing, flesh, bones, and internal organs.

Meanwhile, Larkin inched around the scene of battle in an attempt to be as inconspicuous as possible. His goal was the sales office and the rescue of the dealership's employees. He was a third of the way across the showroom floor when a body bumped into him. He turned and stared into the face of a Swarm member. The soldier snarled and pointed his weapon at the detective's face. Larkin swallowed compulsively, fearing the worst. A brief, regretful thought about Sheena flickered through his mind.

The soldier never fired his weapon. He was torn between scoring a victory and disobeying his Leader's order to take this Tellurian alive. His indecision cost him. "Brother" Horton came up behind him and swung a lead pipe viciously across the back of his skull; the alien fell like a ton of bricks, blood and brains leaking out of the wound. The detective nodded his thanks to his savior, and Horton returned the gesture by way of acknowledgement.

"George," the tinny voice sounded on his cell phone.

"What is it, Chris? I'm a little busy right now."

"I'm sure you are. You should know, however, that the leader of the aliens has one of those cubes Mr. Jones had. He's looking for an opportunity to use it."

"I'm on it. Thanks, Chris." He turned to Horton and directed his attention toward the Leader. "That's the chief demon in this bunch. If we can strike him down, perhaps the others will lose heart and flee."

"I'll get him for you, Brother Larkin," the football coach said throatily and rushed off to confront the "chief demon," threading his way through the melee that the showroom had become.

The detective began inching his way again toward the office, all the while remaining alert to any Swarm member who might be near. He grimaced as he saw another Disciple fall victim to an energy weapon. He also saw the Leader watching him, a look of recognition crossing his face. The alien began inching *his* way across the showroom toward the chief Tellurian, avoiding contact with any of the combatants as he did so. Larkin picked up his pace.

His movements served one useful purpose: distracting the Leader long enough for Horton to catch up with him. A swing of the lead pipe caught the alien on his upper arm and nearly shattered the bone. The Leader yelped in pain and dropped his cube; he attempted to retrieve it but a second swing smashed into his rib cage, breaking two ribs. Horton was poised for a third blow but never delivered it; he was shot by a soldier who had just finished off another Disciple.

The Leader headed toward the main entrance, shouting orders as he went. Those of his command who were able followed him out of the building; those who were not able continued to fight until they were brought down. All who fled ran headlong down the street in the direction of their base. Some of the Disciples started to give chase, but Larkin called them back.

"Never mind those creatures," he admonished. "We know where their hiding place is. We can deal with them later. Right now, we have to re-group and tend to the wounded. Whoever's got a cell phone, call 9-1-1."

He scanned the area and shook his head sadly. The showroom resembled an abattoir more than a place of business. Seven of the Swarm lie crumpled up in pools of their blood as a result of cracked skulls. A low moan from one of the aliens indicated that not all of the Enemy were dead. A Disciple wielding a club "remedied" that oversight with a quick *coup de grace*. The detective then checked out the remainder of the Swarm bodies and determined that they were quite dead.

The Disciples had taken a number of casualties themselves, all by energy discharges from Swarm weapons. Six were clearly dead, and three others – including Horton – were badly burned. Larkin took little satisfaction that the surprise attack had tilted the odds in his favor and produced a greater number of enemy casualties. It still was a disturbing sight, even if it had been necessary. And, he knew, there would be more battles ahead. How many more bodies would he have to look at before this war was over – assuming, of course, that he himself survived it? And survival was not guaranteed, given the nature of the Swarm.

One of his "troops" approached him, carrying an armful of energy weapons and knives he had collected from the alien corpses.

"Ah, battle trophies," he said grimly. "We can use them against the Enemy. As soon as you're trained in the proper use of them, you'll form an elite squadron of warriors."

"But, Brother Larkin," the other murmured, "seven of these against what else those hell-spawn might have?"

"I didn't say it would be easy. But, for every casualty you inflict upon the Enemy, you'll add to your arsenal. Eventually, the squadron will become a company, then a battalion. Have faith, brother."

"Um, speakin' of faith, did I see an…*angel* just before we entered the building?"

"You did indeed, friend. I've seen it twice before. But this was the first time it took an active role in our war with the demons of Hell."

"The Lord truly works wonders. He gave us the victory this day."

Other Disciples who happened to be nearby "amened" that observation. Larkin merely nodded.

With the sound of sirens in the background, he walked away and headed for the last spot the Swarm Leader had occupied when his own person had been assaulted. He spied what he had hoped to find: the black cube, lying forgotten on the floor. Carefully, he picked it up and gave it a cursory examination. It looked harmless enough, but he knew that looks were deceiving. This little gadget could – and did – cause considerable harm to anyone within its range. He'd give it to Monk and let the electronics whiz figure out its operation. In the right hands, the cube would be worth more than ten times the number of hand weapons just confiscated; it might even be worth more than what the Coalition was unwilling to part with.

The day's battle had a positive side after all!

* * *

The intercom buzzed in both Larkin's office and the "snoop room."
The detective was in the latter, catching up on his e-mail.

"Yes, Madge?"

"George, Mr. Smith is here to see you."

"Hmmm. Give me a minute. I'm right in the middle of something."

He frowned at the announcement. If his alien ally was here in person, it meant that something urgent was on his mind; and the only thing that could be urgent from his point of view was Larkin's methods of dealing with the Swarm. If he was here to criticize, he was wasting his and Larkin's time. The alien hadn't provided any guidelines, nor had the Coalition; therefore, the detective was free to handle the Swarm as best he could. And under the "Larkin Grand Plan," the handling was going as well as could be expected.

In any event, he really was "in the middle of something." That something was the latest ramblings of the Quintessential Quark, and it presaged bad news. After whining about persecution at the hands of the local FBI office, "men in black" delusions, and his medical problems, the informant got to the meat of the matter. Two hours ago, the Quark claimed, he observed the arrival of two black SUV's at the Swarm base. Commandant Yowk came out to meet them, followed by a dozen of his troops. The Commandant spoke to them briefly in a highly charged voice whereupon the troops, in full combat gear, climbed into the SUV's and headed east for parts unknown. No further activity was seen. The Quark signed off in his usual fashion.

Larkin found this to be very disturbing news. He could deduce that the local Swarm Leader had reported his losses at the auto dealership and that the Commandant was sending re-enforcements to replace the casualties. But these soldiers were in "full combat gear," according to the Quark. What did he mean by that? If he was going by American standards, that could mean body armor, automatic weapons, explosives, and detection devices. The idea of a platoon of heavily-armed and dedicated soldiers descending upon his city, willing to wreak havoc on an unsuspecting populace in a non-discriminatory fashion sent a chill up and down his spine. In a worst-case scenario, the PDF would have its hands full, if it came to having to use their powers, and there was a high likelihood that he would have to use them and risk casualties to DEDEP.

If the Swarm re-enforcements drove all day – he checked his computer's clock – the SUV's might be arriving in the City in the evening. How much rest would they require before they were ready to carry out the Commandant's orders (whatever they were)? Would they rest at all? It didn't matter, however; he had to alert the PDF to this newest development and to devise an actual battle plan (as opposed to a training exercise) to meet the expected threat.

But first, he had to bring Mr. Smith up to speed.

He logged off and exited the "snoop room." Instantly, he encountered Sheena, who was returning from lunch. She handed him a brown paper bag.

"Since you decided to work through the lunch hour, I decided to bring you something to eat. I hope it meets with your approval."

He peeked inside the bag and discovered a BLT sandwich, a dill pickle, and a mini-bag of potato chips. He grunted in surprise and smiled.

"Not exactly what I would have ordered. But, since you were so thoughtful, I'll eat it with gusto. Thank you."

"You're welcome. One of these days, I'll fix you something you would have ordered." She glanced toward the outer office. "I passed by Mr. Smith. What does he want?"

"I don't know yet. I'll soon find out, though. Do you want to sit in?"

"I have some files that need updating. Fill me in later?"

"Right."

Larkin entered his own office, made himself comfortable, and activated the intercom.

"Madge, you can send in Mr. Smith now."

"Will do, George."

Half a minute later, the pasty-faced alien shuffled in, made his way slowly to a chair, and plopped into it. Beads of oily perspiration dotted his face. He pulled out his handkerchief and mopped his face thoroughly. Then he regarded the detective thoughtfully for a moment.

"Hhhello...Mr....Largin," he began. "Thhhang...you...for...
seeing... me...unannounced."

"Hello, Mr. Smith. You were fortunate to catch me in. I was about
to leave to meet someone, but it's not urgent. What can I do for you
today?"

"Thhhe...Goalition...wishes...to...gonsult...withhh...you...again.
If ...you...will...gome...to...my...base...in...thhhree...hours...I...
will...mague ...thhhe...gonnegtion."

"I'll certainly be there. By the way, is there some other method
we can use to communicate without your having to leave your base? I
realize it's difficult for you to move around."

"Thhhere...is.   Now...thhhat...you...are...a...member...of...
thhhe... Goalition...I...will...reguest...a...portable...gommunigator...
you...gan... garry...on...your...person."

"Wonderful! Now, I have some news for you, but I don't think
you'll like it."

"I...am...used...to...bad...news...Mr....Largin. Tell me."

The detective related the events of the morning, omitting the part
played by the "angel." As expected, Mr. Smith's reaction was one of
distress and frustration, and he squirmed fitfully in his chair. When
Larkin had finished, the silence in the office was deafening.

"Thhhis...is...most...disturbing," the alien murmured presently.
"I ...grieve...of...gourse...for...thhhe...loss...of...your...fellow...
Tellurians ...but...not...for...thhhe...loss...of...thhhe...soldshers...
of...thhhe...Swarm.   Yet...you...must...understand...thhhat...
thhhis...incident...is...anothhher   ...gonseguence...of...your...
orishinal...agtion...thhhe...gilling...of...'Mr....Shones.' Thhhe...
Swarm... will... advance...thhheir...timetable...and... launch...
an...attag...before...thhhe...Goalition...hhhas...gompleted...
its ...preparations."

"Perhaps. But, *you* must understand, Mr. Smith, that we have to
defend ourselves when attacked. We appreciate what the Coalition is
doing on our behalf, but they are far away and can't help us immediately."

"Very...true.   Perhhhaps...thhhese...recent...events...were...
inevitable ...given...thhhe...nashure...of...thhhe...Swarm. Still...it...
is...a...regrettable ...sishuation."

"On that, I can agree. If there is nothing further, I'll see you in
three hours."

After the alien had departed, Larkin heaved a large sigh of relief.
Being blunt was no way to treat a client. One had to couch one's
thoughts in carefully worded euphemisms; otherwise, the client would
become resentful and perhaps cancel the contract. That would not help
one's reputation one bit. But, Mr. Smith was no ordinary client, was
he? Where he came from, bluntness might be considered a virtue; and
the Coalition he represented was entitled to the cold facts so that they
could fine-tune their strategy in the upcoming battle. He didn't like
recent developments any more than Mr. Smith did, but developments
tended to have a life of their own and had to be dealt with accordingly.

A knock at the door interrupted his train of thought. Sheena walked
in, took her usual chair, and waited for him to speak. He quietly told
her what had transpired between him and his client. She frowned all
the while.

"You really can't blame him for saying what he did, George. He's
working off a timetable, not of his own making, and he has people to
report to."

"I don't blame him at all, Sheena. In his situation, I'd probably
react the same way. But we have a timetable too, so to speak, and we
have no one whose shoulders we can cry on." He sighed again. "I stand
corrected. I can cry on the Archdeacon's shoulders whether I want to
or not. And that's what I must do now. I'll see you when I get back."

* * *

When Larkin entered Disciples HQ, he was surprised to see "Sister"
Smithers sitting at the receptionist's desk again rather than another new
face. Perhaps "auditioning" for the post was over, and she had been the
successful "candidate." Not that he cared one way or the other; one
Disciple was as gullible as another when it came to swallowing religious

propaganda, hook, line, and sinker. At least, the girl would not be out on the street proselytizing 24/7. If only the rest of them found something else to occupy their time...

Smithers greeted him cheerfully and informed him how excited her boyfriend, "Brother" Connolly, was to be working with him for the common good. For his part, the detective allowed that Connolly had proven himself to be a dedicated worker and an invaluable assistant, a comment which lit up her entire face. She then buzzed the *sanctum sanctorum* and learned that the Archdeacon was conferring with the Mayor but would be available in ten or fifteen minutes. Larkin said he was in no hurry and took a seat.

While he waited, he delved into the paper bag Sheena had given him, fished out the BLT, and munched away. It was a simple lunch, to be sure, but satisfying. He thought idly that his degree of satisfaction might be the result of the lunch's "delivery service." Sheena had never brought back lunch for him before, although she had hinted time and again about sharing dinner at a local restaurant. Was she trying a new tack in her campaign of seduction? Or was this her way of declaring a truce after their previous conversation? Whatever the reason was, it filled him with deeper longing, and that bothered him more than he cared to admit. Soon, he would have to resolve this dilemma once and for all.

The timing was impeccable. He had just finished off the BLT and was about to tackle the pickle when Smithers announced that the Archdeacon would see him now. He devoured the pickle on his way up the stairs (the potato chips would have to wait until later), rapped gently on the door, and was given leave to enter.

The old man was alone at this time, a rare occasion. Neither his "shadow" (Kincaid) nor his "secretary" (Hedberg) were to be seen. He was relieved on both counts. Kincaid gave him the creeps, and Hedberg made him uncomfortable; having to deal with either one was a formidable task, and anytime he didn't have to was a welcome situation. He took his customary seat on the right-hand sofa. Fogarty waited for him to start the conversation.

"I'm sure you're aware of the incident of this morning, Your Worship. Things happened so fast that I had to take some time to sort them out before I made my report."

"Understandable, Brother Larkin. I heard from Brother Connolly and a couple of others who participated in the conflict, and they were rather incoherent at times. The engagement with the Enemy – and that business with the angel – must have been traumatic."

"That it was, sir. It was a minor miracle that any of us survived. I confess that I looked Death in the face and saw no hope for escape."

"With the Lord, there is always hope, Brother Larkin." He paused for a second or two, then: "Tell me about the angel."

The detective smiled to himself. Chris' little play-acting had painted the picture he wanted to be painted. Keeping the Disciples off-balance was all part of The Plan.

"Ah, yes, the angel. To be sure, I only saw a glimpse of it before we tackled the Enemy head-on, but I could swear that it was the same being who inspired the late Brother Rosansky and his group to become martyrs to The Cause. Of course, I'm no expert in these matters."

"It is clear to me," Fogarty allowed, "that we are indeed in the End Times and that the Final Battle will soon be upon us. The Lord has given us His sign that He is with us, and it is up to us to fulfill our part in His Purpose."

"Yes, sir. I heartily agree, and I stand ready and willing to take the battle to the Enemy."

"Very commendable, Brother Larkin." Another pause. "Now, I want to discuss a more personal matter with you."

"And that is?"

"Your relationship to Sister Whitley."

Well, that's none of your damned business, you old lecher!

"Our relationship is strictly professional. It's…less complicated that way. Why do you ask?"

"If you haven't already guessed by now, Sister Hedberg has taken a fancy to you. I've noticed the way she looks at you and the body postures she assumes when she's near you. Only a blind person could fail to miss these signals."

One blind person hasn't missed them, and she's livid *over them.*

"Is that a problem, sir? Should I not encourage her?"

"No, not in the least. Sister Hedberg is free to make relationships as she sees fit. Oh, I'm aware of all the rumors concerning her and me, and I assure you that there is no truth to them. If you wish to have a relationship with her, you have my blessing."

That's very magnanimous of you, you old hypocrite. Have you gotten all you can out of her and are ready to pass her on to someone else?

"I appreciate your feelings on this matter, Your Worship. I wasn't sure how to react to Sister Hedberg's interest in me."

"I think you two would be well-suited together."

"There is one problem that I can see – my, um, disabilities."

"Yes, I know about the accident that took your arms and legs, Brother Larkin. But the Lord spared your life for a purpose, and that purpose is manifesting itself in the situation at hand. You've proven to be a valuable asset, and Sister Hedberg recognizes that as much as I do."

So, she's not trying to seduce me in order to make a Disciple out of me?

"Thank you for your confidence, sir. Now I know how to proceed."

And that's to keep my distance from that female shark!

The detective was never so glad to leave the Disciple HQ than he was that day. Fogarty's attempt to foist his "secretary" on him was a blatant move to meld him to the Disciple organization closer than he cared to be. The old man may or may not have been truthful concerning his own relationship with Hedberg, but that made no difference. The fact of the matter was that he was pimping for an ulterior motive which made him all the more odious. If Larkin hadn't been a rational person, he might have been tempted to strangle the Archdeacon on the spot.

* * *

When he entered the abandoned supermarket, Larkin experienced a sensation of foreboding. He couldn't quite put his finger on the cause, but he was certain that something unpleasant was about to happen here and that something would change the nature of the war against the Swarm and consequently the unfolding of his Grand Plan. He had listened to Emil Razumov explain psycho-oraculism – the Russian's term for precognition – from the viewpoint of radiopsychology, but he had never believed he had such psychic ability (or any psychic ability at all). He had an eidetic memory, but that wasn't the same thing. As far as he knew, only the blustery Henry Rawlins had the ability to see future events, and even then the events were couched in symbolism which required a great deal of interpretation for complete understanding.

On the other hand, Emil had always insisted that everyone had *psi*-talent of one sort or another. The trick was in unlocking it so that it could be used. For a relative few, such as the residents of DEDEP, psychic ability had manifested itself easily; for the rest of humankind, *psi* had to be coaxed out by an exact set of circumstances, both physical and psychological. In either case, the manifestation had to be dealt with in a rational fashion as the alternative was insanity.

So, what were the circumstances surrounding his feeling of foreboding? He understood that the supermarket and the Swarm were involved. What else? There had to be a linking factor between the two, if only he could recognize it. He supposed he could ask the Director of Research at DEDEP the next time he saw him. But what if the explanation was too late in coming to do anything about the cause of the foreboding? He had to solve the puzzle ASAP, or the war might be lost.

Meanwhile, the here and now had priority. And the "here and now" was the summons by the Coalition. What did they want with him that they needed to initiate contact with their "primitive" ally? Did they have an update on their preparations, a change of strategy perhaps? Had they changed their minds about providing him with offensive weapons, and were they waiting for him to take possession? Larkin felt goosebumps forming all over his body in anticipation.

Again, Mr. Smith was nowhere to be seen, and the detective assumed he was inside the silver-gray cube which held the cold-fusion generator. This was as good a time to continue his examination of the control console and to puzzle out its operation. From his past observations, he had memorized a few sequences which produced specific actions. For example, if he were to press the touch-sensitive point in the upper left-hand corner of the upper-left section, followed by two adjacent points in the middle of the second row, he could activate the "Tinker Toy" tower, enabling him to contact the Coalition's base. Further, if he were to press the point in the upper *right*-hand corner followed by the point in the extreme left of the second row, the point in the extreme right of the same row, and the point in the extreme right of the third row, he could switch on the lesser towers Mr. Smith used to communicate with his fellow agents on Earth. There were other, partial sequences which required more observation before he could commit them to his memory.

Of course, he wasn't about to experiment with any sequence then and there. One, that would be rude of him. Two, that would be unwise of him. He had to gain the Coalition's complete trust before he could make himself at home and play with the gadgets here – if ever that moment came to pass.

Presently, Mr. Smith emerged from the silver-gray cube and shuffled over to the control panel.

"Hhhello…again…Mr.…Largin. Hhhave…you…been…waiting… long?"

"Only a minute or so."

"Egcellent.   I…will…gontagt…thhhe…Goalition…and… Frommar …will…advise…you…of…new…developments."

"Do you know what they are?"

"No.   Frommar…prefers…to…hhhandle…thhhese…matters… hhhimself."

Was there an element of resentment in that remark? Larkin wondered. *It can't be too pleasant to be kept out of the loop where policy is concerned. But then I'm thinking like a human, aren't I? Maybe these alien 'friends' take a laid-back attitude toward everything.*

Mr. Smith tapped the console in the same places that the detective knew would open the channel to the base in the Oort Cloud. On the large monitor overhead, a kaleidoscopic swirl of colors coalesced into a humanoid figure, the same yellow-skinned Oriental-resembling alien he had seen before and was frightened by his human appearance. The new alien puckered his lips upon seeing the human again, and the detective could well imagine that it was exhibiting apprehension/ wariness/suspicion. Mr. Smith activated his translating program and spoke to his colleague briefly. The response was just as brief, and the yellow man moved off-screen.

He was immediately replaced by the neckless Co-ordinator of the Coalition whose mouth twisted in an alien attempt at a human smile. For some reason, Frommar's eyes kept darting from left to right as if he were keeping track of someone/something else's whereabouts. Larkin shrugged. Even extraterrestrials had their little idiosyncrasies!

"Lak'n," Frommar rumbled. "We pleased to sight you one more."

"And I am also pleased, Frommar. What news do you have for me?"

"We announcing that final arrangements made-have been in preparing for engagement of Swarm. All our forces awaiting in your star-space, in the asteroid field, fully armed and fully trained."

The image of the Co-ordinator disappeared, and Larkin viewed a large array of asteroids in varying size and shape. Following this panorama came a series of shots of individual asteroids where weaponry had been installed. He observed short white cylinders projecting from the surfaces of rocks only a kilometer or two in diameter; Frommar's voice-over described them as "pulse cannons" capable of firing intense laser beams which could slice through the hulls of spaceships. Other, smaller rocks bore black metallic hemispheres which, when launched, could attach themselves magnetically to the hulls of ships and be detonated at will. He also spied small propulsion units bolted to small rocks which would send the rocks smashing against ships and rupture their hulls. And finally, the battle fleet of the Coalition – a thousand fully armed ships, Frommar claimed – was interspersed throughout the asteroid field to act as the last line of defense against whatever Swarm vessels survived the gauntlet.

The detective had to shake his head in amazement as the preparations for war unfolded piece by piece. He hadn't seen such an array of war machines since he viewed the final film of the "Star Wars" trilogy, and he couldn't be blamed for believing that he was watching yet another display of computer-generated imagery. He wondered idly if, when the actual battle took place, he could compare it to the scenes in that film. Would the Coalition – *could* the Coalition – permit him to observe the battle as it played out? He hoped so, if only to satisfy his morbid curiosity. The images of weaponry-disguised-as-asteroids faded, and Frommar came on-screen again. The Co-ordinator's mouth was twisted again in the mockery of a smile.

"You observing, Lak'n, how well prepared we. It taken-has many long [*untranslatable*] to install these weapons, but we satisfied that they prove-will to be adequate."

"That is good news indeed, Frommar. Victory seems close at hand."

"It remaining to actualize, but we being confident."

"What do you want me to do?"

"You remaining alert. You notifying us of any new developments of Swarm vanguard on Telluria. Mabel-choo-choo informing us that you wishing to communicate with him directly. That acceptable. We sent-have a device to accomplish such."

"Thank you. But, still no weapons?"

"Not now. It depending on what happen-will in asteroid field. Farewell, Lak'n, and good fortune."

"Good fortune to you, Frommar."

The image of the Co-ordinator was lost in the swirl of color, and the monitor went black. The detective turned to Mr. Smith and regarded him expectantly. In response, the alien pulled a silver disc – ten centimeters in diameter and notched at one point along the rim -- out of his coat pocket and handed it over. From another pocket, he produced yet another sheet of paper and passed that over.

"Thhhis...device...will...allow...you...to...speag...to...me...and... I...to...you. Follow...thhhe...instructions...I...hhhave...given...you."

"Can I speak directly to the Coalition in case something happens to you?"

"Not...at...thhhis...time. I...am...sorry...Mr....Largin...but... for... segurity...reasons...we...gannot...permit...thhhat. At...some... fushure ...date...you...may...be...given...thhhe...appropriate... engoding... program."

"I see. Well, it's better than nothing, I suppose. Thank you, Mr. Smith, and good-bye."

"Good-bye...Mr....Largin."

* * *

The detective was walking across the weed-strewn parking lot, the images of the Coalition's offensive array still playing in his mind, when the familiar buzz of an incoming telepathic message filled his head. He instantly cleared his mind of all extraneous thoughts.

*Hello, George.

*Hello, Paddy. What have you got for me?

*Some bad news, I'm afraid, old darling. I've just received a message from Lacey. It seems the Swarm are taking to hijacking automobiles. Two of the blighters snatched one and drove it downtown. They began cruising the streets until they spotted you in your station wagon and started following it.

*I'm being followed? *Damn!*

*How did they latch onto you in the first place?

*Their leader recognized me during that little tussle we had this morning. I can well believe he assigned two of his men to search for me. *Damn!* but I've been careless – *again!*

*How so?

*I'm at Mr. Smith's base right now, and I've led the Swarm right to it. They'll wonder why I was here and send a team to investigate. And that'll be the end of Mr. Smith.

*What will you do?

*First, I'll lose my 'tail.' Then I'll warn Mr. Smith. After that, I'll have to form a counter-move. In the meantime, you contact Billy Perkins – it's time he chipped in – and have him monitor Mr. Smith's base for every five minutes and report back anything he sees out of the ordinary.

*Will do, old darling.

*By the way, *I've* got some bad news too. The Quintessential Quark informed me that the Swarm at Omaha has sent re-enforcements. They should be here tonight.

Bloody hell!

*You got that right, chum. Now, describe that stolen auto for me.

Larkin finished his walk to the station wagon, keeping an eye out for a dark green sedan with wire-rim hubcaps and a smashed-in left-front fender. He spotted it easily enough; it was parked on the opposite side of the street where he was parked and twenty meters further west. He smiled wickedly. As "tails" went, those two jokers were rank amateurs. He'd lose them in a New York minute!

He pulled away from the curb and made a left turn onto Hill Avenue. A glance in the rear-view mirror told him that his "tail" was keeping up with him. He drove slowly so as not to alert the Swarm members that he was aware of them; he'd sucker them into the trap he was preparing and spring it before they had a chance to avoid it. At Hill and Main Street, he speeded up, ran a red light, and made another left turn. In the rear-view mirror, he saw no sign of the sedan; it had had to halt for east-west traffic on Main Street. But he was not through losing them yet. At Main and Root Streets, he pulled into the parking lot of a Spanish-language supermarket, found an empty parking space in a group of vehicles, and entered it. There he'd remain until he was certain that his "tail" had been completely lost.

He retrieved the disc and the instruction sheet Mr. Smith had given him and studied both intensely. With the notch at the "north" position, he located the spot which, when pressed, would activate or de-activate the communicator. Other spots would increase or decrease the volume, kick in the translating program, and record the conversation for later review. Confident that he knew how the gadget worked, he activated it. The spot he had just pressed lit up and began pulsing in a red glow. Three seconds later, the pulsing stopped, and the glow remained steady.

"Hhhello...Mr....Largin," the alien's voice issued from a hidden speaker. "Are...you...testing...thhe...gommunigator?"

"Hello, Mr. Smith. How did you know who was calling?"

"Eash...of...thhe...gommunigators...produces...a...unigue... sound...whhhen...agtivated. I...gonsulted...my...list...of...godes... to...learn... whhho...was...galling. You...will...be...able...to...do... thhhe...same."

"Ingenious. We have a different method, but it performs the same function. As to why I'm calling, I have a warning for you."

"Whhhat…is…it?"

"I regret to inform you that I've been followed by members of the Swarm. Their local leader instigated an intense search for me since this morning's battle. Your base may have been compromised."

"Thhhis…is…most…distressing…indeed.   I…gannot…be… taguen… alive…nor…gan…my…eguipment…fall…into…thhhe… wrong…hands."

The hair on Larkin's neck bristled with sudden realization of the implications of that statement.

"What do you intend to do, Mr. Smith?" he said slowly and deliberately.

"First…I…must…alert…my…superiors…to…the…dansher. Then…I…will…program…my…gold-fushon…shenerator…to… overload."

The alien spoke in such a matter-of-fact manner that a chill ran up and down the detective's spine. The thought of overloading that generator made him physically ill. The resulting explosion – or was it *implosion?* – would reduce most of the City to a smoking crater.

"I'm afraid I can't allow you to do that, Mr. Smith."

"Whhhat…alternative…do…I…hhhave…Mr….Largin? My… orders… are…guite…specific."

"I have a possible solution. Since this situation is partly my fault, I am willing to offer the use of some…property I own five miles from the City, if you're able to re-locate. The property has a large building that can accommodate most of your equipment, but those tall towers may have to be placed outside. There is also a house where you can live."

"You…are…most…shenerous…Mr….Largin. I…will…hhhave… to… gonsult…with…my…superiors…for…permission…to…re-logate."

"How long would it take to re-locate?"

"At…least…two…hours…perhhhaps…thhhree…hours…to… glose …down…thhhe…array. I…will…reguire…go-ordinates…for… thhhe… transfer. Return…hhhere…and…I…will…provide…you… withhh… logator…beagons."

"All right. Then I'll go to my property and make my own preparations for the transfer. I just hope we do have three hours to work with."

THE SWARM ⊕UT-MANEUVERED

THE PA SYSTEM came alive with the familiar squawk of audio feed-back.

"Jean Fulton," Dr. Razumov's voice sounded throughout DEDEP, "please come to Lab #2 for your next testing session. *Spaceebo.*"

DEDEP's newest "acquisition," in the midst of assisting Freddie with re-wiring the elevator in an effort to get it working again and sparing the residents the tedium of walking up and down the emergency stairs, wrinkled her nose in disgust and turned toward her "mentor."

"Again?" she whined. "Doesn't Boris get tired of testing?"

The handyman straightened up to his full height and gave her a hard stare. He moved the stub of his cigar from one side of his mouth to the other and pointed a stubby finger at her.

"That's *Dr. Razumov* to you, my girl, and don't you ferget it!"

"Well, *hell*, Freddie, *you* don't call 'im that."

"Never mind what *I* call 'im. I paid my dues. Yer still wet behind the ears, far as I'm concerned, so you hafta call 'im by his proper title."

"Yes, sir!" the young woman mocked and threw up a sloppy salute. "Anything you say, *sir*!"

Freddie moved the cigar back to its original position.

"Don't get cheeky with me, Jeanie, or I'll turn you over my knee and spank you."

Jean's eyes went wide with surprise at the dwarf's brazen and ludicrous remark. She hadn't known him all that long, but he hadn't been harsh to her until now. And, when his "threat" finally sunk in, the unbelievable scenario passed briefly across her mind's eye and served to wash away the fit of pique she had just raised. She assumed a demure body posture and facial expression, both of which were semi-feigned.

"Sorry, Chief. It won't happen again. But, really, is all this testing necessary? Doesn't Dr. Razumov know what I am already?"

"He might, and he might not. He's the sort who hasta be absolutely sure. 'Sides, nobody said you'd get a free ride here. We all pay a price for a safe haven from the Disciples, one way or the other. Especially them as got *psi*-talent. So, you just run along and do what the Doc tells you to do, and don't give 'im any shit."

"Can you handle this job by yourself?"

"Prob'ly not. I'll just wait 'til you come back, won't I? Now, *scat!*"

As Jean trudged her way to Lab #2, Freddie's words continued to ring in her ears. The little guy was deadly serious about "paying one's dues." Even her new friend, Joyce Jankowsky, had pointed this out in their few conversations together, and Joyce had given several examples. Lacey Perkins, ex-nurse in the "real" world, was the "chief medical officer" of DEDEP. Her husband, Bill Sr., had been a computer programmer in his former life and so, naturally, he was the facility's webmaster and chief troubleshooter. Christopher Wredling, who was well-read, was the unofficial "school teacher" (albeit by remote control). Even "Fat Henry" Rawlins had a function when he wasn't dream-casting (or complaining about one thing or another); he was the chef in the kitchen, responsible for the daily menu and the nutritional needs of the residents. Most of the adults had skills which weren't needed in their current circumstances, and they were relegated to more mundane tasks of housekeeping.

In a way, DEDEP's organization was modeled after Marx's famous prescription: "To each according to his needs; from each according to his ability." The chief need of all the residents was protection from the religious fanatics who ran the USA, from the President on down to the town mayor. The residents "paid" for this protection with their labor wherever and whenever it was called for. Given the choice of protection by DEDEP or fending for themselves "upstairs," the fifty-plus humans – whether they were gifted or not – had opted for the former. They might grouse now and then about having to live in a hole in the ground, but the alternative was infinitely worse, and they knew it in every fiber of their being.

Deep down, Jean Fulton knew Freddie was right. Life in St. Louis had become unbearable once people realized what she could do, even though she had no control over the ability to discharge tremendous amounts of electrical energy when under emotional stress. The people at the Psi Squad had gone as far as they could with limited resources to provide succor and recommended that she seek out the help of the renowned Dr. Emil Razumov. If he could not find a way to control her ability, then no one could, but she would be no worse off than she had been before.

She sighed. What *could* the great Dr. Razumov do? The electrical build-up manifested itself without warning. Emotional stress was a constant with human beings, caused by a legion of circumstances – fright, anger, sexual arousal, death of a loved one – since the species began. In time, stress could be relieved by counseling, both professional and personal, although some people never recovered. Get rid of the stress, and the "eel" in her would go away. Easier said than done. But control it? How? she would like to know.

The Doctor was setting up the EEG when Jean entered Lab #2. She had already undergone two sessions on that machine. What did he expect from another session? Huh, Freddie?

The Russian acknowledged her presence with a nod of the head and waved her to the chair next to the EEG. She slumped in it and awaited the ordeal. Wordlessly, he attached sensor pads to points on her skull he intended to examine and switched the machine on. The "needles" danced across the monitor. Jean strained to see what he was seeing – as she had done in the previous sessions – but she didn't notice any difference in the markings. Only when her emotional level had been elevated would there be any difference, but she hoped there never would be. She could dream, couldn't she?

"Now, *ryebyonka*," the old man said at last, "I want you to think, first, of the most pleasant experience you have ever had and, second, of the most frightening one."

Was he serious? she wondered. *Did he want me to* deliberately *have an emotional moment?*

And then Freddie's voice came ringing back into her head. "Pay yer dues, kiddo. The Doc is here to help you – if ya *want* to be helped." She sighed deeply.

"Well, that's easy enough, 'cause both happened at the same time. I kissed a guy I wanted to kiss for a long time and nearly fried 'im."

"Think deeply about that incident, Miss Fulton. Let it fill your mind.

Despite her forebodings, the memory of that day came unbidden, and she replayed it once again.

Eddie van Meter. Now, there was a hunk! Good looks. Great body. Easy smile. Inviting eyes. Friendly as hell.

For Jean, it was love at first sight. Eddie didn't pay much attention to her at first. He was a senior in high school, and she was only a freshman. He was captain of the football team, the basketball team, and the baseball team, and he could have his pick of girls. God knew a lot of them flocked around him, all hoping for the same thing from him.

He finally did take notice of her, but not because either of them had planned on it. She was hurrying to a class before the tardy bell rang. And wouldn't you know she dropped two of her books? She almost burst into tears at her clumsiness, but it was Eddie van Meter to the rescue! He came up from behind her, assessed the situation, stooped, and picked up the errant books. He said "Here you are, little lady" in a voice like syrup, and she immediately became tongue-tied. She rushed off without thanking him and later kicked herself (figuratively) for not doing so.

Imagine her surprise when, the next day, Eddie approached her in the cafeteria at lunchtime and asked if he could join her. Oh, God, yes! He started the conversation by asking if she had dropped any more books lately.

She blushed right down to her toes, and he apologized for embarrassing her. They exchanged personal data, and she spent the rest of the day walking on the clouds.

Thereafter, they met casually in the hallway and had brief conversations. Sometimes, they were going in the same direction, and the conversations were lengthier. On those occasions, she noticed that other girls glared at her — out of jealousy, no doubt — but she didn't care, because she was in seventh heaven. She hoped he would ask her for a date, but for some reason he just wanted to be friends.

And then, the unbelievable happened. He asked her if she would like go to the school dance that would take place after the upcoming football game with the crosstown rival. Yes, yes, yes! Oh, God, yes!

The Big Day couldn't come any too soon. She rushed to the stadium in order to get a front-row seat near the fifty-yard line — not an easy thing to do when the girlfriends of all the other players had the same idea — and she had to settle for a seat on the forty-yard line. The game went too slowly to suit her, and the action on the field became a blur. Her eyes were fixed on Eddie, and she followed his every move, even if he were just standing around waiting for his time to go back on the field. He scored two touchdowns after taking long passes, and she screamed and jumped up and down like everyone else — and maybe a little more.

Finally, the game was over, and she rushed to the gymnasium where the dance was to be held. She headed immediately and briskly to the entrance of the locker room (along with the other girlfriends) and waited for Her Man to come out. An age passed — how long did it take to shower up? — before the players emerged from the locker room and hooked up with their girlfriends. Eddie was in the middle of the pack, and it seemed like another age passed before he was able to separate himself from his buddies. He spotted her, flashed a big toothy smile, went to her side, took both of her hands in his, bent down, and kissed her firmly on the lips.

Oh, ecstasy! She couldn't believe this was happening to her. If she were dreaming, she didn't want to wake up. She had overheard some of the older girls talking about sex. They had described the tingling feeling in their loins when a guy turned them on. When Eddie kissed her, she too felt that tingling.

Then the horrible thing happened -- in spades.

Her lusting after Eddie van Meter had made her forget temporarily what she could do to people when she became emotional. And sexual arousal was a very strong emotion. The tingling in her loins gave way to the familiar tingling in her head which grew until it affected her entire body. When it reached a certain point, the electricity would discharge and radiate outward in all directions. If the charge struck an object, it crackled and caused the object to smolder as if it had been set on fire; and, if it touched a living person, that person was shocked from head to toe – the nearer the person was, the greater the shock.

She had to get away from Eddie before she hurt him severely. But Eddie was holding her close to him, enjoying the moment. She struggled to break free, and he looked at her questioningly. She confessed that, if he didn't let go of her, he risked serious injury. And all the while the sensation grew and grew.

She finally broke free of his grip and backed away from him. But it was too late. She discharged a large amount of electrical energy then and there. Although she had managed to put six feet between him and her, the charge hit him with a force which caused him to stagger backwards and fall to the floor, his clothes smoldering. She screamed, turned, and ran out of the gym as fast as she could.

The next day, her parents kept her home from school at the school's request pending an investigation. She learned that Eddie had suffered second-degree burns all over his body and was in intensive care in a local hospital. The police investigated, refused to believe her version of the incident, and turned the matter over to the department's psychiatrist. The school requested that she be pulled from the school; her parents immediately acquiesced and planned to put her in a private school. Eddie's parents, upon learning that the police had determined that the matter was a mental-health issue and would not be filing criminal charges, sued her parents for wrongful injury. When she learned that they were acquiescing in that as well, she ran away from home and wandered the streets of St. Louis where the Psi Squad found her.

The horrific memories were overwhelming, and Jean felt the build-up of electrical energy forming inside her. The thought of what it would do to Dr. Razumov filled her with panic, and the panic accelerated the build-up. She reached up to pull the sensor pads from her skull, but the Doctor with a surprising strength for a man his age gripped both of her arms and held them fast.

Up to this moment, he had been fixed upon the recording of Jean's brain-wave patterns. From the normal alpha-wave stage to the beta-wave stage, the "pens" showed no significant activity; once they passed beyond the beta stage and into the gamma stage, they went wild. He was both fascinated and concerned – fascinated because his suspicions about her "eel-ness" had just been confirmed, concerned because what might happen if he allowed the phenomenon to reach its inevitable conclusion would be disastrous. It was time to initiate his solution to Jean's problem, and he hoped it wasn't too late!

"*Nyet, ryebyonka.* You must not run away. You must fight for control."

"I can't control it," she protested in an agonized tone. "It's too strong."

"*Fzdor!* It is a product of your body. Therefore, you can control it."

"How?" she squeaked.

"Use your will power to make it go away. You have done it before." Now his voice took on a soothing tone. "Think of something pleasant. Concentrate on it. Let the pleasant thing fill your mind. Embrace it as you would a lover. Draw it nearer to you. Feel its warmth and softness. Think of flowers – how colorful they are, how lovely they smell, how beautiful they are."

Flowers? she mused. *Was he serious?*

Almost instantly, an image formed in her mind, an image of her mother tending her flower garden. Mom was always fussing over her flowers, and hardly a day passed that she could not be seen puttering in the garden, weeding, aerating the soil, watering the plants, applying fertilizer and insecticides. She regarded her flowers as her "special children" and always said that, if she didn't watch over them, they would become "spoiled brats."

Jean nearly laughed out loud at the thought of flowers as children. And she would have, but for the change she felt inside her. Incredibly, the horrific build-up was subsiding; she could literally feel it draining out of her. The relief she experienced served to accelerate the subsidence until she could no longer feel it at all. She relaxed in her chair and gazed into the Doctor's smiling face and eyes.

"What made you think of flowers?"

"It was in the report the Psi Squad sent me about you," he answered as he released his grip on her. "They observed how fascinated you were by the flower arrangements in the safe house they put you in. It may not have been very scientific of me, but I played a hunch, as you Americans say. It was a moment of intuition as defined by my General Theory of Radiopsychology."

"Well, whatever it was, it worked. I'm cured."

"No, not yet. This is only the beginning of the curative process. In future sessions, you will practice creating and dissipating the force within you."

"But I don't want to create it! It's – it's...*frightening*!"

"Of course it is. And that is why you must learn to bring it to life and to send it away at will. In time, you will cause it to serve you rather than to control you." He smiled again. "Your salvation is within you, *ryebyonka*, if only you reach out for it."

"You make it sound so simple."

"Did you not dispel the build-up just now? How simple was that?"

Jean thought about it for a moment. He had her there. Thinking pleasant thoughts instead of awful ones was the key. Why hadn't she realized it before? The answer to the question came immediately.

Because you were too busy being frightened, you ninny!

"Yeah, it was, wasn't it? OK, Dr. Razumov, I'm convinced. But, what's this business about it serving me? For what reason?"

"I shall tell you another time. Now, you are dismissed to go back to your duties."

Once Jean had departed, the Director turned his attention to his EEG. He ordered up a hard copy of the readings before, during, and after Jean's experience and sat down to study the long strip of paper.

The read-out was a perfect picture of symmetry. In the beginning was a plateau of alpha waves. During the exercise, the lines increased in intensity through the beta and gamma and peaked in the delta stage. Afterwards, when he brought her down, the pattern reversed itself until it reached the alpha stage again. The picture was exactly as he had expected it to be, given the descriptions of the sensations Jean had provided to him. Only this time, the process had not left her a nervous wreck, hating the power within her, hating herself for possessing it. This time, she had turned a corner. Soon, she would no longer be a slave to inexplicable forces but rather the mistress of explained powers.

How her power could be fitted into the scheme of radiopsychology was yet to be resolved. It could be done, of course, with a bit of thought. Ah, the life of a scientist – to be justified in all that he did!

"Emil," came a familiar voice from the doorway, "got a minute?"

"For you, George, always. What is on your mind this time?"

"A matter of great urgency, I'm afraid." The detective updated his colleague, concluding with the promise made to Mr. Smith. "I came here directly after leaving his base."

The Russian fell into a deep frown and rubbed his jaw repeatedly. Larkin had made many requests of him – some of which he was very, very reluctant to grant as they would have impacted on the health and safety of DEDEP – but this newest one seemed to be the most outlandish one of all. Allow an alien being to "set up shop" on DEDEP's premises? That would open the facility to Swarm attack (albeit unintentionally but devastating nevertheless) and put an end to everything he had devoted his life to achieve. What had George been thinking when he made such a promise?

"George, *moy drug*, you should not have made this promise without first consulting me – or our benefactors. They might – how do you say it? – "pull the plug" on us if they do not approve."

"I understand, Emil, but consider the alternative. Mr. Smith will overload his cold-fusion generator which would certainly end any Swarm attack, but it will also reduce the City to a smoking hole in the ground."

"Surely he would not carry out that threat."

"These are aliens, Emil. They don't think like us. Why else would they choose the Solar System for their last-chance battleground? We're just a bunch of 'primitives' to them – 'collateral damage.'"

"*Bozhu moyu!* What a choice!" The old man rubbed his jaw some more. "No choice, it would seem. How would you proceed?"

"First, we organize a work brigade to clear enough space in the barn to accommodate most of Mr. Smith's array. The large pieces will have to be placed outside."

"How much time to we have?"

"Three hours, tops."

"And Mr. Smith can move everything in that short a time?"

A brief smile played on Larkin's lips as he described the nature of the Coalition's "transportation" system. The Doctor's eyes widened with surprise, and he searched the detective's face for signs of foolery. He saw none, slumped in his chair, and stared at the ceiling for a long time.

"Now we are entering the realm of science fiction, George. I cannot believe this."

"Is it any less believable than radiopsychology? Remember, you're here because your former associates at the APA hooted you out."

"*Oo tyebya pravdy.* Very well. Since I have accepted the reality of extraterrestrials, I must accept other unbelievable things. I shall go now and recruit your work brigade. *Do sveedanye.*"

No sooner had the Doctor departed than Larkin received an incoming message from one of the Twins.

*George.

*Paddy. What's up?

*More bad news, wouldn't you know? Lacey has reported that the Swarm is on the move – the remnants of the original lot plus the re-enforcements. Judging from the direction they took, she believes they're on their way to Mr. Smith's base.

*Damn! Then the base *was* compromised.

*What's the game plan, old darling?

*I'll have to warn Mr. Smith right away. You call Sheena and have her contact 'Brother' Connolly. I want some 'troops' on Ridgeway ASAP. As soon as I warn Mr. Smith, I'll head back to the City.

*Righto. Be seeing you.

So much for our three hours, unless I can divert the Swarm's attention in time, he thought worriedly. *Otherwise we're headed for a four-star disaster.*

He pulled the alien communicator out of his pocket, thumbed it into the 'active' mode, and entered the Coalition agent's code. It seemed like forever before the alien responded.

"Hhhello…again…Mr.…Largin."

"Hello, Mr. Smith. I have another warning for you."

"Whhhat…is…wrong…now?"

"My informants tell me that a group of Swarm soldiers is heading your way. They will probably reach you in half an hour." A lengthy silence ensued. Larkin quietly counted to twenty before speaking again. "Mr. Smith?"

"I…apoloshize…for…not…responding…sooner…Mr.…Largin. Thhhis…news…is…very…upsetting. I…am…afraid…I…must… do…whhhat …I…had…orishinally…planned. It…hhhas…been…a… pleashure…working …withhh…you. Perhhhaps…we…will…meet… again…in…thhhe… world…beyond."

"No, wait, Mr. Smith! Don't give up just yet. There is always hope."

"Hhhope? Whhhat…hhhope…is…thhhere?"

"I'm creating a diversion that will buy you more time to make your preparations."

"Whhhat…sort…of…divershion?"

"We Tellurians have a saying. 'The best defense is a good offense.' I'll send some of my people to attack the Swarm base. They can't have left it completely unattended. The guards will alert their comrades, and hopefully they'll return to protect their ship."

"You…would…sagrifice…your…own…people?"

"We're allies, Mr. Smith. That is what allies do. Besides, it's a better solution than total destruction of you, your base, and the City."

"I…do…not…envy…you…your…decishon…Mr.…Largin…but… you …hhhave…shust…given…me…hhhope. Do…whhhat…you… must."

As soon as he had broken connection with the alien, the detective was on his cell phone calling Sheena. She answered breathlessly.

"George! Where are you?"

"I'm at DEDEP. I'll explain why later. Did you get hold of Connolly?"

"Yes. He said he'd start rounding up the Disciple task force for whatever you have in mind. What *do* you have in mind?"

Larkin tersely explained the emergency and heard a sharp gasp on the other end. He had expected a scream at worst or a long moan at best. Perhaps the scream would come later when the implications of the situation sank in.

"You're sending those Disciples to certain death, George. The Archdeacon won't be pleased."

"He's already aware of the necessity of my actions. Besides, they've been primed for martyrdom by the load of Disciple propaganda they've been spoon-fed since they joined up. Would you rather see the City reduced to a smoking – possibly radioactive – crater?"

"No-o-o-o, of course not."

"I didn't think so. I'll do what's necessary for the greater good."

"I know," Sheena said softly. "When are you coming back to the City?"

"As soon as I hang up. 'Bye."

* * *

"Brother" Connolly bent as low as he could as he crept toward one of the side windows in the abandoned factory. He was sweating every step of the way, and it had little to do with the temperature of the day. He was desperately trying to keep a low profile so that the Enemy would not spot him and confound the assault on their base of operations. He was not confident of success; but he knew he had to persevere or else the plan "Brother" Larkin had outlined would fall into ruin, and Evil would triumph over Good. As a true believer in the Light of Purity and all that it stood for, he was obliged not to allow that to come to pass.

The plan was simplicity itself. The Enemy had just launched a new front in its conquest of Earth, he had been told; but, rather than chasing after them and wasting energy better used for actual battle, his group was advised to attack the Enemy's base of operations and force them to return here. And, when they did return, they would be set upon by his guys and utterly destroyed. On the off-chance that some of the Enemy remained behind to guard the base against intruders, a cautious approach was advised.

Connolly finally reached the window and raised himself to peer inside. What he observed both alarmed and comforted him – alarmed by the presence of the Enemy's chief weapon of destruction capable (he was told) of shooting flames and missiles in vast quantities and destroying whole populations, comforted by the presence of only two of the Enemy standing guard. He knew they had fearsome personal weapons – he had witnessed their use earlier at the auto dealership – but he also knew that his guys had the element of surprise. Those two would be quickly overcome and sent back to Hell, and the task force would wait patiently for their comrades to return and meet a similar fate.

What a blessing Brother Larkin was! He knew exactly what to do to prevent Evil from gaining the upper hand. He and his (Connolly's) guys would win the war for sure.

Connolly chuckled to himself at the thought of "his guys." Physically, he was a scrawny fellow, not good material for a sports team like many of the Disciple males, least of all for a militant task force like this one. In a different context, he would have been taking orders instead of giving them; the members of the task force would have looked upon him with contempt for not being able to keep up with them. In the present context, however, he had the comfort of the Light of Purity, which rendered all men as equal before God, regardless of their physical or mental abilities. And, though he had not expected to be thrust into the limelight but sought to contribute however he could, thrust he had been. He was almost tempted to bask in the limelight, but the Archdeacon had cautioned against prideful behavior. Still, his new position gave him a thrill he couldn't contain well. He was the Archdeacon's personal messenger, and people listened to him instead of ignoring him. He – and Brother Larkin, of course – were calling the shots, and "his guys" were marching in lock-step!

The two guards inside were doing nothing in particular, or so it seemed. They were just standing around, talking to each other. That was a plus, Connolly thought; the element of surprise would be enhanced by an element of laxity.

He looked over his shoulder. "His guys," two dozen strong, were holding their positions along the railroad track which lay about ten meters west of the factory. All of them were armed with a variety of blunt instruments, and all of them were anxious to employ those instruments. Connolly had been able to round up more than what was left of the original task force; many of the present company had friends who had been lost in previous forays against the Enemy and so had volunteered to form a new, fully functional force and to seek revenge --a most unspiritual attitude, to say the least, but Connolly was pleased that so many had answered the call so promptly.

Now he signaled them to join him. As one man with one purpose, they moved forward and assumed the low crouch their "leader" had. When all had gathered around him, he divided them up into two groups; one group would advance to the rear of the building in a clockwise direction, while the other would do so in a counter-clockwise direction. Quickly, they set off as directed with Connolly leading the counter-clockwise group.

Presently, they rejoined at the loading dock. With Connolly still in the lead, they squeezed, one by one, through the doorway with as much stealth as muscle men could muster. Slowly and cautiously, they maneuvered through the debris of abandonment, taking care to use whatever cover lent itself to remaining out of sight of the two guards. They reached the limit of the available cover and were about to rush the Swarm soldiers when the element of surprise dissipated in an instant.

For whatever reason, one of the guards had decided to make his way toward the rear of the building. He rounded a large, empty packing crate and collided with Connolly. Both individuals stared at each other in shock for the space of two seconds. Then the alien shouted out a warning to his comrade, drew his hand weapon, and pointed it directly at Connolly's head. But, before he could fire, the Disciple closest to his "leader" rushed forward and delivered a smashing blow to the Enemy's skull with a steel pipe. The latter sank to the floor, a purplish liquid oozing out of the wound, and lay still.

The other guard had the presence of mind to grab his communication device and alert his Commander to the situation before he leaped into action. After the initial shock of confrontation and possible death had passed, Connolly noted with pleasure that the Enemy was reacting exactly as Brother Larkin said he would, i.e. causing the main force to retreat and return to base. At once, he signaled a charge, and all of "his guys" sprang forward to dispatch the remaining guard. The Swarm soldier managed to draw his weapon and get off two shots before being overwhelmed and pummeled to death. Both shots had found their marks, and two Disciples achieved martyrdom in the form of gaping holes in their chests.

Connolly directed the bodies to be covered as a temporary measure and posted guards at the windows in the front of the building.

Then the wait began.

* * *

The Commander surveys the abandoned and dilapidated supermarket with his kind's version of binoculars. He slowly sweeps the area from one side to another in hopes of spotting any sign of activity. He sees nothing, however, and wonders idly why in the six hells of the Universe anyone would choose to make a base out of this ruin. But, of course, he answers himself, that is the perfect camouflage, for no one would suspect activity occurring in a place which might collapse at any moment. The Tellurian who leads the white-clothed rabble has been very clever indeed.

The members of his re-enforced unit stand behind him, awaiting his order to advance and assault the supposed Tellurian stronghold. All are eager to engage the resistance force and deal a crushing blow; they have already lost a number of their comrades to simple fools waging war with makeshift weapons, and they seek revenge. Revenge will be as slow and as painful as they are able to make it, and the Tellurians will know, even as they are dying, that the Swarm is an irresistible force, not to be taken lightly.

The Commander now addresses them. He gives them their order of battle which differs from the usual Swarm tactic. They are to capture unharmed the leader of this rabble and bring the fellow to him for intense interrogation; all others are to be dispatched however it pleases them. To a man, the unit grins wickedly at the thought of the mayhem to come. The Commander then tells them to spread out, to advance slowly, and to be alert for any counter-measures.

The Swarm is halfway across the broken tarmac when the Commander's communication device sounds. He answers the call and listens in alarm as one of the guards he had left behind at the base informs him in a voice filled with panic that the base has been invaded by the white-clothed resistance force and that the other guard has been killed.

The Commander curses himself as he realizes he has been made a fool of by his Tellurian counterpart. The clever fellow's being at this ruined building had been only a ruse to lure his unit away from their base so that his rabble could seize it with impunity. They now have possession of all of the Swarm's equipment – and their warship. The clever fellow may or may not understand the functioning of Swarm technology, but that is beside the point which is that he must not be given the opportunity to understand it.

He gives new orders: one man shall remain here to keep watch in case the Tellurian leader returns; the rest will return to base on the double.

* * *

Larkin knew he was driving faster than he ought to, but he was gripped by a sense of extreme urgency. Matters were moving at a more rapid pace, and he needed to be on the scene where those matters were occurring in order to assure that they were moving according to his Grand Plan and not taking off on a tangent. One matter in particular was pushing Mr. Smith along a suicidal path which threatened to include all humans within a ten-kilometer radius. He had calmed down the pasty-faced alien, but there was still the off-chance that the Coalition agent might still panic and self-destruct. He hadn't seen any explosions yet – although he was near enough to catch a glimpse of the fireball before he himself was incinerated – so Mr. Smith was still in control of himself. But why take chances?

It was probably his imagination but, as he traveled along Main Street, it seemed he was catching all of the red traffic signals in the world and encountering one traffic jam after another. He had to force himself to relax his grip on the steering wheel; he didn't need to be stopped by the police and arrested for reckless driving.

As he approached the Coalition base, he was glad to see that it still existed, but he saw no sign of activity. That could mean one of two things: one, the diversion had been successful, the Swarm had returned to their own base, and Mr. Smith was back to making his preparations for transfer of his array; or, two, the diversion had not worked, the Swarm had captured Mr. Smith before he had had a chance to self-destruct, and the Coalition operative was either dead or wishing he was.

Think positive, George old sock!

He parked the station wagon in the usual place -- no need to break the routine as that might cause suspicion amongst the locals -- and marched across the tarmac. Once inside the building, he was alert for any sign of unusual activity – or as unusual as it could be where extraterrestrials were concerned. He was instantly relieved when he discovered nothing of the sort.

Mr. Smith was engaged in conversation with Frommar. Both were being translated in each other's language, and he had no idea what they were discussing. The Coalition's Co-ordinator spied him first and broke out in his facsimile of a human smile. He said something to the local agent, and the latter turned and greeted the visitor.

"Hhhello…again…Mr.…Largin. You…are…bag."

"Yes, I wanted to make sure my diversion worked."

"It…must…hhhave. I…hhhave…not…been…disturbed…at…all."

"Great. Might I speak to Frommar?"

"Certainly. One...moment...please." He made an adjustment on his control board. "Go...ahead."

"Greetings, Frommar."

"Greetings, La-k'n. We understanding you made-have an interesting offer."

"I have, and the offer still stands. This location may have been compromised."

"We feeling that true. Your location having sufficient space for our equipment?"

The detective did a quick scan of the array. In his mind's eye, he was placing each piece in the barn in as close proximity to its current position here.

"Most will fit in the interior of the largest structure on the property. That tall tower will have to be placed outside. Would that be a problem?"

"We not thinking so. We approving. How soon you transfer-ready?"

"Two" – he checked himself when he was about to say "hours" as it probably would not have translated into Frommar's language – "time units from now. Is that sufficient?"

"Yes. We begin-can the transfer in [*untranslatable*] from now. Mabel-choo-choo give-will you a locator beacon which you setting up at your location. When the beacon activating, the transfer begin-will. Farewell, La-k'n, and good fortune."

"Good-bye, Frommar. Good fortune to you."

The Co-ordinator's image disappeared in a swirl of color, and the monitor went dark. Larkin turned to Mr. Smith.

"I...was...not...sure...thhhat...thhhe...Goalition...would... approve ...your...offer...Mr....Largin. You...must...hhhave... made...a...larshe... impression...on...Frommar."

"I certainly hope so. Now, about the locator beacon?"

"One...moment. I...shall...obtain...it...for...you."

Once again, the alien retreated into the cold-fusion generator housing. Half a minute later, he re-appeared with what for all the world looked like a twenty-centimeter-long popsicle stick. But this stick was either metallic or plastic and silver in color. He handed the detective the beacon who regarded it with wonder.

"Whhhen...you...are...ready...for...thhhe...transfer...press... thhhe ...nodule...on...thhhe...top...of...thhhe...beagon."

Larkin examined the device, located the nodule, and touched it lightly. He nodded in understanding.

"Great. I'll return to my property now and start setting up for the transfer."

"Good-bye...Mr....Largin."

Once he was back in the station wagon, the detective slumped in his seat and made contact with the Twins.

*Kenny, Paddy.

*We're here, old darling. We were...

*...just about to call *you*.

*What's the latest?

*Well, Sheena is frantic. She thinks that...

*...you're in over your head with this...

*...plan of yours, now that the Swarm...

*...has gotten belligerent of late.

*I know what I'm doing. What else?

*Lacey reports that the Swarm unit has...

*...nearly reached their base and that...

*...they look meaner than usual. She...

*...thinks your ploy worked too well and...

*...that the blighters will unleash all...

*...sorts of mayhem on the Disciples.

*That can't be helped. Anything more?

*Good God, George, but you're being cold-...

*...hearted about these developments.

*I'm in command here. I can't afford to wallow in emotionalism.

*Humph! Well, here's one more tidbit...

*...which should chip away at your reserve. Billy...

*...reports that the Swarm left one of their...

*...group behind in order to keep an eye on...

*...Mr. Smith's base, for what reason we can only...

*...surmise. That's the end of our report, old darling.

*Thanks, guys. I'll 'talk' at you later.

Larkin straightened up quickly and peered out the window. So, the Swarm Leader left a watchdog behind, eh? Undoubtedly, he was hedging his bets, watching for Tellurian resistance fighters here while he returned to engage them at his base. This was a good thing. The watcher was sure to report having seen the "Tellurian leader" here, and his chief would wonder if the abandoned supermarket was worth investigating after all and be thrown into a state of confusion. Of course, in two hours' time, it wouldn't make any difference what the Swarm Leader decided to do.

He continued his scan of the area. Fifteen seconds later, he observed his quarry standing behind a telephone pole on the other side of North Avenue. He snorted in derision. The joker may have been a highly efficient soldier but, when it came to surveillance, he was a complete amateur. The question was what to do about him. The answer was, nothing. The watchman could stand there until he collapsed from sheer fatigue as far as Larkin was concerned. Right now, he had to inform "Brother" Connolly that he was about to have visitors.

CAPTURED!

THE COMMANDER HALTS his troops in order to answer a call. It is from the sentry he left to observe the alleged headquarters of the Tellurian resistance. The sentry reports that the leader of the resistance had re-appeared, entered the dilapidated building, stayed there for the space of one [*untranslatable*], and exited. Further, the Tellurian had remained in his vehicle, *unmoving*, for the space of a quarter [*untranslatable*] before speaking to someone on his own communicator. After that, he had driven off.

The Commander takes this report with an air of disgust. Did the Tellurian [*untranslatable*] think he could fool the Swarm twice? The Commander will not play this silly game – not while his own base is being occupied by the white-clothed rabble. He orders his sentry to remain at his post. If the resistance leader returns, he is to be captured and held for interrogation. *Under no circumstances* is he to be given a chance to communicate with anyone or to self-terminate.

He now gives his troops an update and their final marching orders. In all likelihood, the rabble at the base has been forewarned of their return; therefore, they are to follow Attack Sequence #5D: dispatch all enemy combatants in the shortest time possible – with one exception. If the resistance leader has re-joined his own forces, he is to be seized, *unharmed*, and immobilized. Failure on this last point will result in summary execution.

The Swarm unit resumes its quick-march. A half [*untranslatable*] later, it is within sight of its base. The Commander halts it and surveys the scene with his "binoculars." All seems quiet, but that could be deception on the part of the resistance. Still, the sooner the base is re-taken, the better. He signals his troops to initiate Attack Sequence #5D.

* * *

"Brother" Connolly nervously paced back and forth in the empty space between the Swarm warship and the front entrance to the building. To break the monotony, he occasionally circled the awesome weapon of warfare and cast a furtive glance at its sinister presence. He had been doing this ever since he and his guys overcame what little resistance the Enemy had presented and established control over his base.

The waiting for the main force of the Enemy to return wasn't the only matter weighing on his mind, nor was it the uppermost matter. What really bothered him was the very idea of being in a firefight with an Enemy who, according to Brother Larkin's description, never took prisoners. He wasn't a fighter; he was just a go-fer, a message boy, and – he had to admit – a flunky. The Disciples had already lost many of their membership in confrontations with the demons, and they were sure to lose some more very shortly – including, perhaps, himself. The Archdeacon had explained that martyrdom in the cause of spreading the Light of Purity might be necessary, but Connolly had not believed it would happen to *him*. He didn't want to die, if truth be told, for any reason; he just wanted to marry Sister Smithers and raise a family.

If the worst-case scenario occurred, what would become of her? Would she mourn his death for the rest of her life and never marry at all? Or would she find someone else to love? Too many questions – not enough answers.

His fretting was abruptly interrupted by the *beep-beep* of his cell phone. A glance at the caller ID told him the call was from Brother Larkin. Did his nominal superior have good news or bad?

"Brother Larkin," he murmured, "I've been hoping you'd call. We've secured the Enemy's base, according to your plan. What's next?"

"My ploy worked, Brother Connolly. The Enemy went off on a wild-goose chase, and now they're on their way back."

"My guys will be ready for them."

"I want you and your guys to evacuate the building as soon as they show up. Do you have sentries posted?"

"Yes. But, I thought you wanted us to ambush them when they did return."

"I've re-evaluated their forces, and the odds of success are against you. What you need to do is to hold them at bay until I round up more re-enforcements to swing the odds in your favor. If those devils go after you, you retreat and keep them occupied until the re-enforcements show up."

"Will do, Brother Larkin. How soon will you be joining us?"

"I've got one more errand to run. Then I'll hook up with you."

With the thought of impending doom dissipated, the young Disciple breathed a sigh of relief and made the rounds to check on his sentries. There was a distinct jaunt in his step. Fifteen minutes later, one of the sentries called out to him.

"Brother Connolly! I see the Enemy approaching!"

"All right! Everyone, out of the building!"

"We're not going to fight them?" another Disciple asked.

"We are, but not here and not now. As soon as Brother Larkin sends us some re-enforcements, then we'll take those hell-spawn out. Let's move, guys!"

None of the burly group fully understood what was going on. They all wanted to stay and take the fight to the Enemy. But Brother Connolly was in charge, and he said to move. So, they moved.

* * *

When Larkin returned to DEDEP, he discovered a beehive of activity in the barn. It looked like all of the adult male residents and half of all the adult female residents, plus a few teenagers of both sexes, were pitching in to clear a space large enough to accommodate the lion's share of Mr. Smith's equipment. He idly wondered what Emil had told them to motivate them so. Even Joyce Jankowsky was present, doing what she could; from the perplexed expression on her face, however, he deduced that she was just following someone else's directions and not having a clue as to *why* it had to be done. Freddie seemed to have appointed himself as the straw boss of this outfit and was directing traffic; the sight of his many gesticulations made the detective laugh out loud, but not too loudly to attract attention to himself. In the midst of all his manic motions, the dwarf spotted him anyhow and waddled over to him.

"You seem to be enjoying yourself," Larkin remarked off-handedly.

"Always wanted to be a boss of somethin'." He grinned. "Now I am. How soon is Mr. Smith's stuff arrivin'?"

"As soon as I activate the locator beacon he gave me."

"A locator beacon?" Freddie scowled. "What's that for?"

"You know how they moved things on 'Star Trek'? Well, that's how this alien set-up is being transported."

The handyman's jaw dropped open, and he stared at Larkin for a long moment, speechless. The detective suppressed a smirk which was building up and maintained a serious demeanor.

"No *shit*!?!" Freddie finally found his voice. "You mean they're actually goin' to *beam* that stuff down? Be damned! This I gotta see!"

"You and me both, chum. The explanation knocked me for a loop too. Ah, there's Emil. Excuse me."

Larkin hastened over to the Director's position near the emergency exit. The old man was scanning the activity with a keen eye and a sense of wonder which would normally have been the reaction of a child at a circus. He looked this way and that, not daring to move lest he miss something important. At one point, he had to dodge Bill Perkins, Sr., carrying an armload of scrap lumber; otherwise, he would have been knocked to the floor, because Perkins' vision was obscured by his load. Larkin had to dodge in his turn. Perkins mumbled an apology in both instances and kept moving.

"I haven't seen this much activity since the last fire drill."

"Nye ya [nor I]" the doctor murmured as his attention was drawn toward yet another interesting activity. "I have outdone myself this time, *moy droog.*"

"What did you tell them they were preparing for?"

The Russian peered at his colleague in surprise.

"Why, the truth, of course. What should I have told them? At first, they were obviously skeptical, but I reminded them that recent events, while out of the ordinary, had required a project no more or no less impossible than what had preceded them."

"Well, it worked. The barn is almost cleared away."

"How soon will Mr. Smith's equipment be transported?"

"I'm going to call him now and see if he's ready."

Instinctively, the Russian looked upward as if he could spy the spaceship involved in the transport.

"Bozhu moyu!" he whispered. "That I should live to see more wonders than I even dreamed possible."

"You and me both, chum," the detective repeated himself. "It looks like the work is done. Let's hold a meeting."

While the Director made the rounds to inform the residents of the impromptu conference, Larkin called Mr. Smith.

"Ahhh...Mr....Largin. Thhhang...you...for...thhhe...respite... you... provided. We...hhhave...hhhad...sufficient...time...to... gomplete...our ...preparations...for...thhhe...transfer. We...are... sharshing...up...thhhe ...[*untranslatable*]...now. We...reguire...one... half...hour...to...fully... sharsh."

"Glad to hear it. We're ready on our end."

"Egcellent. We...will...transfer...thhhe...eguipment...one... module ...at...a...time...in...order...to...gonserve...enershy. Do... you...remember ...thhhe...egsagt...positions...of...thhhe...array?"

"Yes, I do."

"Egcellent. Whhhen...we...are...ready...to...transfer...I...want... you ...to...place...thhhe...logator...beagon...in...your...facility...at... thhhose... logations...beginning...withhh...thhhe...gold-fushon... shenerator."

"Okay. How long will the transfer take?"

Mr. Smith made what sounded like a chuckle. But, where extraterrestrials were concerned, one could not tell what their emotional state was by sound alone.

"No…longer…thhhan…it…tagues…you…to…move…thhhe…logator…beagon…from…one…place…to…anothhher."

"No more than fifteen minutes then. All right, I'll wait for your signal to begin."

Ten minutes later, the remainder of DEDEP (mostly children) emerged from below. Wonder and excitement was written all over their faces as much as on those of the adult residents already present. Everyone gathered around Larkin, who smiled hugely.

"Ladies and gentlemen and children of all ages," he began grandly (Freddie grunted at the traditional opening of a circus ringmaster), "what you are about to see will seem fantastic, something out of a science-fiction movie – transmission of matter by wireless methods, or "beaming," as they used to say on 'Star Trek.' But I assure you that it is all real.

"We've already seen some fantastic things, haven't we? Many of you have *done* fantastic things, but you don't think psychic abilities are 'science fiction,' do you? We're now dealing with aliens from outer space with technology further advanced than our own, and they probably take it all for granted. We've been 'recruited' involuntarily in this galactic war they're fighting – although the Earth's existence is at stake as well – but, if we acquit ourselves with honor, perhaps the Coalition will reward us with the information and technology we need to catch up with them. Any questions so far?"

Henry Rawlins' hand went up immediately. Larkin grimaced. The "dreaming prophet" was going to gripe some more!

"I got two questions, George. First, does this…Coalition know about DEDEP? And, second, why don't they work with government in this war of theirs?"

"The answer to your first question, Henry, is 'No – definitely no.' And they're not going to if I can help it. All they do know is that I am loaning them the use of 'my property' to re-locate their local base of operations. It's only fair, I suppose, since I'm the one who compromised their original base. I'll see to it that Mr. Smith does not wander about when he isn't working with his array.

"As to the second question, all of us here are fairly intelligent, and we still had trouble accepting the existence of intelligent life on other worlds. Imagine the reaction the Coalition would provoke if they presented themselves to the political animals that run most governments on this world. And I will remind you of who's running *our* government. The Coalition sees us as 'primitives', and so they operate in secret here as much as DEDEP does. Any more questions?"

"I have one, George," Dr. Razumov spoke up. "How do you plan to keep Mr. Smith from discovering us?"

"Mr. Smith will be put up at the house. I'll make it clear to him that he must remain there when he is not operating his equipment so as not to interfere with the operations of 'my farm.' And I'll have either Monk or Ted escort him back and forth from the house to the barn. Anyone else?" Before another question could be asked, the alien communicator sounded. "Ah, that's Mr. Smith now. Hold your questions until after the transfer has been made." He pressed the "receive" nodule. "Hello, Mr. Smith. Are you ready to transfer?"

"Yes…Mr.….Largin.   Place…thhhe…logator…beagon…on… thhhe… first…logation…and…agtivate…it."

"All right, folks. Move back toward the walls. You don't want to be caught in the middle of this."

The residents quickly complied, murmuring excitedly to each other as they did so. When Larkin was satisfied that he had a clear space in the center of the barn, he made a quick scan of the area and sighted the first location, for the cold-fusion generator. He strode deliberately to that spot, bent down, set the beacon on the floor, and pressed its activating nodule. The thing lit up like a Christmas tree and issued three musical notes. He assumed they were musical notes, although he had never heard "music" like that before.

"All done, Mr. Smith."

"Egcellent.   Now…place…thhhe…beagon…at…thhhe… position …of…thhhe…gontrol…gonsole."

"Check."

If a poll had been taken among the residents with the question, which was more spectacular, the appearance of the psychic gestalt or the reality of wireless transmission of matter, quite possibly there might have been a split right down the middle. The latter may have been favored because the former had appeared suddenly and therefore had been a bit frightening. When the first piece of alien technology arrived as if by magic, the residents were expecting it and eagerly awaiting it. They had to wait six minutes before something happened.

The first inkling that something spectacular was about to occur came in the form of a crackling that static electricity makes. The second inkling – which followed quickly on the heels of the first – was the *sight* of static electricity hovering over the spot where Larkin had set the locator beacon. The third inkling was a brilliant white flash which temporarily blinded the residents. When the flash faded away, the piece of technology stood there in all of its awesome magnificence. And, if another poll had been taken with the question, have you ever seen a cold-fusion generator, the result would have a unanimous "No!"

The detective paid no attention to any of this as he was too busy dancing around the barn and setting the beacon in the prescribed places. Six minutes after each setting, a new piece appeared. Inexplicably (at least to the residents), Larkin strolled outside and re-entered a minute later. In due time, a barely visible flash of white light lit up the sky. With each new sighting, "ahhh's" and "ohhh's" rippled through the assembly with the wonder of it all. The detective resumed his place in the center of the barn and spread his arms wide.

"Ladies and gentlemen and children of all ages, behold the *eighth* wonder of the modern world! Feel free to examine each module but please don't touch. This is very delicate stuff. When you are finished, I'll explain what function each module performs."

Slowly, the DEDEP'ers split up into small groups and began wandering around the barn like tourists at a museum. Larkin took it all in with bemusement even though he could have related to the sense of awe, having been down that road himself not too long ago. The buzzing of his communicator interrupted his smugness.

"Thhhe...process...is...gomplete...Mr....Largin.   Is... everythhhing... in...order?"

"Couldn't be better, Mr. Smith. Except for the different surroundings, you'd think nothing had been moved."

"Egcellent. As...soon...as...I...'tie...up...some...loose...ends'... as ...you...Tellurians...say...I...will...shoin....you."

"You're going through the same process? Isn't that dangerous?"

"It...was...whhhen...thhhe...tegnoloshy...was...first...developed. It...is...guite...safe...now."

"Well, you would know best. Do I need to use the beacon again?"

"Yes. Selegt...a...point...between...two...established...positions."

The Coalition agent signed off, and the detective frowned. There was no telling when Mr. Smith's transfer would take place. Which meant that his "lecture" concerning the functions of the array would necessarily have to be a brief one.

"OK, everybody, gather around, and I'll brief you on the functions of these gadgets."

The assembly gave him their full attention. To a man, woman, and child, they were enthralled by what had just arrived in their midst by a most mind-boggling method, and they wanted to learn all they could about it. Larkin was pleased by how quickly they had accepted the reality of alien technology; it would make his "lecture" much easier to present.

"I'm going to leave the first piece to arrive for last," he began. One, there's a certain order that must be followed and, two, I want to save the best for last. I'll start with the control module over there."

He pointed to the module, and all eyes followed the pointing finger. With as much detail as he could remember, he explained what the thing did and how it worked. As he did so, he observed the facial expressions of his audience. Most of the group seemed to have taken the explanation in stride; the rest exhibited puzzlement – which was not too surprising – and Larkin imagined there would be many questions asked after the "lecture" – and perhaps beyond. Then he went down the line to the smaller monitor and the translator towers. The larger monitor and the

"Tinker Toy" were next, followed by the EMF generator. He paused dramatically before gesturing at the silver-gray cube.

"Ladies and gentlemen and children of all ages," he announced grandiosely, "I present the *piece de resistance* –technology that our own scientists and engineers have been working on for decades but have never been able to construct a working model – a cold-fusion generator!"

Those who were familiar with the concept gasped audibly and goggled at the sight of the real thing. Those who were not murmured amongst themselves and expressed much apprehension. All of them moved away from the machine a step or two as if to get out of harm's way. The detective remained in place and smiled a reassuring smile. The crowd relaxed somewhat.

"That's the 'grand tour,' people. I'm sure you have questions."

Predictably, "Fat Henry" Rawlins took a half step forward, a worried look on his face.

"Is that thing…really *safe*, George? I've heard that cold-fusion generators are inherently unstable."

"Our alien 'friends' seem to think so, or they wouldn't carry one around with them."

No further questions were forthcoming. The awe which the cold-fusion generator had produced put them on hold for a while. Larkin was relieved since he had no idea how soon Mr. Smith would call back and inform him that he was ready to transfer. He invited everyone to take one last look at the array before returning "downstairs."

Bill Perkins, Sr., joined him. Accompanying him was his younger son, Wilson. Both were shaking their heads in disbelief. The detective regarded them with bemusement.

"It's hard to believe," the elder Perkins remarked softly, "that I'm looking at an actual working model. I've seen the computer models – hell, I've done a few myself – but no one could get them to work."

"The mathematics are really complex, Dad," Wilson remarked casually. "It took me a whole month to grasp them."

Larkin stared at the eleven-year-old in amazement and could not believe his ears. The boy's father laughed.

"This son of mine is quite the genius, George."

"I guess," Larkin whispered. "He certainly fits in with everyone else in DEDEP."

"That's not all. If you ever want to hack into the Disciples' computer files, let me know. I'll have Willie work his wonders for you."

"You're kidding?"

"Nope. He knows more about computers than I ever will, and I've got a drawer full of awards for my accomplishments."

"Well, thanks for the offer. I'll get back to you when I'm ready."

Soon – all too soon for most of the DEDEP'ers – it was time to return to their hole in the ground in order to avoid being spotted by the alien soon to be their "guest." Even though they were upset that they couldn't "see the sights" a little bit longer, they knew that remaining hidden from the outside world – not to mention from outer space! – was of prime importance. Someday, it would not have to be this way. Someday…

The detective waited until everyone had departed, then retrieved his cell phone and punched up a number. It was the Archdeacon's private line.

"Hello?" the old man answered tentatively.

"Larkin here, Your Worship."

"Ah, Brother Larkin. What do you have to report?"

"So far, everything is going according to plan. Brother Connolly and some of the fellows are at the Enemy's base, waiting for the signal to attack. I've held off on giving that signal because I think we'll need a larger force to increase our chances of success."

"Very wise of you. How many extra people do you need?"

"Another two dozen should be sufficient."

"I'll have Brother Kincaid see to it immediately."

"Thank you, sir. I hope I'll have good news to report shortly."

He disconnected again and smirked. Yes, indeed, everything *was* going according to plan – *his* plan, not the Archdeacon's!

* * *

The Swarm unit approaches the east side of the abandoned factory with utmost caution, using all available cover and keeping alert to any signs of the opposition. What they expect, however, fails to materialize.

In the Swarm "war playbook," Attack Sequence #5D called for approaching an enemy position where the strength of the enemy is unknown with a series of incremental advances. One pair of soldiers establishes a "ground zero" point and provides cover fire for the next pair to advance; the second pair advances a specified distance, holds its position, and provides cover for a third pair. The unit leap-frogs by this manner until all members have surrounded the target. Attack Sequence #5D never allowed for approaching an Enemy who possessed no sophisticated weaponry – it never occurred to the High Command that organized resistance could be formed without it – but it was the closest plan of action which fitted the current situation.

The Commander intends to bring up this matter at the next war council, once this backwater planet has been destroyed, although he feels foolish in doing so. What kind of an Enemy restricts themselves to blunt instruments and inflicts death and injury by bludgeoning? He might have expected such tactics to be carried out by a mob acting spontaneously. This rabble have not acted spontaneously so far; rather, they have a leader who organizes his forces into carefully calculated attack vectors. The clever fellow took over the Swarm base by a ruse and a prepared attack. The Swarm could – should – learn from this experience.

But that is for the future. The present demands that the base be re-captured and the white-clothed rabble inside annihilated with all possible speed.

When the unit has moved into their final positions, the Commander signals for the assault to begin. The soldiers thrust their weapons into open windows (or break open those still paned) and fire carefully aimed blasts of energy. After one [*untranslatable*] of sustained fire, one-half of the unit break off and head for the rear entrance; the remainder resume fire as a distraction to whoever is inside.

The former group enters the building and maneuvers cautiously toward the front, watching for signs of the opposition. It is shocked and disappointed to find no one inside. One soldier happens to glance out a window and spots the opposition retreating toward the west. Hastily, the soldiers fire their weapons, but the white-clothed rabble is out of range.

The Commander, when he has been informed of this unexpected development, is furious. The clever fellow has played him for a fool for a second time, and he is determined more than ever to get hold of the Tellurian and torture him in every way possible – not to gain intelligence, however, but to enjoy himself.

* * *

Larkin arrived at the abandoned factory at nearly the same time as the re-enforcements. Half a dozen automobiles were just pulling up on the opposite side of the street. All of the passengers quickly piled out and waited for their leader to exit. "Brother" Kincaid did so with a flourish; slowly and deliberately, he eased out of the lead vehicle, straightened to his full height, and carefully scanned his surroundings with a grim expression on his face. The detective had to hand it to the man; whatever else Kincaid was – and he was still a mystery as far as Larkin was concerned – he knew how to make an entrance.

The detective parked the station wagon behind the vehicles of Connolly's group for no other reason than this was as close to the building as he cared to get. He exited just as slowly and deliberately and walked over to Kincaid's position; in his case, however, it was due more to physical limitations than to one-upmanship. The number two Disciple watched him (as always) like a hawk its prey.

"Brother Kincaid," he said ingratiatingly, "that was quick action on your part."

"It pays to be prepared, Brother Larkin, and we came prepared."

He stepped to the rear of the car and yanked open the trunk door. Larkin goggled at what he spied inside: a large stack of automatic rifles. How in the world had the man gotten his hands on this mini-arsenal? Clearly, the Disciples *had* been prepared – prepared to use force in case persuasion failed to keep Americans in line. One by one, Kincaid's group lined up to receive a weapon which he placed smartly in their eager hands. After all were armed, the supply had not been depleted. Kincaid peered at Larkin with a raised eyebrow.

"Help yourself, Brother Larkin."

"Um, I've never handled long arms before. I do have a pistol in my station wagon."

The Disciple leader smiled insincerely and turned to Connolly's group.

"You fellows, there are plenty of rifles to go around. And there are fully-loaded magazines in the back seat."

There was no hesitation. Connolly's group nearly stampeded in order to get a high-powered weapon into their hands. Their "leader" followed but was not as anxious to be armed; he was anxious, but for a different reason. When everyone had procured a rifle, Kincaid opened the rear door of the car.

"Take three magazines each. We'll keep some ammo in reserve, just in case." He regarded Connolly with a hint of disdain. "What's your pleasure, Brother Connolly?"

The young Disciple swallowed compulsively, and Larkin could almost feel sorry for him. Connolly was a fish out of water in this setting, and he didn't bother to disguise the fact.

"Sorry, Brother Kincaid, but I've never handled a gun in my life. I…never had any use for one."

"Suit yourself. You'd better stay out of the way then. Things are going to get hot around here pretty soon." He turned to the detective. "I assume you have a plan of attack."

Larkin thought fast. He had a plan – as always – but he hadn't counted on Kincaid's taking a personal role in the assault or Kincaid's arming the Disciples with heavy-duty weapons. If it appeared to the rank-and-file that he was undercutting the authority of the Archdeacon's deputy, the latter might take exception to anything the detective might propose; trouble might soon follow and cause Fogarty to have to choose between them. Fogarty would naturally choose his deputy since he had known the man longer than he had known Larkin, leaving the latter in a lesser position and ruining the trust he had so diligently worked to instill. Better to give the appearance of seeking the man's opinion to avoid any friction between them and let him make his own mistakes which might reflect positively on the detective's position.

"Well, yes, I do. But you've been a strategist longer than I have. What do you suggest we do?"

Kincaid scanned the factory again. His facial expression remained neutral, but Larkin knew that mental gears were shifting at maximum speed.

"This situation calls for a pincer operation," the number-two finally remarked. "My group will line up in front of the building, fire at will, and draw the Enemy's attention away from Brother Connolly's group. They will enter at the rear of the building and catch the Enemy in a crossfire. You can position yourself anywhere you like. What do you think, Brother Larkin?"

The detective's facial expression did not change either. Mentally, however, he was amazed. Kincaid had just outlined the very plan of attack *he* had been about to propose.

"Talk about birds of a feather. That's exactly what I had in mind. Lead on, Brother Kincaid."

Instantly, the number-two began issuing orders to his group. Each of them loaded a magazine into his rifle and pocketed two more. They were instructed to switch to single-shot mode in order to conserve ammunition. The group then crossed the street, approached the factory cautiously, and took what cover was available. Kincaid brought up the rear with a rifle of his own. Larkin noted that he was handling it very professionally.

Meanwhile, Connolly designated one of his group to be "deputy leader" – a choice he made strictly at random because he hardly knew any of them – and had him proceed with the rest of the battle plan. After loading their rifles, those Disciples returned to where their automobiles were parked and from there stealthily (or as stealthily as poster children for body-building products could achieve) advanced toward the rear of the factory. Connolly stayed close to Larkin, who sought the safety of his own vehicle on the pretext of obtaining his pistol.

A sudden movement appeared at one of the front windows, followed by a flash of light. One of Kincaid's group fell to the ground, screaming in agony; his right arm and shoulder had nearly been burned off. The Swarm had "scored" first in this contest.

"Open fire!" Kincaid shouted. "Retreat!"

His group began firing at will, all the while moving backwards toward the safety of their automobiles. Two more of their number were struck down. Connolly's group also retreated to their vehicles and joined in in the barrage of firepower. Two of that group never made it.

Larkin watched the drama unfold with as much stoicism as he could muster, but dismay nibbled at his consciousness. His and Kincaid's plan was unraveling at a rapid pace. Eventually, the Disciples would run out of ammunition. Then what? Kincaid, he thought, should have brought a couple of rocket launchers; they would have been equalizers in what was now an unequal firefight. He did notice one odd thing, however; there seemed to be only three or four of the Swarm actually firing their energy weapons. What were the rest of them doing?

In a low crouch, he maneuvered toward Kincaid's position. When he reached it, the number-two gave him a deep frown.

"So much for 'Plan A,' Brother Larkin," he remarked humorlessly. "Have you got a 'Plan B'?"

"Other than an orderly retreat, no. We could leave without incurring any more casualties. I've noticed that the Enemy's response has been sporadic. They're up to something, but I don't know what. This would be a good time to retreat and regroup."

"You may be right. Pass the word that we're pulling out."

What happened next Larkin would never forget as long as he lived. As he moved down the line to give the order to retreat, he heard a *thrum-thrum-thrum* emanating from the factory. It grew louder by the second. He looked back and gasped in shock. The Swarm's warship was rising through the hole in the roof the aliens had made earlier; as soon as it had cleared the roof, it swung around to face the resistance group. The detective didn't need to have a picture drawn for him; he had Eve's vision in his memory banks, and he knew and dreaded what was coming.

"Kincaid!" he shouted, dispensing with formalities. "Get your people out of here! Now!"

The number-two and his group stared at the alien ship briefly in confusion, but he quickly reacted to Larkin's warning. He ordered an immediate evacuation of the area, and his group piled into their vehicles without question. The detective walked as fast as he could toward his station wagon. Connolly and his group were also staring in shock at the sight of the warship.

"Everyone out of here!" he ordered. "Connolly, you're with me. Get into the station wagon. Move it, man!"

The young Disciple didn't have to be told twice. He obeyed without saying a word.

Larkin looked back to check on the movement of the alien vessel and the progress of the evacuation and wished he hadn't. The craft slowly approached the line of resistance and opened fire on it. Gouts of flame from the forward ports washed over one of the Disciples' vehicles, setting it on fire; two seconds later, the vehicle's gasoline tank ignited from the heat and exploded. Screams of agony followed, but they were short-lived. Car parts and bodies flew in all directions. Relentlessly, the Swarm weapon pressed the attack. One by one, on down the line, cars exploded and created more charred bodies.

The detective had seen more than enough. This cause had become hopelessly lost; the Disciples were totally outgunned. He jumped into the station wagon and started it up. Since it was facing east, he had to take the time to turn it around for a westerly retreat. Because his disability made maneuvering difficult, he cursed under his breath at the slowness of the vehicle's response but managed the turn and began to pull away. Briefly, he glanced at Connolly. The young man was gripped by sheer terror and prayed fervently for salvation. Had he been a religious person, Larkin might have joined him in prayer.

Forward motion of the station wagon was brief. An exploding vehicle behind it sent a chunk of burning metal into the rear end and spun it around. Larkin tried to brake, but the vehicle careened into a tree with great force. The impact knocked the detective sideways, and his head struck the driver's-side window. He lost consciousness instantly.

* * *

The detective regained consciousness and found himself in a very strange place. He was lying on the floor of a small room half-filled with metallic-like objects. The floor, the walls, and the ceiling also appeared to be metallic. The room was obviously a storage room, but for what? The room was also obviously in the interior of a larger structure, but what kind of structure?

He tried to sit up but discovered that he was bound head and foot. The bindings were as strange as everything else here; they didn't look like rope or cords or tape, but they secured him quite sufficiently. He craned his head this way and that but saw no clues as to where he might be. All he knew for sure was that he was a prisoner.

A prisoner of the Swarm, most likely – there was no other possible explanation.

He was alone in this strange room. What had become of Connolly after he had blacked out? Were any of the Disciples at the factory still alive? He replayed mentally the last thing he remembered: the Disciples' vehicles exploding one by one as the flame-throwing ship worked its way down the line with deadly precision; scorched bodies flying through the air; the screams of agony of the dying. He shuddered at the memory. No one could have survived that onslaught.

Why then was he still alive? The answer came as soon as the question was given form. The Swarm needed a prisoner they could interrogate in order to learn the extent and strength of the resistance on Planet Earth. That had been Mr. Jones' intent when the detective had temporarily been his captive. Now he had been caught again. How soon would he be subjected to questioning and torture?

As if on cue, a panel in the wall opposite his position slid to one side, revealing what seemed to be a passageway, dimly lit. Three Swarm soldiers entered the room, and the one in the middle was the last person on Earth – or any other world, for that matter – that Larkin wanted to see: the Leader of the local Swarm contingent. The flanking soldiers were grim enough, but the man with the long wicked scar on his face was grimmer still. The detective shuddered again.

The Leader stood over him, regarding him with feral eyes for a long moment. Larkin maintained eye contact for no other reason than he had nothing to lose by doing so. Abruptly, the Leader broke out in a wicked grin, showing yellow teeth and twisting his scar into a grotesque shape.

"So, Tellurian," he said in the same harsh and gravelly voice Mr. Jones had used, "we have you at last."

Time for some false bravado, George old sock. Perhaps I can provoke him into revealing some useful intel – not that I might not be able to use it.

"Temporarily, I can assure you. Your agent – whom we called 'Mr. Jones,' which is an insult on our world – thought he had me too. But, he didn't have me long. I escaped and, in the end, destroyed him."

"Brag all you want, Tellurian [*untranslatable*]. It will not save you this time. Soon you will tell me everything you know about your puny little resistance force."

"Ha! All you need to know is that we will kill you." He eyed the other two soldiers and sneered. "*All* of you."

"We shall see who kills who, Tellurian. Now, will you volunteer the information we seek? If you do, your death will be quick and painless. Or must we resort to…more persuasive methods?"

"Do your worst, monster. It won't do you any good."

"Very well. My subordinates here are experts in 'persuasion.' They will –"

The Leader was interrupted by the opening of the panel again. Another soldier stepped inside, approached his superior, and spoke to him in a low voice. The Leader scowled in response. He then spoke to his "expert persuaders," and the pair stationed themselves near the entrance to the room.

"You have gained a brief respite, Tellurian. I have an urgent matter to attend to. Use the time to re-evaluate your attitude."

The Swarm officer left, and Larkin speculated on what the "urgent matter" was. Whatever it was, it seemed like a set-back to the Swarm's plans. It also provided him with the opportunity to effect his escape. He relaxed, closed his eyes, and opened his mind.

*Kenny. Paddy.

*We're here, old darling. What in the world…

*…have you gotten yourself into? We've just…

*…received a report from Lacey who has been…

*...monitoring the Swarm base almost non-stop. And...

*...she's described what has happened there in more...

*...detail than she or we have cared to have. The poor dear...

*...is beside herself with horror. And we had to calm her...

*...down with one of our unpatented 'mental sedatives.'

*She should be thankful she didn't have a 'ringside seat.' It was bloody awful, to say the least.

*Lacey said the station wagon was wrecked and...

*...and that you might be injured. She couldn't...

*...take any more and broke off. So, where are...

*...you now? We haven't got a fix on you.

*You don't? That's odd. I thought you could track anyone you wanted to. The Swarm captured me, and I'm tied up somewhere.

*We can track anyone anywhere on the planet. Good...

*...God! George, you're not on the planet at all! You're...

*...*off-planet*. You must be inside the Swarm space-...

*...ship. You're right, old darling. This *is* bloody awful!

*That's not the half of it. They intend to torture me in an effort to make me tell them what I know about the 'resistance movement.'

"What do you want us to do? [Kenny asked].

*Well, first of all, you have to locate me. Widen your search pattern until you find me.

Silence ensued. Ages passed. Larkin fought to remain calm – not an easy task because the Swarm officer could return at any minute and interrupt his "conversation." Then:

*George! We've located you. You're in orbit around...

*...the Earth, approximately fifty kilometers away.

*That makes sense. Isolation is a form of psychological torture. All right. Contact Sheena and bring her up to speed. Have her contact either Monk or Ted and get one of them to pick you and her up and take you to DEDEP. The PDF will have to force the ship to land however they can. Once the Swarm is on the ground, they can make a frontal assault. I'll -- Uh, oh! Company's coming. Talk at you later – I hope!

The Swarm Leader entered the room, strode over to Larkin, and regarded him with a vicious gleam in his eyes. The detective took a deep breath and initiated a yoga technique he had learned while working on kidnap cases at the Chicago Police Department. The technique was supposed to insure one against pain, but he had never had the occasion to put it into practice – until now.

"Well, Tellurian, are you going to co-operate?"

"I need more time to think it over."

"You have had all the time you deserve."

The Leader motioned to his subordinates to step forward. As one, both of them withdrew a long, slender white rod from their tunics and pressed one tip of it; the opposite tip glowed red. Larkin braced himself. One of the soldiers placed his rod against the detective's left "leg," while the other did the same to his right "arm." Larkin felt the circuitry in both "limbs" being disrupted and then the loss of sensation in both. His fear turned to surprise over the Swarm's choice of body parts to affect. He smiled, eliciting a deep frown from the Leader.

"Um," the detective remarked casually, "that tickles."

The Leader barked a command, and the soldiers made an adjustment on their devices. They re-administered both "limbs." Since the circuitry had shut down, Larkin felt nothing.

"That feels good," he rejoined. "Keep it up!"

The Leader gave another command, and the soldiers adjusted their rods to what appeared to be the maximum setting. The detective chuckled.

"If I had known you were going to 'torture' me by tickling me to death, I'd've volunteered right away."

The Leader uttered something short and vicious sounding. Then he stepped forward and grabbed Larkin's "arm." As soon as he felt the artificiality of it, his eyes widened in shock. Quickly, he pushed back the sleeves of coat and shirt to expose the steel rods which had long ago replaced flesh and blood.

"By the Swarm!" he roared. "You are a cyborg!"

"I could have told you that, but you decided to be difficult about it."

"This changes everything, Tellurian. I will not use this form of torture any more. I will have to transport you to our main base for the proper tools."

"And how long will that take?"

"Longer than I care for. You have only delayed the inevitable."

The Leader turned, signaled to his subordinates, and left the room. The detective heaved a sigh of relief. That had been a near thing – too near for his tastes. It wasn't often he appreciated having artificial limbs, but this had been one time that he had. How much of a respite he had before the Swarm discovered that he wasn't a "cyborg" after all and took revenge for the deceit by choosing more vulnerable body parts was indeterminate, but he intended not to waste a minute of it. He relaxed once again.

*Kenny, Paddy.

*Yes, George. Are you all right? Did they…

*…hurt you badly? We were worried.

Quickly, he related his "torture" experience which set both of the Twins to laughing -- which gave him a headache.

*One supposes that you *are* a 'cyborg,' old darling. It…

*…could have been worse, however. You could have…

*…been labeled a 'robot,' a mere machine one could…

*…turn off and on whenever one wanted to.

*The Swarm intends to turn me 'off' one way or another. Which makes it all the more imperative that we get the PDF moving. Fortunately, we have a bit more time.

*We did brief Sheena while you were 'away,' and…

*…she's crying her eyes out over your situation. Her…

*…feelings for you run deep, old darling, and, if we…

*…come out of this business with whole skins, you…

*…really ought to reciprocate. Take it from those…

*…who care about both of you from time to time.

*I will – *if* we come out of this with whole skins. In the meantime, assemble the PDF. Can your abilities work with alien minds?

*We've had limited success [Kenny answered].

*Good. See if you can influence the Swarm to return to Earth, where we'll welcome them with open arms. [He laughed now]. Artificial or otherwise.

The Twins' laughter echoed in his head.

CHAPTER TWENTY-THREE

RESCUED!

As I HAVE *demonstrated in chapter four concerning "ghosts" and "hauntings," radio energy generated by the human brain can be imprinted upon an individual's environment, either in visual or audio mode. If the individual is a strong radiator or has died a violent death, (s)he can make an imprint indirectly upon whatever material is at hand. These imprints can then be seen/heard by those who are sensitive to the frequency at which the imprint was "recorded"....*

....What Lethbridge did not discover (either by neglect or by unawareness) was that there is another method by which radio energy can be imprinted, and this through direct means. I refer to the physical handling of objects and the subsequent transfer of radio energy to the objects touched. It goes without saying that the more times an individual touches a given object, the stronger the imprint becomes. Thus, a ring or an article of clothing can be "read" and a great deal of information about the owner learned. This ability to glean the information has been called "psychometry," but I choose to call it "psycho-visualization."

...I have discovered that psycho-visualizers are a rare breed for the simple reason that one must sift through a myriad of energy frequencies in order to obtain a true picture of the individual (s)he desires to "read." It may seem strange to think that, in the case of personal items, there should

be a difficulty. After all, how many persons would come into contact with someone's personal possessions? But, it does happen more often than one might think. Therefore, a true psycho-visualizer must be trained, either by him/herself or by a knowledgeable outsider, to sort through the hodge-podge and pinpoint the desired frequency.

…Psycho-visualization serves two purposes. The first is identification of a distinct individual….

…The second is more important because it involves a person's memory. *As I have discussed in the previous chapter on "re-incarnation," absorption of radio energy by the indirect method provides a profile of a person's life experiences (whereby the untrained sensitive mistakenly believes (s)he has lived a "past life"). This same process applies also to psycho-visualization. By this means, one can extract a sort of "biography" that cannot be edited or misconstrued….*

* * *

Joyce set aside Dr. Razumov's book wearily, not because learning about psycho-visualization was uninteresting or incomprehensible (even though it was because that was her view of the entire subject of radiopsychology in the first place). She did have an interest in this particular *psi*-talent since her son's "partner-in-crime" had that ability, and anything that concerned her son brought out the maternal instinct in her, even though she was not entirely free to exercise it.

She had to put the book aside because she couldn't concentrate. Too much was on her mind, not the least of which was Stan's going off with Eve and Freddie for hours at a time and because he and Eve whispered to each other like co-conspirators in some illegal business. She would have given anything to know what those two were up to. On second thought, maybe she wouldn't, given the nature of the current environment in which she labored. Still…

Then there was the matter of this "paranormal defensive force" that Stan had so eagerly volunteered to join – along with Eve – in the belief that their combined abilities to conjure up that mysterious (and sinister?) gestalt was needed to combat the aliens invading Earth.

Fighting the Swarm who had highly advanced weaponry was dangerous business, and a child ought not to be involved in it. That child should be getting an education and playing games with his peers, not hobnobbing with adults and saving the world. She was helpless in the face of this situation, especially when the leadership of DEDEP was encouraging everyone to volunteer for the PDF.

What was a mother to do?

Joyce had one consolation: she had someone with whom to commiserate. Jean Fulton, the newest member of DEDEP, was just as confused as she was by the strange circumstances in which she found herself. The younger woman had turned to her for advice, believing her to be an "old hand" here; their daily conversations were full of Jean's questions about how Joyce had gotten involved with DEDEP, what she thought about the facility, the staff, and the residents in it, and – most importantly – how to keep from "going nutso" by the fast pace of recent events – not to mention the events themselves. The older woman had tried to answer the questions as best she could; but, more often than not, she had floundered and told Jean that they were in the same boat and had to cope with their predicament together.

She was on firmer ground when the conversation turned to their personal interests. She and Jean discovered that they had several things in common, not the least of which was their abiding admiration of George Larkin. Joyce considered him to be thoughtful and compassionate, whereas Jean simply said he was a "hunk" she'd like to cuddle up with (and both of them giggled over that wishful thinking). Jean wondered aloud if he was "available," and Joyce had no answer for that but floated the idea that he and Sheena might have more than a professional relationship – or not. There was nothing to indicate one way or another. Of course, being cooped up in a hole in the ground limited one's observations of much of anything.

Joyce sighed and gazed at the Doctor's book. She ought to pick it up and start reading it again, but she was worried about Stan. At the moment, he was with rest of the PDF. The Director had called an emergency meeting of it, and the little imp had dashed out the door before she could stop him. Something was up, something not very pleasant (but what wasn't these days?), and Stan was rushing headlong into it.

What was a mother to do?

She wished Jean was here, so that they could commiserate some more.

* * *

Rarely did Sheena appreciate having to wear "blind person's" glasses – it was all part of a ruse to cover up the fact that she could "see" better than most sighted persons – but this was one of those times. The glasses covered the rims of her eye sockets which were bright red from excessive crying. She had started crying the moment Paddy informed her of Larkin's capture by the Swarm, and she hadn't stopped all the way out to DEDEP. Only when she entered the facility's conference room #1 did she make an attempt to calm herself and present a picture of cool detachment to the rest of the PDF. It wasn't easy to do.

She wanted to die the minute Paddy broke the news. She could scarcely believe that her darling George was in the hands of those – those *monsters* after all he and she had been through. She would rather have believed that he had escaped the Swarm's clutches and that, any minute now, he would be walking into the office with the grim look on his face which meant that he was hatching yet another of his awesome schemes to even the score.

You have got to get real, girl, she had berated herself. *He's gone missing and expecting you to come to his rescue.*

But what if it's too late? she had argued with herself. *What if he's already* – dead? *Oh, God! I can't live without him, even if he has a hard time telling me he loves me.*

Damn you, girl! she had cursed herself. *You tried to pressure him into revealing his true feelings, and he resented it. He didn't say so in so many words, but you could tell he did. Now, he may never get another chance, and you'll be alone for the rest of your life.*

She had replayed that little repartee over and over on the way to DEDEP, but it was time to stop feeling sorry for herself and come up with a plan to rescue George if it weren't too late. And if it were, she had to devise a method to avenge him and destroy those alien bastards!

Sheena studied the other members of the PDF with her psychometric abilities as they entered the conference room by ones and twos. The most common signals she was receiving were concern and apprehension. The Twins already were aware of the situation, and they remained impassive as was their habit. And Lacey and Billy Perkins had also learned what had happened on Ridgeway Avenue via their psycho-occulism; they radiated mostly concern. The others, not yet in the know, were apprehensive at this sudden calling of a meeting – further enhanced by their not seeing Larkin, whom they would have expected to make the call – with one exception. Freddie was upset at having been called away from whatever project he had been working on, and he wasn't bothering to disguise the fact.

What happened next surprised Sheena. A new signal was impacting her senses, and it was following Freddie's signal closely. It came from the new member of DEDEP, the "eel," Jean Fulton. Why was she here? She hadn't volunteered when George first formed the PDF, and neither of them had expected her to. Sheena supposed she would find out soon enough, but first she had to deliver the bad news.

"Thank you for coming on such short notice," she began tremulously. "*I* called this meeting, and not George, because of what has happened to George." A murmur of alarm rippled across the group. Sheena took a deep breath to remain calm. "George has been...captured by the Swarm. He's in their spaceship in orbit around the Earth."

The murmurs escalated into gasps of shock and cries of despair. Hands clutched other hands, and heads bowed in grief.

"George," she pushed on, "as Kenny and Paddy will attest, is still alive. He gave them a report on his condition and instructions on what we need to do to rescue him. It is now up to me, the deputy leader of the PDF, to follow his instructions."

"What's the plan, Sheena?" Lacey asked.

"We're to force that ship to land so that a ground assault by us can take place. I've given some thought to the *how*, and I think that a show of force in the form of our gestalt will do the job. Eve, Stan, can you accomplish that?"

"Yeah," the boy piped up. "We c'n use a tactic from one of my video games. It's called 'Aerial Attack' and takes place during World War I, where one pilot gets an enemy pilot to follow him and leads him into a trap. Eve 'n' me can get the Ent – uh, the gestalt to do the leading."

"Brilliant, Stan," his "partner" opined. "We'll lure the spaceship to some isolated place outside of the City and attack it far from prying eyes."

"Excellent," Sheena enthused. "Chris, are you there?"

"I am," the tinny voice issued from the PA system, "standing ready and able to do my part."

"Good. Your part will be to harass the Swarm after they've landed and keep them occupied until the rest of us show up."

Kenny cleared his throat for recognition and received it.

"George wanted to know if Paddy and I…"

"…could plant 'suggestions' in the mind…"

"…of the Swarm leader. We don't know if…"

"…we can, but we're willing to try."

"Thanks, guys. Now, the hard part is dealing with the Swarm once we've engaged them."

"I can use my psycho-kinesis," Stan offered. "I'll throw rocks at 'em!"

"And I can throw illusions at them, Ms. Whitley," Billy chipped in.

"*I* can 'throw' a lot more than rocks and illusions," Jean declared suddenly.

"I was going to ask you why you're here. You didn't volunteer when George first made the call."

"No, but I'm volunteering now. For one thing, I owe George for rescuing me from the Swarm. And for another, I owe those bastards for scaring the hell out of me. I've already burned one of them, and I'd like to burn a few more."

"I hope it doesn't come to that, but we'll accept your 'membership application.' Okay, people, let's get to work!"

* * *

From the diary of Christopher Wredling:

I've seen some marvelous sights in all the years I've psycho-projected. Whole cities, both by day and by night. From mountain tops looking into valleys below. The crowns of forests full of birds and small animals. A hurricane whipping across the ocean. A volcano belching lava. And so much more.

But looking down at the Earth from the edge of space is one sight I'll never forget. Not for nothing is our world called the "blue planet." (Actually, it's blue and white, but let's not be picky!) I could have stayed up there and gazed all day long at the panorama and at the various cloud formations (one of which was a thunderstorm over Europe); but I had a task to perform and, reluctantly I tore myself away from the sight-seeing.

I must qualify a preceding statement. I was not really on the edge of space, but a mile below it. Just as I cannot cross high-voltage lines and electromagnetic fields, so I am halted by the ionosphere. Think of the places I could go if that were not the case! The possibilities would be, well, infinite. *Ah, well.*

So, there I was, keeping an eye on the Swarm ship which was *on the edge of space. The game plan was that I would report on any movements of the ship and relay them to Kenny and Paddy; they in turn would relay the information to Stan, and he would then send the gestalt to harass the Swarm to the point where they would chase the sphere to where we would be waiting for it.*

This was the first 'mission' of the PDF. And who'd've thought it was to rescue our fearless leader?

George has always been careful not to over-extend himself in order to avoid putting himself in harm's way. Up until now, he had been successful. But then he had never come up against aliens from outer space. They were an unknown variable, and their behavior was not like human behavior and therefore could not be predicted. His first rude awakening was his capture by the late Mr. Jones, but some quick thinking on his part got him out of that jam.

If his plan of harassment didn't pan out, he might not survive the second encounter. He was counting heavily on us to carry the day. The ball was in our court, so to speak, and we had to play it with all the skill we possessed.

I was the 'lead-off man,' and so I projected up, up, and away and found the Swarm ship exactly where the Twins said it would be. I contacted Sheena and told her I was in position. Ten seconds later, I spotted the gestalt ascending toward the ship.

I have to give Stan a lot of credit. For a ten-year-old, he can be pretty innovative when it comes to using his psi-talent. Once the sphere reached the ship, it started bobbing up and down, then rocking back and forth. After that, it circled the ship several times and made physical contact with it once every orbit. Using the images planted in his mind by Kenny and Paddy, he could follow the progress of his directions to the sphere and create new patterns to annoy the Swarm.

And annoyed they were. Once, when the gestalt came around to 'face' the ship, it was fired upon. They missed, of course, because Stan kept it moving constantly. (Later, he told us that it was like playing one of his video games in which the 'hunted' tried to avoid the 'hunter.')

Once Stan had 'hooked' the 'fish,' he began to 'reel' it in. He moved the gestalt away from the ship, then toward it, and away from it again; and all the while, he made slow but steady descent. The Swarm followed it down, firing at will; once, it was nearly struck, but Stan reacted instantly and moved it out of danger at the last second. It was all I could do to keep up with these maneuvers and relay timely updates.

Down, down, down both sphere and ship went until finally the former was on the ground where the PDF was lying in wait. The Swarm were still firing randomly and would surely have hit it; but, at Kenny's sudden command, Stan and Eve broke contact, and it disappeared in an instant. The ship came to rest on the ground near the spot where the gestalt had been and remained there for several minutes. I called Sheena and asked if I could lure the soldiers outside. She OK'ed it, and I projected an image of my true form inside the ship. I was quite surprised that I could do so; it meant that the Swarm, in their over-confidence, had not thought to shield their ship electromagnetically as they had done their ground bases. That proved to be their undoing.

In retrospect, I always hesitate to project an image of my true form. In the first place, it's ugly and repulsive and gives the mobiles a false impression of me. In the second place, I feel shamed and embarrassed, even though I had no choice in its creation. And, in the third place, I prefer the images I can create.

But, I had a reason for doing what I did, distasteful as it was. And it worked.

* * *

Larkin had no need to look out a window (even if there had been one to look out of) to know the Swarm ship was moving erratically. He was being bounced around like the loose object he was; being bound and unable to brace himself, he was quite helpless. What was going on?

The answer to his unspoken question came when the Leader marched in with a fierce scowl on his face. At his command, the two guards seized him and yanked him roughly to his feet. The Leader pivoted and marched out again. The detective was half-pulled and half dragged in his wake. Captor and captive moved through a narrow corridor until they reached the bridge of the ship. Though the controls were totally unfamiliar to him, Larkin could easily deduce that he was in the heart of the ship; the pilot was doing his damnedest to keep an eye on a monitor and the other on his control panel and not go crazy in the effort.

The detective peered at the monitor and nearly laughed out loud. The gestalt was in plain sight – although the image bounced in all directions as the pilot fought to keep it on dead center – and Stan was making it perform like a whirling dervish. There was one other in this compartment, and he was firing one gout of flame after another in order to score a hit on the sphere and neutralize it. He was obviously shooting wildly, unable to pinpoint a rapidly moving target. Larkin allowed himself a smirk.

"What is that thing, Tellurian?" the Leader growled. "What purpose does it serve?"

"That's what your agent wanted to know – just before it killed him. It's a weapon – a *dangerous* weapon – and, if you persist in trying to destroy it, it will destroy you as easily as it did your agent."

"You underestimate the military prowess of the Swarm."

"Uh-uh. I know exactly what you're capable of – and what you're not. You're out of your league here, my friend. I suggest you withdraw before it's too late."

"Your forces would not sacrifice you for the sake of just one ship."

"I'm expendable. The defense of my world is all that matters. You've got the choice of withdrawing – or surrendering."

Larkin was bluffing, of course. The PDF would hardly down the ship while he was still aboard, but he had to convince the Leader that they would for the "greater good." He regarded the Swarm officer with feigned coolness and could almost see the mental gears turning. Several of the latter's facial muscles twitched in rapid succession.

"No!" the other declared, unnecessarily loudly. "The Swarm does not withdraw from a battle, nor do they surrender to an inferior force. We fight until the goal is achieved."

"Suit yourself. But, don't say you weren't warned."

The Swarm ship followed the gestalt toward the ground. Larkin saw that the landing site was a wide clearing in one quadrant of the forest preserve south of DEDEP. He assumed that the PDF was close by, hiding amongst the trees and waiting for the ship to land before effecting a rescue. On the monitor, the gestalt remained immobile. The Leader barked a command to his fire-control officer. The latter furiously worked at his targeting controls. The detective forced himself to relax.

*Disengage the gestalt! [he thought forcefully]. *Now!*

And, just as the fire-control officer pressed his firing button, the sphere popped out existence. The Leader uttered several harsh sentences. Larkin did not need to understand the language to know that the fellow was cursing a blue streak.

"Last chance, my friend. Surrender, or die."

"Never!"

What happened next surprised even Larkin and put the Swarm into a sheer panic.

When Christopher Wredling materialized inside the ship, the first individual to be aware of his presence was one of the detective's guards who was only half a meter away. The guard caught a movement out of the corner of his eye, turned, and spied the most horrendous sight he had ever seen – a rail-thin, small-bodied, naked creature with an enormous head, spindly arms and legs, and a cadaverous complexion. His eyes widened in abject fear, and he let out the most blood-curdling scream in all of Creation. In his haste to move away from the apparition, he lost his footing, dropped to the deck, and tried to push himself across it, all the while moaning and whimpering.

His terror caught the attention of the others. The soldiers reacted much like their comrade; the Leader showed fright but held his ground and instinctively drew his sidearm.

Larkin was surprised not so much by Chris' appearance – he was used to that – as by his projection of his true form. The detective was one of only three known persons cognizant of Chris' abnormal birth and life, but he was used to seeing a projection of a smiling blonde-haired young man dressed in casual attire. Still, he realized immediately what the psycho-projectionist had in mind: frightening the Swarm to the point of releasing their captive lest something dreadful happen to them.

And it seemed to be working.

"What – what," the Leader stammered, "is that...*thing*?"

"Him?" Larkin replied nonchalantly. "Oh, he's my pet. He missed me so much that he had to come aboard your ship."

"But – but, how did it get in?"

"He simply thinks about being in a place, and he's there. It's called 'teleportation.' That's not your main worry, however. He looks hungry and wants to feed."

"Feed? What does it eat?"

"Well, 'eat' is the wrong word. He absorbs energy to sustain himself, including the energy from your weapon. He particularly savors the life energies of living creatures. The older he grows, the more energy he requires. When he's through feeding, all that's left is a shriveled-up husk."

Deep down, Larkin was enjoying the impromptu scenario he had made up, even under the present circumstance, pulling the wool over the Swarm officer. His greatest effort was in keeping a straight face while spinning a fantastic tale; he really wanted to laugh at the Leader's confusion.

"I do not want it on my ship."

"You'll have to release me then. Buster – that's his name – won't leave without me."

The Leader regarded him balefully. He was caught between his duty as a soldier of the Swarm and his fear of the Unknown. Ordinarily, he would not have backed away from danger but met it head on. His kind had seen any number of life-forms during their marauding -- some fair to look at, some quite disgusting – but they had never seen the likes of what was standing before them at this moment. And it was hungry!

"Curse you, Tellurian! You seem to have gained the upper hand – for now. I shall release you, if only to save my men from a horrible fate. But, I promise you, we shall meet again."

"I await your pleasure," Larkin replied grandiosely.

He signaled to Chris, and the apparition disappeared. Instantly, the Leader barked a command; and the guards, now relieved of their fears, seized the detective and dragged him to the entry hatch. They opened it and shoved him out of the ship, and Larkin hit the ground like a sack of potatoes. As soon as he heard the whine of the ship's engines increase in intensity, he rolled a few meters away from it; he watched as it rose slowly out of the clearing and sighed in relief at being free again.

At once, he heard a clamor behind him, and he twisted around to observe the PDF rushing toward him, all smiles. He grinned in response. It was great to be wanted!

Sheena was in the forefront of the "welcoming" party. Without any sense of propriety or embarrassment, she knelt down, wrapped her arms around him, and pressed her body against his. The warmth and softness she provided provoked the feelings he had experienced before but had suppressed in order to avoid false hopes. How easy it would be to just let himself go and luxuriate in the moment! Someday, but not today.

"Oh, George," she whispered, "I wanted to die when I heard what happened to you – after all the things I said to you earlier. I'm so sorry."

"You don't need to apologize, Sheena. *I'm* the one who should do the apologizing for the things *I* said."

"Hey, you two!" Freddie chortled. "Not in front o' the children. Get a room!"

"We'll take that under advisement, chum. Now, will somebody please untie me?"

"George," Lacey spoke up, "the Swarm ship is getting away. Shouldn't we send the gestalt after it and destroy it while we've got the chance?"

"I'm not sure that's possible, Lacey. The gestalt has acted in self-defense one time. Whether it will go on the offense is an unknown. I wish we could communicate with it and find out if it will aid us against the Swarm."

Eve and Stan glanced at each other knowingly, but no one else caught the gesture.

"Besides," Larkin continued, "there were only five of them aboard. The rest must be at their base. I want to take all of them down at once and be done with them."

"We're in complete accord, old darling. So what's…"

"…our next move, according to the 'Larkin Agenda'?"

"*My* next move is to get some rest. Being a prisoner tends to take a lot out of one, don't you know?"

* * *

Come fly/run with me, the Entity whispers to him/her.

"You're back!" (s)he exclaim(s). "I'm/we're glad."

I am gratified and pleased to meet with you again.

"Have you considered my/our request for assistance against the creatures who are attacking me/us? (Female)

I have consulted with my cohorts. They are debating the question.

"It's kinda urgent, mister. They've got real nasty weapons now." (Male)

I shall relay this information to my cohorts. Now, I wish to make you a proposal.

"Yes?" [(S)he in unison]

I should like you to become members of my organization which we call the 'Communion.'

"What's that?" (Female)

It is a group of entities like myself who monitor the multi-verse and prevent instability wherever it arises. Each of us is responsible for a universe. I am responsible for this one.

"How long have you been doin' it?" (Male)

We have been here since the Beginning of All Things.

"How is that possible?" (Female)

It is difficult to explain to a young species such as yours is. You must accept what I tell you as the truth. First, you must join the Communion on a provisional basis. In time, once you have been trained in its protocols, you will understand.

"What kinda training?" (Male)

The training involves the purposes and the methods by which we operate. At the end of the training, we will test you to learn if you are worthy of permanent membership. If you pass the test, we will welcome you as equals, give you your assignments, and show you how to access all the universes that are.

"Assignments? What sort of assignments?" (Female)

Mostly monitoring, as I do.

"Will we look like you?" (Male)

When you are accepted into the Communion, yes, you will be... transformed. *That is the only way you will be able to move about the multi-verse.*

"Will we ever see our home again?" (Female)

Only during your training period. The training comes in stages, each one more intense than the previous one. We allow you a rest period between stages, and you may do whatever you like.

"Will us two see each other again? We're kinda like a team." (Male)

Only during convocations of the Communion. The nature of our duties preclude any fraternizing.

"Why me/us?" [(S)he in unison]

You are unique in this universe. You were able to summon me from the VOID, an exceptional talent.

[Silence in the VOID for a second/eon. Then:]

"Do you have a name?" (Male)

A 'name'? Please elaborate.

"A name is what I/we call each other to identify me/us." (Female)

Ah, a designation to distinguish one being from another.

"Yeah. Like I'm Stan, and she's Eve. Those are our names." (Male)

I have no 'name' that you would understand. I am simply referred to as '121.1.'

"Why that?" (Female)

That is the frequency by which your universe vibrates. Since I am the monitor of this universe, I have been given this designation.

"Will we have such…'designations' if we join the Communion?" (Male)

Yes. It is part of the acceptance. Now, are you ready to fly/run with me?

"Yes, I/we are." [(S)he in unison]

Then open your minds.

* * *

The VOID.

Emptiness.

Darkness.

Solitude.

Silence.

Infinite sameness stretching across and through infinite numbers of dimensions of EXISTENCE.

An eternal sameness which transcends TIME itself.

Without boundaries, it simply is.

Nothing has disturbed the VOID for uncounted [time periods].

Until now.

Three images appear. One image represents an adult female humanoid. Another represents a juvenile male humanoid. The last is not humanoid at all; it is a large, glowing white sphere.

The humanoid images regard the non-humanoid image with awe and wonder – and with reverence. How the non-humanoid image regards the humanoid images is open to speculation and, in point of fact, is irrelevant.

"As before, children, you may have two choices each."

* * *

A multitude of colors – all the colors of the rainbow and all their shadings.

Swirling and twisting and looping and criss-crossing each other in no discernable pattern.

Dimming and brightening and fading out and fading in in no discernable pattern.

It is a hodge-podge, a riot, a melee, a kaleidoscope – chaos in technicolor.

The viewers are awed/astonished/amazed/astounded/bedazzled/ dazed/ overwhelmed/stunned/stupefied beyond belief.

(S)he stand(s) in the exact center of this multi-hued display, craning her/his neck this way, then that way, in a futile effort to take it all in at once. The light show envelopes her/him in a sphere, and (s)he cannot see in all directions at once. At length, (s)he give(s) up the effort and concentrate(s) on one section or another of the display.

Blink! *The display vanishes and is replaced by:*

A mass of cold air drifts southward across the land. A mass of warm air rises slowly to meet it.

The cold air struggles to descend to the ground. The warm air struggles to rise higher. Equal but opposite pressures cause movement in a rotary fashion.

Rotary movement increases as the opposing pressures increase. A dark funnel of air is created, spinning rapidly, and it begins to move laterally across the landscape in an effort to alleviate the unbearable pressures.

The funnel twists this way and that way, following no particular pathway. The force of its movement creates a vacuum at the points where it touches ground. All loose objects – animate and inanimate – in its path are swept up and thrown in all directions.

The funnel carves out a huge swath of destruction until the pressures have been alleviated. The landscape below lies in ruins, and many lives are lost.

Blink! *The display vanishes and is replaced by:*

The star, once a medium-sized, yellow sun in the main sequence, has come to the end of its life. It has exhausted all of its hydrogen fuel and is slowly but steadily morphing into a red giant. It expands and floods nearby space with the last of its stellar energy.

This energy is still hot enough to burn everything in its neighborhood to a crisp. The star possesses a number of planets and moons orbiting about it. Two of the planets, plus their moons, are in imminent danger. The star's energy embraces the innermost planet, and that world is quickly reduced to a cinder. The next planet suffers the same fate.

Had either of those worlds been inhabited by sentient beings? If so, were they able to escape the holocaust in time? What became of them? Do they wander still, seeking out a new home?

Once all of the energy has been expended, the star collapses in upon itself. It is now a white dwarf until the end of the Universe.

Blink! *The display vanishes and is replaced by:*

A seed is planted. It has been picked up off the ground by a hungry bird and swallowed along with other seeds. The bird fails to digest the seed and so excretes it in a place far from its original location.

The seed lies on the ground and waits patiently until wind and water create a pocket in the soil for it to nestle in.

The soil contains nutrients which are absorbed by the seed. The nutrients react to the chemical compounds within the seed's core, producing germination.

The seed sprouts and sends out tentative roots which anchor it and enable it to grow larger. A stem pushes up through the soil to receive sunlight. Through photosynthesis, a bud is formed at the top of the stem.

The bud opens up to expose a brightly-colored centerpiece surrounded by long, narrow petals.

The seed has become a flower.

Blink! *The display vanishes and is replaced by:*

Far off in space, a nebula gathers in a huge quantity of dust and hydrogen gas. The dust and hydrogen gas are all which remains of exploded stars, sending its constituent parts in all directions.

The nebula is called by astronomers a 'stellar nursery,' for here is where the remnants of dead stars will coalesce and form new stars.

The dust and hydrogen gas through the force of gravitational attraction form a coherent mass. The size of the new stars, their chemical make-up, and the amount of thermal energy generated depend upon the amount of dust and hydrogen gas available.

In the fullness of time, the mass reaches its optimum size, and internal friction produces sufficient heat to ignite the hydrogen gas. The star burns brightly, although it may burn more or less brightly than other stars which have 'hatched' in this 'nursery.'

If the circumstances are right, the new star will leave the 'nest' and drift off into space to join a galaxy or a globular cluster. If not, it will remain in the nebula and assist in attracting yet more dust and hydrogen gas.

Blink! The display vanishes and is replaced by:

A multitude of colors – all the colors of the rainbow and all of their shadings.

Swirling and twisting and looping and criss-crossing each other in no discernible pattern.

Dimming and brightening and fading out and fading in in no discernible pattern.

It is a hodge-podge, a riot, a melee, a kaleidoscope – chaos in technicolor.

The viewers are awed/astonished/amazed/astounded/bedazzled/dazed/ overwhelmed/ stunned/stupefied beyond belief.

* * *

"Amazing!" (Female)

"Cool!" (Male)

That is one more sampling of what lies before you once you join the Communion.

"We'll have to think long and hard about joining." (Female)

"Yeah. We'd be leavin' a lot o' friends behind." (Male)

I understand. Take as much time as you need. There is no hurry. The Communion has existed for countless eons. It can wait a few more.

"Don't forget our request – 121.1." (Female)

"It's real important." (Male)

I will not forget – Eve and Stan. Now, I will return you to your own plane of existence.

* * *

Eve and Stan left their respective rooms and met in what had become their secret hiding space – the sub-basement beneath the utility level. They regarded each other silently for a long while, attempting to fathom each other's mind. Finally:

"What do you think, Stan? Should we join this Communion or not?"

"Jeez, I dunno. We'd go on a lot of adventures and see things nobody else has ever seen. And maybe we'd meet some other people like us. But..."

"But, we'd have to give up what we have here – forever – especially you."

"Whattaya mean?"

"You're young. You've got your mother. She'd miss you. My family disowned me long ago because of my power. I have no one who will miss me."

"How about the rest of DEDEP? *They'd* miss you."

"Perhaps. Like 121.1 said, we ought to take our time before we make any decisions. Besides, the Swarm is still out there, and the PDF needs us."

"Uh-huh. OK, that's the plan."

* * *

Larkin had just settled down on the sofa in the farmhouse's living room and gotten comfortable when the alien communication device sounded. He activated it with much reluctance as he really wanted to take a nap before the evening meal "downstairs."

"Hello, Mr. Smith."

"Hhhello...Mr....Largin. I...am...ready...to...transfer."

"I had thought I could just drive over and pick you up. It would've been a lot easier. Unfortunately, my vehicle is...out of service at the moment."

He had debated whether or not to tell his client what really happened to the station wagon. But that would have included the Swarm attack, his capture, and the subsequent rescue by the PDF. Since he wanted to keep the PDF out of the discussion, he couldn't talk about prior incidents until he had thought of a plausible lie to fill in the gaps. Sometimes, webs of deceit could be altogether entangling. He was already up to his nose in webbing with keeping the Disciples on the hook; he didn't need another web just now.

"It…would…hhhave…done…you…no…good. I…am…not…in… my base…at…thhhe…moment."

"You aren't? Where are you then?"

"I…am…at…anothhher…of…thhhe…Goalition's…listening… posts …gonferring…withhh…Frommar."

"And with your equipment here, you have to use someone else's."

"Egsactly. As…I…said…I…am…ready…to…transfer."

"All right. The locator beacon is still in the barn. I'll head over there and switch it on."

"Thhhang…you…Mr…Largin."

So much for the nap, George old sock

Moments later, he was in the barn surrounded by Mr. Smith's array. The first thing he did was to check DEDEP's emergency entrance/exit for any sign of activity near it. He heard or saw nothing. The residents were probably preparing to go to the dining room. Lucky them! They hadn't had to have not eaten since breakfast and so were not having their stomachs growling in protest.

He placed the locator beacon in the exact center of the array and activated it. Five seconds later, the crackle and sight of static electricity which indicated an incoming transmission filled the barn and was replaced by the brilliant white light. Larkin immediately turned away. When the light faded, he turned back and saw the pasty-faced alien standing there looking quite relieved at having endured the bizarre transference. At his feet was a trunk-like object, made of a shiny brass-colored metal, half a meter on all sides.

"Welcome to my farm, Mr. Smith, your new home until the Swarm are defeated."

"Thhhang…you…Mr….Largin.   I…will…not…to…be…a… burden…on…you."

"You won't be – although my…farm workers might be alarmed by your appearance at first."

"I…understand. I…trust…thhhey…will…not…disturb…my…my…eguipment."

"I've already cautioned them about it. They'll keep their trips to a bare minimum."

"Egcellent."

"You'll be staying at the house when you're not working with your array. Did you bring your personal belongings?"

The alien gestured at the trunk-like object.

"Thhhis…is…all…I…hhhave. I…am…'traveling…light'…as…you …Tellurians…say."

"Hmmm. I see you're picking up local slang nicely. There are two other persons living in the house, my…co-managers. They will see to your needs while you're here. Um, what about meals? I don't know if you can handle human food."

"I…hhhave…a…supply…of…nutritional…wafers…in…thhhis…gontainer. I…reguisitioned…thhhem…from…my…golleague…in …Brasilia."

"Wafers? That's all you eat?"

"Whhhen…we…are…in…thhhe…field…on…distant…worlds…thhhe …Goalition…supplies…us…withhh…a…gombination…of…nutrients… suited…to…our…indivishual…metabolisms."

"Don't you miss your native foods?"

"Of…gourse. Whhhen…our…tours…of…duty…are…gompleted… we…are…permitted…to…return…to…a…world… whhhish…serves… our…native…food. We…live…thhhere…until…we…are…galled…bag …to…duty…again."

"Just like being in the military, eh?"

"We…*are*…an…army…Mr….Largin…an…army…of…venshful… beings…whhho…seeg…one…gommon…goal…to…rid…thhhis… galagsy…of…thhhe…Swarm."

Mr. Smith's tone of voice took on a measure of stridency when he uttered that last remark, and it caught the detective by surprise. Until now, the alien had spoken softly and politely, and he had never shown any propensity for harshness. The change in attitude puzzled Larkin briefly but then he remembered Mr. Smith's past; the loss of his family and the destruction of his planet was something he could not suppress every minute of every day. Like a pressure cooker, he had to release the pent-up energy inside, even if it were only through a few harsh words.

"Um, I'll take you to your room now, if you like."

"Thhhang…you…Mr.…Largin…but…first…I…must…inspegt…my … eguipment… to…see…if…it…withhhstood…thhhe…transfer."

Mr. Smith shuffled over to the control console and began pressing key pads. The detective whipped out his cell phone and called the house.

"Monk here. What's up, Georgie?"

"I've got our alien friend here in the barn. I want you or Ted to prepare the guest room for him. I told him he should stay there when he wasn't working with his array. Either of you should watch him when he's out of the house. We can't have him wandering about and poking his nose here and there."

"Gotcha. Is everything in place there?"

"It is. You'd like to take a gander at it, wouldn't you?"

"You bet your last dollar I would."

"OK, but do it on the sly. I don't want to upset our friend any more than I have to."

"Oakie-doakie, Georgie."

Larkin waited patiently – or as patiently as he could, while his stomach continued to growl – while the Coalition agent made his rounds and examined every piece minutely. When he had finished, he picked up his "luggage" and regarded the detective expectantly. The latter led the way to the farmhouse, walking slowly so that his "guest" could keep up.

When they entered the house, they encountered the horse-faced Ted, who had just finished filing the monthly report to the Department of Energy in Washington, D.C., his nominal employer. The detective introduced him to the alien and identified Ted as the farm's live-in "co-manager." He told Ted what the house rules were regarding Mr. Smith's presence here, and the DOE man assured him he'd take good care of the guest. Just then, Monk appeared with a shocked look on his face. Larkin also introduced him to the alien as the other "co-manager."

"I'll take…Mr. Smith upstairs, George," Ted said.

"Thanks, Ted. Good night, Mr. Smith."

"Good…night…Mr.….Largin."

When the pair had left, the detective peered at Monk, who still wore the expression of shock.

"What's the matter, Monk?"

"I just saw on the local TV station that the police are looking for you."

"What for?"

"You're wanted for questioning about what they're calling a 'war zone' on Ridgeway Avenue."

CHAPTER TWENTY-FOUR

BREATHING SPACE

LARKIN AWOKE THE next morning feeling surprisingly refreshed, despite the fact that he had been relegated to sleeping on a sofa and that he had spent some time mulling over what he ought to do about the police search for him. Obviously, he had to make a public appearance sometime; he had a business to run if for no other reason. But, explaining why his station wagon was at the scene of a horrific battle between the Disciples and the Swarm was going to be a hard row to hoe. What could he possibly say to avoid being labeled as a madman?

Well, you see, officer, it's like this. Some Disciples and I discovered this hide-out for aliens from outer space who were planning to conquer Planet Earth. We attacked them because they weren't good Christians and had to be led to the Light of Purity by any means possible. But they countered with their spaceship that spat out balls of fire and destroyed all of the Disciples. And, before I could escape, the bug-eyed monsters captured me, put me in their spaceship, and tortured me. They would have killed me, except some friends of mine who have super-powers came to my rescue. They hid me out until the aliens left.

What wasn't there to believe?

He wasn't about to tell *that* story to just anyone. He had to tell it to someone who wouldn't consider him a lunatic out of hand. And there was only one person who fit that bill: Deputy Mayor Joaquim Torres. Jack already knew there were extraterrestrials on Earth and in the City. He'd listen to the story before making a judgment. Not the *whole* story, of course – the detective had to omit the part that DEDEP had played and come up with a different version of his escape. He hated to lie to his friend, but he was obliged to maintain the integrity of his other friends.

First, breakfast. He was famished, having gone twenty-four hours without a bite to eat. There was nothing like being captured and tortured to whet one's appetite!

When he entered the barn, a new problem surfaced and had to be resolved before too much time passed. Living in a hole in the ground had its advantages and its disadvantages. Chief among the former was the safety of the dwellers in the hole; another was the possibility of ambushing any snoopers in the area. Among the latter was the unhealthiness of living in a hole. The human organism required sunlight, fresh air, and exercise for optimum health; the last could be obtained with a make-shift gymnasium, but the first two could not. Artificial sunlight and recycled air could never replace the real thing, as Dr. Razumov had pointed out at the founding of the facility.

To this end, the Director had worked up a schedule whereby the residents could get out of their hole and walk around the farmyard for an hour each day. It was especially crucial to allow the children to return to the surface and run and jump and roll around – as all children were wont to do – not only to preserve their health but also to relieve the tensions and frustrations as a result of their artificial environment. And the adults could benefit as well.

This schedule had now been thrown into a cocked hat with the introduction of a stranger in their midst. While Mr. Smith was not entirely free to come and go as he pleased, there was always the danger of his being at work with his electronic array at the same time as residents were emerging from "downstairs" for their scheduled walk. The sight of a group of humans coming seemingly from nowhere was bound to raise suspicions in the alien's mind and to his asking for an explanation.

Larkin was not prepared to provide him with an explanation – not yet, anyway, if at all – because, in the war against the Swarm, DEDEP was Earth's ace-in-the-hole (all puns aside!).

The detective thus had to confer with the Doctor, and the two of them had to re-work the schedule of both the residents and the "guest" so that their paths would never cross. Quite possibly, a look-out might have to be posted at the emergency entrance/exit to monitor Mr. Smith's comings and goings – a difficult and possibly an unpleasant task, but Larkin could see no other way around the problem at the moment.

At this point in time, however, the barn was devoid of any living beings. So much the better – he could disappear "downstairs" without raising any suspicions. Returning to the surface might pose a problem, but he'd cross that bridge when he came to it.

He did not expect the reception he got when he entered the dining room and, to his dying day, he remembered it with a profound sense of gratitude and not a little self-satisfaction. All of the adults in DEDEP were there; and, to a man and woman, they stood and applauded him. The children were there also; the older ones who were in the know concerning recent events joined in the accolades. All then gathered about him and, one by one, hugged him or shook his hand or slapped him on the back and wished him well. Even the disputatious Henry Rawlins solemnly offered his hand. Though he was extremely embarrassed by this outpouring of good cheer, he gracefully acknowledged it and thanked each person in his/her turn.

As soon as the individual well-wishing had concluded, the Twins conducted a round of "For he's a jolly good fellow," singing in the same manner as they always spoke. He thought that was a bit over the top, but he accepted it with aplomb.

Lastly, the Director stepped forward and pressed his cheeks against Larkin's after the Russian fashion. The detective looked at him with suspicion.

"Did you plan this, Emil?" he accused.

"*Nyet!* Why would I do such a thing? DEDEP loves you, George, and is pleased to see you safe and sound. This was entirely a spontaneous reaction."

"Yeah, right." To the assembled crowd, he said: "Well, spontaneous or not, I'm happy to be back in the world – literally – amongst good friends."

That prompted another round of applause and a fresh rendition of "For he's a jolly good fellow." At this time, his stomach sent him another reminder, and he excused himself to the serving line. He took a little of everything on the breakfast menu and found a seat. Instantly, all of the PDF (minus Chris) sat down beside him. While he ate, he asked each one to give him his/her view of the PDF's first "mission"; when they had done so, he thanked Sheena for taking charge and welcomed Jean into their ranks.

"I wasn't sure the plan would work," Sheena responded demurely, "but I followed your lead. I – we were so worried that we might lose you."

"I couldn't have done it better myself. You deserve as much praise as I do." He paused to switch mental gears. "We have a new problem to solve before we move against the Swarm again." He outlined the dilemma Mr. Smith's presence presented and reiterated a possible solution. "What do you think?"

"I mebbe got an answer to that, Georgie," Freddie piped up. "Now that I got me a helper" – he patted Jean's hand – "we been workin' on fixin' the elevator. Jeanie's handlin' the wiring –"

"It's like a plate of spaghetti in there," she interrupted, "and I had to spend a whole hour tracing every single wire."

"Yeah," the dwarf continued, unperturbed by the interruption, "and I dug up an old welding torch. Been freein' up the elevator doors whenever I had a coupla minutes to spare. Another day or so, we might have the damned thing runnin' again."

"Great!" Larkin enthused. "That certainly would solve a lot of problems. Where is the elevator located above ground?"

"The one place on a farm that can accommodate an elevator – the silo. When the Feds took over the property, they cleaned out the silo, excavated the ground beneath it, and installed the elevator shaft. Nobody in the world woulda suspected it was the entrance to an underground facility. Monk found the drawings in an old filing cabinet and gave 'em to me. I took it from there."

"OK. Keep at it. Now I have a personal problem to resolve – as soon as I finish stuffing myself."

He related Monk's message to him the day before. Worried looks passed back and forth across the table, especially from Sheena, who laid a hand on his shoulder and did not concern herself with how the others felt about the gesture.

"You'll weather it, old darling, as you…"

"…usually do. We've great confidence."

"Thanks, guys. How this will turn out is anybody's guess, but I'm glad I have your backs. It gives me the strength I need to carry on."

After he had stuffed himself, Larkin made his way to the Doctor's office. He rapped on the door and eased himself in. The old man was holding a sheet of paper in his hand, but he appeared to be in a daze. The detective approached his desk quietly. The Russian took cognizance of him and broke out in a rare smile.

"George, *moy drug*, you are just in time to hear some interesting developments."

"Somehow I get the idea you're being sarcastic, Emil."

"*Konyechno*. You will never guess what arrived in the mail for me personally." He held up the sheet of paper. "The American Psychological Association wants to re-instate my membership."

"No kidding?"

"No kidding. A quaint American expression, that. There has been a change in the administration of the organization, and the new one believes that my dismissal was too hasty an action. This letter was signed personally by the new president of the APA (he was the senior vice-president at the time of my dismissal), and he apologizes for the whole affair."

"Are you going to accept?"

"I have not made a decision yet. I would first like to know if the attitude toward radiopsychology has changed."

"Good luck."

"*Spaceebo*. Now, what can I do for you?" Larkin informed him of the search by the City's police department. "Hmmm. This sounds very serious, George. In my country, we always reacted to such searches with extreme dread, as you might imagine. It is fortunate that Americans have a history of freedom to protect them – notwithstanding the possibility that your freedom is rapidly falling victim to the Disciples. What do you plan to do?"

"I'm going to call my friend, the Vice Mayor, and explain what happened to him. He's the only one in City Hall I can trust to keep the wolves at bay."

"An interesting analogy. Now, it is *my* turn to wish *you* good luck."

The detective returned to the farmhouse and dialed Jack Torres' private number. The phone rang several times before it was answered.

"Hello?" a cautious voice said.

"Jack, it's George."

"George! My God! Are you all right? Where are you?"

"I'm all right, and I'm with friends."

"I was worried stiff when the Chief of Police reported what had happened on Ridgeway and that the investigating officers had found your station wagon wrapped around a tree. What *did* happen?"

Larkin told him almost the whole story – the attack by the Disciples on the aliens' base, the counter-attack, his attempt to escape the destruction, his losing consciousness and waking up in the aliens' spaceship. At that point, he told his best friend a real whopper, i.e. catching the aliens off-guard and making good his escape.

"Now, I learn I'm wanted for questioning."

"That's right, old son. Everybody from the Mayor on down to the cop on the beat would like to get their hands on you."

"I can imagine. That's why I called you, Jack. You're the only one who would believe my story. I'll turn myself in, but only to you."

"Huh! I don't know what I'll tell the Chief – or the Mayor. It's hard for me to believe."

"I have an idea. It's wild, but it might work."

"Yeah?"

"Yeah. We get the Archdeacon in on this."

"Are you serious?"

"I am. He already knows about the aliens, but I've convinced him that they're really demons from Hell and that this is the beginning of Armegeddon."

Torres whistled.

"Man, oh, man! When you come up with a story, you don't mess around."

"I wouldn't get any fun at all otherwise. Look, Jack, I'm going to head for the City as soon as I hang up. I'll meet you at the usual place. OK?"

"OK, old son. I'll be there with bells on."

* * *

In the VOID, five points of light appear in a circle. After a brief moment/eon, a sixth point appears in the center of the circle.

One of the points in the circle brightens slightly.

-- REPORT.

The point in the center of the circle brightens slightly.

--This One has initiated Phase Two by explaining to the candidates the existence and purpose of the Communion and offering membership in it.

A second point in the circle brightens slightly.

-- Are they agreeable to the offer?

-- They seem to be, but they require time to come to a decision.

A third point in the circle brightens slightly.

-- Why do they hesitate?

-- They and their allies are under attack by a hostile force, and they believe that they must first defeat this enemy before they are free to join the Communion. They have requested assistance from this One in this endeavor.

A fourth point in the circle brightens slightly.

-- The Communion does not ordinarily interfere in parochial matters, as you well know. Are the candidates in imminent danger from this hostile force?

-- This One believes so. This One also believes that their destruction would represent a great loss to the Communion.

The final point in the circle brightens slightly.

-- The Inner Ring will take the matter under advisement and make a ruling. You are dismissed.

The point of light in the center of the circle winks out of existence. After a brief moment/eon, the remaining points are extinguished.

Only the VOID remains.

* * *

Ted dropped Larkin off first, in front of the City's war memorial, and then drove off to deposit Sheena and the Twins at their respective places of business. The detective ambled over to the stone bench where he and Jack Torres had long ago designated as their covert meeting place and sat down cautiously on its hot surface. He pulled out his large red handkerchief from his back pocket and laid it on his lap in preparation of wiping away the perspiration he knew would soon form on his face.

For no particular reason, the memory of another meeting with the Vice Mayor popped into his head. That had been the day he met his first extraterrestrial. Was it really only less than a month ago? The extraordinary events which followed since then seemed to have raced by. One supposed that it was just a matter of perspective; for the active person, time speeded up but, for the idle one, it marched slowly.

And, most definitely, George Larkin had been a very active person the past few weeks. He hadn't been this active since his days with the Chicago Police Department as a consultant helping to solve kidnappings. A private investigator, on the other hand, required a slow and patient pace. Now, in the midst of a galactic war in one's backyard, the pace had picked up considerably; he had had to hatch more emergency plans than ever before in order to keep up with quickly developing events and prevent those events from overwhelming him and those around him. So far, he had succeeded, but it was still early in the game; the Enemy was still out there, biding his time, planning his own next move, and marshaling his forces. One could not let one's guard down for a single minute.

He casually gazed at the scene about him. With his powers of keen observation and eidetic memory, he could discern volumes of information with a single glance. Quite often, he could project a future action by actors on the scene based on previous experience and a knowledge of human behavior. He wasn't a highly successful private investigator for nothing.

What he was seeing this morning was definitely out of the ordinary. He should have seen some pedestrians braving the tremendous heat of a summer day in the year 2018 in order to conduct whatever private business occupied them at the moment. He should have seen the usual amount of vehicular traffic, private and commercial, going about their business as well. It was as if all of the City's residents had decided to take the day off and stay home. On a hot day like this one, no one could have blamed them for not wanting to go outdoors. Yet, it was not a normal scene he was looking at. What *was* going on?

A number of cars were parked at the curbs on all four corners of the near-by intersection. Nothing too unusual about that, was there? Except –

His keen sense of observation kicked into high gear. There were people inside those cars, *and they were just sitting there, doing nothing.*

Larkin had been on any number of stake-outs with the CPD to know what one looked like. And he was looking at one just then. Obviously the Chief of Police wasn't taking any chances of his "pigeon" flying away; all the possible routes of escape had been covered, and now his police were waiting for the signal to close in on the "pigeon." He, George Larkin, was wanted for questioning concerning a major criminal act, and by damn! he was not going anywhere until some answers were forthcoming.

In one sense, the whole situation was laughable. The detective had been as much a victim of that criminal act as those who had died. He had nothing to fear from an official interrogation. Jack had assured him of protective custody. In another sense, however, the situation was deadly serious. And he had to emphasize the word "deadly." In light of recent events, the City's police department had investigated some rather unusual deaths involving some rather unusual victims, and they were at their wits' end trying to understand them. Now, they had what they were calling a "war zone" unraveling on the City's south side. Larkin would have been very surprised if all of the occupants of those parked cars weren't armed to the teeth and prepared to use deadly force at the least provocation.

Well, Mrs. Larkin's little boy wasn't about to give them that provocation. He was just going to sit there quietly and wait for the said occupants to make the first move – even if it meant drowning in his own sweat!

No sooner had he thought that thought than the occupants of the car directly across the street from him obliged him by getting out and walking toward him. One was wearing plain clothes; the other was wearing a gold-braided police uniform. He recognized both of them: Vice Mayor Joaquim Torres and Chief of Police Walter Barnwell. They were both grim-faced, the Chief more so than the Vice Mayor.

"Good morning, Mr. Torres, Chief Barnwell," he addressed them amiably. "Another hot one today, eh?"

"It'll be even hotter," the Chief grumbled, "if you don't co-operate."

"Now, now, Walter," Torres admonished him, "we agreed that Mr. Larkin would be treated fairly." Barnwell grunted in disgust. "Mr. Larkin has told me what happened on Ridgeway yesterday. He'll repeat his story for you. Won't you, Mr. Larkin?"

"Of course, Mr. Torres. I'm always glad to co-operate with the authorities. What happened, Chief, is that a group of hell-spawn collided with a group of Disciples. As you may know, Archdeacon Fogarty has stated that we are in the Last Days and that Armageddon is upon us."

Barnwell nodded in agreement. He was, in fact, a Deacon himself; and Larkin, knowing that, was playing on his gullibility.

"So," the detective continued, "the Disciples knew that the factory on Ridgeway was the base of operations for the first wave of Satan's forces and took it upon themselves to meet the threat without going through the proper channels. The demons countered with hell-fire and got the better of them. Our side lost many good people."

"But you escaped."

"Just barely. One of the blasts of hell-fire forced my station wagon off the street and into a tree. I was dazed but I managed to crawl out and find a hiding place until the coast was clear."

"What was *your* connection in all this?"

"Ah, well, in the course of pursuing one of my cases, I learned from one of my informants that strange-looking creatures were at the factory. I told His Worship, and he passed the information on to his people."

"But why were *you* there?" Barnwell persisted. "You're not a Disciple."

"No, I'm not. But I've been working with His Worship for the past two weeks on this matter, and he requested I monitor whatever action the Disciples took against the hell-spawn. He'll vouch for me."

"And," Torres put in, "I'm aware of Mr. Larkin's activity, Walter. I'll vouch for him as well."

The Chief worked his jaw muscles for a minute or two. The Vice Mayor was nominally his superior, and it would have been impolitic to doubt him. And, as a Disciple, he couldn't very well doubt the Archdeacon either. The story seemed plausible; the City's Coroner had bodies in his morgue whose physiology he couldn't explain. They might not be human after all. He'd have to discuss it with the Archdeacon – *discreetly*, of course – and try to fit the pieces together.

Larkin smiled to himself. He could just picture the Chief's mental gears grinding away. Pulling the wool over the eyes of a toady like Walter Barnwell was a job worth doing, and an enjoyable one to boot. He glanced at Torres, who smirked briefly.

"All right, gentlemen," the Chief finally spoke, "I'll accept this report – for the time being. Mr. Larkin, if I have any more questions, I can count on your co-operation?"

"Most assuredly, Chief. I'll do whatever I can to keep the City safe for decent folks."

The Vice Mayor almost laughed out loud at the double entendre but caught himself in time. It was Larkin's turn to smirk.

Barnwell excused himself, turned, and signaled to all of the members of his stake-out to leave. One by one, the vehicles pulled away and disappeared down the streets.

"Are you coming, Mr. Torres?" the Chief asked.

"I need to discuss another matter with Mr. Larkin – um, concerning the upcoming elections."

Barnwell nodded in acquiescence and returned to his own car. Soon, he was out of sight.

"Thanks, Jack, for playing along with me."

"Think nothing of it, old son. Anything I can do to discomfit a blowhard like Walter Barnwell, I'll do." He frowned then. "D'ya think he'll talk to the Archdeacon and verify your story?"

"He may. But I intend to speak to old man Fogarty first and let *him* decide how to deal with the toady."

"Good luck. Let me know how it works out."

"Will do. See you later, Jack."

* * *

If Dorothea Hedberg could have leaped from the second floor landing to the first floor rather than waste time using the stairs, she would have done so. The receptionist -- not "Sister" Smithers, however (was this her day off?) – had greeted Larkin cordially enough before announcing his presence; but he had seen, not surprisingly, worry in her eyes. Ten seconds after the call to the *sanctum sanctorum*, the door flew open, and Hedberg dashed down the stairs. He marveled that she didn't lose her balance and *fall* down the stairs. She rushed over and unabashedly threw her arms around him.

"Oh, George!" she whispered. "I – *we* were so worried when we learned you had disappeared after that awful incident on Ridgeway."

"How did you know about that? I didn't think there were any other survivors."

"Brother Kincaid survived, and he reported right away."

"Well, it *was* a near thing, Dorothea. Let's go upstairs so I can make my own report."

When he entered the Archdeacon's office, he spied "Brother" Kincaid sitting in his accustomed place, bandaged up here and there. He gaped at the man, but the number-two remained stoical.

"How did you manage to escape, Brother Kincaid?" he asked disingenuously. "You were right in the thick of it."

"As soon as the first car blew up, I hot-footed it toward the old ball field. A couple of others got away as well but, sad to say, we lost the rest of the fellows."

"What about Brother Connolly? He was in my station wagon when I lost consciousness."

"He seems to be the only one still missing in action. I saw him get out of your station wagon and run west on Ridgeway. No one's seen him since."

"We're pleased that you're safe and sound, Brother Larkin," the Archdeacon finally spoke. "Do you have anything to add to Brother Kincaid's account?"

"Of course, Your Worship. As you can imagine, it's still fresh in my mind – too fresh, I should say, for my comfort. First of all, I want you to know that I take full responsibility for our defeat. I...underestimated the strength of the Enemy and did not formulate a more effective plan of attack."

"I appreciate your admission, Brother Larkin, but we *are* dealing with all the fiends of Hell. Therefore, we must trust in the Lord to guide us. I believe He allowed this defeat to occur for a reason which we have yet to understand. Do not concern yourself with responsibility. All will be revealed to us at the proper time."

"Thank you, sir. I am greatly relieved."

The detective sat down in *his* accustomed place (and Hedberg snuggled up beside him) and proceeded to tell the old man the same story he had told Jack Torres (leaving out the involvement of DEDEP), except that he substituted the word "demon" for the word "alien."

"After I escaped their clutches, I hid out at a friend's house. Then he heard that I was wanted for questioning about the incident. I duly turned myself in half an hour ago and told them just what I told you. Frankly, sir, I didn't know who in the police department I could trust with the truth. They might not have believed me but locked me up as a lunatic. I did say that you'd vouch for me."

Fogarty remained stiff as a statue all the while and did not respond immediately. He too, like Chief Barnwell, was attempting to assess the "facts" of the matter. One could have heard insects scurry across the floor for all the lack of sound in the office.

"In certain cases, Brother Larkin," the Archdeacon spoke at last, "a little white lie might have been the proper course to take. Not every member of the police department embraces the Light of Purity, and so they are not ready for the Truth at this time." A pause. "Once more, the Enemy has inflicted losses upon us. I have no doubt that he believes himself invulnerable. In the end, he will suffer mightily for his arrogance."

"Yes, sir, that he will. What do you want me to do next?"

"You should rest after your ordeal. However, I am concerned about Brother Connolly. You're the expert in locating missing persons. Will you help?"

"I'll be glad to, Your Worship. He's been of great assistance to me this past week. I…feel he is destined for greater things."

"You may be right. Good day, Brother Larkin."

Hedberg walked the detective out of the office, arm in arm, down the stairs, and to the front door where she planted another kiss on his lips. He mumbled his good-byes and left hurriedly.

So, Kincaid survived the holocaust, he mused. *I wonder what reason he gave Fogarty for running away? Was Fogarty as forgiving of him as he was of me? That bit about accepting responsibility might have done the trick. My luck is still holding out.*

*George [Paddy's "voice" buzzed in his head], has your libido cooled off?

*Excuse me?

*You're getting awfully chummy with that Hedberg bird.

*Huh! I can tell you that the 'chumminess' is all one-sided. It's embarrassing the way she fawns over me. I can never tell if it's just a ruse for some ulterior purpose, or if she's really infatuated with me.

*Some chaps have all the luck, old darling.

*So you say. What news do you have for me?

*Some rather interesting developments concerning our Swarm 'friends.' I've just received an update from Lacey. The blighters have abandoned the factory – cleaned out all their equipment. Apparently, things got a little too hot for them there – in more ways than one.

*Where did they go?

*Ah, now that's the interesting part. They've removed themselves to Mr. Smith's old lair.

*That *is* interesting. First, it puts them far from downtown, so we're not likely to see many of their patrols from now on. Secondly, they're in a dilapidated building, and a good stiff wind would bring the roof down on them.

*Or a good stiff blow from our resident psycho-kinetic.

*You got it, chum. Anything else?

*Well, I've heard there's another psycho-communicator wandering about town – a female who, incidentally, can talk to animals as I can.

*That's worth investigating, but it'll have to be put on the back burner for the time being. And speaking of investigations, the young Disciple who's been my unwitting assistant in my Grand Plan – 'Brother' Connolly – has turned up missing. The Archdeacon wants him back, and so do I. Do a scan, will you?

*It'll be my pleasure, old darling. Ta-ta!

* * *

Kenny and Paddy re-enter the metaphysical "universe." The blackness is punctuated with a multitude of points of light, mostly dim lights reflecting mundane minds. How long they search for a particular point of light is academic; Time does not exist here, and a second of "normal" time is as long as an eon.

But they do locate their target on the periphery of a large collection of points of light. This tells them that the target is on the fringe of the City, far from the madding crowd. They deduce that he is in hiding. *Where* he is exactly remains to be seen.

*There's the bloke, dear heart [Kenny announces]. We'll access his optic center and get a clue as to his whereabouts.

They easily enter Connolly's mind and encounter the usual flotsam and jetsam which clutters the average human mind. They both wince in disgust, not so much from the run-of-the-mill thought processes as from the hodge-podge of Disciple propaganda. Above all, however, this mind is gripped by abject fear. The Twins do not wonder at the fear they perceive; Connolly has witnessed an event beyond his limited comprehension, an event for which he thanked his god of surviving.

*If this chap weren't a Disciple [Paddy remarks], I'd feel sorry for him.

*Be charitable, dear heart. He's just a lad, don't you know? Our dear George will know how to deal with him.

They access Connolly's optic center and peer at the outside world through his eyes. The Disciple is in a living room of a house. The room is adequately furnished, but not extravagantly. Connolly is looking at a young female whom the Twins deduce from prior descriptions is the young man's girlfriend, "Sister" Smithers. She is crying and speaking at the same time.

*Do we need to access the auditory region? [Paddy asks].

*No. I'd rather not have to listen to a lot of blubbering. Hmmm. I can't get a location fix from this angle. Plant a suggestion in his mind, dear heart. Tell him he needs to look out the window.

Paddy complies. Instantly, the field of vision is elevated as Connolly rises to his feet. He walks over to a front window and stares out at the street. The Twins observe other houses in both directions.

*Bloody hell! [Kenny growls]. I don't recognize this neighborhood at all. Plant another suggestion. Have him think he needs to report back to the Archdeacon straightaway.

Through Connolly's eyes, they observe the sudden alarm on Smithers face, to be replaced by grudging acceptance. Connolly heads for the door, opens it, and walks down the front walk. He turns to his right and continues down the street.

*Kenny, I see a street sign.

*Yes. As soon as he moves closer to it, we'll be able to pinpoint his location.

Connolly approaches the intersection ahead, and the wording on the street sign becomes legible. It reads "Prairie Street/Orchard Road."

*Aha! We've got him! As soon as we leave this bloke, we'll contact George and give him the location.

They withdraw from Connolly's mind and locate Larkin's familiar mental signature.

*Mission accomplished, old darling, and…

*…we're reporting back to you PDQ.

*That didn't take long. Where is he?

*He should be heading east on Prairie. He…

*…was hiding out at the Smithers bird's house.

*Good work, guys. I'll take it from here.

*What would you like to do now, dear heart? [Kenny asks as soon as they break contact with Larkin].

*Well, we should – uh-oh!

*What's wrong?

*Look there.

Kenny follows his brother's direction and spies a very bright point of light moving toward them.

*Is that who I think it is? [Paddy inquires].

*That would be my guess.

They remain stationary. The mobile point of light approaches near to them and vibrates slightly for the space of a few heartbeats. Then:

*WE MEET AGAIN, HUMANS [the "voice" booms]. ARE YOU TRAVELING ONCE MORE?

*We are. We were seeking a friend of ours. We have…

*… found him and have just finished communicating with him.

*If we may ask, what are…

*…your duties as Monitor?

*I OBSERVE ALL THAT OCCURS WHEREVER IT OCCURS IN THIS [undecipherable] ZONE AND RECORD IT.

*You must know a great deal [Kenny remarks].

*I DO.

*And to whom do you report what you have observed? [Paddy asks]. YOU ARE VERY INQUISITIVE, HUMANS.

*It's in our nature to be inquisitive, and…

*…that is how we know what we know.

*SO I UNDERSTAND. NEVERTHELESS, I AM NOT AT LIBERTY TO ANSWER THAT QUESTION. I BID YOU FAREWELL. WE SHALL MEET AGAIN.

The point of light retreats until it fades from view. The metaphysical "universe" becomes very still again. A long moment passes before either brother desires to speak.

*Bloody hell! [Paddy exclaims in sudden rage]. A most disagreeable blighter, that one!

*Perhaps. If we encounter him again, we should try a different tactic. Let's go home.

* * *

Relieved that "Brother" Connolly was still alive (and ready for possible use), Larkin visited the nearest car-rental agency and took possession of the least expensive vehicle on the lot. Eventually, he would have to replace the station wagon, but that was for the future when the current situation had been resolved. Right now, he needed to return to DEDEP and update Mr. Smith on the new developments.

His arrival at the farm prompted both Monk and Ted to dash out of the house with pistols on their hips and grimness on their faces. Not surprisingly, they did not recognize who was driving the unidentified vehicle until they peered in the window. Both relaxed considerably.

"For a hot minute there, Georgie," Monk explained, "we thought you might have been from the DOE, checkin' up on us. We ain't been inspected since the facility was closed down. If an inspector did come here and spotted that alien tech in the barn, we woulda had to answer some embarrassing questions."

"Not to mention bein' hauled off to Washington to answer them," Ted added.

"If it's an announced inspection," the detective assured them, "I'll have Mr. Smith 'beam' the stuff away until the 'all clear.'"

"And if it's an unannounced one?"

"I'll have Kenny or Paddy put a few 'suggestions' in the inspector's mind."

Both of the DOE men went wide-eyed at the thought of mind-control but said nothing. They couldn't be sure if George was joking or not.

"So, where is Mr. Smith?"

"Um, he's still in his room," Ted replied. "Ain't seen 'im since last night."

"OK. Thanks for being alert. These are perilous times."

The detective entered the house, lurched up the stairs to the second floor, and rapped gently on the guest-room door. Half a minute later, the door opened, and the pasty-faced alien peeked out. Immediately, he broke out in a smile.

"Good...morning...Mr....Largin. I...was...shust...about...to...gall ...you. I...hhhave...some...interesting...news...for...you."

"Good morning, Mr. Smith. And I have some for you."

Without hesitating, Larkin launched into the same story he had told Torres, Barnwell, and Fogarty (minus the involvement of DEDEP) and finished with the report by his "informant" concerning the abandoned supermarket. The Coalition agent seemed very distraught by it all.

"I...must...tell...you...thhhat...thhhis...behhhhavior...by...thhhe ...Swarm...is...guite...inegspligable. Thhhey...hhhave...never...gommitted ...agts...of...violence...until...thhhey...attagted...in...full...force. Whhhat...hhhad...you...done...to...provogue...thhhem?"

That sounded like an accusation. Under other circumstances, Larkin might have reacted with resentment. Under the present circumstances, however, he suppressed his indignation; it would have benefitted no one to alienate an ally – even a non-human one – and risk the possibility of being abandoned by the Coalition and facing the Swarm alone.

"We did nothing to provoke them, Mr. Smith. They provoked *us* when they sought to avenge the death of Mr. Jones. We were only protecting ourselves."

"Thhhis...matter...is...getting...out...of...control...Mr....Largin." He made a gesture which may have been the alien equivalent of a shrug. "Neverthhheless...whhhat...is...done...is...done. No...use...to...gry...over...spilled...beer...as...you...Tellurians...say."

"Absolutely. We need each other more than ever before. What's your next move?"

"I...hhhave...spoguen...to...Frommar...about...a... gontinshency...plan...if...anythhhing...should...happen...to...me."

"What could possibly happen to you? You're safe here. Only I – and my co-managers – have knowledge of your whereabouts."

"I...agree. But...withhh...thhhe...Swarm...so...glose...by...it... is ...best...not...to...tague...any...shances."

"What's the contingency plan?"

"I...hhhad...reguested...permission...to...train...you...in... thhhe ...use...of...my...eguipment...in...thhhe...barn...and... Frommar...hhhas ...given...it."

To say that the detective was stunned by this pronouncement would have been a colossal understatement. The fact of the matter was that he was overwhelmed by this contingency plan; it meant that the Coalition trusted him – a mere "primitive" – enough to share their technology with him. And to say that he was delighted by the prospect of operating sophisticated alien technology was also a colossal understatement. The fact of the matter was that he was positively ecstatic and not a little anxious to get his hands on it. Of course, he'd have to be modest about accepting the proposal; if he even hinted at being overly eager, Frommar might withdraw the offer.

"Mr. Smith, I'm – I'm overwhelmed by this offer. And I appreciate your confidence in me. Although I still think nothing will happen to you, I'll be happy to serve as your back-up. When do we start?"

"Right...away...if...you...hhhave...thhhe...time."

"I do. Lead on, MacDuff."

The alien regarded him with puzzlement at the unfamiliar expression but made the previous gesture again and led the way. Upon entering the barn, he headed straight for the control console, stood before it, and contemplated its darkened screen for a minute or two. Larkin alternated his attention between him and the console, fighting to keep the other from knowing how much he wanted to get started. Finally, Mr. Smith ended his meditation.

"You…will…observe…Mr….Largin…thhhat…thhhe…gonsole… is…divided…into…four…segtions.   Eash…segtion…governs… specific…fungtions. Thhhis…one" – he indicated the upper left area   –   "governs…thhhe…gommunigation…between…thhhe… logal…ashent…and…thhhe …Goalition. Thhhis…one" – the upper right area – "governs… gommunigation…between…logal…ashents. Thhhis…one" – the lower left area – "governs…thhhe…gomputer… fungtions. And…thhhis…one" – the lower right area – "governs… agcess…to…thhhe…data…bases."

"Hmmm. Very efficient."

"Yes…it…is.   Now…you…will…observe…thhhat…eash… segtion… gonsists…of…ten…pressure…points…thhhree…golumns… of…thhhree …points…and…one…point…in…one…gorner…of… eash…segtion. Thhhe …gorner…points…serve…two…fungtions. Thhhe…first…is…to…agtivate …and…de-agtivate…the console… itself. You…start…withhh…thhhe… upper…left…point…and… press…all…four…in…a…glockwise…fashion… to…turn…thhhe… gonsole…on. You…reverse…thhhe…seguence…to…finish. Agtivate… thhhe…gonsole…Mr….Largin."

With exaggerated motions, the detective pressed the corner points in the desired fashion. When the fourth point had been pressed, the console lit up like a neon sign. Each section had its own color – red for the upper left, orange for the upper right, yellow for the lower left, and green for the lower right – and they all glowed steadily and brightly. Larkin congratulated himself for mastering his first lesson but instantly admonished himself for thinking so highly of a simple exercise.

"Very…good.   Now…to…agtivate…a…partigular…segtion… you… press…thhhe…gorner…point…in…thhhat…segtion. Let… us…begin… withhh…thhhe… agcess… of… thhhe… data… bases."

Larkin did so. At once, the corner point dimmed, then re-brightened, and the nine other points brightened.

"As…you…might…imashine…from…thhhe…number…of… points …in   eash…segtion…thhhere…are…many…possible… gombinations. We…ashents…are…egspegted…to…memorize…all… of…thhhem."

"That must have taken a long time."

"It...did. Some...of...us...hhhad...to...study...very...hhhard. For ...thhhe...purposes...of...*your*...training...I...will...show... you...our... 'gode...book.' We...ashents...often...agcess...it...in... order...to...learn ...if...a...new...gode...hhhas...been...added... or...an...old...one...shanshed ...or...deleted...and...to...refresh... our...memories." He smiled unexpectedly, and Larkin regarded him expectantly. "Thhhe...first... gode...I...will...show...you...will... agcess...thhhe...'gode...book.' Pay... glose...attention."

He then proceeded to press all nine points in that section, beginning with the top one in the left-hand column and ending with the bottom one in the right-hand column. When he had finished, he smiled again. Larkin stared at him in disbelief.

"You must be joking," he grumbled.

"Not...at...all...Mr....Largin. Frommar...himself...greated... thhhis ...gode...in...order...to...facilitate...agcess...to...thhhe... 'book.' I...thhhing ...*hhhe*...was...thhhe...one...maghing...a...shoke."

"Huh! Hoorah for him!"

The detective now looked at the monitor. On it appeared the cover of the "code book." At least, he thought it was the cover; all he saw were a few characters in an alien script. He looked at Mr. Smith questioningly.

"Thhhis...is...my...gopy. It...hhhas...been...translated...into... my ...languashe. Whhhen...I...hhhave...shown...you...thhhe... basig...fungtions...I...will...reguest...a...gopy...translated...into... Ingles. Now ...thhhe...segond...most...important...gode...you... must...know...is... thhhe...one...to...gontagt...thhhe...Goalition."

The Coalition agent now pressed the corner point in the section governing Coalition communications and five other points, a sequence Larkin had seen before and had already memorized (although he had never told his ally that he did). The Coalition base responded in due time. The being who took the call was even thinner than Mr. Smith and had a bluish tinge to his skin. The latter pressed the corner point of the section governing computer operations and four other points (which he explained was the code to activate the translator), then spoke to his colleague in his own language. The other being acknowledged Mr. Smith and signed off.

"It...may...tague...a...few...days...for...thhhe...translated... gopy... to... be... transferred... to... thhhis... base. In... thhhe... meantime... I... will ... gontinue... your... training... and... prepare... some... egsercishes... for... you... to... perform."

Larkin nodded agreeably and rubbed his hands in anticipation. He could hardly wait to sink his teeth into this project.

CHAPTER TWENTY-FIVE

THE PDF TRIUMPHANT

FROM THE DIARY of Christopher Wredling:

I have to believe that it was the strangest battle ever fought on this old planet. I'm no student of history, but I know enough to realize that most battles in Earth's past have involved masses of men and weapons that are thrown at each other by so-called 'master strategists' who make decisions to go to war but do not have a personal interest in the destruction war inevitably brings about.

The battle DEDEP fought against the alien Swarm on a summer day in 2018 involved only a handful of combatants on either side. But both sides possessed strange and awesome weapons that they deployed as best they could. The Swarm relied on technological weapons and skills, while DEDEP used the power of the mind to meet the greatest challenge humanity ever faced.

It was a most unequal contest, and I leave it to posterity to decide which side had the edge.

The damnedest thing about this particular contest was that it was waged in secret. Oh, the newspapers were full of press releases from the office of the Vice Mayor of the City which suggested that 'terrorists' using the abandoned supermarket on Hill Street had, while constructing bombs to rid the City of the Disciples of Purity, gotten careless and blew themselves up. Not a word was mentioned about anyone else being present. Of course, the PDF was pleased by the lack of publicity; otherwise, the press would have had a field day reporting about the 'mutants' in their midst using 'devilish' abilities. We'd have had to leave the City and set up shop somewhere else that may or may not have been less vulnerable to attack.

Our 'master strategist' was able to save the day that day!

* * *

DEDEP's "master strategist" gazed at his "army" with a decidedly grim expression. He had called this meeting because he was going to ask them to accept a very dangerous mission. He had even asked the Director to attend because he needed to know what was going to be asked of his "wards." The PDF was properly attentive, unaware of what was going to be asked of them. (Perhaps the Twins knew what was running through his mind, but they maintained their usual stoical selves.) Larkin took a deep breath and began with a recap of recent events, beginning with the holocaust on Ridgeway, his kidnapping and rescue, the abandonment of the Swarm base in favor of Mr. Smith's former base, and ending with his training on the Coalition's technology in the barn. It all sounded boring in his ears while he spoke; and, in the back of his mind, he wondered if it sounded boring to his "troops." Yet, no one exhibited any such emotion but hung on his every word.

Now to lower the boom, he thought, *and watch the sparks fly.*

"I'm telling you all this because I want to instill in you the gravity of the current situation and to explain why I'm going to ask you to launch an attack against the Swarm."

Gasps of shock and murmurs of concern greeted that pronouncement. The detective expected no less and braced himself for the inevitable wave of protest. The first to speak was Emil Razumov.

"George," he said solemnly, "it was my understanding that you intended to continue to use the Disciples as 'shock troops,' as unappetizing as that sounds. Why do you now alter your strategy?"

"I'm not altering anything, Emil. I'm simply adding a new variable to the equation. Also, I think the Archdeacon is becoming suspicious of my intentions after losing so many of his followers. But the main reason I'm proposing this move is that we're the best qualified to defeat the Swarm."

"How so?"

"The Swarm has, in my estimation, no defense against our psychic abilities and our gestalt. They won't know what kind of attack is being used or where it's coming from."

"Excuse us, old darling, but ain't we supposed to be …"

"…a strictly *defensive* force against an attack on us?"

"It still is. But, consider that, with the presence of the Swarm on Earth, we *are* on the defensive. Look, people, I've given this a lot of thought, and I'm sticking to my guns. Only if all of you are against this change of strategy will I back down."

A long silence followed. The detective held his breath.

"Perhaps," Dr. Razumov interjected, "we ought to retire to consider the proposal further."

"*I* don't need any more time!" Jean exclaimed, as she jumped to her feet. "I may be the new kid on the block here, but I'm the only one – besides George, that is – who's had a run-in with those alien bastards. They owe me."

"Jean hasn't been told of our harrowing…"

"…experience. The Swarm owes us as well."

"And she hasn't learned of *my* experience either," Chris' voice issued from the PA system. "I've got a 'debt' to repay too."

"I have to stand behind my partner, Emil," Sheena declared, "even though I'm scared stiff at the prospect of going up against those scumbags."

After a brief, whispered conversation, Eve and Stan also got to their feet. Freddie was floored by their action.

"You'll need the…gestalt, George," Eve said in an even voice. "Stan and I are ready."

"Yeah," the boy concurred with a big grin. "It'll be like playin' a video game."

"It's far from bein' a 'game,' kid," the handyman muttered, "but, if you two are goin' on this joy ride, I guess I'll hafta go along – just to keep you outa trouble."

Larkin regarded the Perkinses. They in turn had a brief, quiet conversation.

"I don't like it one bit, George," Lacey said at last. "It's too risky to suit me, and I have my family to consider." She paused and bit her lip. "But, if the rest of the PDF is willing to take that risk, Billy and I will make it unanimous."

"Yes, sir, Mr. Larkin," the teenager agreed. "I got a few tricks up my sleeve I've been wanting to try out. This'll be a good opportunity to test my powers of illusion."

The detective did not speak for a long moment. His head was awhirl with the quickness his "troops" had accepted his proposal, but he was nevertheless relieved and pleased by the outcome.

"Well, I thank each and every one of you. Rest assured that, if I see the first sign of danger to anyone, I'll sound the retreat and run like hell."

The image of George Larkin running anywhere brought on a chuckle from all present – except the Doctor, who was frowning furiously. The detective turned to him.

"Emil?"

The Russian threw his hands up.

"*Eto sumasshedshy* [this is insane]! You are throwing your lives away!"

"Will you try to stop us?"

"*Nyet*. You have made your decision, and I must respect your decision. I only hope you live long enough to regret it."

With that, he turned and left the conference room. Larkin shook his head sadly. He had really wanted Emil's blessing on this venture. The idea that the old man was withholding his blessing weighed heavily on him. Still, the Swarm had to be dealt with as only the PDF could do it.

"All right, people. Get some rest. We'll be moving out after lunch."

* * *

Larkin cautiously emerged from the emergency entrance/exit in order not to be spotted by Mr. Smith and to avoid having to come up with an explanation of where he had been. He saw no sign of the alien which struck him as odd, since the Coalition agent was seldom far from his array, puttering around with one module or another if not actually operating it. He supposed that Mr. Smith was still in his room. He had no clue as to the other's sense of time; perhaps his "circadian cycle" was different than that of a human. Whatever the reason, the coast was clear, and the detective nonchalantly exited the barn.

On a hunch, he decided to look up Monk and learn if he had discovered anything new from the purloined Swarm array. As he approached the farmhouse, Ted came out to stretch his legs. He told Larkin that Monk was probably in the basement tinkering with the alien equipment, a new pastime for him since acquiring it. Larkin went around to the rear of the house and entered the basement from there.

Monk was indeed tinkering with one of the modules. And he wasn't alone. To the detective's great surprise (and not a little concern), Mr. Smith was right beside him, peering over the adjacent module. This was a curious development. For one thing, the DOE man hadn't cleared with him the alien's presence here; he had no problem with the latter's investigation of Swarm technology – he might discover something useful to The Cause – but he would have preferred to be consulted beforehand. For another thing, he had no idea what the alien would make of anything he learned or if he would share his findings with his human ally. This whole business was highly irregular in the extreme to his way of thinking, and he intended to upgrade the rules of conduct.

Both investigators looked up as Larkin appeared and gave him a friendly greeting.

"Hiya, Georgie," the human one said cheerfully. "I'm glad you're here. Got somethin' new to show ya."

"Hhhello...Mr....Largin," the alien one said cordially. "As...do...I."

"How is it that Mr. Smith is here, Monk?" the detective asked in an accusatory tone.

"Ah, well, he came lookin' for me. Seems there's a loose electrical wire in his room. He saw me and followed me down here."

"I...apoloshize...for...thhhis...intrusion...but...I...did...not... know...whhhat...you...hhhad...done...withhh...Mr....Shones'... eguipment. Do ...you...wish...me...to...leave?"

"No, no, you're fine. However, I wish you had asked me first. I suppose I should have told you what I did with this stuff, but I've been pre-occupied lately. So, what have you learned?"

"Well," Monk began, "it seems that Mr. Smith has seen similar equipment before, and I picked his brain for techniques on accessing the data in these modules. With his help, I found another set of maps, and they'll knock your socks off!"

So saying, he turned to the control panel he had been investigating and tapped out a sequence different than the one Larkin had seen before. The monitor lit up and revealed a map of the Western Hemisphere of the Earth; a number of red dots punctuated it, and they were accompanied by characters from the Swarm language.

"This is a wide view," Monk explained. "Other maps show individual countries and regions within countries."

"The dots are specific locations of Swarm activity, I presume."

"Yep. You're lookin' at every Swarm base in the world."

"Now...thhhat...we...know...egsagtly...whhhere...thhhey...are... logated...it...will...be...a...simple...matter...to...destroy...thhhem... one ...by...one. Thhhe...main...Swarm...fleet...will...not...be... able...to...strigue...withhh...thhhe...impunity...thhhey...hhhave... been...aggustomed...to."

The detective studied the map closely. He noted that the dots in the United States corroborated the recent UFO reports. Each country in the Western Hemisphere had at least one dot; the more technologically developed nations had more than one. He nodded in agreement with Mr. Smith's assessment.

"Indeed they won't, Mr. Smith. What's more, we'll be able to destroy any of their ships that might survive the ambush the Coalition has planned – although I hope it doesn't come to that."

"I...agree...Mr....Largin. We...very...mush...want...to...destroy... thhhem...all...withhh...one...powerful...blow."

"I'm in favor of that as well. What have you learned from the module next to you? I believe it's a communications station."

"You...are...gorregt. It...is...similar...to...thhhe...one...in...
thhhe ...Goalition...base. I...thhhing...it...gan...be...agtivated...in...
thhhe...same...fashion."

He pressed a sequence of pressure points (which Larkin quickly memorized), and the monitor lit up. What was displayed was a simple geometric pattern, a series of interlocking hexagons.

"I...suspegt...thhhat...thhhe...Swarm...stole...thhhis...
tegnoloshy ...from...a...world...whhhish...hhhad...previously...
shared...it...withhh ...some...of...the...member...worlds...of...
thhhe...Goalition...before...it...was...attagted."

"When I first snooped around Mr. Jones' base, it suddenly activated, and I was face to face with the Swarm officer who's leading the unit currently in the City. That's why he wants me so much – to find out how much I know about their plans. I don't recommend that you press any more pressure points. You might accidentally contact a Swarm operative and compromise our position."

"I...do...not...intend...to...Mr....Largin. I...shall...egsamine...
anothhher...module...instead."

"A good idea. Keep me posted. I have other business to attend to."

As the detective left the basement, he took pleasure in this new development, even if it had been an unwelcome surprise initially. With the alien probing the Swarm technology and satisfying Monk's curiosity about him personally, the barn would be clear when the time came for the PDF to move out and launch its attack against the Swarm. He couldn't have planned it any better.

* * *

In the VOID, five points of light appear in a circle. After a brief moment/eon, a sixth point appears in the center of the circle.

One of the points in the circle brightens slightly.

-- It is decided. You will protect the candidates by any means at your disposal.

The point of light in the center of the circle brightens slightly.

-- This One thanks the Inner Ring for its wise counsel. This One will comply as the need arises.

A second point in the circle brightens slightly.

-- What is the current status of the candidates?

-- They, and their allies, are preparing an assault on the hostile force which threatens them. This One shall await the opportunity to assist them.

A third point in the circle brightens slightly.

-- You have our permission to act without being summoned.

-- Again, this One thanks the Inner Ring for its wise counsel.

A fourth point in the circle brightens slightly.

-- When the hostilities have ceased, you will bring the candidates before us so that we may examine them.

-- This One will comply.

The final point in the circle brightens slightly.

-- You are dismissed.

The point of light in the center of the circle winks out of existence. After a brief moment/eon, the remaining points of light are extinguished.

Only the VOID remains.

* * *

Larkin had told everyone else to get some rest, but he hadn't followed his own orders. Instead, after he had left Monk and Mr. Smith to their own amusements, he got into the rental car and drove back to the City. He was much too restless to lie down and do nothing. On the way, he continued to mull over the plan of action he wanted to pursue once the PDF arrived at the new Swarm base. He picked the plan apart sequence by sequence, examined each one for fatal flaws, and considered alternatives for each one. The plan had several inherent risks, not the least of which was the terrain upon which the PDF would be fighting. The former supermarket was surrounded by a large parking lot, and his people would be clear targets for any counter-attack which was sure to come. He paid close attention to that knotty problem and settled on the least risky sequence.

As luck would have it, as soon as he reached the western edge of the business district, he spied two familiar faces, and he craned his head to catch a better view. One was the "heretic" he had located for the Archdeacon. The man was no longer dressed in the ice-cream suit of the Disciples but wore "civilian clothing." Either he had quit the organization or he had been "de-frocked" by old man Fogarty. In either case, why was he still running loose and preaching his "heretical" views? That's what he was doing at the moment. A large crowd of Disciples and non-Disciples surrounded him hanging on his every word. The second familiar face was "Brother" Connolly; he was still wearing his white suit, but he seemed to be as enraptured as the rest of the crowd. The detective grunted. The Archdeacon would have a serious fit if he learned of this gathering. Perhaps he'd send "Brother" Kincaid out to "rectify" the situation.

Quickly, he pulled over to the curb and waited until the crowd broke up and went their separate ways. Connolly headed east while the "heretic" went north. The detective honked his horn and waved at the young Disciple to get his attention. As soon as he recognized Larkin, Connolly dashed across the street, oblivious to any oncoming traffic, and jumped into the car.

"Brother Larkin," he said breathlessly, "am I glad to see you! What happened to you? How did you escape?"

"I'm glad to see you too, my friend. And I can ask you those same questions. But I'll go first."

He then related essentially the same story he had told Vice Mayor Torres and Chief of Police Barnwell. As he described his experience at the hands of the Swarm, the young man's eyes widened with fright and his face turned ashen.

"My...*God*! How horrible! I'm surprised you escaped at all."

"It was...God's Will, Brother Connolly," Larkin forced the words out of his mouth. "He has other plans for me."

"Yes, I've suspected that for some time."

"Your turn."

"Well, when your station wagon crashed and you fell unconscious, I – I panicked. May the Lord forgive me, but I was scared to death. All that destruction – all that death. I got out as fast as I could and ran, and I prayed that those vile creatures would not follow me. I ended up at Sister Smithers' house. Fortunately, her parents weren't at home – they're over-protective of her, and they don't like me much – so I could stay there until I calmed down. I'm afraid I upset her more than I should have.

"While we were trying to comfort each other, the idea came to me that I should report back to His Worship and confess my cowardly behavior. But, when I got downtown, I spotted Brother Franco –"

"Who?"

"You remember him. He's the one on Union Street who said that the Light of Purity was a false message and that we should follow a new path to salvation."

"Ah, yes. I never did catch his name. Go on."

"Anyway, I stopped to talk to him. And the more he talked, the more sense he made." He looked at Larkin pleadingly. "Can I confide in you?"

"Of course."

Tell me all of your secrets, chum, and I'll make good use of them.

"Thank you. Well, I'm ready to quit the Disciples and join Brother Franco's group. It's growing every day and soon will be able to challenge the Archdeacon to a debate."

"You'll be taking a great risk, Brother Connolly. Archdeacon Fogarty is a force to be reckoned with."

"If the Lord is with us, all things are possible."

"Good luck. Can I drop you off somewhere?"

"Thank you, no. I'm meeting Sister Smithers at the Broadway Restaurant for a late breakfast."

The detective shook his head in amazement as soon as Connolly went his own way. A new religious movement in the City to challenge the authority of the old one was certainly an interesting development. And it all had started with Paddy's little prank! This old town wouldn't be the same from now on – that is, if this old town survived the Swarm.

He returned to his office. The kidnapping had caused him to neglect his business longer than he cared for. When he walked in, Mrs. Watson looked up in shock.

"Oh, my God, George! Where have you been? I was so worried."

"I…was called out of town in an emergency. I didn't have time to notify anyone – not even Sheena."

"I haven't seen much of her either lately."

"No? Maybe she's working one of her cases."

"I suppose. Well, you don't seem to be any worse for wear, George."

"Thank you, Madge. Hold any calls, will you? I've got play catch-up."

In the "snoop room," he quickly fell into his usual routine. Half a dozen phone messages were waiting for him; all but one were from clients who were anxiously waiting for an update from him concerning their cases. The one exception was a call from Gordy marked "Urgent." He pressed the reply button. The phone on the other end rang four times before anyone answered.

"Hello, George," the former FBI agent spoke. "Thanks for getting back to me promptly."

"Hi, Gordy. What's the urgency?"

"My connection at the Bureau just got his pink slip. They made up a few legalistic excuses for the firing, but he and I both think it had to do with passing Bureau files to outsiders."

"So, where does that leave you?"

"Dunno, old buddy. But I got to keep a low profile for a while. You probably won't hear from me as often as I'd like. Just so you know."

"That's a damned shame, chum. I was hoping to get more information on UFO's."

"No can do. Look, I can't stay on the phone too long. Those bastards might try to trace this call."

"OK. Take care, Gordy."

He disconnected and treated himself to a few well-chosen disparaging remarks about the Federal Bureau of Investigation, bureaucracy in general, and the current Administration. He ignored the other phone messages and went straight to his e-mail. There were a dozen messages, most of which were more demands from clients for updates. He ignored them as well and examined the two which were not from clients. He smiled when he saw that one of them was from the Quintessential Quark.

The Quark was his usual paranoid self (maybe a bit more so this time around) and rambled on about being "monitored" by extraterrestrial beings lurking in his neighborhood. He opined that he was not long for this world. He did, however, have one intriguing bit of information. He was continuing to spy out the Swarm base in Nebraska; and the last time he was there, he saw what he described as an "alien convention." There were, he said, three of the ships he had described before (which Chris had corroborated) and "hundreds" of aliens going through their military drills. "The invasion's on!" he typed in capital letters. "We're doomed!" He signed off with his usual "benediction."

The detective furrowed his brow at this "news." Obviously, the Quark in his drug-induced paranoia was exaggerating; yet, he had seen something out of the ordinary (for him), and it frightened the hell out of him. An "alien convention," he said. Was the Swarm mobilizing for some soon-to-be-realized activity? If so, how soon? More importantly, was this the prelude to the planned invasion by the main fleet? He'd have to consult with the Coalition about this. Perhaps they could confirm his concerns.

The other message was just as alarming (if not more so). The sender – who identified him/herself as "The Watcher" (where did these people get their online monikers?) – claimed to be in the know about the Quark's activities, but (s)he chose not to elaborate on that point. And (s)he chose not to elaborate on how (s)he had gotten Larkin's e-mail address. Was (s)he a hacker? If so, what was his/her game? His/her message spoke of kidnappings by aliens who were attempting to locate the leaders and the bases of operation of the anti-alien resistance groups. Was that a reference to DEDEP? Unlikely. Or was there another organization in the country which was aware of the Swarm presence and was making preparations to repel it? Plausible. He'd respond to "The Watcher," but very, very carefully. This person might or might not be fishing; either way, (s)he posed a potential danger to DEDEP. The detective made a mental note to track this joker down.

When he had finished with the "paperwork," he left the office and headed for Disciples HQ to bring the Archdeacon up to speed. He hated to rat out Connolly and Franco – they were providing dissension in the ranks of Fogarty's little empire – but he needed to score some points with the old man after yesterday's debacle. Upon arrival, he noted that yet another new face was at the reception desk – a young male this time. Was there a new round of "auditions" taking place? Or was "Sister" Smithers simply on "administrative leave"? He didn't care, one way nor another, but it was a curious situation.

As soon as he had been announced, Hedberg bounded down the stairs, rushed over, and pressed herself against him. He endured this "greeting" as best he could and mumbled a "hello." The walk upstairs was awkward as she insisted on walking up with an arm about his waist. He was glad to enter the Archdeacon's office where he could disentangle himself (somewhat) from this female shark.

The old man greeted him perfunctorily, and Kincaid gave him the usual nod. The former's mind clearly was elsewhere. Larkin knew that this was not a good time to bring bad news, but he persevered out of necessity.

"What can I do for you, Brother Larkin?" the Archdeacon asked in a neutral voice.

"I've encountered Brothers Connolly and Franco a short time ago, Your Worship. I thought you had them in tow."

"No, I have not," came a curt reply. "I haven't seen Brother Connolly since yesterday morning. I'd like to, of course, so that I may have his views on yesterday's...incident. As for *Mr.* Franco, I had him 'in tow' only briefly. A group of his followers whom he has corrupted snatched him away from the man I sent after him. Where did you see them?"

"They were both at Main and Oak, along with a large group –perhaps the same group that spirited Franco away – and holding a discourse."

"*Humph!* Re-enforcing his heretical views, I should judge."

"If it's any help to you, as I passed by, Franco headed north on Oak and Connolly went east on Main."

Fogarty turned to Kincaid.

"Get on it. And try to hold onto them this time."

"Yes, sir," the other responded with determination.

"Perhaps we can still salvage something out of this tragic affair, Brother Larkin."

"I certainly hope so, sir. I wish I could have contributed more. I haven't been very useful of late."

"There are bound to be set-backs, because there are so many variables. But, if we are faithful to the Light of Purity, the final victory will be ours."

"I'd like to believe that. But I need to come up with a better plan, one that doesn't cost so much in blood."

"I have confidence in you, Brother Larkin."

"Thank you, Your Worship. Um, I have another appointment now. I'll keep you posted about the new plan."

And you won't like it at all, he added.

Hedberg escorted him downstairs, again wrapped around him. Before he departed, she gave him a longer kiss than before.

"I hope this terrible business is over soon, George dear. I so want to spend more time with you."

"Be patient, Dorothea. I have a feeling that things are rushing toward a conclusion. See you later."

If I'm unlucky, he added.

He was quite relieved to be walking away from that place. How long he could keep up the pretense of being the Archdeacon's trusted accomplice and of being charmed by Hedberg's blatant moves on him was anybody's guess. As the old man had said, perhaps something could be salvaged out of this business. He certainly hoped so. He was being worn down by the web he had spun.

Right now, however, he had to hurry back to DEDEP, enlist Ted to chauffeur some of the PDF, and then meet the Swarm head-on. The very idea gave him the shivers.

* * *

At the appointed time, the PDF gathered in front of the farmhouse. None of them appeared too worried about their prospects in the coming battle; in fact, they were all chatting amiably amongst themselves. When Larkin emerged from the house with Ted in tow, they gave him their immediate attention.

"OK, people, off we go. Alpha Squad, in my car. Beta Squad, with Ted."

"I sense that you're too tired to drive any more, George," Sheena observed. "Why don't you let me drive and get the rest you prescribed for us?"

"I'll accept that offer, Sheena. It'll give me a chance to go over the battle plan again."

The PDF clambered into their assigned vehicles and moved out. The drive back to the City was made in almost complete silence as each member mentally rehearsed their upcoming roles – and their fates. The lone exceptions were Eve and Stan in the back seat with Larkin who were engaged in whispered conversation all the while. The detective was too tired to listen in, but he wondered for the dozenth time just what those two had to say to each other.

All too soon, the two vehicles reached their destination and halted a few meters shy of the intersection of North and Hill Avenues. The abandoned supermarket still stood out like a monument to human folly but now had taken on a decidedly sinister appearance. Inside were creatures whose only purpose in life was to destroy what others had created. Larkin was at once fearful and angry. How could the Universe allow such creatures to exist? And why was it necessary to sacrifice everything in order to oppose them?

The PDF piled out of the cars and gathered around their leader. He scanned the area for a moment before giving them their marching orders. Then:

"The first thing we do is to collapse the roof and force the Swarm out into the open. Stan, can you do that at this distance?"

"Jeez, I never moved anything more'n ten feet away. But, I'll try, Mr. Larkin."

The boy faced the building and concentrated. What he hoped to do first was to gain a mental image of the interior; then he would locate a weak spot and focus on that. After a couple of minutes, he shook his head.

"Ever'thing is hazy. I can't get a fix on it. Sorry, Mr. Larkin."

"No need to apologize. You just need more training. Let's try something different." He reached into his pocket, pulled out his cell phone, and tapped out a number. "Hello, Chris. We're in position. I want you to scan the interior of the Swarm base."

"Will do, George," the tinny voice replied. Presently: "I'm inside now. The Swarm is here, old 'Scarface' and a dozen-and-a-half of his thugs. It looks like they're going through a weapons check. That seems ominous."

"Uh-huh. I'm going to have Kenny hook up with you in order to get the same image you're getting."

He nodded at the psycho-communicator. The latter faced the supermarket, reached out with his mind, and made contact. Chris yelped.

"Whoa!" he exclaimed. "That tingled!"

"Yeah. Been there, done that. Have you got a clear image, Kenny?"

"I do, old darling."

"All right. Now, I want you to send that image to Stan's mind. Brace yourself, Stan."

The boy's eyes widened in a mix of shock and surprise.

"Wow! Cool!"

"Does that help any?"

"Yeah. I got a real clear picture. I'll give it another try." Again he concentrated. "Nope. I got to get closer, Mr. Larkin."

"Very well. It's going to be risky, though. You and Billy walk slowly toward the building. No one will pay much attention to a couple of kids poking around. As soon as you get within your range, do your thing."

Stan nodded in acquiescence and looked at Billy. The teenager nodded back, and the two started meandering in the direction of the supermarket, chatting idly as they went. When they came to within twenty meters of the building, Stan stretched one arm above his head. The detective took that as the signal that the psycho-kinetic was about to make another attempt. Stan tested his ability, then advanced closer;

at ten meters, he and Billy halted, and he signaled again. He tested his power and got results this time.

The old supermarket began to quiver as it was caught in the grip of Stan's mind, and a faint groaning could be heard. Stan focused all of his mental energy on a weak spot he had discovered above where the Swarm ship was sitting. The building shook furiously under the assault. Plaster showered the area inside. Empty shelves tipped over and crashed to the floor. And still Stan plied his *psi*-talent as he had never done before. The creaking and groaning intensified, and an interior wall collapsed. The latter action produced a domino effect as the portion of the roof attached to that wall sagged, wrenched free, and dropped to the floor. As the roof fell, it pulled the exterior walls with it, and the entire building collapsed with a thunderous sound.

"George!" Chris exclaimed. "That's done the trick! Many of the Swarm were caught in the wreckage and crushed. Old 'Scarface' and one of his soldiers got into their ship when the debris started to fall. The others ran for any exit they could find."

"Thanks, Chris. Kenny, tell Stan and Billy to retreat as fast as they can." He addressed the remainder of the PDF. "OK, people, we've flushed out the 'pheasants.' Now comes the hard part: we pick them off, one by one."

Six Swarm soldiers emerged from the collapsed supermarket, dazed, confused, and unaware of their surroundings. They were also grime-covered from head to toe. Once in the open, they stood still and tried to get their bearings.

Larkin directed his "troops" across Hill Avenue to confront them. This action posed the most risk, but he had felt it was necessary; there was too wide a gap between them and the Enemy to apply individual *psi*-talents effectively and efficiently, as evidenced by Stan's use of his psycho-kinesis. Whatever was the optimum range for any of them had to be achieved or they faced certain defeat and/or death. The risk was calculated, however, because the detective had his alien force-field generator to protect against Swarm energy weapons. And, if the soldiers got too close, he'd just sic the Twins on them.

He halted the group halfway between the street and the ruined building. The soldiers, having recovered some of their wits, spotted them and slowly advanced in their direction, weapons at the ready. He took a deep breath, let it out quickly, and issued his very first "combat" order.

"Billy, you're up first. Whatever tricks you've got up your sleeve, go to it."

"You betcha, Mr. Larkin," the teenager responded with a grin. "Watch this."

The boy went ramrod stiff and concentrated. Almost at once, the Swarm found themselves surrounded by the most hideous "creatures" they'd ever seen. Billy had conjured up every film monster he had viewed and was serving them to the opposition. The Frankenstein Monster, the Creature from the Black Lagoon, the Wolf Man, the Invaders from Mars, the Crawling Eye, the giant Tarantula, the Trifids, the Living Dead, and much, much more. All were walking, crawling, slithering, and lurching toward the frightened soldiers with the most menacing demeanor possible.

"Oh, God!" Lacey whispered to no one in particular. "I knew it was a bad idea to let him watch those horrid movies."

"But it's paying off, Lacey," Larkin assured her, even though the sight was sending shivers up *his* spine. "The Swarm is totally disoriented. Look!"

The soldiers reacted in the only way they knew how, the way they had been trained to do. They pointed their weapons at the advancing "creatures" and fired repeatedly in all directions. Their actions were futile, of course, since they were firing at thin air. And the closer the "creatures" came, the more wildly they fired.

"OK, Chris," the detective spoke into his cell phone, "you're next. Use the same image from yesterday."

"Roger, fearless leader."

The Swarm were so engaged by one "menace" that they failed to see yet another one materialize in their midst. Chris had re-created an image of his true form and was maneuvering it behind one of the soldiers. When the image was positioned where he wanted it to be, he let out an eerie screech via the cell phone. The soldier who was the target paused in his futile discharging of his weapon to wonder what that sound was; he turned around slowly, spied the horrific image, and let out a screech of his own. Frantically, he aimed and fired at the image; the blast passed through the illusion and struck one of his comrades full force. The latter collapsed, a gaping hole where his spine used to be.

Another of the Swarm reacted to the screeching also, saw the image, and thought to come to the rescue of his comrade. That one fired and, instead of destroying the "creature," killed the screecher.

"Two down, four to go," Larkin murmured, at once horrified and satisfied by his handiwork.

"Mr. Larkin," Billy said hoarsely, "I don't think I can maintain the illusions any longer."

"That's all right, Billy. Shut down. I've got some tricks of my own."

The illusions disappeared immediately, leaving the Swarm even more confused. They looked this way and that way and saw only their dead comrades. Then they realized that the Tellurians were still present, and they resumed their forward march to get within firing range.

"Kenny, Paddy," the detective ordered, "your turn. Use your abilities as you see fit."

"With pleasure, old darling, we'll…"

"…show those blighters who's who."

But before the Twins could act, the Swarm suddenly broke into a trot, firing their weapons as they closed the gap. Some of the bolts of energy came dangerously near two of the team. Larkin reacted instinctively, turned toward Sheena, and ordered her to step back. She did not hesitate and moved toward Hill Avenue. The detective then ordered Freddie to activate the force-field generator; the dwarf did so and adjusted it for maximum range. The light-blue energy screen quickly enveloped the group. Bolts from the Swarm weapons struck it and were deflected back at the point of origin. Two more soldiers dropped.

Frustrated by this new turn of events, the remainder of the Swarm approached at a more cautious pace and halted before the energy curtain. One of the remaining soldiers, perhaps braver and bolder than his comrade reached out and lightly touched the force-field. He felt nothing but a slight tingling sensation. Emboldened, he stepped forward and passed through the screen unharmed. He grinned wickedly.

This was what Larkin had dreaded the most about the alien technology he had been given: it was limited in its usage. The screen blocked all forms of energy, but not physical objects. The situation called for desperate measures. Reluctantly, the detective reached into another pocket and pulled out the pistol he normally kept in a desk drawer in his office.

It was safe to say that George Larkin had never fired a gun at any living being during all the years he had worked for the Chicago Police Department and later as a private investigator. He had never had a reason to fire one. It simply wasn't his style to shoot first and ask questions later, despite the image the general populace had of one in his profession as a result of decades of Hollywood thrillers. The current dilemma was another matter, however; it was literally a matter of life-and-death – his and the PDF's or the Swarm's. His choice was easy enough, however much he abhorred it, and he raised the pistol to fire it.

The Swarm soldier also raised his weapon. His Commander had shown all under his command an image of the leader of the "Tellurian scum" and promised a great reward for the one who captured the obstacle to their dream of conquering this backward planet. The soldier, in his mind, was already spending his reward. But, who would fire first?

The answer, as it happened, was neither one. Jean Fulton had watched anxiously as the Swarm drew closer to the PDF's position. Memories of the incident at the transportation center filled her mind. The fear she had felt then was now layered with anger as she envisioned the deaths of her new friends (and her own). These raging emotions served to create the build-up of static electricity which she had railed against all her life. This time, however, she saw a need for the incredibly destructive power within her and allowed it to well up to its maximum charge. At the moment she felt it reach that level, she rushed headlong at the soldier.

Both Larkin and the soldier were taken aback by this seemingly foolhardy move, and both held their fire. For the detective, it was a fear of hitting Jean; for the soldier, a female surrounded by a red haze was a complete surprise and a fatal error. Jean came within a step of the soldier at the precise moment of discharge. A sharp and loud crackling filled the air, followed by a scream of agony from the intended target as he was literally roasted alive. His charred corpse crumpled to the ground.

It was also safe to say that the witnesses to this death were horrified beyond belief. They had believed, quite erroneously, that the "eel" produced the same sort of electrical shock one created by shuffling one's feet across a carpet. Never in their wildest imaginations would they have believed that their newest member was in reality an organic dynamo, capable of producing thousands of volts of electrical energy. The fact that she was was quite sobering, and none of them would ever look upon Jean Fulton in the same way again.

In particular, the remaining soldier slowly backed away but kept his eyes firmly fixed upon this strange female who killed people who got too near her. Transfixed as he was, he (and most of the PDF) were unaware that the Twins, who quickly took advantage of the distraction, had surreptitiously exited the protective screen in order to put their own incredible powers into play. Kenny and Paddy both focused on the soldier.

The brothers Smythe had already had the unpleasant experience of entering the mind of a Swarm member. They recalled with a shudder how filled it had been with evil intent, violence, lust, obscenity, and vile thoughts and thus braced themselves for the cesspool they found necessary to enter. In the previous incident, they had entered the alien mind together, and so they had had each other to comfort them. This time, they had the added impetus of impending danger to both themselves and their friends, and so they did not hesitate.

With all deliberate speed, the Twins headed for what for the Swarm passed as the cerebral cortex, the thought center. Along the way, they ignored the filth they encountered as best they could but soon found themselves in the midst of it. Their goal was simple: to plant a thought in the mind of this warmonger to the effect that he would eliminate himself. Specifically, they "told" their target that a large number of the Enemy was advancing on him and that self-immolation was the only avenue of escape. For good measure, they also planted an image by which the soldier would "see" the advancing Enemy. As soon as they were finished with this task, they quickly exited the Swarm mind.

And not a moment too soon. The soldier, under the influence of the mind alteration, raised his arm, pointed his weapon at his head, and fired. The headless corpse dropped without making a sound.

As horrific as Jean's action had been, this bit of mental assault was stupefying. Of all of DEDEP, only Emil Razumov and George Larkin knew the full extent of the Smythes' *psi*-talent – and that by mutual understanding. The fewer who knew what they were capable of, the safer they were. Now that they had been moved to demonstrate the more sinister side of their abilities, the rest of the PDF had an inkling of the potential danger they posed to humankind, and none of them would ever look upon Kensington and Paddington Smythe in the same way again.

"Two more of them left," Larkin said somewhat callously to mask his inner thoughts. "They're in their ship. That means extra precautions." He ordered Freddie to shut down the force-field. "Eve, Stan, stand by to call up the gestalt."

"George!" Lacey cried out. "I see the ship now. It's just emerging from the rubble."

All eyes turned toward the ruined building. All eyes observed the alien craft as it rose into the air and move in their direction.

"George!" Sheena exclaimed from her safe vantage point. "I'm picking up a low-frequency humming sound. I think they're powering up their weapons system."

"She's right, old darling. We've just scanned their minds…"

"…and old 'Scarface' has given the order to fire at will."

"All right. Eve, Stan, call up the gestalt."

It was debatable who was the most surprised by what occurred next. Certainly, the gestalt-makers were thunderstruck for a second or two before their bodies stiffened and their eyes glazed over in the same manner as when Mr. Jones had been confronted. The rest of the PDF were thrown into confusion.

Without warning the black sphere materialized before Eve and Stan could join hands and shimmered above their heads. And, while the humans were gripped with wonder, it shot up into the sky straight toward the Swarm ship. When it came within ten meters of the craft, it halted and hung motionless. Then…

* * *

Alert!
This One recognizes a threat to the Summoners.
Investigate! Analyze! Protect!
Investigation: the Summoners have identified this machine as a danger to them and their allies. This machine possesses a [undeciperable]*–generating capability of lethal proportions. The* [undecipherable] *cannot harm this One, but it can harm the Summoners.*
Analysis: this One is commanded to protect the Summoners by any means necessary so that they may survive to join the Communion and fulfill their destinies. This One has been authorized to take independent action to fulfill the mission.
Protection: based on the nature of this machine, this One will generate a sunstorm in the [undecipherable] *range.*
Initiating sunstorm.

* * *

…the spheroid became mottled with yellow splotches which rotated and zigzagged in kaleidoscopic fashion.

"Cover your eyes, people!" Larkin called out. "Something's about to happen."

Even as he spoke, the yellow mottling ceased its St. Vitus dance and faded away entirely. Instantly, a brilliant white light burst forth as a single colossal pulse of energy lit up the sky. As quickly as it had appeared, the pulsar winked out of existence, leaving only the sphere in the vicinity; the sphere returned to its normal coloration before it too de-materialized. The detective saw no sign of the Swarm ship, but he thought he saw a cloud of particles of – *something* – raining to the ground. He shook his head in amazement at this second demonstration of the power of the gestalt.

"What in God's name just happened, George?" Sheena asked as soon as she had re-joined the group.

"I'll tell you when we get back to DEDEP. Right now, we've got to leave before the authorities – and the curiosity-seekers – arrive."

No one speaks for a long time.

When the PDF left the scene of their victory over the Swarm, Larkin had contacted the Director and given him a brief account of the battle, including the fact that the gestalt had acted on its own and placed Eve and Stan in a trance-like state again while it acted. Upon their arrival at DEDEP, Dr. Razumov had met them at the entrance to the barn, and he and the detective had rushed the stricken members to the infirmary.

The remainder of the team now await their leader in conference room #1, each in his/her own private thoughts. After what seems like hours, the "master strategist" puts in his appearance. He looks haggard and does not make immediate eye contact. Sheena bites her lip in anguish; she is distraught, not only because of the recent events but also because of his emotional state. The Twins, stoic as ever, are undoubtedly communicating privately. Freddie and Jean sit side by side, her head on his shoulder. The Perkineses embrace each other. Chris flickers on and off in an effort to remain visible for as long as he can.

Larkin walks slowly to the head of the table where they sit and now glances at each one in turn. A long pause follows. Finally, he speaks.

"Well, boys and girls," he says in an attempt to inject a little humor into the room, "we won our first battle. That's a positive note. Eve and Stan are still in a trance – again – but they're all right. That's another positive."

"What about my question, George?" Sheena is quick to ask. "What's going on with the gestalt?"

The detective pauses again. He himself is not too sure what had "gone on" with the gestalt; he had been as surprised as everyone else by its behavior. Not only could it act in self-defense, but it also could take the offensive *on its own initiative*. And the only ones who could shed some light on the matter are indisposed. He can only make an educated guess.

"The gestalt has sprung another surprise on us, which leads me to believe that it is a sentient creature." A sharp gasp of shock ripples through the group. "Yes, I know that's a quantum leap in logic, but I can't think of any other explanation for its behavior. Whatever it is and wherever it came from – and I'll tell you that I think Eve and Stan know more about it than they're letting on – it seems like the creature has 'adopted' us and is looking out for our welfare. *Why* is another large question I don't have an answer to."

"How can you be sure it's intelligent?" Lacey asks.

"The fact that it did act of its own accord without being called up or directed by Eve and Stan. That's the mark of a self-aware creature."

"Does that mean I'm out of a job?" Freddie pipes up.

"Maybe, chum. It all depends on what Eve and Stan tell us – if they are willing to tell us anything at all."

"Well, I hope so. That thing was takin' up too much o' my time. Um, are we gonna celebrate our victory?"

"We can. We should. You guys look too somber to suit me."

That brings a smile to all of the faces. They begin to brag about their roles in the late battle. Larkin takes a seat next to Sheena and clasps her hand. She smiles and squeezes it.

Printed in the United States
By Bookmasters